HOLY WAR

"Action-filled thriller." —*Manchester Evening News (UK)*

"A profound tale of war ... Impossible to stop reading."
   —*British Armed Forces Broadcasting*

"A terrific book ... The smells, taste, noise, dust, and fear are
   communicated so clearly." —*Great Book Escapes*

"A supercharged thriller ... A story to chill and haunt you."
   —*Peterborough Evening Telegraph (UK)*

"A tale of fear, hatred, revenge, and desire, flicking between
   bloody Beirut and the lesser battles of London and Paris."
   —*Evening Herald (UK)*

"If you are looking to get a driver's seat look at the landscape of
   modern conflict, holy wars, and the Middle East then this is
   the perfect book to do so." —*Masterful Book Reviews*

"A gripping tale of passion, hostage-taking and war, set against a
   war-ravaged Beirut." —*Evening News (UK)*

"A stunning novel of love and loss, good and evil, of real people
   who live in our hearts after the last page is done."
   —*Greater London Radio*

SNOW

"A captivating story of three friends on opposing sides of a betrayal ... a well-paced tale with intricate storylines." —*Kirkus*

"A complex interplay of fascinating characters." —*Culture Buzz*

"An action-packed adventure, but also a morality tale of what happens when two men who should know better get entangled in a crime from which they can't escape." —*Denver Post*

"More than just a thriller, Snow lights up the complexities of American culture, the tensions of morality and obligation and the human search for love and freedom, all of which makes it clear Bond is a masterful storyteller." —*Sacramento Bee*

"Exploring the psyche and the depths of human reasoning and drive, Snow is a captivating story." —*BookTrib*

"An action-packed thriller that wouldn't let go. The heart-pounding scenes kept me on the edge of my seat." —*Goodreads*

"A simple story at its heart that warps into a splendid morality tale." —*Providence Sunday Journal*

ASSASSINS

"An exhilarating spy novel that offers equal amounts of ingenuity and intrigue." —*Kirkus*

"An epic spy story ... Bond often writes with a staccato beat, in sentence fragments with the effect of bullet fire. His dialogue is sharp and his description of combat is tactical and detached, professional as a soldier's debriefing. Yet this terseness is rife with tension and feeling ... A cohesive and compelling story of political intrigue, religious fanaticism, love, brotherhood and the ultimate pursuit of peace." —*Honolulu Star-Advertiser*

"Packs one thrilling punch after the other ... A first-rate thriller." —*Book Chase*

"Powerful, true to life, and explosive ... The energy is palpable and the danger is real ... A story that could be ripped right out of the headlines." —*Just Reviews*

"Bond is one of America's best thriller writers ... You need to get this book ... It's an eye-opener, a page-turner ... very strongly based in reality." —*Culture Buzz*

"Riveting, thrilling ... so realistic and fast-paced that the reader felt as if they were actually there." —*NetGalley*

"The action is outstanding and realistic. The suspense flows from page to page ... The background is provided by recent events we have all lived through. The flow of the writing is almost musical as romance and horrors share equal billing ... I wish everyone could read and understand this book." —*Goodreads*

SAVING PARADISE
(PONO HAWKINS BOOK 1)

"Bond is one of the 21st century's most exciting authors ... An action-packed, must read novel ... taking readers behind the alluring façade of Hawaii's pristine beaches and tourist traps into a festering underworld of murder, intrigue and corruption." —*Washington Times*

"A complex, entertaining ... lusciously convoluted story." —*Kirkus*

"Highly recommended." —*Midwest Book Review*

"A rousing crime thriller – but it is so much more ... a highly atmospheric thriller focusing on a side of Hawaiian life that tourists seldom see." —*Book Chase*

"An intersection of fiction and real life." —*Hawaii Public Radio*

"An absolute page-turner." —*Ecotopia Radio*

"An unusual thriller and a must-read." —*Fresh Fiction*

"A complex murder mystery about political and corporate greed and corruption ... Bond's vivid descriptions of Hawaii bring Saving Paradise vibrantly to life." —*Book Reviews and More*

"Saving Paradise will change you ... It will call into question what little you really know, what people want you to believe you know and then hit you with a deep wave of dangerous truths." —*Where Truth Meets Fiction*

KILLING MAINE
(PONO HAWKINS BOOK 2)

FIRST PRIZE FOR FICTION, *New England Book Festival:*
"A gripping tale of murders, manhunts and other crimes set amidst today's dirty politics and corporate graft, an unforgettable hero facing enormous dangers as he tries to save a friend, protect the women he loves, and defend a beautiful, endangered place."

"Another terrifically entertaining read from a master of the storytelling craft ... A work of compelling fiction ... Very highly recommended." —*Midwest Book Review*

"Bond returns with another winner in Killing Maine. Bond's ability to infuse his real-world experiences into a fast-paced story is unequaled." —*Culture Buzz*

"Quite a ride for those who love good crime thrillers ... I can't recommend this one strongly enough." —*Book Chase*

"The suspense, mystery, and intrigue will keep you on the edge of your seat." —*Goodreads*

"Bond tackles many important social and environmental issues in a fast-paced, politically charged plot with a passionate main character. Killing Maine is a twisting mystery with enough suspicious characters and red herrings to keep you guessing. It's also a dire warning about the power of big industry and a commentary on our modern ecological responsibilities. A great read for the socially and environmentally conscious mystery lover." —*Honolulu Star-Advertiser*

"Sucks in the reader and makes it difficult to put the book down until the very last page ... A winner of a thriller." —*Mystery Maven*

"Another stellar ride from Bond; checking out Pono's first adventure isn't a prerequisite, but this will make readers want to." —*Kirkus*

GOODBYE PARIS
(PONO HAWKINS BOOK 3)

"There's tension, turmoil and drama on every page that's hot enough to singe your fingers." —*New York Times* Bestseller, Steve Berry

"A rip-roaring page-turner, edgy and brilliantly realistic." —*Culture Buzz*

"Another non-stop thriller of a novel by a master of the genre." —*Midwest Book Review*

"A stunning thriller, entrancing love story and exciting account of anti-terror operations." —*BookTrib*

"Doesn't stop until it has delivered every possible ounce of intelligent excitement." —*Miami Times*

"Fast and twisty, and you don't know how it's going to end." —*Arizona Daily Sun*

"Exhilarating." —*Kirkus*

"With non-stop action and strong character development, Bond's take on terrorism is addictive and timely." —*NetGalley*

"Mike Bond is my favorite author ... and his books are nothing short of works of art ... I could not put this book down once I started reading it." —*Goodreads*

"A great book with normal special forces action and thrills, but what makes it great is the integration of Islamic terrorism." —*Basingstone Reviews*

"An action-packed story culminates in an exciting ending." —*The Bookworm*

"Thrills ... crisp writing and intelligence." —*St. Louis Today*

THE LAST SAVANNA

FIRST PRIZE FOR FICTION, *Los Angeles Book Festival:* "One of the best books yet on Africa, a stunning tale of love and loss amid a magnificent wilderness and its myriad animals, and a deadly manhunt through savage jungles, steep mountains and fierce deserts as an SAS commando tries to save the elephants, the woman he loves and the soul of Africa itself."

"A gripping thriller." —*Liverpool Daily Post (UK)*

"One of the most exciting portrayals of Africa yet ... Dynamic, heart-breaking and timely to current events ... a must-read." —*Yahoo Reviews*

"Sheer intensity, depicting the immense, arid land and never-ending scenes ... but it's the volatile nature of nature itself that gives the story its greatest distinction." —*Kirkus*

"One of the most darkly beautiful books you will ever read." —*WordDreams*

"Exciting, action-packed ... A nightmarish vision of Africa."
—*Manchester Evening News (UK)*

"A manhunt through crocodile-infested jungle, sun-scorched savannah, and impenetrable mountains as a former SAS man tries to save the life of the woman he loves but cannot have."
—*Evening Telegraph (UK)*

"Unrelenting in its portrait of the modern African reality."
—*Mystery File*

"A powerful love story set in the savage jungles and deserts of East Africa." —*Daily Examiner (UK)*

"The central figure is not human; it is the barren, terrifying landscape of Northern Kenya and the deadly creatures who inhabit it." —*Daily Telegraph (UK)*

"An entrancing, terrifying vision of Africa." —*BBC*

"From the opening page maintains an exhilarating pace until the closing line ... A highly entertaining and gripping read."
—*East African Wild Life Society*

"Tragic and beautiful, sentimental and ruthless, *The Last Savanna* is a vast and wonderful book." —*NetGalley*

HOUSE OF JAGUAR

"A riveting thriller of murder, politics, and lies." —*London Broadcasting*

"A terrifying depiction of one man's battle against the CIA and Latin American death squads." —*BBC*

"A high-octane story rife with action, from US streets to Guatemalan jungles." —*Kirkus*

"Outstanding and entertaining ... Intriguing, exciting, captivating, sexy ... absolutely incredible ... a great thriller."
—*NetGalley*

"Vicious thriller of drugs and revolution in the wilds of Guatemala, with the adventurer hero, aided by a woman doctor, facing a crooked CIA agent." —*Liverpool Daily Post (UK)*

"Tough and tense thriller." —*Manchester Evening News (UK)*

"A riveting story where even the good guys are bad guys, set in the politically corrupt and drug infested world of present-day Central America." —*Middlesborough Evening Gazette (UK)*

"Based upon Bond's own experiences in Guatemala. With detailed descriptions of actual jungle battles and manhunts, vanishing rain forests and the ferocity of guerrilla war, *House of Jaguar* also reveals the CIA's role in both death squads and drug running, twin scourges of Central America."
—*Newton Chronicle (UK)*

"Grips the reader from the very first page. An ideal thriller for the beach, but be prepared to be there when the sun goes down." —*Herald Express (UK)*

TIBETAN CROSS

"A taut, tense tale of pursuit through exotic and unsavory locales." —*Publishers Weekly*

"Grips the reader from the very first chapter until the climactic ending." —*UPI*

"An astonishing thriller." —*San Francisco Examiner*

"A tautly written study of one man's descent into living hell ... a mood of near claustrophobic intensity." —*Spokane Chronicle*

Holy War

Holy War

MIKE BOND

BIG CITY PRESS
NEW YORK

Big City Press, New York, NY 10014

Published in the United States by Big City Press

LIBRARY OF CONGRESS CATALOGING-IN-PUBLICATION DATA
Bond, Mike – author
Holy War/Mike Bond

ISBN paperback: 978-1-949751-16-1
ISBN ebook: 978-1-949751-17-8

Cover design by Alan Dingman
Book design by John Lotte
Author photo by © PF Bentley/PFPix.com

www.MikeBondBooks.com

for Jude, Lucas, and David

God is well able to effect his purpose,
but the greater part of men do not understand.

—KORAN, XII

Ye lust, and have not: ye kill,
and desire to have, and cannot obtain:
ye fight and war, yet ye have not.

—JAMES, IV

Time's short your life's your own
And in the end we are just dust n' bones.

—GUNS N' ROSES

BEIRUT was a paradise when I first arrived there as a very young man. The golden sun and brilliant sea, the ancient streets, the hubbub of cultures, the food and wines, the tanned and sensual young women, the perfume of many million flowers, the pine hills and cold white peaks, all imbued it with a near-sacred substance. This, I felt, is a place where all peoples come together, vibrant with history, wisdom, lust, and delight.

It was soon a battlefield of smashed buildings and bloody streets, its Phoenician treasures blasted, its forests and vineyards burned, its people huddled in bombed-out basements or sniping at each other from shattered windows, hating, killing, raping, pillaging. I survived by luck, by tricks, even in dark places where discovery was death. Everywhere I lived is gone, every good friend is dead. I refuse to let them die, to see it gone, without a testament, a memory.

As the years went by, broken-hearted by Beirut, I tried to understand – why do we war? Now, after having covered wars on three continents, I can find no answer beyond the experience itself. What I mean is this: only when we have *lived* war do we hate and know it well enough to make it stop. For in every country, every city, neighborhood and family, Beirut is waiting.

If everyone could *live* Beirut, I thought, we might war less. If I could tell one small true story of Beirut, let the reader fear the bullets, crouch beneath the thundering bombs in airless cellars as the concrete floors come crashing down, see loved ones die, grope for passion and belief amid terror and death, that it might make a difference.

Every book must be a failure because it fails to say so much. Today fiction withers because it is too literary, and ceases to be relevant. But if we are to learn we must do so through the heart, not through the mind – a book that does not touch the heart conveys no experience at all. If readers turn away, we need look no further than ourselves.

Like many people I still live Beirut every day, every night, and will probably the rest of my life. I have tried in *Holy War* to tell its story.

Holy War

1

THE TROUBLE'S SYLVIE, Yves decided. How she's never happy with what I am, what I'm doing. Wants me home.

He stretched in his army cot, twisting his back to let the muscles flex up and down his shoulder blades. Shards of sharp blue through the sandbagged window. Another lovely day in the lovely Levant. Red-golden sun through the pines, the green hill sweeping down to the sea. Incense of cedars, salty cool wind, warm earth; *promise* in the fragrant air, the buzzing insects, the gulls crying over the waves.

Off duty. Luxury of nowhere to go and nothing to do. Nowhere to go but a sandbagged perimeter and sentried corridors, maybe a quick trip to town in an armored car, the machine gun nervously scanning, the driver watching through the hot slit for an RPG, some mad kid with a Molotov. *Vive la France*, damn you, for sending us here ...

He rolled out of his cot and ambled down the corridor to the WC. Why do all urinals smell like Beirut? Ask the philosophers, he decided, the ones with all the answers. Yawning, scratching his overnight whiskers and under his arms, he wandered to the officers' mess, found a dirty cup and rinsed it, clamped fresh espresso into the machine, drew up and pulled down the handle, two streams of black gold dribbling into the cup.

Makes you feel better already. He filled the cup to the brim and stood by another window, peering through chinks in the sandbagged concrete blocks at the day growing bright blue. Sylvie would still be in bed, the Paris light gray through the blinds. He imagined waking beside her, her lovely sleepy smell, the roughness of her morning voice, the smoothness of her skin.

In Normandy, Papa would already be out in his garden, watering, picking on the weeds, Mama taking fresh *brioches* out of the oven, Papa coming in with a handful of onions and leeks, taking up his coffee cup in his big fist. André on maneuvers somewhere, playing at war. Trying to get stationed back here, where there's plenty of war. But none for *La France*, for the Multinational Force, impartially observing the slaughter. The United fucking Nations: you want to murder each other, we'll pay to watch.

He made a second cup, loitered back to his cot and slipped into his thongs, tossed a towel over his shoulders and headed for the showers. A thunderclap cracked, the floor lurched, shivered, the thunder louder. Christ, we've been hit, he thought, dropping the cup. He raced to his cot, snatched his FAMAS, the explosion shaking the sky, men yelling now, down below.

The earth was shaking, an earthquake; he raced up the stairs to the roof, smashed into a sentry coming down. "It's the Marines," the sentry screamed. "A bomb!"

From the roof he couldn't see the U.S. Marines' compound to the south, just a great billowing dark cloud. He raced downstairs to the radio room. Chevenet, the communications chief, was crouched speaking English then listening to the headset as he loaded his rifle. "A truck," he said, "somebody drove up in a truck. The whole building. *The whole fucking building!*"

Yves sprinted down the corridor and down the stairs. "Battle stations!" he screamed. *"Battle stations!"* Pumping a round into the FAMAS he dashed across the lobby into the parking area. Dark smoke filled the sky. "They hit the Marines!" he yelled to the sentries at the gate. "A big truck!"

A Mercedes truck, the kind used to collect rubbish from the embattled streets of Beirut, geared down and swung into the parking lot, snapped the gate barrier and accelerated toward him. A ton of *plastique*, he realized as he fired from the waist exploding the windshield but the driver had ducked, the truck's grille huge in Yves' face as he shot for the engine now, the distributor cap on the right side, the plugs, the fuel pump. It was too late, the truck would have them. His heart broke in frantic agony for the men inside, the men who would be trapped, crushed to death, the Paras, *fleur de la France*, his beloved brothers. The universe congealed, shrank to an atom and blew apart, reducing him to tiny chunks of blood and bone, never to be found.

2

IT'S YOUR LAST NIGHT, Neill – please let's not fight?"
Beverly poured the noodles into the strainer and dumped the
strainer into a bowl. "Can you get the butter?"

Her close-cropped round head made him think of an eel
peering from its hole. Waiting to sink her fangs. "It's just three
weeks." He spoke carefully, not letting the whisky slur his tongue,
upbeat at the end. "Good to put a little distance between us."

She took the butter from the refrigerator. "There's been no
lack of that."

He turned as if to hold her in his arms, opened the freezer
door and took out the ice cubes. Everything you say, he told
himself, she turns right back on you. He twisted the ice cube
container and popped some into the low octagonal glass. She
spun round. "There's wine with dinner."

He poured in extra Knockando, for what she'd said. "What
I mean is we'll have a little time to see how it's like, living
alone ..."

"I'll hardly be alone with two teenagers to cook and clean for,
to drive around and worry about when they're not here and try
to run my own office at the same time."

Under their feet the ground rumbled, a District Line train

slowing for Earls Court Station. He took a sip. "And slip Timothy a quick fuck when you can."

"And you! With that Dutch bitch!"

"Hardly, in darkest Beirut."

"You'll find somebody there. You always do."

He tossed back the whisky and put the glass in the sink. "There's no point, Bev. We can't keep this up."

She came close, took his elbow. "For all the years we've had, Neill, let's not take it out tonight on the kids? Let's have a quiet evening and then in the morning you can go and we'll see what happens when you get back? Please?"

"You know they damn well don't care whether I go or stay."

"Yes, they do. They'd rather you go."

"Thanks."

"The way you've been, can you blame them?"

"I blame you." The phone was ringing. "Imagine, some day we could've been buried side by side."

"We *have* been!" she snapped.

"Mum!" Edgar called. "Phone!"

Neill opened a bottle of wine and took it into the dining room. "Yes," Beverly was saying in the living room, into the phone. "Yes, yes."

"You didn't put out wine glasses," he said to Edgar.

"Sorry." Edgar bent to the buffet, took out a glass.

"Two," Neill said. "Since when doesn't your mother drink?"

"Sometimes." Edgar put a second glass on the table. "Mostly with you."

He smiled at Katerina. "See how he is, your brother?"

She glanced back at him. "No wonder."

"That's *it*, don't you see? No wonder at this magic life of ours!"

The children looked at him. Beverly sat and began serving the peas, the noodles. "This *case* ..."

"That's why I'll never be a lawyer," Katerina said. "You see what she has to go through?"

Neill sat back. "You mean me, or her job?"

Beverly's hand undulated through the plates and glasses, caught his. "We made a deal ..."

"I made no damn deal. I never made a damn deal that I couldn't say what I think." He took a forkful of meat, chewing gristle, turned on Edgar, this son, he thought, I love who hates me. I didn't always drink, my son, I didn't always hate your mother. "What do you think?"

"It's not worth saying," Edgar said, "what I think."

"Even with me?"

Katerina stopped chewing. "*Especially* with you."

He smiled at her. "*Et tu*, Brute?"

"Now, don't pick on your father," Beverly said. "He'll be gone three whole weeks, and if the news desk takes all his articles maybe when he gets back we can go up to the Lake District, unwind together."

"That, Mother," Katerina answered, "is impossible."

"Promise to study?" he said to Edgar.

"You were the one," Edgar said, "who told me school was like what that caste does in India – maiming their children young so they'll always be able to earn a living. As crippled beggars."

"That's true." Neill rubbed his head, imagined the gray hairs growing silently, ruthlessly. "I said that."

"You say lots of things." Katerina tossed him her best smile, one she practiced in the cloakroom mirror before going out to that nauseous little creep with the curly Afro and the earring. Trying to slip his puny prick into my daughter. Go ahead, he told her silently, with his eyes. Go ahead and see what you get.

The phone rang and in a single fluid motion Beverly was up and after it.

"It's just a circus," Neill said. "We play the clown, the tightrope walker, you name it. In the end the audience goes home."

"*What* is?" Edgar said.

Beverly returned. "Just Timothy."

"Just Timothy."

"Same case, different argument."

Château Lascaze, the bottle said, *1981*. He emptied it and scanned the buffet for another. "In October, 1981, where were we? Does anybody remember? When these grapes were plucked from the sun –"

"School," Edgar said.

Katerina nodded. "School."

"I must've been bent over my desk at *The Times*, pounding out my daily thousand pointless words, beside Quilliver and his bloody cigarettes and graveyard cough – you know, they've found passive smoke's more cancerous?"

"Because it isn't filtered," Edgar said.

He smiled at Beverly. "That was long before Timothy. What in heavens, my dear, had *you* to do back then?"

She made a show of thinking. "October '81. That wretched accident case. Woman lived but her husband didn't. Nine months of plastic surgery. Sued the drunken driver in the other car and lost."

"Long, sure hand of the law. Rewarding the guilty. Justifiably flailing the innocent."

"She said the strangest things. They reanimated her in hospital, dead but they brought her back. Said she'd risen up out of her body and traveled down a tunnel toward the light, but decided to return. Do you suppose –"

"Journalists aren't supposed to suppose." He went to the kitchen and brought back another bottle.

"Neill," she whispered.

"Even if you *did* care I wouldn't –"

"Don't have so much, Neill."

From his pockets Neill extracted a Swiss Army knife, opened it and uncorked the bottle. "Long swift arm of the law. Furious fist of timorous Timothy."

"You're never serious. Except when you're talking about yourself. Your deep problems of love and death."

Across the table Katerina yawned. Edgar rose like a butler

who'd momentarily forgotten himself and sat at table with his masters. "The dishes call."

Neill poured a full glass, raised it to the light. "Don't answer."

"Afterwards can I go and play music?" Edgar said. "Just till midnight?"

"Be on the last Tube," Beverly said.

"And you?" Neill turned to Katerina.

"Going to Max's. We have a calculus assignment."

And fiddle his liverish prick, he said for her. See the Crusader departing for the Holy Land, shunned by his own kind. "Whatever happened to the time-honored idea of figuring things out for yourself?"

"She does better over there," Beverly said.

"With his own place," Katerina added, "why would he want to come here?"

"Nothing left," Neill smiled at Beverly, "but for you and me to have our quiet evening at home."

"I've got to work on that case."

They carried the dirty plates into the kitchen, loaded the dishwasher and turned it on. It started with a self-satisfied hum. To be so inanimate, Neill thought, so free. Please God, where are we? These stars we travel through, this universe of magic and sorrow, what *is* it? We this amalgam of cells and dreams, this falseness.

Upstairs in the bathroom he poured the last of his wine into the toilet, felt guilty and drank the dregs. Just don't understand. Dear God, I just don't. Right away the answer came to him: all that counts is *wrath*.

Love doesn't matter? he asked.

No, came the answer, it surely doesn't. Drink no more.

But what would that change? What else do you have?

He took a leak and flushed the loo, the red and yellow liquid sucking down. Every drop of the Thames goes through nine people, says the National Rivers Association, between the

Cotswolds and the Channel. Drinking piss, we are, cradle to grave.

Clasping the empty glass to his chest he wandered back down the corridor with the blue-red Persian runner that Bev had paid good money for, to the head of the stairs. At forty-two he shouldn't be afraid of tripping down the stairs. Trick is to have each foot well posed. Like each question posed but never answered. Dear God, if I could only understand.

THE DOOR SWUNG OPEN, damp urine odor rushing out, no light. Broken glass underfoot, tinkle of a bottle cap. Smell of corpses beneath the rubble.

It was a long low cellar with a gaping window at the back. Footsteps clattered into the alley behind her; Rosa ducked into the cellar, shut the door. The men dashed past, three or four, frightened, gasping. One tripped on debris and fell with a crash of metal then ran onward, wailing.

Streets away a Kalashnikov barked; death seeking someone. A whoosh and wham of shells against the next hill. A scream – no a ricochet; anguished metal hunting a home in flesh.

More men ran into the alley, panting, halted, clink of steel on steel. A crackle of Hebrew on the radio. "*Damn* you," she said, pressed herself back into the corner of the cellar, beside the window, reached under her raincoat into the sack round her waist and took out a grenade.

A rocket swooshed over. The ground shivered, a roar split the night. Chunks of wall and ceiling pattered down, one punching her shoulder.

Bullets whacked and crashed into the alley, an M16, uphill. Galils chattered back, someone called out, Israeli. Again the Galils roared, the noise deafening through the street door. A man was moaning, as if he'd had the wind knocked out of him. Another whispered, Israeli, then harsher, louder. Ahead, the

Galil spat more bullets down the alley. She bent over her sack of grenades, trying to cover them, fearing the noise would explode them.

Sounds of choking, ripping cloth, someone speaking fast in Hebrew about a medic in five minutes and a recoilless rifle; she couldn't understand.

A spent round pinged down into the street. Stab of light under the door, fifty-caliber bullets hammering off distant walls.

The Israelis broke the door and dragged the wounded man into the cellar. They shut the door and snapped on a flashlight. One tall and broad-chested, on the floor, gut shot. Another trying to compress the wound while a third held the light, tearing open a medical kit.

Her heart was beating so hard she couldn't hear what they said. Steps thumped across the ruined floor overhead – more Israelis taking up positions. No. The Israelis in the cellar were silent, holding their guns, listening. The wounded man's legs began to quiver and another put a hand over his mouth, shut off the flashlight.

She took a deep, silent breath. Two grenades clicked together in her sack; she held her breath; the Israelis didn't hear.

A shell came down sighing and smacked into the next street, the earth shook, staggered, a building began to fall. In the roar Rosa crawled quickly through the window, over a tile roof that had fallen in one tilting piece, then down the next alley, listening, moving ten feet and listening again. A Mirage came in low and dropped napalm, the sky bright as a hearth, wind roaring through the streets toward the seething flames, the screams, the wail of metal, stone and flesh bending, breaking, melting. So this is Hell, she thought, running up the narrow street under the boiling red clouds, her sack of grenades clasped tight to her belly.

3

NEILL WOKE WITH HIS STOMACH AFIRE. There was a distant, nearing rumble. A 747, the first United from New York. In that plane the passengers would be waking, stretching, gathering their things after a night over the Atlantic. Not the same as the first time he had crossed fourth class in the *SS Statendam*, a kid of seventeen deserting Cleveland for the London School of Economics and a world of excitement and anticipation.

The plane passed over rattling the glass. What if he'd stayed in the States – how could it have been worse than this? What would he have become, an editor on some local paper, chasing down dog-bite stories, living in some split-level suburban slum? He'd have never gone to Beirut, Czechoslovakia, all those other places, have never met Bev.

He got up and closed the window. "I was going somewhere with Jonathan Tremaine," Beverly mumbled. "In his Austin Healey. The wind was blowing our hair."

"Good old Jonathan." Neill got back into bed, wondering if in the dream she'd slept with him. A 707, a charter maybe, crisped over, closer to the Thames, landing lights blinking as it crossed the window.

Without Bev he wouldn't have had the kids. He thought of them sleeping in their rooms above the ceiling. If he never came back would they miss him? They'd grow up fine without him. Or is even a lousy father better than none? Edgar already had too much of the world on his broad young shoulders. And the boys like sharks round Katerina – a fatherless girl is always easier to screw. Even if they don't think so they *need* you. More than you give.

But you always feel like this before you go. A total coward, always have been. Admit it. You may be a world-jaded journalist but you've hated or feared or been bored by nearly every moment of it.

And aren't kids better with a father who does what he wants, instead of one who's always afraid? He noted the triumphant smile of peace on Beverly's sleeping face. Would that I could. He raised his knees but the knot in his stomach wouldn't go away. Beverly a believer in twenty-year cycles. Ready to slip from him to the next. He sat up, feet cold on the carpet, rubbing his stubble. Can I shower without waking her?

A SHELL SCREAMED over like a siren, Syrian from the hills, aimed *here*, coming down louder, louder, shaking the night, shuddering the earth, shrapnel shrieking through the streets.

Beneath her raincoat Rosa cradled the sack of grenades closer. "You're crazy," the Christian guard said.

He had a scar down one cheek, under the stubble. It cut into his lip and in the early morning light made him seem petulant. She adjusted her weight. "He's still in there, my father. Rue Lebbos –"

"We've cornered some Shiites there. You can't go in."

"He's blind. I have to get him out."

He tipped up her chin with his rifle, watching her eyes. "There *is* no more Rue Lebbos."

"He's in a cellar."

"They've all caved in. There's no one there any more, sister." He glanced at the round belly beneath her raincoat. "Bring us new life. Forget the old."

He seemed kind, despite his scar, maybe not one of the Christians that murdered the two thousand Palestinian women and children and old people here in Shatila last year. She pushed round him, over the broken concrete. "You'd treat *your* father so?"

He pointed the rifle at her belly, nudged the muzzle up to her face, tapped the trigger as he swung the muzzle up and the bullets spattered over her head off the wall and up into the sky. Chunks of clay fell down on her head and shoulders. "It's for your child, sister, that I didn't shoot you. Perhaps I still will."

"Shoot me, then." She turned and walked between the broken houses, tensed for the bullets to bore like rods of fire through her belly, spine, and brain, the grenades blowing up and spreading her in tiny chunks of flesh and bone.

A shell roared down and slapped the next street, shrapnel singing off the buildings. She ducked, straightened slowly, walking still, cradling her belly of grenades beneath the raincoat, the rush of her breath and hustling footsteps and the clicking of the grenades loud in her ears.

The guard would wait till the last moment before he fired. Till she crossed the ruined orchard at the top, full silhouette. Giving her time to think about it, turn back.

Steadily up the steps cut in the clay hill, no houses now, splintered lemon stumps, her footsteps whispering, the sun's red crescent up out of the towering Shouf, spilling like dusty lava down through wracked pine forests and smoky ruined villages. Not looking back she passed the crest, beyond the guard's field of fire, round a blasted tractor, a ruined almond orchard with demolished stone walls and the carious upjutting jaws of a burnt house. Someone had dragged olive boughs to the path to cut up for firewood. There was the stench of death, human or animal, she couldn't tell. She went in dawn's light down the far side of the hill into the outskirts of Beirut.

"THIS *WILL* BE THE LAST TIME," Beverly said. She took a sip of her coffee and it left a creamy mark on her upper lip. Neill forced down the annoyed urge to wipe it away. Let her look how she looks.

"I've tried, too, Bev," he said softly. His leaving made everything here seem easy, made him feel affection for it all. With the back of a finger he wiped the milk from her lip. All was packed, the kids already gone, no reason to linger but for some moment of clarity that never came.

He put his dishes in the dishwasher, went upstairs, brushed his teeth, took a leak, as if marking territory for the last time, he thought, and came down with his bag over one shoulder.

"I said I'd take you to the airport," she said.

"You've got clients this morning."

She fingered half a caress down his temple and cheek. "Thank God you're going ..." She gave him her reluctant half-shy smile, the one to make him feel guilty for her having to smile. For her having to overcome the sorrow of living with him.

He kissed her, thinking of when their kisses might have meant something. The house felt dusty, full of ashes and chill; he couldn't breathe he was so anxious to leave, the knot in his stomach something he could nearly reach inside and tear out.

"Remember how you always said, Neill, we have to choose between being kind and winning? See, you've proved yourself wrong: you've done neither."

He went down the front steps into the early morning street and turned toward Earls Court station, across Cromwell and right at the corner into Hogarth Road, glancing back at the traffic.

A taxi slowed but he waved it on. Another, a red one, came idling up and stopped beside him. He glanced into the back, opened the door and got in beside a short stocky balding man in a gray suit and mac. The man held a black hat, *The Times*, and a briefcase on his lap. The driver turned into Earls Court and continued past the station. The small man opened his briefcase, raising its lid so the driver could not see inside it. "Came in last night. Bloody perfect."

Inside the briefcase was a photo of a dark-bearded man, high forehead, clear expression, narrow deepset eyes, thick long nose, sharp lips in a wide mouth. A straight-ahead, fear-nothing face. Staring toward the camera but not seeing it, not squinting despite the sun in his face. Behind him, out of focus, a clay brick wall.

"What if this guy *didn't* blow the Marines' barracks, the French paratroopers?"

"That's what we'd like to find out."

"I still don't understand why you've got the hots for him –"

"You let *us* worry about that. Just get to see him."

"*Us?*"

"You don't have to be British to serve the Queen, Neill. We appreciate what you've done, over the last twelve years …"

"Screw the Queen, Adam. I do it for the money."

"That's an honorable motive, too. We respect that."

"If I see him, I'm doing it *my* way."

"Then we can't back you up."

"Even after twelve years, Adam, I wouldn't depend on you."

"Nor we on you."

"That's a bloody lie!"

Freeman sat back in the taxi seat with a pricked stiff face. As if, Neill thought, I could ever hurt *them*. "What I meant," Freeman said, "is I don't know how far we can leverage for you."

"First time you want you'll drop me dead. We both know that."

"And you'll drop us too, any time *you* want."

"Everybody shafts everybody, Adam. What are you getting at?"

"It's two stitches up under your arm. Nobody will ever see it or know it's there. Soon as you come back we take it out."

"Until then, every second, you know where I am –"

"Most of the time we couldn't care less. But if you're in trouble we can be there."

"You blind bastards couldn't rescue the PM from the Royal Loo. You don't even dare show your ass in Beirut since the Hez came."

Freeman smiled, a teacher tolerating the tantrum of a child. "We've decided that if you want to go through with it, we need you wired."

"I'll go without you. Do my interview with Mohammed for the paper and leave."

"I can't imagine you giving up ten thousand that easily."

"So that's what you're saying? No transmitter, no money?"

"Imagine how *we'd* look if you got into trouble."

The taxi swerved round a bicycle, a girl in a brown suit and long black scarf. "Whatever happens," Neill answered, "you're clean. You know that or you wouldn't be here."

"It takes about five minutes and you're on your way. You won't even feel it. By the time you reach Amsterdam you'll have forgotten all about it. But it could save your life. Do it for *us*."

Neill watched the traffic, the grim dirty fenders and windshields, sheets of the *Telegraph* windscattered along King's Road, the wind-wrenched boughs and muddy grass behind the curb, the sense of living on decay. How good it would be, he thought, to start anew. "Once and for all, Adam, tell me who *us* is?"

"I do and I'll be out of a job and in prison. Official secrets, all that."

"Just between me and you, Adam? After all these years –"

"There *is* no between you and me." Freeman nodded at the taxi roof. "We're on record."

Neill stared out of the window, seeing nothing. "Fifteen thousand."

"It isn't a money thing, Neill. For this protection, we should ask *you* to pay."

Neill smiled. See, there is a God, for only a God would have invented *us*. "Fifteen thousand, instead of the original ten. If you want to follow me around, that's what it's going to cost you."

"I'll speak to them."

"No *speaking*, Adam. I want your agreement, now. Half sent now and a half later."

Freeman checked the locks on his briefcase. "We've always tried to bend over for you, Neill –"

"Don't say that, Adam. Makes you sound like a fag."

Freeman snorted, turned away. Neill could not find him in the mirror. Beside Neill a Mini throbbed, dark-haired girl inside, red scarf, red lips; beyond her and around them cars, trucks, and buses floated in a writhing gray sea that had risen up and stained the buildings, the morning sky. Under the Albert Bridge the Thames was dirtier than the sky. Dirty as our lungs, Neill thought.

At Gatwick they went into a locked hospitality suite. Inside was a short slender balding young man with gold rims and a dark beard. "This is Dr. Kane," Freeman said. It was a narrow room with a yellow-green convertible couch, a self-service bar, and a window with closed curtains of yellow and white acrylic.

Dr. Kane opened his black briefcase. "I need you to strip to the waist and lie down on the couch. We'll have you back on your way in a sec."

4

"THE MORE I GET TO KNOW YOU," Monique said, "the less I know."

André lay back, watching her, the espresso cup in her hand, the strap of her silly nightgown across her arm, her hair all tousled, a sleep crease shadowed by the morning sun down her cheek. She shook back her hair. "You're always disappearing."

Since Yves' death everything irritated him, even Monique. "I don't go anywhere. I've told you that."

"You shack up with somebody?"

"They were training exercises – cowboy stuff. Preparing for the day Corsica attacks France."

She finished her coffee, leaned out of the bed to put the cup on the floor. "When we decide to, it won't do any good to be prepared –"

"I've quit the Paras. The biggest danger I face now is probably your husband."

NEAR THE RUINS of the prison and the Université Libanaise some merchants had set up shop in rubble-walled shacks with tin roofing. A man was selling pens from a paper bag. Another had spread lemons, oranges, peppers, and eggs in the sun under half an awning; a cat sat in a shred of stone window, its yellow tail hanging down.

"Hey, young mother!" the fruit man called, "I've got meat!"

"What meat?" Rosa said.

"Goat, mother! Came through Israeli lines. Come, have a look!"

She followed him into the shade of the half-awning, where a stringy black foreleg hung. He waved at the flies. "It's dog," Rosa said.

"Where are you going?"

She glanced at his eyes, troubled and brown, in creases of dirty skin. Druze, down from the Shouf. Lost everyone too, have you? She nodded toward the smoky southern heights of Ras Beirut. "What do you hear?"

"Hezbollah still has the southern side and Amal the north. There's Palestinians trying to fight their way out of Hamra. When they're not shooting each other, Hezbollah and Amal are killing the Palestinians. Christians are shelling from the east, Syrians from the hills, Druze from the Shouf, and Israelis from the south."

"Nothing new, then."

The creased eyes dropped to her belly. He held up the black foreleg. "Young mother like you, needs her meat."

THE DAMP AIR at Schiphol Airport made Neill's underarm hurt even more. It had been five stitches, not two, up under the hair. Liar. The stitches rubbed when he walked and tugged when he carried his bag, and the lump under the skin was swollen like a nodule. He stopped at a bar for a quick gin to swallow down two of the Klaricid Kane had given him, "so there'll be no infection," and two Paludrine for the malaria he had first caught at nineteen in Beirut, and that came back with any quick change of climate, any new exposure. He downed a second gin and caught a taxi to Prinsengracht.

Number 39 was a four-story house one room wide leaning over the root-fissured brick pavement, propped up by narrow houses on each side, and facing across the sycamore crowns and brick street, the leaf-dirty cars, and the cold canal to another façade of other tall grim houses. He punched a code into the door, opened it, climbed to the top floor and let himself in.

The long thin apartment was bathed in near-sepulchral light. Too calm – the goldfish coasting slowly in their bowl, the shiny kitchen counter, the fine rugs and polished floors, Amsterdam's saline sky through diamond-paned windows. "Inneka!" he called, but no one answered. He left his bag by the bed and went downstairs and along Reguliersgracht over the double humped bridges where two canals met, toward Rembrandts Plein and the river, the wind at his back.

THE PRIEST was droning on and André's glance wandered to the pale limestone walls downcast with sun, the stained stone bleeding its slow calcium rot, the time-gnawed lion and human gargoyles on the column crowns, stone faces that had leered down on so many centuries of humans reaching up for God, sneering for centuries at the same human hunger, pain, and sorrow. Is that hatred in their eyes, he wondered, or only irony?

The gray midmorning Normandy light spilled through the faded glass, streaking the pale walls. This imitation, he thought, of the first temples at this ancient curve of the Seine, hallowed rock beneath the oaks, the eye following their columns upward to the arched leafy boughs and the azure of a ceiling you could take for Heaven, if you wanted.

This church at Les Andelys that Richard the Lionheart had built after he came back from the Holy Land and prison in Dürnstein, after he'd built Château Gaillard on the limestone promontory above – two years to build the castle then two months for the church, the castle incorporating the most advanced military defense techniques he'd copied from the

Saracens in the Holy Land. Like Richard, André realized, like his brother Yves, now he too was leaving Normandy for the Holy Land. But not to defend it.

Richard taught that to serve the cause of vengeance is to serve the cause of God: build a church or castle, it's all the same. Richard came back from Lebanon with the secrets of Saracen defensive architecture, but they didn't save him. Yves came back in shreds in a black box. Who am I avenging, really? And how will I come back?

Bread and wine into body and blood, every word so sharp that everyone inside this church hears it with a single heart, one mind, for these few moments. He saw the crewcut rugged soldiers in the far pews, some bored, some in conscientious attention to the priest whose words washed over them like so many words over so many souls over eight hundred years inside these same stone walls. The children sucking thumbs and wheedling, old people rapt or diligent in prayer, the priest's prayer now for Pierre Duclair, the sports teacher, forty-three, with a wife and four children, fallen dead on Tuesday as he waited for medicine at the chemist, the priest's prayer for all those hungry and despairing, his admonition to see the scorned beggar at the roadside as Christ, and André made a mental note that this was foolishness because if you did you'd soon be a beggar yourself – but then wouldn't you be like Christ?

A woman in front of him, with three kids, young and pert with short blonde hair curled over her ears, a pretty young body despite the kids. Beyond her another, a little older, tall and slim, hardly any breasts, with a composed ravenous look – which would he spend the night with, if he could?

He chose the young blonde, thought of *croissants aux amandes* and a *café crème* to break his fast, after Communion. He could meet Monique at Le Central, but she wouldn't want to with Hermann coming home; at lunch today there'd be fine St. Emilion to go with the lamb, Papa bringing up an armful of bottles spiderwebbed and dusty from the *cave* – the way they painted the church walls in the twelfth century, you could still see it, frail and dim, the reds last longest, color of wine, color of blood, or is it just that everything turns to that?

The Host in the priest's hands in the mordant light, boys passing each other in the Communion line with quick glances of complicity, coming and going round him the people he'd grown up with, the couples of his early youth now older and tenuous, the girls he'd been a boy with now with girls of their own, lines of worry and comprehension graven in their faces – it was all there for him, hadn't he understood it, at the moment of the Host, the full mystery and miracle of life?

Filing into the street, there was a patter of tires on cobblestones, rain soft as a woman shedding silken clothes, a sad hunger for vengeance and the dry taste of the Host at the back of his throat.

5

AT A CAFÉ by the river Neill bought a 25-guilder bag of Afghani grass and sat smoking on the terrace with a cappuccino. Across the street cars were lined along the canal, parking meters spaced among them like guards among prisoners on a work detail. On the far side of the Amstel rose the stone gingerbread and brick of the Hotel de l'Europe; everywhere cars, bicycles, and trucks were fleeting back and forth as if seeking somewhere to go, people hustling past, the tall slender women with beautiful chiseled faces and red lips set off by their blonde hair; he smiled, imagining their cool long naked skin.

The grass was chunky and sticky and didn't roll easily, the smoke sweet and powerful down into his lungs out into his blood, putting all in perspective, Bev and Freeman and Inneka and the newspaper and the kids and this trip and his forty-two years crowned with no success, no future. It didn't matter, your future, if you could understand *this*, live fully in *this*.

Across the street policemen with two trucks were towing away first a gray Toyota then a red Lada. One tall bearded cop had a key that opened the Lada's door instantly. Oh to have a key, Neill thought, that opens everything. A few passersby watched half curiously, a man in a tan beret complaining quietly and rancorously. On the radio a man was whining over some woman's desertion:

> *And if you leave me now*
> *You'll take away*
> *The very best part of me*

A tall slender black man, athletic, passed by with a smaller dark-haired white man – a laughing young-hearted couple. How can I look down on that? Neill thought. Then a blonde girl in a camelhair coat, black high heels, black foam pads on wires over her ears. *"You don't have to be alone,"* sang the café radio, a husky woman's voice.

Two girls sat at the next table, drinking espressos and smoking hash from a clay pipe. "Hey!" one of them said, and he looked up, but she was calling a young long-haired guy on the pavement who smiled and came over, kissed them and sat down, his hand on one girl's thigh, smoking their hash. I'm the kind of graying soft-faced man, Neill realized, that nobody notices. He caught his reflection in the café's side window: soon an old man, ripe for defeat.

The joint was too resiny and kept going out; he relit it, inhaling the sweet smoke through his nostrils, tasting it. The CIA had shipped Afghani weed like this to Europe to help pay for weapons to defeat the Russians in Afghanistan. Like everyone in Lebanon was selling opium and hash to pay for their weapons.

Through the smoke everything seemed clearer, the blue Jaguar that had parked where the Lada had been towed away, half up on the pavement, the wet leaves on the dirty stones, the rail beyond and the Amstel River gray slate, an orange houseboat chugging up it, the Hotel de l'Europe primly awaiting a change of season, the weary houses, wet streets beneath damp clouds.

For a moment he'd been happy just to let the game of life go on around him.

BY AFTERNOON IT WAS SUNNY and the dew had dried out of the garden. They set the long wooden table on the stone patio, with wine and salad and bread, lamb and potatoes and peas, André's mother not wanting to sit because then there'd be thirteen at table. "Don't be silly," he said. "You think we'd eat without you?"

She waited till the others, his sisters and their husbands and children, had filed through the kitchen to the patio. "You're going again, aren't you?"

"Just a little while, Mama. Down south."

"Your father knows but he won't tell me."

How savage age is, he thought, seeing her lined face, the pallid flesh and dark worry under the faded eyes. "Papa doesn't know anything because there's nothing to know."

"You've resigned your commission."

"You know why, Mama. Because they did *nothing*. After the bombing."

He saw that the word hurt her and regretted it, took her hand, her skin cold, the flesh bony. When we get old, he thought, the sun doesn't warm us anymore.

"It's because of Yves you're going back," she said. "But there's nothing you can do, *mon cher, cher fils*. And instead of losing one of you now I'm going to lose you both."

"YOU COULD HAVE LEFT me a note," Inneka said.

"I thought you were gone all afternoon," Neill answered. "So I —"

"I just went down to Shopi to get you some beer! I get back, wait two more hours before you come. I could have been at work today, for all the good it does!"

"I'm sorry, Inneka."

"I don't care you're sorry!" She slapped a hairbrush down on the sink. "How do you think I ever want to build a life with you, when I never know where you are?"

Neill followed her into the bedroom, realized what he was doing and stopped, went instead to the window, tucked aside the curtain, watching the umbrellas like black toadstools diagonally cross the street. A gull bobbed on the canal, something white in its beak.

"It's after two," he said. "In eighteen hours I have to be at the station."

She came into his arms and they stood there, swaying slightly, silently.

Even when I do think of her, he realized, it's still for *me*.

ROSA COULD NOT CROSS Rue Madame Curie in the open before dark, and the route she'd planned to take behind the old houses had been hit by Israeli 500-pounders.

A rumble at the far end of Rue Alfred Nobel grew louder through the shelling, the singing inwhistle of Katyushas, the mortars' irregular rattle and thud making the ground pulse like a heart. With a prehistoric roar a Syrian T-34 ground up the hill of ruined houses, its turret gun swinging down Rue Nobel as its treads shuddered and clanked toward the mound where she hid, and all the greatest fears she'd ever had came to one, the great crushing treads, the engine's throaty snarl coming toward her, but if she got up and ran they'd surely shoot her. She had to stay, stay in this hole as it crumbled in the tank's nearing vibration. She had to use the grenades, *that* would stop them, but the sack wouldn't untie and she should have thought of it earlier. Thrashing the earth the tank passed her by, concrete and steel crunching and writhing under its great steel paws, its sour exhaust in her face. It halted, swung its gun uphill.

They're looking for me, she thought, hearing the rumble of

a second tank, a louder higher engine. It swung over the top of the hill and down the flattened street behind her and she darted up and across Rue Madame Curie hoping maybe they wouldn't see her, for a half-fallen building was blocking them. The tank's snout came round the edge of collapsed stones as she leaped into a well, smashing down some kind of stairs that broke the grenades loose when she fell. I'll die now, she thought, scrambling down the stairs after the grenades, they'll explode and me with them. She found the sack and there were three, five, six, seven – they were all there, the thirteen grenades. Holding her breath, she felt for the pins – all there. If they hadn't been it would already have been too late.

Loose stone banged down as the tank neared, shuddering the earth. She scrambled feet first down the stairs into the blackness – it was a courtyard, not a well, this earth above and around her the debris of houses. Fumbling along a wall, she found a window, barred, then a door to smash open and here was an open corridor, chunks of ceiling and something – dishes? – on the floor. Chairs, furniture in the way but she scrambled over them as with a white *wham* a grenade went off in the courtyard and a wall cascaded down between her and it. The tank overhead ground into gear and rumbled away.

Plaster and rock clattered down around her, the air thick with dust. Her ears roared, deafened. Bent over the grenades, she held her breath as long as possible then tried to breathe through her veil. When the air cleared and things stopped falling she tied the grenades up again under her raincoat and peered round her in the shallow darkness. Along one wall was a buffet with dishes and crystal, along the next a coat rack with a man and a woman's long coats and children's jackets. In the middle of the room was a wooden table, set with six plates, silverware, and glasses, all covered with dust.

6

THE GRENADE the tank crew had thrown into the courtyard had imploded the front wall of the living room and the facade of the other floor had dropped in on it. Rosa could find no way out. She felt her way back through the dining room to the kitchen but the next building had fallen in and filled the back door and windows. Her watch said 19:21; already she was late. She put the sack of grenades on the table and began to dig a hole through the rubble blocking the courtyard.

Every handful of rubble she pulled aside only made more tumble down. But cool air was coming in and she scrambled up to it – a fistful of night. She pulled and punched at it, forced the hole wider, slid back down for the grenades and squeezed out through the hole, went down into the courtyard then carefully up its stairs to the gap she had earlier thought was a well. Beneath this opening she listened. There was no sound of the tanks, of footsteps, bullets, or shells. For a moment there was no sound at all, no rifle or mortar anywhere, nothing but the night. Then one round hissed down. No bang: a dud. Or a delay. She tried to decide where it had landed.

A flare burst, half-lighting the street and across it a stairway. Without thinking she crossed the street and climbed the stairs, the light shifting up the steps as the flare fell. The flare died and darkness leaped out at her from the head of the stairs as she caught a glimpse of a vast low room of hunched machines.

She stepped into the room. No sound. Slowly then faster she walked down the aisle alongside the machines. They were like huge animals sleeping, making her afraid to wake them.

Another long low room to the right, then a corridor climbing beyond, then stairs to a dark passage; beyond it a broken door, another dark room.

Wind came through the broken door and chilled her back. She could just see the rectangle of greater darkness that was another door beyond. In between was dark shadow, lumpy, rubble maybe, from the roof through which the tiles had fallen, leaving only a few rafters with splintered crosspieces, a skeleton's ribs black against the sky.

Toward Ras Beirut a machine gun opened up, throaty bursts like migraine jolts, then a long twisting fusillade, answered by the metallic chatter of Kalashnikovs, the hot spat of Galils. She imagined the bullets smashing and clattering through shattered walls and piles of concrete, snatching innocent flesh by hazard, tearing and splattering it.

Someone came through the door behind her and stood, panting.

Whoever it was hadn't seen her. Or he'd seen her and was waiting. To see what she'd do.

She twisted round silently to face him, sinking to her knees to drop her profile from view. He hadn't seen her because he was just standing there. Now he was looking around – she saw the dark shadow of his head move. Automatic rifle in his right hand, smell of burnt oil and powder. Pale shirt, stink of his sweat, cigarette breath. Surely he must smell her too?

He coughed softly, his head moved, and he spat spraying her face. He lunged on ahead, down the corridor into the night.

When his footfalls had cleared the room ahead she followed, toeing her way in and around the smashed concrete, along a path many feet had hardened. Before the next door she halted, expecting him to be there. But he'd gone on, a stripe of moonlight skidding off his shoulder. Twenty yards ahead now, moving fast.

Three more rooms, rubble, splintered beams, starlight, silence, the quiet of roaches and rats, of all that feed on corpses. She imagined them eating, the little shreds of flesh, flesh that had made love, had held children and danced to music, then felt the chill of death.

Ahead a sudden scuffle, a gasp, grunts, three men at least, a voice: "Calm down, brother! Tell us, what religion are you?"

The man in the pale shirt kept gasping, trying to gain time to decide if these men who had grabbed him out of the darkness were Christian or Muslim, Druze or Hezbollah, Sunni or Shiite, Maronite, Syrian, Palestinian or Israeli.

"Answer right and I kiss you," one of them said. "Answer wrong and you die." The others closed up behind him, one's shape blocking the corridor. Rosa edged back into the rubble of the room, knelt down, reached under her raincoat and untied the sack of grenades.

"Just going to Rue Hamra," whispered the man in the pale shirt. "Please, brothers."

"What religion?"

"Truly, brother, I don't care about religion."

"One last time, brother, before I shoot. What religion?"

"*Allahah akbaar*," the man sighed.

Clink of pistol cocking. "Recount the faiths."

"Do not hurt. Do not lie. Do not steal."

"Which of those are you doing tonight?"

"I was just going to Rue Hamra. My family –"

"You are truly a Muslim, brother?"

"Truly."

"You're in luck, brother: so are we."

Rosa took three grenades from the sack, laying them side by side on the ground. She retied the sack tight around her abdomen, put a grenade in each pocket and took the third in her hand.

"Allah be praised," the man in the pale shirt kept repeating.

His voice was shivering. The other men were joking with him now, about his being almost shot for a Christian. "Those pigs!" he said, "eat their own children's entrails."

"How do you know, brother?" one of the men laughed.

"Because I've made them do it."

"Really, now?" One voice took interest. "Tell us."

"No, not really. Just joking ..."

"It is a joke, really," another put in, softly. "The joke is that *we're* Christians."

"And you're a filthy little Muslim," said the first questioner, "who sucks his own cock."

"Please, brother, oh God, please! I'll help you – I've got money –"

"Open his legs!" one said.

The man was screaming then moaning through something, then choking. "See!" one laughed. "I told you Muslims suck their own cocks!"

"That's homosexuality," another said. "You know the sentence for that."

"Certainly." There was a sharp, three-shot burst.

Beretta parabellum, Rosa decided, 9 mm, Israeli issue. Thus perhaps truly Christians. No way could she go back up the shattered corridor without them seeing her shadow cross the opening where the roofs had fallen in. Stay here and sooner or later one of them would light a match, a flashlight, and see her. Or circle round, to take a piss, run right into her.

The grenade was a hard, perfect weight in her hand. But even then could she be sure? Should she move back into the rubble by the wall of the room and wait for them to leave? She put down the grenade, cupped a hand over her wrist and slipped back the sleeve to check her watch: 21:42.

She felt behind her with her toe for a clear place in the broken concrete, stopped when it made a slight hiss against plaster and cement dust. She found another place for her foot, further back, slowly shifted her weight and moved a step backward.

7

RAIN STREAKED the windows. Holland is the only place on earth, Neill thought, where the rain comes down sideways.

In Beirut there'd be no rain now. The wind down from the hills, pine and lavender, the cafés on Rue Hamra full of espresso and cigars and sweet liquor and sex, the sounds of traffic, music, laughter.

No, Hamra's barricaded and bombed. And the only people who go out become the dead ones on the pavements.

"You've been married nineteen years," Inneka said. "No one else I know, but for my parents, their generation, has stayed married so long. How are you going to explain divorcing to Edgar? Even worse, to Katerina?"

"They'd barely notice if I went." He slid his hand slowly up the curve of her waist. So smooth, he thought, nothing stops you.

"I refuse to be the one who makes that happen. If you're going to break from her, do it for yourself, not me."

"I'm crazy," he let his hand fall, "to be thinking of going from one of you to the other."

"You're the one you have to learn to live with, darling."

They dressed in the hesitant glow of the streetlight through the window; he couldn't find one sock till she put on the lamp. "We'll have to go all the way to Rembrandts Plein," she said.

The rain had cleared, white clouds dashed across the moon. Wind cut up Prinsengracht, ruffling the black canal, sharp as a knife at his neck. She wrapped her coat tighter, hugging his arm as they walked. "You should've worn trousers," he said.

A bell tinkled coming up behind them on darkened Keizersgracht by the Advent church, making him jump up on the pavement. "Just a bike," she said.

It was a black rattletrap ridden by a girl in a long blue wool coat who took the bridge across Reguliersgracht, parked the bike and went into the Coffeeshop African Unity.

"It's because you don't want to go on this trip," Inneka said. "That's why you're so jumpy."

The Rhapsody on Rembrandts Plein was still open. At a chilled table on the terrace they ate Greek salad, tournedos and *spaetzle*. The couple at the next table were arguing gently in Italian, under the Motown on the café stereo. On the pavement an electric sign of a woman in blue, a gray cat, and a red-labeled black bottle of instant coffee: "*Sheba. Een teken van liefde.*" The sky had lifted, the moon's light slinking down the slate roofs, the wind chasing scraps of paper and dust around their ankles. On the far side of Rembrandts Plein flashed a red neon sign, "*La Porte d'Or – Live Music*", and he realized he'd been thinking of going in there as if it were a place where he could forget everything, as if there'd be a truth there. A secret.

A trolley ground past, absurdly painted. "Damn graffiti," she said.

"This used to be a nice town."

Behind them three dealers were talking low in French, one with great wide hairy ears. "Seventy *balles*," another said, "I'd take that."

"We should try seventy-five," great ears said.

The first pointed at a car outside. "Look at him, turning round in the street!"

"Like Paris, do whatever they want."

The third raised a finger. *"Je veux dire un truc, moi.* Let me say something."

"But he's not so great. He hustles sometimes but then he just lets himself go ..."

"Nah, nah, nah, nah, nah, nah, still on your side," sang the stereo.

"That's four thousand *balles* each." Great ears held up his cigarette, shrugged. "Not so bad."

The third raised his finger. *"Moi, je veux dire un truc."*

Going down Reguliersgracht, the canal kept catching the moon, its reflection ducking under the bridges. Cars passed furtively like hunted animals. Inside the tall peaceful living room windows, books stood seriously on shelves, pictures hung meaningfully on white walls, and people dined under crystal chandeliers at long tables, all talking animatedly. What, Neill wondered, do they have to talk *about?* What can they *believe?*

Outside a girly bar a kid in jeans with torn knees, a cloth cap, and holey coat was playing a beaten white Strat hooked to a twenty-watt Peavey, the wind so cold his fingers were blue, his caved-in junkie face all caught up in the music that soared out of the black box as the blue fingers raced up and down the strings. A shorter man in a white jacket came round with a cup.

"Amazing," Neill said.

"My student," the man in the white coat said.

Neill dug out his change. Three guilders. "All I have."

The man nodded peremptorily, moved toward another couple. "He's amazing," Neill repeated.

Inneka tugged herself closer to him as they walked. Why am I so nervous? Neill asked himself. Is it about this trip, like she said? He should've given more money to the guitarist – it'd been a lie, about the three guilders; he had guilder notes in his wallet. He could have given him five guilders, even ten. You don't hear that every day, someone so connected to God. To hear someone play like that. It was as if it was a lesson, a test, to see if you were willing to pay for what you get.

"Why do you keep turning round?" Inneka said. "What are you afraid of?"

TEN TO MIDNIGHT but the men hadn't left. Four of them, Rosa had decided. With M16s and handguns – Christians hiding in a deserted factory while Beirut raged around them and their brothers battled to their deaths.

One of the Christians kept too far apart, a sentry – she couldn't be sure to get him with the first grenade, he might have time to dive among the rubble, and then it'd be his rifle against her grenades. She should have disobeyed Walid, brought a pistol. But a pistol in this darkness was like having a flare to show people where you are.

If she used two grenades there'd only be eleven left, and Mohammed's men would be angry. But if she waited any longer the grenades might be too late. Then she'd never get to see Mohammed.

She eased the pin out of one grenade and placed it softly on the ground. One man farted, another laughed. "I'm a happy married man," said a third. "I wouldn't even *look* at his sister."

"Now we know you're a liar. To have said *happy* and *married* in the same sentence."

"For someone who complains so much about his wife, Sylvain, you're always ready to go home."

"Who wouldn't be when *you're* the alternative?"

Holding down the lever of the first grenade she took a second from her pocket, pulled the pin with her teeth and spat it quietly on the ground. A grenade in each hand, she inched on hands and knees toward the voices.

"I have to admit," one was saying, "Muslims cook the best lamb."

"So why are we killing them?"

"Because they're killing us, remember?"

She reached the last jumble of concrete before the open

doorway, their voices five yards beyond. Fighting down her fear she released one lever, then the other.

One second plus one makes two. Two seconds plus two makes three. Three plus three makes four. Four plus four and you always have an extra half a second and she threw one far and one near and dived behind the broken concrete.

A clatter of steel, a yell. The air sucked in, glared white and the *boom* threw her up and smashed her down among flying chunks of steel and concrete in the first grenade's enormous roar that grew and grew, crushed through the hands she'd clasped over her ears down into her skull, her heart, her soul. Great pieces of concrete were smashing down as the second grenade blew, cleaner, hot steel ringing off the shuddering walls. She tried to roll to her feet but couldn't.

Something warm and wet on her neck made her reach up for the wound but it was only a piece of one of the men. Chunks of ceiling kept ticking down. None of the men was moving; their guns were smashed. She stumbled through boiling dust and smoke out the back door of the warehouse into what could be Rue Hussein, she couldn't tell. In the moonlit rubble she could not discern where the Roman arch had been, the square where the old stone houses had grown together like ancient married couples, like old trees.

She could hear nothing, as if at the bottom of the sea, new pain shooting through her ears with every pulse. Mohammed's men would surely be angry that she'd used the two grenades. Four hours late too. Lazy, cowardly slut, they'll have given up on you. She crossed the street and entered the darkness of battered houses on the far side. In four years she'd never been caught; don't start now.

"You can stop now," a voice whispered, behind her.

"*Right* now!" said another.

"Please, sirs, I'm hurrying home –"

"Hah! Abdul, it's a wench!"

"Lucky you didn't kill her!"

A match scraped, flared toward her.

8

"I'M A MOTHER." She forced down the quaver in her voice. "Trying to get home."

In the light of the match she saw a red dirty hand, a smudged candle stub. "Keep your arms up," the other one said, *"mother."*

"I must get to Rue Hamra. My father –"

"He can wait. No doubt he's had a few pieces too in his life."

"What are you? Israelis, Syrians? I'm carrying a child!"

"Was it a nice fuck – the one that knocked you up?"

In the greasy candle light she couldn't find their faces, only shapes, one against the wall, the other closer. She reached for a grenade. "Get undressed," he said.

"I *can't*."

"We'll teach you what a big one feels like. Two of them."

The muzzle he shoved against her was short and hot, an Uzi's. "Either we do it nice," he said, "or we do it nasty. One way you live, one way you don't." His fingers brushed her breast, traveled downwards. She pushed the hand away. "Watch it, *mother*," he said softly.

"*Please ...*"

He tugged her hair. "I'm running out of patience."

"I'll lie down in darkness, over there. You, by the wall there – you come first."

She undressed in the darkness, laying the grenades and her clothes to one side.

"Where are you, chicken?" he whispered. He had a soft young beard and hard hands. "You're not pregnant!"

"It was a pillow, I didn't want *this*." She was shivering so hard she feared she'd throw up.

"Hurry!" the other whispered.

The first finished, facing away as he pulled himself to his feet, stepped back to his gun. The other came forward, knelt, sliding down his pants, his gun loose in the crotch of his arm as he took in her body, leaning his belly down on her. With the heel of her hand she snapped his head up hard, snatched the gun, rolled out from under him and shot the other three times, hearing the bullets smack, then shot this one on the ground, the bullet bouncing back up through his head. He kept squirming so she shot him again between the eyes but he wouldn't stop, even when she leaned down and shot him through the back of the neck.

The air stank. She crouched in a corner to urinate. Animals, she swore. All of us.

THIS IS NOT SO BAD, Neill thought, not realizing it was a dream, stepping into the next street where there was nothing but one house far out on the smashed burnt landscape. In a rubbled square stood a wooden shed with a sign that said *Bill*. He wandered the dirty streets of Beirut, astonished to remember so much. So many houses were gone. He went to the post office with a friend who then met a black girl and left with her, and Neill found a French 10-franc piece on the floor and put it on the counter and the clerk bit into it to see if it was real.

He gave money to a Muslim and a Christian boy in a blown-down street. In a building full of old people and wounded, a wrinkled ancient couple lay naked on a bed in the heat; Neill went downstairs to the desk and recognized the place as a hotel he'd used to make calls back to the UK, years ago.

On the upstairs screened veranda he sat beside a woman in black garters and green underpants with a tattoo on her arm. "I've been shooting tomato juice," she explained. Three men came in. One had a stack of heroin syringes up under both sides of his Levi jacket. He handed her one then another and she injected them into her neck. She must have shot all the veins in her arms, Neill thought. When the last syringe was empty, the man wiped the bloody needle on Neill's knee. The heroin, Neill wondered, did it come from the Bekaa?

Something stood behind Neill but he didn't see it till the last moment: Death smiling down, no escape. He thought he'd left the door open and started to get up, but it was just another dream. It was because of these damn dreams that he couldn't sleep.

He switched on the lamp, thinking if Inneka's got lamps on both sides of the bed then she must have another guy. From the yellow light a skull leaped at him with jaws bared – no, *this* wasn't a dream, just the skull on Inneka's desk, seedy in the malarial light, jaw downhung in disappointment. Her little *memento mori*.

On the ceiling the streetlit shadows of the last sycamore leaves leaped and lurched in the wind. Through the barely open window came the rumble of a car's tires down the wet bricks of Prinsengracht, of clamoring leaves and jostled branches, hiss of cold air over water.

The quilt rustled as Inneka snuggled her back tighter against him. A spray of rain hit the window, as if thrown from a bucket. The leaf and branch shadows lunged harder, writhing against themselves like men being torn apart. His armpit was sore; he pulled his arm from under her head and moved it down between them.

Rain clattered on the roof tiles. Centuries of rain falling on these tiles, he thought, these crooked tall houses stooped like old men. This room of stone, beams, and leaded glass had once been a hayloft where sixteenth-century kids and lovers rummaged. He tried to imagine how they'd looked, felt, acted. Their loves, doubts, and pains. Whom they killed and how, and how they died. How they made love, each time, all of them.

He felt Inneka's warmth settle against his arm, thought of this attic swallowing the two of them also in its silent history.

There was no reason to lose his nerve about this trip. Nothing to fear, nothing he'd be doing that was as dangerous as driving across London. He'd either get to talk to Mohammed or he wouldn't. Give it his best shot. If he did, he'd have a good series for the paper and fifteen thousand from Freeman. But if it fell through – the thought gave him a shiver – he could still come back, pick up where he'd left off. Beverly's client meetings and the kids busy with homework, and every article he wrote exactly the same. Politics – men in gray suits, hapless craven argumentative souls like filthy mirrors casting back a tainted version of all they see.

His mouth felt dry and he thought of getting a drink of water in the bathroom; even the pipe-warm, bleached taste would be great. At dawn would be the chilled station, the train swinging across flat Holland in gray cold rain, from Europe's northern coast up its great river through its cold mountain heart toward the sun.

Bratislava then Beirut. If he was lucky, people in Bratislava could tell him the best way into Beirut. The way to find Mohammed. What was the old saying – about the Mountain coming to Mohammed? Couldn't remember. In Bratislava there'd be Michael Szay – he was selling guns to Mohammed, Freeman had said. And there was Tomás. If anyone in the press knew where to find Mohammed, Tomás would be the one.

Beirut. Like Amsterdam once so innocent and light, now ready to kill you so quickly. Even if you get to see Mohammed, he told himself, there's no way he'll know about Freeman. You're just a journalist, in and out.

Nothing to be afraid of.

The clock on the dresser said 4:44. His underarm felt so damn sore. Burnt out. He'd sleep on the train. No one would be following. Not here.

"I always knew if Bev got in touch with her feelings she'd realize she didn't want to be with me," he'd told Inneka.

"You always said the unexamined life's not worth living," she'd answered.

PRINSENGRACHT was slippery with mist off the canal. Gripping his arm like a hostage's, Inneka walked beside him to the corner up to Vijzelstraat, her raincoat tight over her bathrobe, her leather boots half-zipped, her hair straggly and damp. "There's going to be a taxi right away," she said, "and I'll never have time to say how much I love you but I get mad because you're never here and I love you so much I get angry because *she* has you all the time and doesn't love you and I –"

"She loves me."

"Not like *I* do!" Inneka caught a heel in a crack between the bricks, yanking his arm. "Sometimes it's a month I don't see you! It doesn't even *bother* you."

"Sure it does. I'd rather be with you."

"You have *her*. I have *nobody!*"

"Like I said, you should have somebody, I wouldn't mind. I'm not afraid I'm going to lose you."

"You bastard, I hate you –"

"I meant I love you."

"You don't even understand what you mean."

Down wide wet Vijzelstraat dawn was breaking over the disconsolate trolley wires and vapid windows, the loitering rubbish bins, a solitary high-tailed black cat stalking an alley. The bag tugged his stitches. It would give them time to heal, the train. "Nothing I do I understand – you want me to understand *this?*"

"All the things I said – *we* make them worse."

"Let's just have what we have while we have it."

"I fear for us." She clutched him harder.

"We'll stop if you want. But I think life's too short, too rough, not to do what we can, what we want. I *want* to keep seeing you. I don't want to grow old and die not seeing you."

"We have all eternity, Neill, to be apart."

THE BITCH nosed the puppy but it didn't move. It was cold and she knew it was dead but she kept pushing its rigid chilled body in a dusty circle. She trotted with it in her jaws across the ruins of Bab El-Edriss to a place where stolen vehicles had been parked in the blasted ruins of a goldsmith's shop, and laid it among four others.

From a crest of a collapsed apartment building further up the Rue du Patriarche a pack of dogs watched her go back down through the ruins. She stopped to sniff where once someone had defecated, but it had already been eaten. She loped round the corner into Avenue des Français, glancing back once. A large thin black male trotted after her; the others sniffed the wind and followed.

ANDRÉ TOOK THE BACK ROAD toward Paris, letting the car slide through the dew-wet curves, beech leaves slick on thin macadam, thinking *should've changed the back tires, tread's too slick*. A doe bounded through an apple orchard over leaf-yellow ground, pushed low by the hunters; there was a furl of silver from a roadside stream, trout there if you had the time, a stretch of dairy barns, beams and straw. The engine was hard and hot now, hungry for it, snarling into the curves, baring its teeth as it tore out of them, roaring into the high gears, into the blur of life. *You're going to kill yourself*, he realized and backed it down through the gears, against the engine's banshee wail of disappointment. The road swung round a low beamed house with a plume of smoke and dropped down a steep bouldered slope into a forest.

From Gaillon he took the A13 over the rolling half-forested Normandy hills. There were no cars and he let the Alpine out to 250, till it wanted to fly, the front end planing, the broken line a solid blur, the car vibrating ecstatically, the wind roaring like an engine. The glove box fell open, a flashlight tumbling out, papers. A truck flashed past, "Barboizon & Fils – Démenagements", a faraway jet was a twist of foil in the early sky. Again he let the Alpine back off, down to 200, 180, 150 – there was traffic now, a 735i came up and he dropped it back then slowed and let it pass, its driver choleric and fleshy, a cigarette drooping from his lips.

9

THE DOGS TRACKED the bitch along l'Avenue des Français toward the rubbish dump where the Hotel Normandy had been. She'd seen them and was running now, through a façade of brick and down an alley – but that was wrong because a building had fallen in at the end, and she had to scramble up the rubble and swing round to face them at the top.

They came bounding down the alley and she saw a way out along a slim standing wall, ran across it knowing they'd gain, across a wide square of blasted cars and truncated palms, houses of blackened windows, into a shop with no door, no one to run to, under a hole at the back and across a collapsed building up the trunk of a fallen tree to another wall. One of the dogs snatched her back foot but she pulled free, ripped at his muzzle, dove off the wall and squirmed under a burnt car, the others trying to reach her but she hunched up in the middle and they couldn't get her till one shoved far in and grabbed a front paw. He dragged her out and they tore into her, ripping, crunching up her bones.

The big black thin male dragged away one shoulder, others fighting over ribs, legs, intestines, brains, scraps of skin, smears of blood. They circled the big male, worrying at him, and each time he snapped at one, another darted for the meat; he caught one across the neck and it squealed away but another feinted in. He snatched the meat and dashed back down the alley, the others alongside snatching at the meat; he ducked into a stair corner and dropped it, faced them.

They were three across in the narrow stairway – the young Belgian shepherd male and two red females, the rest behind. Growling, teeth bared, he backed tight into the corner, realized he shouldn't and tried to move forward but one red bitch had edged closer and if he went for her the others would have his neck. He leaped over them but one got him by the scrotum, the Belgian shepherd by the jaw, dragging him down – he couldn't shake it loose. The others were at his belly now, his groin, his thighs, pulling him down under their tearing weight and he was trying to protect his belly but they rolled him over and tore out his throat, snarling and ripping at each other for pieces of him.

A human came out of the building and the dogs backed away, snarling, dragging pieces of meat. A female human. It stepped round the big male's body, and the young Belgian shepherd male circled closer, sniffing for a wound, but this human was healthy, with only the smell of sex and fear about it.

ROSA KEPT GLANCING BACK but after a block the dogs stopped following. The ground crackled beneath her feet. An AK47 snapped nearby, shocking under the early hot sun. Now there was a jet, far away, the crunch and rumble of artillery in the Shouf. She wondered who was shelling whom, and why.

Rue Chateaubriand was blocked so she turned up an alley where the yellow-bricked Phoenician wall still stood waist high. At the top a gray Mercedes sat in the driveway of a wrecked house. There were four Hezbollah in the Mercedes and others in a broken apartment building behind the house. The plane buzzed closer and one of the men in the apartments fired at it. A man in gray shirt and sunglasses got out of the Mercedes. "You're late."

"I've got a message for Mohammed."

They drove fast, dodging the rubble and barricades, uphill toward the Grand Serail, stopped at a truncated building on Rue de France. In one room bodies lay bandaged among sandbags. There was a little room of medical supplies, a radio room and then the captain's office.

"Mohammed doesn't see messengers," the captain said. "That's my job."

"I got through their lines and know how to get out. We can build a supply line – I must tell Mohammed."

He had a nice smile, this captain. His beard was clipped away from his lips, a scar ran across his forehead and another between two right-hand fingers, his camouflage shirt was dark with sweat. "We need you and the others to keep coming through the infidels with your bellies full of grenades, Rosa – that's *your* job."

He gave her his playboy smile again and she decided maybe she didn't like him. His hands were too big, his nose was wrong: you couldn't trust him. "If I can speak to Mohammed about how to get outside, come at them from behind, cut them in two –"

"A woman's writing strategy now?"

"*You* could find your way in here, with a sack of grenades?"

"*I* can't act pregnant."

No, she certainly did not like this squalid little man, his sharp beard and pointed chin. That was the trouble with militia – the killers ruled, the sordid ran behind. "*You'd* do just fine, being pregnant," she sneered, "if you half tried."

THE TRAIN TILTED into a curve, naked poplars running along a ditch, pigeons casting away from bare furrows under a wet wind, distant rain slanting against a sky of cotton wool.

Geese and sheep huddled in a flooded field, God hanging dead over endless cemeteries, trains of rain-shiny new cars on the sidings, camouflaged hunters afoot in mean, close-cropped fields. There were hedgerows, copses, orchards, yellow and blue snub-nosed Dutch trains, nuclear power plants, empty warehouses with broken windows and rusty galvanized roofs, brown stolid rivers, a yellow derrick with the name "Verhagen" in a grove of soggy, chilled birch. Why, he wondered, do the top leaves always cling the longest?

That was the best of Islamic teaching, it clung to fundamental decencies, to an ancient branch of life: take care of the poor, the disinherited, alleviate corruption, simplify and purify our souls ...

But the Koran left nothing unanswered, even that which had no answer. The prophet Mohammed received inspirations to questions posed by himself or others; these inspirations, the *suras*, became a rigid structure of belief learned by repetition, whose challenge was punished by death on earth, eternity in Hell.

The Crusaders went to the Holy Land to deliver it from this heresy, to slaughter the infidels. Those who came back brought the techniques of cathedral architecture, which led to the Gothic enlightenment and the principles of advanced castle construction, which led to a more advanced rate of slaughter. They also brought *rattus rattus*, the black rat, which in turn brought the Black Plague: God's way, Neill had always thought, of punishing the Europeans for the sin of Christianity.

A rusty railroad engine huddled in brush on an abandoned siding. How many lives had it carried back and forth across Europe? What did they come to, each of them?

Three American men were talking loudly in the seats ahead, trading dirty gay jokes in the mistaken impression no one could understand English, or perhaps not even caring. One was being teased about curling his eyebrows. "You go to Paris to make *money*," he said. "Like Tokyo. The catalogues, fashion shows, magazines, even TV. Madrid too – you can make money there, though not as much as in Paris."

"Do you really curl your eyebrows?" another said.

Ubiquitous greenhouses flitting by, amid grimy cities and prim little towns with patches of muddy green between them. "Have to have the clothes," the first added. "*Have* to have the clothes." One made a farting sound with his mouth; they laughed. Rain loud as hail struck the train roof, the window

ANDRÉ LEFT THE ALPINE on Boulevard des Invalides near the Musée Rodin, and crossed against the light, Napoleon's gold-domed crypt afire with sun. He turned into the courtyard at 57 *bis* Rue de Varenne and took the elevator to the third floor, to a bright office with rooms along one side looking down into the courtyard.

"You don't even speak Arabic," St. Honoré said.

"But I know Beirut. And it doesn't matter they've got him surrounded, he'll get away. I know where he'll go."

"Where, pray tell?"

André smiled at St. Honoré's silly envy of a desk man for those who come home with blood on their hands. "It's a waste to tell you; he'll break through one sector, slip round it and get them in the backs."

"The Israelis'll bomb him to the stone age."

"They've been trying for two years. Look at the result."

"Same as yours will be."

"I'm one man, Christian! I can weave right into that crowd."

"With your blue eyes and fluent Arabic."

"I know enough people and you know it."

"So how's Haroun going to help you?" St. Honoré leaned further back in his chair, as if obeying the dictate never to act interested unless you need to. "He's got Palestinians and Hezbollah and Druze and Amal and every other kind of Arab under the sun crawling down his throat. Just because you were with him before isn't going to bring you much."

"That's how you decide who to revenge?"

"The President and the Palestinians, they're hot right now."

"Hezbollah's *not* the Palestinians."

"Iran's making overtures. Foreign Affairs is wrapping up that billion-dollar reactor debt. The Iranians are moderate now."

"You *know* they did it, Christian! *Everyone* knows!"

"That's the trouble with you military guys, you're hung up on truth. Do you understand the place we're in – *la France*? We burn over twenty billion francs of natural gas a year. A third of it comes from Russia, another third from Algeria – both unstable. Any day now we could lose two-thirds of our supply. Literally overnight. We have to diversify."

"And you think Iran's more sure?"

"Iran has seventeen trillion cubic meters of natural gas, the world's second largest reserves."

André thought of St. Honoré when they'd been little, at Institut Suffren. When St. Honoré's mother drove up every morning in the big white Porsche and made him lift up his little *tablier* and piss on the tree outside before he went in to school. Running across the Champs de Mars, skinny knees, *tablier* caught in the wind. The Fields of War – how long since I've thought of it like that?

"The Government's negotiating a pipeline deal with the Iranian National Gas Company," St. Honoré said, "that could eventually supply one-third of our national need, at two billion francs a year cheaper than the Russians. Against that, André, how much do you think your brother's death should weigh?"

"Forty-seven French paratroopers died when Hezbollah blew those barracks, not just Yves."

"France has always required her young men to lay down their lives – whenever *she* wants. The Government would argue, in the long run, that even Yves' death was for the good of France. When we're called, we don't get to choose how we might die."

Again André thought of St. Honoré's little black *tablier* sailing in the wind. St. Honoré'd lost something, and he, André, had found it. But he couldn't remember what it was. "When were you ever called, Christian?"

St. Honoré was listening to traffic on Rue de Varenne. "We go back a long way, *mon cher*. But I don't ask you to like me. I just ask you to understand that your plan gets no sympathy here. In fact, if you go ahead with it, we're going to get badly in your way."

"You'd *tell* him? Via your bedmates in Tehran?"

"He's overstepped his bounds, this Mohammed. Other people out there want him. The Russians, maybe, surely the Israelis, the Americans. But not *you*. We don't want *la France* mixed up in this."

André felt sweaty, as if he'd been driving too fast. "If *la France* doesn't care about Yves, screw *la France*."

"Unless you drop this idea, we have to do what it takes to stop you." The phone buzzed; St. Honoré's hand fell on it. "All the way from the top, *mon cher*, the rule right now is don't piss off Hezbollah."

André shrugged, stood. "I didn't come to ask your advice. I came to tell you." He smiled. "So you don't shoot me by mistake."

"If and when we shoot you," St. Honoré smiled back, "it won't be by mistake."

10

A SYRIAN 240 came over the Green Line, caught people running; a machine gun coughed, tracers darting among the runners. Three bodies lay in the street, one dragging itself backwards till the machine gun coughed again.

Rosa backed from the window. "Despite being surrounded, you seem to have lots to eat."

One of the men crouched round the fire turned, mouth full of bread and lentils. "You've got plump enough yourself, on the outside."

A round cracked across the ceiling. Mortars thudded, one, two, three, onto the roof.

"We're going to break out soon," one said.

"He's got a plan," another answered, chewing. "The people outside, they'll break in."

"If you believe that," Rosa said, "I've got another story for you."

"And you think *he'll* listen to you?"

She returned to the window, edging her face round the frame, thought of a sniper's bullet hitting her head, how *hard* it would feel. Darkness had fallen on the Green Line, shrapnel wailing through the streets, sound of a chopper – no, two – beyond the Israeli lines, the metallic plaint of a buoy out to sea. Then she remembered that all the buoys had been sunk, and whatever the sound was it wasn't out there to save lives.

She heard a rush and patter in the street below. Fearing an attack she glanced down quickly and saw dark shapes, low, fast. She ducked back, against the wall, breathless. Dogs. The ones she'd seen – when? This morning?

She wanted to glance out again but it was too dangerous now; if there was someone out there with a night scope, next time she looked out he'd get her. That's how bad this situation had become, she realized; even an attack here seemed possible. While Mohammed awaited the word of God.

AN OLD MAN in a thin djellabah crouched on the cold concrete quay of Duisburg Station, selling cassettes from a packing crate, AC/DC on a black JVC beside him,

> *You're only young*
> *but you're gonna die.*
> *I won't take no prisoners,*
> *won't spare no lives.*

"Where do you get them?" Neill said.

The man glanced up, surprised by the Arabic, the European face. "Wholesale."

"They're illegal copies."

The man looked up and down the quay, shrugged. "Surely not."

"Where you from?"

The man watched him. "Sidon."

' *"Poor Saida, so close to Israel, so far from God ... "* '

Despite himself the man smiled. "There are many viewpoints."

In a station café Neill ate steak and onions and drank Kaiser Pils till his train was called. A single compartment, first class, the window streaked with rain as the train meandered the bombed medieval memories of Cologne and followed the Rhine canyon south through the soft rolling Rheinisches Schiefergebirge, forests and castles on their crests, steep swathes of grapes below, past Koblenz, the ancient roots of European reason, the Odenwald, and he had again the sense he'd had in Inneka's bedroom, of the generations upon generations who had lived here. Like the sense of all the lives the rusted locomotive had towed across Europe. Here in these German hills, it seemed, was lost the ancient reason for man. Houses flitted by, singular and ephemeral as souls. There was no reason and no rule, no reason for man, falling in space, reaching for anything.

What was he reaching for, with Bev? With Inneka? They were going to die too, maybe before him. He was contorting his mind with worries about who to love, who to live with, for nothing. So that he didn't have to think about death.

He closed the window, took up the Arab newspapers he'd brought in Duisburg Station, and began to read them carefully.

PASTIS IS THE PARAS as much as the bullets themselves, André thought, watching its golden trickles down the inside of his father's glass. The hard friendships, the smoldering anger, the fun. "Michel!" his father roared. "*Encore deux!*"

"Got to go, Papa."

"One more? Come on, *mon fils*, it does us good!" His father grinning his broad-jawed silvered teeth, chubby cheeks curling up into his eyes. "Leave these women alone, for God's sake!"

"Don't cast stones."

His father tilted his pastis glass, contemplated it. André thought of the Red Indians, how supposedly they had learned the art of silence. How right his father had been to teach it, a soldier's gift. "I've known Haroun thirty years," his father said. "Never had a reason not to trust him. But I've never learned who you can trust, for sure, until it's too late."

"I don't trust anybody, Papa."

"You saw your friend?"

"He's not my friend."

"They're so in love with political solutions, those boys at Matignon." His father drained the pastis, smacked his lips – it made him seem a huge gregarious bear with a silver crewcut, gray-bristly cheeks and merry little black eyes. "People who've never been to war, you never can tell what they'll do. How they'll decide to prove their courage." He raised his glass and nodded at Michel. "No matter how many other people's lives it takes."

Michel refilled their glasses and laid a pack of Gauloises on the counter. André's father tore it open and lit one. "Such shit –"

"Don't smoke them then."

"This pastis. Not like the old stuff," he raised high his glass like a scientist examining a test tube. "The old stuff, it made your veins sing." He put the glass down. "All those herbs crushed to-gether – the *essence* of Provence, basil, rosemary, thyme, anise, sage – ah!" He smacked his lips. "This!" He raised the test tube again, downed it, wrinkling his lips. "*La merde!* Factory-made! *La nouvelle France* – Arabs, niggers, drug addicts, pederasts, thieves."

André glanced down the bar. "See you, Papa."

His father laid a fifty franc bill beside the empty yellow glass. "Coming with you."

Outside the early darkness was damp and fresh, the pave-ments filled with people hurrying home with children and handbags and briefcases and bread and bags of vegetables and fruit and cheese and wine. "Nobody on the other side," his fa-ther said, "is going to believe your story, once they tie you to Haroun."

"He's just a *point de départ.*"

They came to Emile Zola, a taxi splashing through the cross-walk. "Start saving *now* for your burial expenses," an electric sign said. "Spare your family." His father was short of breath, hissing through his nostrils, trying not to show it. "I told your mama if there's one chance in a thousand of losing you, I wouldn't want to take it. And I don't."

"It's not Oran, Papa. Not Hanoi. I know Beirut."

"I knew Oran. That didn't keep me from losing two hundred men there. Each with a family and dreams. And another twelve hundred wounded. A lot of them ruined for life."

André nodded. "And just like Beirut, we took a beating and ran away. When *we* were the stronger! Killing our own brave men for nothing."

"Nobody wins all the time, even the strong. We're lucky to win at all."

"You don't believe that." André embraced him, his father's bristly cheeks against his own.

His father seemed to be chewing something far back inside his mouth. "Let me know, what happens." He turned and walked toward the *métro* entrance, suddenly a bowed-over burly man who hesitated at the stairs, looked back and nodded, a wink perhaps, André couldn't see, and stepped down into the teeming maw as into a freshly turned mass grave.

11

"YOU? LEADING MUJIHADEEN?" Mohammed said.

"You'd be leading them," Rosa answered. "I just know the way to safety."

"I don't care about their safety. Nor do they."

"If they're dead, how can they fight?"

Static rose and fell on the radio, the operator bent over it as if praying, Rosa thought, awaiting the *Word*. Four mujihadeen were playing cards on a piece of cardboard set on a broken box. Like rodents, Mohammed's fingers burrowed into his gown, joined. "She fears for your safety, Hassan!" he called to the guard at the door.

Crunching a pistachio shell in his teeth, Hassan looked straight at Rosa, back to Mohammed, spat the shell.

She curled her lip. "*I* want to win."

Mohammed's head tilted back, shadowed in the yellow lamp-light, his blue eyes seeming to look down his face, his full beard, to hers. "Win?"

Long and pale-whiskered in his white gown, he looked both taut and empty of everything, as if not really there – only the maroon pillows on which he sat, the torn carpet littered with cartridge casings, the guard picking his teeth with a broken match, a European country scene in a shattered gilded frame hanging sideways on the graffiti-covered wall.

"We had a picture like that, when I was a girl," she said. "Of a woman walking a path toward a straw-roofed cottage, with purple hills behind. Made you feel warm, going home."

He yawned, covering his mouth. "And?"

"It was in our farm at Ramalla. Where my mother and father moved in 1950 after we escaped from Beersheba. Then in 1967 we escaped to Nablus, and the mule died, and then to Zababida where we had to live in a tent camp and my father caught tuberculosis. Then they moved us across the Jordan to another camp where both my sisters died, and then to Tiberias where my father dug a farm out of the rocks and boulders, but they took that away and chased us across the Golan and up the Jebel ech Cheikh to Mount Hermon where my father and mother died, in Ain Aata, when the Israelis bombed us. And you ask *me* what it means to *win*?"

"God grant peace to the souls of your family," Mohammed said mechanically. "What was it like, in Ain Aata?"

"Everyone made us feel outsiders. Going home from school the boys hit me with rocks."

"There were too many of you, coming up from Palestine."

"If I have to tell you what winning means ..." She paused, a shell coming like a distant train's whistle, something that could take you somewhere, far from it all. For a very long time it came no nearer, wailing in mid-sky, then dived at them shrieking, seething metal louder than a comet rushing down; she rolled over on her side clutching her head as the building shuddered and heaved in the roar of falling concrete in the next street, plaster crashing down.

She sat up, head covered, held her breath till the ceiling stopped falling. Bullets cracked along a wall, plaster flying. Another shell was screaming down; her ears were blocked with plaster dust, she couldn't hear; the shell fell a few streets away, the building shuddering anew like a crazed dancer. "You should be ashamed!" she yelled. "To let them shell us like this!"

Mohammed brushed plaster chunks from her shoulders. "That was Amal, from Shatila. A mistake –"

One of the guards relit the lantern, throwing the room into jagged boiling shadows. Somewhere overhead a machine gun fired, then a Kalashnikov, a long, rattling salvo. "Shooting at nothing!" she fumed. Another shell was dropping; they keep coming, she thought, like homeless children, like hunting dogs. "Don't you *care*?" she screamed. The shell fell like a dying airplane into the next street, knocking her to her knees, new plaster tumbling. He said something she couldn't hear over the waterfall rumble of a building collapsing. It takes so long, she thought, for a building to fall, like a man dying.

Mohammed was brushing plaster from her shoulder again, and she sensed suddenly how much he did care that this was happening, that the way to make him gentle was to hurt him. A bullet sang off the window frame into the room, seeking flesh. "You're going to lose us all," she said.

"Kill the light!" he called.

"We'll have to move down a floor," a guard yelled. "The other side."

"Can't see from there."

"He's in the Life Building over there, your sniper," Rosa shouted.

"We can't get him from here!" Hassan snarled. Bullets punched through the wall, fifty caliber, and she dove hitting her head on chunks of plaster. The bullets had crossed right through, in the front walls and out the back; she lay gripping a gun then realized it was a piece of the gilded frame.

She followed them down the dark plaster-piled stairway to the next floor. They were smashing open a door to a back apartment. The wood splintered and gave. An enormous *bang* knocked her to her knees, the floor wobbling.

"Just a rocket, up there," Mohammed said calmly, as if he'd found the simple answer to a complex problem. "Lucky we moved."

The new apartment was well-furnished. Like an archaeological dig, Rosa thought, a tomb not yet looted. "Damn!" Hassan said, lighting the lantern.

More mujihadeen were coming down from the upper stories. "They've located you," one said to Mohammed.

An old man came running up the stairs and into the room, knelt before Mohammed. "Cut that out," Mohammed snapped.

The old man stood, panting. "Hekmatyar says send a hundred men. Fifty rocket grenades. Or we can't hold all night."

"Tell him to pull back now. To Soutros Soustani."

Another rocket hit upstairs and the old man clasped his ears. Rosa shoved him aside, yelled at Mohammed, "I'll shut your snipers up. Give me a *gun!*"

"My son's there," the old man said, "with Hekmatyar."

"He'll pull back now. To safety."

Rosa snatched Mohammed's arm. "You're abandoning the Green Line?"

"I don't have the men to hold it."

"Put the wounded here?" someone called.

"Basement!" Mohammed yelled. Another rocket smashed through the upstairs and out the back, exploding in air, pieces howling down.

"Who's on the roof?"

"Dead!"

"Who's upstairs?"

"None."

"Got to go!" someone was saying, over and over. "Go!"

Rosa shook Mohammed's arm. "Give me a *gun!*"

"The basement," someone yelled.

"No!" Mohammed thundered through the plaster dust and echoing explosions. "I want an outpost *here!*"

She snatched his beard in both hands and shook it. "Do you want to kill those snipers?"

"Quiet!" he snapped.

"It's Christians in the Life Building," she seethed, "with anti-tank rockets and a fifty caliber! Give me a *gun*, and I'll get them!"

"You?" Hassan was coughing from the dust. "You?"

"If I get them," she said to Mohammed, "will you follow my plan?"

Another rocket hit and he pushed her down. "Go back to Mount Hermon, Rosa! Leave us to fight."

WET COBBLES HISSED AND RATTLED under the tires, a cat's eyes flashed from beneath a parked Citroen, a big dog bent over a trash can – then André saw it was an old man. "You're going to kill yourself with those cigarettes," he said to Monique.

"Can't stop," she said.

"If someone said stop or they'd shoot you, wouldn't you stop?"

"You always think one more won't hurt you."

He pushed the button to open her window a crack, to suck her cigarette smoke out. "Funny it's what we love that kills us."

"Sometimes I think it's the reverse: we kill what we love." She took a last drag on the cigarette, tossed it out of the window. "You ever think where you want to be when you die?"

"Buried?"

"I want to be in Corsica, a rocky hill high over the sea. I told Hermann that, but he couldn't give a damn – thinks we're all going to live forever."

He turned into Rue Etienne Marcel, shifted into second, letting the car snap them back, slid his hand up her short skirt, the lovely silky thigh perfect against his palm. "I like the sea."

She put her hand over his. "You'd be buried there?"

"Down with the fish and octopus, the sharks, flesh of their flesh."

A taxi shot out of a side street and he braked hard, the Alpine sideskidding. Should have switched the rear tires, he reminded himself angrily.

"That's it, isn't it?" She pointed up at a crooked tower over the narrow twisting street. "The *tour de Jean sans Peur?*"

"He built it with a fortified room at the top, to spend his nights."

"Who'd he kill? I forgot."

"His cousin, the Duke of Orleans, in the Rue des Francs-Bourgeois."

"Imagine, never daring to sleep, for fear you'll be knifed to death."

"He was killed anyway, by the Armagnacs." He geared down, hit the high beams. "Has to be here." On one side of the next street, tall leaning stone façades, on the other a wall two stories high with a great red carved door. André pulled up on the paved drive, and sounded the horn and the door swung open.

Inside, cars were parked in a broad cobbled square lit by the tall windows of a great house with a double curving stone staircase. "Whatever you do," she said, "don't say who I am."

12

THE MAP WAS BLOODY and torn across Shatila, Rosa noticed. Where they'd slaughtered so many. For an instant war seemed insane, like facing a mirror and smashing your image till you bleed to death. Here at Rue Weygand the map was worn by many fingers having moved across it, fingers seeking ways out, ambushes, corners, dead ends, ways to get caught and ways not to, the brutal business of death. How far can that rocket reach? How long can he breathe with a 7.62 through his lungs?

"It's a firestorm," the boy was saying. He was dirty and thin, a tail of *keffiyeh* over long curly blond hair, a Christian cross chained to his neck in case of capture. He couldn't stop his lips from shaking; he kept pinching them with his fingers, and the tears were streaking his cheeks, making him seem even younger. Every time he started to talk his lips would shiver and the tears ran.

"You don't have to go back," Mohammed said.

A rocket came down clattering over by the Serail, only half blew. "Send us more men."

"There aren't any."

"Here?" The boy glanced round. Bullets drummed into the front wall; upstairs someone fired back.

"I have ten men for a command that should have fifty," Mohammed said. "Every man I take from here risks losing a hundred elsewhere."

"I understand."

Mohammed hugged him across the shoulders, pulling him close, touched his forehead to the boy's temple. "Go quickly and carefully." He stood back. "Look at me!" When the boy glanced up, Mohammed looked straight into his eyes. "I *order* you not to die."

The boy glanced down as if contrite.

"And tell Abou Hamid," Mohammed said, "to pull back to Riad Solh, except for the one building that makes the L at the corner. Tell him no matter what don't lose it. Retreat to it if you have to, but don't lose it."

"If we do, we can't get across –"

A bullet snapped overhead but Mohammed did not duck. "Keep the three buildings around it – you'll see, there's three in a box. They're all stone with small windows. If you keep the upper stories you can sweep the streets and nobody's going to come in, and until they get the Israelis or the Americans on you you're OK. Keep the M60 on the top floor of the building on the right and one Katyusha the next floor down in the middle. Two riflemen at least in the place on the left, one top, one middle."

A man with a bandaged head came in, winded from the climb. He hugged Mohammed and the boy, one guard.

'Go on," Mohammed told the boy. "Tell them no rock 'n roll."

"Full automatic? We don't have the ammo."

"Do you want to speak to Al-Safa?" the radio man called.

Mohammed took the phone. "Allah!" He turned to the boy. "I'll be there at midnight."

"Don't come –"

"Tell them to pull back," Mohammed said into the phone.

"We lost the fifty caliber," the bandaged man said.

"You *what?*" Mohammed put down the phone.

"A mortar. We don't know whose. Three more men gone; we're down to two magazines each."

"Like I told Emmaus, no full automatic."

The man snorted. "You really think those poor kids are going to be into a paradise of solid pussy, where you're sending them?"

A rocket screamed into the floor upstairs and after the explosion there was a long roaring sound like oil catching fire and with a great shrug the floor above them fell outwards. "You heard me," Mohammed said. "I told them to pull back."

"To that building that makes the L," the man said. "And where the hell are they going to pull back to from there?"

Another rocket blew out the ceiling and people were leaning out of the windows to escape from the fumes but the Christians in the Life Building saw them and raked the windows just as Rosa ran screaming at them. "Get down! Get *down!*" And now there was another to add to the pile of thin young men who lay in the corner uncomplaining, dressed in their own blood.

"Get that sniper!" Rosa screamed.

"More sandbags!" someone was yelling down the stairs. *"Bring up more sandbags!"*

It was the radio operator who'd been hit, half his head taken off, like a biology textbook, she thought, "Look inside your brain". But now they couldn't send messages and Hassan ran downstairs to get the girl off the machine gun in the street who knew the signals.

Skidding on blood, Rosa ran into a bedroom. There was a canopied double bed and two dressers with a crucifix high between them. She tore the spread off the bed and swept the snapshots off the dressers into it, some clothes from the drawers, silk scarves, an alarm clock, a pair of heels, tied it all up tight. Bullets were hitting the front of the building like rain, singing up and down the stairway like lost birds. She took down the crucifix, broke it in two, shoved half in the bag and half in her gown.

Back in the living room people were stacking sandbags against the front wall. An AK47 stood against a wall beside a stack of 30-round magazines. Its stock was split and had been wrapped carefully with black tape. Rosa set it to single and crossed halfway to the sandbagged window, aimed across the smoky darkness at a shred of window in the hulk of the Life Building, fired a shot, thought she saw a spark ten feet high, to the left. She backed away and stood rubbing her shoulder where the splintered stock had punched it.

She took one extra magazine. Mohammed was talking into the radio, gave her a surprised look as she left. She went down the seven sets of stairs to the front hallway and stopped ten feet from the door. The hallway was a vaulted dark tunnel to the shallow darkness of the street; something lay on the floor – rubble maybe, or a person. No, just sandbags, two of them, broken.

She crept nearer the door. A chunk of glowing metal fell into the street, writhing and twisting. In its light she saw a burnt car on bare rims, behind it a tall façade with sky through its windows. A rocket hammered overhead, stone crashing and crunching into the street.

Her hands were shaking, her thighs shivering, the rifle kept sliding off her shoulder. She felt as if she'd throw up any moment. She started back up the stairs but forced herself to turn round, go down to the door, look out. Men were running down the street, one with a rocket on his shoulder – *fedayeen*. She ducked into the hallway, waited till they passed, and edged forward to the door.

More footsteps – a fast shuffle, uneven. Dogs, she worried. No, a single man, bent over, leaving a black trail on the street. Bearded, dirty, head uncovered, unseeing, stumbling, clenching his stomach. Shia? Amal or Hezbollah? Palestinian? Just another refugee?

If she followed him he'd attract snipers before she did. Head down, she stepped into the street holding the bedspread of trinkets loosely over the AK47. The man wobbled and weaved down the hill between the narrow burning buildings, his trail of blood glinting. The way it was spurting and slacking, it had to be an artery, an artery in his gut.

He fell over a pram lying sideways in the street and writhed, shrieking. She ducked into a doorway. If anyone was going to shoot him, they'd wait now, let him suffer. Watching him grovel sideways, in a circle, she was suddenly shocked by this idea of suffering: we *like* to make others suffer. That was war. *That* was its purpose.

But why do we like to make others suffer?

He'd risen to his knees. A few rounds whined down the street, twanged off a façade. In a collapsed building somewhere someone was screaming. With a faraway *whoosh* a Mirage was climbing after a bombing run. The man stood, clenching his gut, stumbled bent over in a circle, looking for his way. He fell, got up and continued down Rue Weygand toward the Green Line.

At the end of the street the glowing carcass of a tank lit up the dark stumps of buildings on Place des Martyres. Tracers were trading tiny yellow and red fires, like electrons, Rosa thought, back and forth. A shell hit a building, a red-white flash and contorted black smoke boiling up. The man staggered boldly out into Martyres, stumbled over something, straightened, and fell down.

He lay flat and unmoving in the red glare of the tank; she couldn't tell if he'd been shot or had just died. Maybe he was resting. Anyway she couldn't chance it.

She backtracked to the first row of standing buildings and turned south. She'd go down Rue Basta and cross at the Museum, hide the gun before she went across and get another on the Christian side. From a corner she glanced back but could not see Mohammed's outpost. Rockets were still coming over, a big recoilless rifle hitting near, 155s in Martyres now. Even if she reached the Life Building it might be too late, and she'd lose him. No, she decided, Mohammed would never be so stupid as to let the Christians kill him.

13

THE RECEPTION ROOM was bigger than his parents'
Normandy farm, a three-story ceiling with crystal chandeliers
and a double staircase spiraling down from a gallery where a few
guests ambled arm in arm. There were Louis XIV chairs and set-
tees and ancient Persian rugs on the polished herringbone oak,
Renaissance tapestries on the stone walls.

The whole place curdled André's stomach. Over the heads of
well-dressed silver-haired men and hard-smiling jeweled women
he looked for Monique but couldn't see her. Her kind of place,
really. Her husband would eat it right up.

Hammurabi, as broad as he was tall, held court on center
stage, an eager flock around him. Humans just like roaches, André
thought; a little excrement pulls them right in. A little money.

Walid Farrahan, code-named Hammurabi in French secret
service files, had plenty of that. Every war is fought primarily for
profit, and Hammurabi had always been one of the first to shove
his face into the trough. Fancy receptions in his Marais mansion to which company presidents and members of Parliament
and ministers and ambassadors from nearly every country came
scurrying by the hundreds, to clasp his great hard paw and beg
for the tools of death.

And for the really lucky there were the *soirées intimes* in the mansion's back rooms, the saunas and spa rooms, the swimming pool on the roof. A French citizen now, Hammurabi was, they couldn't throw him out. Even if they wanted.

"Ah, the Legionnaire," Hammurabi rumbled out of his great chest when André forced his way through the throng. "My office told me. Enjoying yourself?"

"Of course."

Hammurabi waved a sausage finger at the others. "Give us a moment?"

Magically they vanished. "I'm leaving in a few days," André said. "I don't want to promise anything I can't do."

Hammurabi fondled a piece of metal round his neck, beneath his tuxedo – a huge diamond-studded cross. "My staff has already confirmed you." He squeezed André's arm. "See how fast we work? When you get to Beirut and have your order, cable it through with payment. Normal procedure," he smiled. "Don't worry, my dear Legionnaire, you'll have your scramblers."

"Conforming to specs?"

"A laser-guided bomb works on very simple principles, as you know. I wouldn't offer you scramblers if they didn't work, would I?"

WATCHING FOR MINES Rosa crossed over the shattered crest of Beirut on Rue Basta and down to the Museum, stored the AK47 in the side-street ruins of a store called Anita's Gifts. There was less war here, just the constant whiffle and swish of things going over, the rattle of guns and thump of mortars. There was a line of overturned buses across Avenue Abdallah Yafi with two armored cars and at least one tank lurking in caves in the rubble, their snouts pointing into the street, and machine guns and rockets in the windows behind. Beyond the shell-shocked intersection, on the Christian side, it was the same.

Behind the overturned buses was a space with gleaming concertina wire and sandbagged positions with fifty calibers. A mujihadeen checked Rosa's papers and spoke on the radio while she sat quietly on a sandbag and it seemed as if the whole cool heavy night weighted down her neck and shoulders. She let it wash over her, told herself she would do this one last thing and no more. It would be enough and if it weren't, she'd tell them she'd given up.

The mujihadeen came back. "You really need to go?"

"My father's in a basement by the Sacre-Coeur."

"There's surely people there ..."

"The building's empty. He's confused, doesn't understand, won't leave." She looked down, at the mujihadeen's dirty yellow-blue running shoes, how they wouldn't stand still on the ground littered with empty cartridges and cigarette butts.

"They're animals," he said, "over there. Shot a Palestinian girl last night. Twenty-three, going over to look for food."

"She looked up into his fair, troubled eyes. "You remind me of my brother."

"How was he?"

"Very sweet." She stepped round him past the barricade and down the middle of the wide, bludgeoned avenue. Now she was in Christian rifle range, a Muslim woman rushing toward them with a bundle of something.

She was almost running but it took forever, lugging the loaded bedspread, tripping on chunks of stone, shreds of metal, a dead cat, broken bricks.

The blasted chassis of a car crouched against the Christian curb like a chastised dog. The muzzles of the Christian guns followed her to the first line of smashed cars and concrete. Behind this barricade were Phalange who checked her papers and looked into the bedspread. The captain, younger than the others, with a burn scar across his cheek, took out the clock.

"It was my mother's," she protested.

"You know I can't let it through."

"It's for my father, to give him a sense of time."

"Better having no time these days."

"That's why he's so mixed up."

"My mother won't eat," he said, "because she's afraid we're running out of food. Things are hard but we have food … but she won't eat."

"Make her exercise. We spend all day crouched in our basements –"

"If she'd just go up to Jounié. She has a sister there."

"Can you lend me a flashlight? *They* took mine." She pointed behind, at the Muslim lines.

He sucked in a breath. "I can't."

"Please? As soon as I've seen my father I'll bring it back. And pick up my clock."

"What about my batteries?"

"I'll charge your batteries."

"How soon?"

She smiled, seeing his face light up. "Two hours?"

He unbuckled the flashlight from his belt. "I'll be here."

She climbed the steep street past the Hotel Dieu Hospital and the Hotel Alexandre. It was so strange to see the buildings undamaged, cars in the streets, the fighting almost distant like a summer storm.

She went down l'Indépendence and across to Fouad Chehab at Tabariss. Now the guns were louder and she could hear the crack of individual shells against stone. The sky above the black buildings was pink, red, yellow. A rifle fired from a roof and she heard it hit on the Muslim side.

The big front gates of the Sacré-Coeur had been blasted open and there was nothing in the courtyard. She went up to the first floor and through the corridors till she found four nun's habits on knobs, stuffed one into the bedspread and went out through a side door into Youssef Hani, turning right toward the Life Building, the Place des Martyres three blocks on her left, across the Green Line, Mohammed and his men only three blocks further.

Unless they'd pulled back. If they had, it wouldn't matter what happened to the snipers at the Life Building. Mohammed would be beyond their range, beyond hers.

A Katyusha struck in the next block before she could cover her ears and the *wham* seemed to slice off the top of her head. She crouched on steps going down to a cellar, crying and clasping her ears till the pain dimmed. She took off her gown and put the black habit on. It was dark and confining, like wearing chains; her body couldn't breathe. She hid the bedspread under the stairway and went to Nahr Ibrahim, looking down it to the Place des Martyres where the gut-shot man had fallen, two hours ago, in the glow of the Amal tank.

Mortars were falling there now. She took the trench across Nahr Ibrahim, the habit cloying at her knees. There were Phalange in the basements going up to the Life Building and machine guns at both ends of the street. Bullets and rockets kept ricocheting down into the street. A Phalange grabbed her arm. "No more."

"My father's in that basement, by the Life Building."

"A 240 went all the way to the basement before it exploded. There's nothing there, sister."

"He could have moved to the next basement ... the Life Building. I've got to try."

"I've been there. It's just storage."

"Storage?"

"You can't stay here, sister. *Please.*"

She pulled the two halves of the crucifix from her habit. "See what they did? They broke the tree on which the Lord died. But we will join it back together. I swear to you, on this broken cross ..."

He backed away a little, watching her, slightly raised the rifle. "I can't let you in, sister. You go home now. Back up to Sacré-Coeur."

She scanned the Life Building, the other streets coming in, all guarded. With a chuckle another rocket left the top floor, swooshing toward Muslim lines. The key to Mohammed. She backed away. "You should have more pity."

"Don't beat a dead horse ..."

She went round the corner and halfway up the back street till she found a sewer manhole but she couldn't pry it open. At the corner of Nahr Ibrahim she was back in the view of the Phalange at the Life Building but here was an open manhole with steel rungs down into moldy cold darkness. At the bottom, ten feet below the street, tunnels led off in five directions. In one direction, toward the Life Building, was a tiny distant light. Not using the flashlight, she crawled toward it. Tendrils of mud and wire hanging from the ceiling dragged across her face, snatched her hair. The sandy muck at the bottom was jammed with plastic bottles and plastic bags in clumps of twigs and broken glass bottles and again something dead – another rat, she thought. Her fingers bumped a fat, soft, short stick that she tried to pull out of the way but it was someone's hand.

She pulled back in pure terror then realized it was swollen, dead. *That* was the smell. And the reason why she hadn't been able to see more light was that he was blocking it.

She lay trying to catch her breath, the top of the tunnel heavy on her back, cold muck soaking her chest. She could hardly breathe, her lungs wouldn't open.

She'd have to slow her pulse somehow and calm down but she was dying from no air. She had to breathe, let the thick cold air go slowly in and out. Slowly, she told herself, feeling the blood slacken, the arteries relax. It's just a bad idea that you're dying.

She crawled closer and tried to peer round the dead man. The light was from a wider tunnel beyond him, one that angled toward the Life Building. Taking a grip with her feet and knees at the sides of the tunnel she squirmed hard against him; pushing his shoulders, his blubbery face against hers.

He wouldn't move. She squirmed backwards, inched the habit up round her hips and finally over her shoulders, and crawled forward dragging it behind her. She jammed tight against him, forcing her shoulders forward along him, her belly against his, his soft slippery flesh rolling against her, bubbling gas each time she pressed herself along him, making her hold her breath against the horrible stink. It wouldn't go away and finally she just breathed it, squeezing herself along his wet bulbous mass, pushing the air from her lungs and his to inch her way down him. She caught on his belt buckle and it was too narrow to breathe and she couldn't back up with his face in her crotch and hers in his and she realized someday someone would find them like this, two skeletons enmeshed, and the terror of it jammed her forward past his fat legs, free, gasping and free, dragging her legs away from him, down the tunnel into the light.

14

SHE SQUIRMED to the edge of the larger tunnel, lay sucking in air. There was a light up ahead, out of sight, and one far behind, barely glimmering. A black cable ran along the tunnel. She waited a few minutes longer but no one appeared and she squirmed into the larger tunnel, dirt tumbling down each time a shell hit overhead.

The light was a bulb pinned halfway up on one side. Beyond it was a wide faint corridor that led to an open chamber loud with the fighting above. Voices were coming down, boots thumping wooden stairs, a flashlight darting and stabbing. Four men came into the basement and in their light she could see a series of open-faced rooms stacked with artillery shells, rockets, jerry cans of fuel, crates of rifle cartridges. The men loaded rocket shells on wooden frames on their backs, slid tumplines up their foreheads, and climbed slowly, unsteadily, back up the stairs.

Had the dead man in the tunnel stunk also of cigarettes? It seemed that he had but she couldn't remember. She scrambled back up the lit tunnel and squeezed up to the dead man. In his shirt pocket were cigarettes but no matches. Again she squashed herself along him, wormed a hand into a trouser pocket. A box of matches that rattled when she shook it. She crawled back to the main tunnel, checked the matches in its light. Four, skinny and blue-headed in their little cardboard box.

In the main basement she unscrewed jerry cans and tipped them over, the foul liquid soaking her feet, rising up her socks, sinking into the soil and sliding out into the ammo rooms, and with each new mortar hit above she thought it was people coming down. Trying not to breathe the fumes, she lugged one jerry can back along the main tunnel, pouring it out, then up her side tunnel, squeezing past the man. She dragged the can behind her and all the way to the end, poured the rest of the gasoline down the tunnel, and climbed the steel rungs up to the street.

It was quieter, tracers departing and arriving, the skies darker. She went back down the ladder, lit a match and tossed it into the tunnel. There was quiet *whuff* then a hiss that slowly died out.

She did not dare to look for fear it would blow in her face. But when she did there was only darkness. She fell against the ladder, felt the sting of tears but they wouldn't come. She couldn't go down there again. It would explode any second. She'd done her best.

She opened the matches. Three. She tossed another in and it huffed and went out. She squirmed back into the tunnel toward the dead man.

It was faster this time, she kept telling herself. The man was easier to crawl past, most of the gas had been pushed out of him. The main tunnel was slippery with gasoline and she was afraid of knocking the light bulb down into it, which might blow it.

There was no one in the basement. She poured out part of another jerry can and carried it back to the main tunnel, cautious not to bump the concrete, cause a spark. She poured more gasoline in the main tunnel and the rest up the small tunnel and over the man.

This is it, she told herself. If it doesn't blow this time I'm leaving.

There was no change in the street. She lit the third match

but the stem snapped and the match fell on the ground. She snatched it and tossed it into the tunnel but it had gone out.

Voices far down the tunnel. Someone yelling? She held the last match carefully, by the head, scratched it across the side of the box and tossed it in. A great tongue of flame roared out of the tunnel and leaped across the sewer main and seared the far wall. There was another roar, much deeper, growing, thundering – and again the tongue of flame lashed out, the far wall cracking. The earth shook, everything moving six inches one way – the concrete, the ladder, herself – then six inches back. Shells were going off like rocket launchers, the earth grumbling and banging. She darted back up the ladder and the whole first two floors of the Life Building were afire, trapped men screaming, pieces of the upper stories falling into flames with each new blast.

She ran to the stairwell where she'd left the bedspread, tugged the muck from her hair, changed her clothes for some in the bedspread, too large in the bust and shoulders, rinsed her hair in a puddle and tried to wash the gasoline from her hands and arms. She pulled on the habit again and went quickly back through the Christian side and down past the Hotel Alexandre and the Hotel Dieu Hospital. A Phalange truck was bringing in wounded, men wrapped in sheets. "Oh dear," she called to a soldier. "What happened?"

He glanced at her habit. "An ammo dump. On the Green Line."

"Oh, how I *hate* them!"

"Not the Muslims, sister. Accident, apparently."

She dropped her head. "How many?"

"Thirty. So far."

"May the dear Lord be with them."

"All very well for you to say that, sister. These were all men with families. Wives and kids. You don't love anyone, just God, as you imagine *Him* to be. You're like those *fedayeen* over there – they think they're going to Heaven."

"Don't criticize what you don't understand," she snapped.

Before she reached the Christian side of the Museum she ditched the habit. Someone came out of the shadows by the big barricade and she saw it was the captain.

She handed him the flashlight. "I didn't even use it."

"So my batteries?" He glanced up as a shell went over like a great bird, hit out in Dora somewhere. "They shoot at bloody anything," he said.

"They think Allah's going to guide it."

He nudged her toward the darkness, where a tank crouched.

"You'll let me through the line again?" she said, reaching her hands up round his neck. It was smooth and young and his hair was short in her fingers all the way up under his beret. Her breasts were itching to be against him and her nails wanted to rip down his back and she could feel him inside already, like he'd be, hot and hard and pumping faster and faster. She dragged him down beside the silent tank, shoving up his shirt as he tore his trousers open and she lay back and let him come in slowly then hard, deeper and deeper till she was sure he was there but he kept coming deeper and she exploded, saw the dragon's tongue of flame, heard the thunder and the screams, felt peace.

"FRÜHSTÜCK!" Knuckles hammered the compartment door; the light flickered, flashed on. The door snapped open, a steward put a breakfast tray on the foot of Neill's bed.

He sat up rubbing the back of his neck. Dark cold shapes flitted past the window. He found his watch, put it on, forgot the time and looked again: five after six. Shivering, he drew the blankets round his shoulders, started to pour his coffee but it had not all run down through the filter, so he waited watching through the rain-beaded glass the cold, flat landscape, the few distant lights, imagined people getting up, farmers and their burly kerchiefed wives, the smell of coffee and coal fires.

It's the girl, he realized, that's why I feel so bad. He'd been with her in the dream. Ardent and slender and brown-eyed, long dark hair. Naked in the glow of the street lamp. Layla.

Was it losing her that had broken his heart? Made him such a cynical bastard who couldn't even love his wife and kids and had no friends? No, that's not entirely true. He set the filter aside and sipped the coffee.

The train's wheels wailed into a curve. And miles to go, he thought, wondering why. Something shone on the pillow and he brushed at it – a silver hair. Can't be mine, he decided, mine's not that gray. These aren't clean sheets.

But the sheets were newly washed and starched. He hadn't seen Layla for many years but in the dream they hadn't grown older, both of them beyond ecstasy to be naked together after so long missing each other, her skin, her lips, her hair, her sighs, the softness inside her, her passionate young lips seeking his. In his dream three men had broken into the room, tall and drunk, tripping over the bed and grabbing Layla. He fought them off, fought them into the hall and beat them one by one. But when he'd gone back, Layla was gone.

Blankets round his shoulders he sat drinking his coffee as Bratislava's ramparts took form against the day.

15

ROSA WAS breathing hard, a wildness in her eyes that made Mohammed want to protect and reassure her. Seeing her pretty, roundish face with its red high cheeks and olive eyes, her smooth young brow, her white teeth and red lips, her dark hair coiling down round her neck into the blush of her chest, it was hard to imagine what she'd just done.

Her breathing calmed. "Thought I'd die, that tunnel." She closed her eyes, leaned back, air filling her lungs. "You never know what a joy it is to breathe till you can't."

"I almost drowned once, when I was a child. Since then breathing seems almost holy."

"What happened to the Christian snipers, on the top?"

"It was so hot up there their ammo was blowing."

She shivered or shrugged, looked away.

"They were using the Life Building as a pivot and you took it from them, and now they've backed off their attack for fear we'll go round them. It was very brave, what you did."

"Bravery's nothing. Only winning matters."

He punched the side of his palm against the back of his neck, loosening the muscles, rubbed them. "You still haven't told me what you think *that* means."

"Palestine."

"And Lebanon?"

"You can tell Christians and Jews apart? After they've warred against us for how many thousand years?"

"We can't drive them all from Lebanon. From Palestine. Not yet."

"Until they go there'll be no peace."

"It was the French who put them over us. It'll never happen again."

"For two thousand years – more, if you count the Romans – they've plagued us."

"When we weren't plaguing each other."

"And you hoped blowing up their embassy and barracks would scare them away? They have no memories, keep stepping in the same hole. Stepping on *us*. Even if they do leave they'll be right back, under the next politician, the next pope."

A 155 was coming over and Mohammed waited for it to hit. "We didn't blow the American barracks. Nor the French ones, as people say."

Her eyes seemed the pale green now of a snow river, the one coming out of the mountain at Yammouné, chunks of green ice crashing inside it. "Anyway, you wouldn't say ..."

"Some day maybe I can."

She moved closer, her smile's warmth making him shiver. "Tell me now."

"It takes time." He let his head drop forward, rubbing the back of his neck. "We've all spent another sleepless night."

She bit her lip. "I can do that for you."

"Sleep for me?"

"Don't be silly! Rub your neck. If you like. I always did it for my father. He'd follow the mule all day, pushing the plough, reins round his neck ..."

Mohammed let his head rotate back, against his hand. "That was where?"

"Tiberias, the Golan, Mount Hermon – like I said." She came

behind him, making him fear for an instant. "Bend forward, let down your shoulders."

"You crossed Beirut tonight and destroyed our enemy." He rolled his shoulders, let them go; her fingers digging round the bone for the hurt muscle and worn tired tendons were like paradise. "Someone should be rubbing your shoulders."

She leaned round, looking at him from the side, kneading the hard muscle at the top of his shoulder blades. "Someday maybe you can." She unbuttoned his shirt from behind, breasts at his back, arms and wrists against his ribs, pulled it up out of his belt and slid it down his back, her hard strong fingers moving up and down the flat muscles on both sides of his spine, neck and shoulder, under the shoulder blades and up the stiff sore neck.

"I forget," he gasped, "how heavy our heads are."

"What a strong back you have – these muscles all across here, down here. You've done a lot of work."

"In the hills I was a shepherd. But when I came to Beirut I worked in construction, carrying concrete."

"Like the Palestinians do now."

"You shovel the trough full of wet concrete and lift it up on your shoulders and carry it up to the top floor and pour it onto the slab. You start at the first floor and then on to the second, building it all the way up, the fifth, the tenth … And then you're going up twenty stories with a trough of concrete on your back, and this whole building has gone up in the sky on your back and the backs of your friends." He stretched, pulling his shoulders forward. "Good for your back, your legs. For a while, it's even good for your head. And you can look at the building and know how it's built, and how you can take it apart."

"What's it feel like, walking back down?"

"You can't take much time because they're paying you by the load and so you run down the steps, trying to fill your lungs and stretch your back and see the city far below down there."

His muscles were so thick she could almost separate them, like ropes. Almost hard enough to stop a bullet.

"You have strong hands," he murmured. "You have wonderful hands."

His body loosened, relaxed, she had a sudden fear of losing him, but he had just drifted off to sleep in mid-sentence, and it made her want to soften her touch, stroke his brow. It was so easy, caring for a man, to make him a slave. He already had a wife, the famous Layla, Mother of the Revolution. But what man is ever satisfied with a famous wife?

NEILL STOOD in the middle of Staromestska Street, two fast lanes of cars whizzing past his back, two lanes in front, just the yellow line between his feet to keep him alive, with no cover and no way back. Cars sucked at the air as they rushed by inches from his skin, big and little, red and black and white, two-ton chunks of hurtling steel; he saw himself hit and knocked into an oncoming lane. There'd been a newspaper story somewhere, a kid's brain blown right out of his skull when he was hit by a semi.

The light turned red and the last traffic hissed through. He finished crossing as more cars roared out of the side streets like hounds wild to run him down. He jumped up on the pavement and stood in a shop doorway as the lines of cars and trucks screamed past. The shop was closed, tourist pictures of Turkey pasted on its window – crystalline blue bays, the blanched and barren hills, columns spiring toward the sun. There were personal ads for household help and selling a motorcycle and getting laid, for the bridge club of Bratislava, for underground films and lectures.

Before him was a torn poster of a great beast's skull, a man-rat staring down on a city aflame, that he had cloven in two with his huge sword. "Friday 13 March," the poster said. "The Most Terrifying Night In Your Life. Don't Be Late." The rest of the poster had been ripped off, and he glanced down at the dirty tile floor of the shop entryway but the torn part wasn't there.

The lights had changed again and the traffic was roaring up and down Staromestska.

Why was the poster in English? Had it been? He went back to check. Yes.

Snow began to fall in lacy cool flakes; one went down the back of his neck making him shiver. You could have died, he told himself. Because you didn't pay attention. You got caught in the middle of the street because you didn't watch the light.

His hands were cold. He went into a café and ordered a grog and held it but his hands wouldn't warm. The insides of his fingers were hot from the cup but when he held the tops to his cheek they felt like ice. Guys your age, he told himself, are dropping all the time now. Cardiac arrest, stroke; half vegetables wondering who their wives are screwing. Too much booze, no sleep, booze and weed, mostly booze, twenty years of wine and beer and whisky. They were painkillers, really, but what was the pain?

If you didn't have your painkiller, you might have to feel.

He wondered if this was true. If it was, if he'd been drinking all these years so he wouldn't have to feel, then he hadn't *felt*. The man without feelings? God that couldn't be true. Jesus if I felt any more pain I'd crack. I'd just crack.

The café smelt companionably of steamed milk and caffeine and pastries and cigarettes and slivovitz and the perfume of young women in black stockings and black leather boots. His fingers would not warm up. What, he wondered, if you could just face the pain? Feel it?

He walked up Staromestska against the morning stream of shoppers in long fur coats, bags in their hands, a red chill on their cheeks, past an unshaven man smelling of cigarettes and plum brandy. At Number 41 he took the stairs to the top floor.

Michael Szay was so tall he had to stoop in his own office. "You're wasting your time going to Beirut," he said. "Mohammed won't talk to you."

"This could help him, build credibility."

"Since when do you care about his credibility?"

"I hate this war. So does everyone, except you."

Szay sat back, watching Neill, chewing an edge of fingernail. "Meaning?"

"As long as you're making money selling weapons, God forbid it should stop."

"Who says I'm selling to him?"

"Aren't you?"

"He's got stuff coming in from Iran, Riyadh. He takes some from the Israelis, Christians."

"He's getting assault rifles and ammo from you –"

Szay scanned his fingertips, began chewing another nail. "Who says?"

"I've played fair with you, Michael. All along. Whatever you say goes no further. I just need a way in, someone to go through."

Szay tipped forward, stared at Neill across his disheveled desk. "And what do *I* get?"

"He's your client. If he goes under, you lose. He's getting terrible copy – nobody knows what he's doing or why. All the papers blame him."

Szay's ironic little eyes were like badgers in their holes. "He's ducking bullets, that's what he's doing. He doesn't give a shit what some London newspaper thinks."

"I won't write about you, Michael. I never have, not even about Ethiopia, your friends in the Sudan ..."

Szay cocked his head, peered down at his nails, selected a finger and began to chew along the quick. "Write what you want. Nobody reads it."

"If you have any messages, I can pass them."

"Won't do you any good to have messages." Szay spat a piece of fingernail. "Since you won't get in."

Beyond the small leaded panes of Szay's windows the rooftops of Bratislava were an immense haphazard junkyard of tiles, damp in new rain. "I'll get in," Neill said. "I always do."

Szay's little badger eyes rose to Neill's. "Thanks to your friends."

"They could be yours, too –"

Szay hissed irritably. "I wouldn't have them."

Neill stood. "You don't *have* any friends, Michael. I'm the closest you get. And I don't even like you."

Szay smiled, crunching a bit of fingernail between his front teeth. "Take the Damascus road. If the Christians or Israelis cut it you're screwed. If the Syrians cut it you're dead."

"Just give me a lead, Michael. That's all I ask."

"You're going to end up dead on a curb somewhere. That's all the lead I'm going to give you. Or in some Hezbollah stink-hole. And your friends won't even care."

16

EVEN IN LATE MORNING the Paris *métro* was crowded. On the seat before André a black girl was checking her face in a cracked pocket mirror. Beside him an old unshaven Arab held the pole with both hands. On top of his bare skull were brown patches and old scabs. André checked the other faces in the car – less than half were white.

The train stopped at Chatelet and the old Arab staggered across the quai and vomited behind a bench. A girl in a Carrefour ad had lovely long legs with graffiti all over them. There was graffiti on every ad, all down the quai.

A thin black man in a yellow uniform was sweeping butts along the quai. He's come up here, André thought, to make a better life for his family. What if he had to leave France? To go back to what? Was that why Africa was failing? Because the best kept leaving?

France could take ten million Africans and it would make no difference at all to the billions in Africa. But it would ruin France. As soon as you take some away they just make more. You have to admit that's the truth. And France has never sent its people starving to another's door.

Africa's thousand children dying daily in the desert with an outstretched hand. He thought of his little brother Yves ahead on the path, sunny hair and freckles, crossing into the sumacs and down over the stream past the oaks where the young couple slept one night and we didn't know why. Yves carrying his gun up the slope of beeches in the dawn-bright dead leaves, toward the knoll where we'd tracked the boar, the ground splashed with his blood, the dog bounding back and forth, shivering, waiting for the charge.

Motorcycles and symphonies, Yves. Let neither side win. Loving to hunt but hating to kill. Under your calm kindness even you couldn't resolve that. You who always went for what you wanted like a magnet. For what you felt was right.

The only honor I have left, Yves, is in not daring to live without it. No, that's not true. Not completely.

A beautiful girl stood beside him in a long green wool coat. Fair skin and light lipstick, full chestnut hair. Oh if I could make love to you. Oh please if I could. Except I have to leave and you already have someone and you wouldn't want to anyway. If you'd make love to me and be my wife I'd stay here, he promised, wouldn't go to Lebanon.

Beneath her green coat, the dark suit, the white silk blouse, her underclothes and skin, he could feel her lovely body all along him. At the Louvre someone left a seat and the girl sat down and took a leaflet from her purse. He read it over the top of her head, a French consular form.

When she got out of the train at Concorde he started to follow her, but turned round and leaped back in the train, took it all the way to Etoile, to pick up the bus for Charles de Gaulle and the afternoon Cyprus Airways flight to Larnaca.

IN THE COMMAND BUILDING all the apartments had been pillaged, so Rosa waited till the shells slowed and ran across the courtyard to the building at the back. It too had been emptied, the furniture burned in cooking fires, one apartment used as a toilet. Shelling had started again, but on the other side. Someone was firing single shots, even spaced, in celebration. He's shot someone, she realized, that's what he's celebrating. Been waiting for hours and finally got his target. She ducked along the pavement to the next building but the stairway had been blown out and there was no way up to the apartments.

Two buildings further she found an apartment with some rice and dried chickpeas under the sink. There was no furniture, on one wall photos of an old stern man and smiling heavy woman, a new color blow-up of a young man and woman with three children and a picnic basket on a rug, behind them the nose of a blue Fiat and the stiff ridges of Mount Lebanon.

In the dirt on one side of the front steps a daisy flamed yellow in the setting sun. She thought of picking it for Mohammed. No, she decided, it's so lovely; let it live.

EACH DAY with a beginning, middle, and end. That's all I remember. No matter how different they seem they're all the same. You're in a train or a plane and you get to a new place and then you see it's the place you just left, the one you're going to next.

Neill brushed the crumbs from his sandwich off the table and into his palm, emptied them on the floor. What if I'm not an alcoholic? If all along I've been thinking I was but I'm not? What if I just love the taste? Beer came before bread, they say that now.

A couple at the next table were clasping hands, legs enwrapped. What was this crazy craving to be *inside* another, or have them inside *you*? They were staring through their cigarette smoke into each other's eyes. Thinking they're Bacall and Bogart, sucking on the tit of death.

The waiter brought another half-liter of Pilsner in a tall glass, a thick head with a tang of barley malt and the brightness of the sun. A short chubby-faced man in a red scarf came through the door and glanced around, saw Neill wave and came over. He had a pixie smile and a scar to the left of his mouth. He took off his raincoat and draped it and the scarf over the back of a chair.

"So how are you?" Neill said.

"Could be better. These are not good times."

"When have they ever been?"

"There were times, you know, when things seemed to go well."

"The operative word is "seemed", Tomás. We're always fucked, it's just that sometimes we don't realize."

Tomás grinned; there seemed more black holes between his teeth than last time. "I was so pleased you were coming."

"I was just realizing that since I last saw you I've done absolutely *nothing*. The more I try to fill my life, the faster it empties."

"You've done nothing? What about that series on Camp David, on the Paris bombings? Even here at the end of the world, we saw those."

"I'm talking about *me*."

"You mean you and Beverly? Since when has that gone right?"

Neill glanced down at his glass. "Maybe never. No, that's not true." He raised his head. "Anyway, we're each seeing other people – just sticking it out for the kids."

"You think they don't know?"

"It's the best we can do."

"Maybe that's not true. Maybe more important than us," Tomás raised his shoulders in a shrug, "is our kids. Like we would die for them, step in front of a car for them, that kind of thing."

Neill had a sharp tremor of this morning's memory, caught between speeding lanes on Staromestska. "Everybody would –"

"It's the same, then, not to leave them, not to split up. A commitment to life: you bring it into the world, you nurture it." He raised his shoulders. "Far more important than what we journalists do, or governments, laws, analyses."

"I sleep through all that, these days."

"Yet you're the one who told us if society's truly an organism then *we* have to be its neurons."

Neill motioned at the waiter, at Tomás. "What you having?"

"Pilsner. It's very fashionable, forty-five-year old men having a values crisis."

"Don't exaggerate. I'm forty-two."

"Yeah, but you're precocious. Just keep doing the same fine work you've always done, and the rest'll go away."

"Society's not an organism, it's a maelstrom. A horror show."

"You think people don't *know* that?"

"Not enough."

"That's always been your passion – uncovering the worst."

"You want to let it fester?"

"Or heal?" Tomás lit a *papirosi* and the fragrant smoke went up in a circular column. He called out something in Slovak and a woman at another table smiled and turned away. "It's only when people like you are content to see the worst that we can get better. No, that's silly. We'll never get any better. But your seeing us as we are may keep us from getting worse."

"Nullities. Bloody idealism."

"When you came here to teach that course, I couldn't understand why you'd bother. Do you remember – I even asked you?"

"No."

"You said journalists can't be just a mirror of their times, but have to be a guide also. That you'd come to share what you'd learned and to learn from us." Tomás grinned. "I always wonder what you learned from us."

Neill scanned the animated crowd, the smoky misted windows. "Maybe that freedom of the press isn't all it's cocked up to be. There was political control over you but we have commercial control over us – and, finally, there isn't too much difference. You ever see our Tory press during an election?"

"You were the best teacher we had. When we started to build

something new, what we learned from you helped us get beyond who *we* were, to the event itself, how to tell it."

You can like someone, Neill realized, without hoping they
understand you. "So tell me, about Beirut. When'd you get
back?"

"What's today – Thursday?"

"Friday."

"Three weeks ago."

"And?"

Tomás splayed spindly fingers round his glass, craned his
neck. Why are all Slovaks bald, Neill wondered. He looked
around at nearby tables, decided this wasn't true. "I went
through Damascus," Tomás said. "Got stopped at the border
then went further north and got through on a Syrian Army truck
headed for Baalbek. It's all Hezbollah now, up there."

"I always thought of it as Heliopolis, City of the Sun. And
now it's just another military outpost."

"That's what it's been, most of the last three thousand, five
thousand years. Guarding the most fertile valley in the Middle
East."

"So how'd you reach Beirut?"

'Got this crazy man to drive me down to Zahlé in his old
Mercedes. The whole way I wanted to lie on the floor, duck the
bullets, but I couldn't, with him driving. Wouldn't have been
fair. We never got hit."

Neill drained his stein, caught the waiter's eye. "I don't want
to put up with any of that. Too much of a coward."

"Then go home. It's not the time, Beirut."

"As I said on the telephone, if I can talk to Mohammed, get
his position out in the open ..."

Tomás reached across, took Neill's hand. "No matter how
bad the war makes you feel, you can't change it."

Neill waited till the waiter left. "I tried Michael Szay today."

"That bastard."

"He's given me good leads, in the past."

"What's he say?"

"Told me to get lost. That I'll never reach Mohammed."

Tomás fiddled with his glass, scratched his skull. "Why don't you ask Layla?"

It stung like a dentist's probe on a dead tooth – the reminder of past pain. How could it, after all these years? "I probably couldn't even find her. If she's with Mohammed I'd have to locate him first. If she's still with her family, down in Saida, they're behind Israeli lines and I can't get in."

"Go see her brother."

"Hamid? He's the one who did us in, way back then."

"He's still in Beirut. Has an office on Mahatma Gandhi. Number 21."

"He's a goddamn snake."

Tomás was silent a moment. "Crazy, what happened to her. To you both."

Neill shrugged. "So what's the latest?"

"Damascus says they're going to stay and the Christians are begging for arms. The Israelis will fight the Syrians on the Green Line and that will be the final solution for Lebanon."

"How do you read Mohammed?"

Tomás lit another cigarette, dropped his lighter, and fished for it under the table, and Neill could see down the back of his neck, under the brown wool collar, the long thin black hairs. "He's about forty," Tomás said. "Very driven, very cold. Yet strangely open-minded, in a way – wants an Islamic Lebanon but isn't too doctrinaire. Some people say he's in it for the power, others say he actually cares."

"Should I try getting through Damascus?"

"The Syrians may let you go as far as Masnaa, somewhere like that. After that you'll have to deal with field units and they may shoot you first and then ask you where you're going. After that you have to deal with Hezbollah. And they aren't going to let you anywhere near Mohammed. They don't even admit he exists."

"Maybe with the Syrians I can go down the coast."

"One way or the other you'll have to pass through Hezbollah. And now, if he's cut off like they say, you've got to pass through the Christians *and* Hezbollah to get to Mohammed, and by then the Syrians and Israelis will have shot you." Tomás smiled, bringing down his empty glass. "You'll be able to excise a lot of guilt."

"Guilt, the gift that keeps on giving –"

"That's the virtue of religion and patriotism: they allow us to do evil without guilt."

"So where do you stand on all this, these days?"

"It never changes. The Israelis have no choice, they have to fight. In all my years in the Middle East I've never met a Moslem who agrees with Israel's right to exist. Not one."

"Me neither," Neill said. *"We will drown the Israelis and their children in the sea* seems to be the general approach."

"And the Holocaust taught them not to rely on anyone but themselves, that at any time the whole world can turn against them."

"As it always does. The last time even America and Britain sent them in their ships back to die. We wouldn't bomb the rail lines, stop the camps…"

"And I'm tired of the Palestinians fussing over what they never wanted till they lost it. I'm tired of people with long memories, people with 'love for the land'. Even back ten thousand years, the forest tribes of central Europe – we'll never stop fighting over territory. I'd like to live on the moon for a while, the dark side of the moon, so I wouldn't have to look down on this." Tomás switched back to English. "Like Arafat once told me, 'There'll never be peace in the Middle East as long as there's Israel. And there'll never be peace in the Middle East even if there is no Israel.'"

"Shit, that unshaven little fucker. The people in the camps, Gaza, the Territories, barefoot in human muck holding up *his* photo!"

"The smart ones all got out, became camera merchants in New York or rug sellers in London or leaders of international guerrilla movements."

"Everybody's has to have a pope. If we could all just have the *same* one."

"When was the first Muslim schism? Within days of the Prophet's death! Even his own family couldn't agree."

"Most wars begin in the family." Neill tried to see through the bar's steamy windows, couldn't tell if it was raining. "Tell me what to say," he drained his glass, dropped a hundred koruna note on the table, "so they let me see him."

"Just like you said: tell them he's getting a bad deal in the press. That it doesn't help the cause of Allah to have so many people unfairly turned against him."

"He wants them all to die, the unbelievers: *O prophet, stir up the faithful to war –*"

"And that on the international level it could impede his arms shipments and cause him trouble consolidating his gains."

Neill shuddered, a premonition somehow. "Suppose it's true, what Arafat said?"

"What, that there'll never be peace in the Middle East even without Israel?" Tomás shrugged: it's obvious.

The bar had filled; to leave they had to squeeze past women in tight leather skirts and men in dark suits, two men in motorcycle jackets, Neill holding his breath against the smoke. A cold wet wind was coming down the sidewalk; looking up he could see an early star.

17

LARNACA SMELLED of diesel, orange blossoms, and sea. The road was uneven and it was hard not to trip on the Roman paving blocks half-covered with old asphalt that glistened with dampness off the sea, with trickles of light from the port.

Across from the port and up a side street was a whorehouse and a bar with people laughing and singing, another street of missing cobbles and drooping façades, dirty windows of anchors and ropes, food and drink, women and sex. Whores, sailors, merchants, children, dogs, trucks, braying cars, and donkeys in the streets, flocks of teenage boys arm in arm, harsh music and Madonna, excrement and bay smells, crude oil, charcoal, diesel and dust.

André started to cross, a horn blared and he jumped back, swearing as a little white car churned past, a cold feeling inside him. You could have died. Looking the wrong way. This insane driving on the left.

Watching both ways he crossed and turned up Nikiolatis. After a block it passed a cemetery and turned to dirt, with low warehouses on both sides, people passing to and fro in the semi-darkness. Everywhere was the sweet addictive perfume of orange blossoms, the fruit fallen on the street and crushed by cars, the wind hissing in the tall palms.

Halfway up was a café with three steps down into a wide low room with a fire at one side, the air thick with rank tobacco smoke and *raki*, spiced with basil and garlic from a lamb stew cooking on the fire. Three men sat smoking at one table, two at another. The other three tables were empty. No one looked up. He went to the bar, feeling tensely out of place in his leather jacket.

No one paid him any attention. Then one of two men at one table got up and came to the bar. "You shouldn't come here," he said in English.

"The anchor man –"

"No matter what you want, he sent you to the wrong place."

"I'm going to Somalia, I need protection."

'Go home. That's the best protection I can give you."

André went back up the three stairs, feeling foolish. A dry dusty smell was coming down from the hills on the evening wind. Never should have come down here alone, he told himself. Never do this yourself.

"What you want?" a voice called. A man on crutches, one-legged, came out through the strollers. "I get you anything you want."

"Like what?"

"You from Brooklyn?" The man looked up at him. "I'm Butch. Once I was to Brooklyn."

"I'm not from Brooklyn," André said.

"Looking for women? I can get you. Looking for a little smoke? I can get you." He kept step beside André, swinging his single leg forward on his crutches through the crowd.

"*Ta bo taa go shaarn,*" someone said, passing – Norwegians maybe, tall blond men shouldering their way, mixing into other tongues, Arabic, Greek, Spanish. We all come to Larnaca, André thought, like rats running from everywhere else.

"Where *you* from, Butch?"

"Me?" The little man was suddenly quiet. "Beirut. But I don't go there anymore."

"What side you on?"

"Me? I didn't care. Just stepped on a mine."

"You know anything about guns?"

"I can get you. You want a hundred? A thousand? I get you the best deal. Don't talk to any of these other guys here, they're cheats. I'm the only one here with a license. You wanna see?" He slowed, propped on his crutches. Behind him a Coca-Cola sign glistened on the pavement. There was a corner kebab stand with a sticky counter and bowls of oranges, the smell of burnt fat and paprika.

"What kind you got?"

"You tell me what you need. We find it."

"Just a sidearm. Good caliber. Some ammo."

After three blocks they turned left, back toward the sea, down a narrow alley lit by the reflections of the port lights off the low clouds. He made Butch go first. There was a fishing boat up on dry dock and a garage at the end of the alley. A blotch of white came toward them. It was a man in a white T-shirt and trousers rolled to his knees. "So what you want?" Butch said to André.

"I'm going down south, need something fast and strong."

Butch translated into Greek. They went into the garage. The man in the T-shirt tugged a cord that lit a bulb in the ceiling. The walls were bare concrete blocks. He led them through a door into a little room with a sink and water jug at one end. It smelled of urine from the sink and of rotting dirt from under the sink. "We wait here," Butch said.

André went back outside. A searchlight was shifting under the heavy, bruised clouds. Someone was singing in another street, another language.

"Hey! Pal!" Butch called. André went back inside. The man

carried a heavy burlap bag into the room with the sink, and eased it off his shoulder onto the floor. He opened it and let the guns slide out.

"Jesus!" André said, reaching down to lay them on top of the burlap, out of the dirt – an Uzi, pre-war, a Makarov, beat up, boxes of cartridges, an engraved Browning .38, a new Daewoo feeling off-balance in his hand. Then he saw it, his hand automatically going for it, the Israeli Jericho in its brown camouflage, but he pushed past it as though not noticing, not wanting to draw the man's attention. He picked up a Mauser – no, a Merkuria. "How'd you get this?" he said.

Butch asked the man, who reached down a spindly long-nailed finger. "That one," André said, pointing to the Merkuria.

"He says it came off a ship," Butch said. "In Larnaca everything comes off a ship."

"How much?"

Another translation. "Three hundred Cyprus pounds," Butch said. "Five hundred dollars."

André riffled through the others, held up the Browning. "Seven hundred dollars," Butch translated. He pointed to the Jericho. "Why you not want this?"

"Don't like Israeli guns."

"They are the best."

"This Merkuria, I'll give you four hundred."

Again the translation. "No," Butch said. "He need four fifty."

The man spoke again. "He say hurry up," Butch translated. "We have troubles with the police, they're looking for guns."

"These others, they're too much. How much that Israeli piece?"

"It's nine hundred, the Jericho. Comes with two types of bullets, he says."

The man dug in the sack and brought out two boxes of Fiocchi 9mm parabellums. He took a bullet from each and André saw one was a shotshell and the other a slug. Now he wanted the gun very badly, to rescue it from this seamy squalid hole with this man who didn't understand that it had been the personal weapon of a professional, one who mixed shotshell and slugs in the same magazine, one to maim and one to kill, whose finely crafted understanding left no room for mistake. But he must have made a mistake somewhere, or why would the gun be here?

The mistake he'd never counted on making. And here was his gun, alone as a hunting dog without its master, its other half.

"TEHERAN DOESN'T WANT war right now with the United States," Mohammed said. "Nor yet against the Jews. And we can't take back Palestine because there is too much Western guilt about the Jews."

"You don't *care* if we get Palestine back!" Rosa said. "You're ready to make your separate peace. A bigger part of Lebanon for giving up Palestine, like Jew shopkeepers with a dried fish. The dried fish that once was Palestine!"

"Israel made the deserts bloom. You're just a bunch of lazy Bedouin with no camels, good for nothing but theft and complaining."

"If you don't hate the Jews, why are you fighting?"

"I do hate the Jews, Rosa. Infinitely and irrevocably. But even worse I hate the ones who put them over us. Who hadn't the courage to take them into America, into Britain. Who let Hitler kill them and then out of guilt sent the rest down here to thrust you from your homes. So you have come up here to thrust us from our own. Even together, Rosa, we don't have the strength to take back Palestine. But *they* can't shove us under, there's too much Muslim oil."

"There's none in Palestine."

"Palestine, poor in oil, so rich in heart."

"Hearts grow big from being filled with grief."

"Or joy. You're too young, Rosa, to be so serious. In any case, over the years Western guilt will continue to diminish, while Western hunger for oil will continue to grow."

"In the meantime, we're not getting closer to Palestine!"

"No. You must *see*. We keep up this pressure so we can eat Israel slowly, from within. While everyone is so preoccupied by the danger we present outside, they never notice what goes on inside. In a hundred years, I promise you, there'll hardly be a Jew in Palestine."

The mujihadeen with the close-cropped beard, the captain Rosa did not like, had come into the room, nodded respectfully at Mohammed, waiting for him to finish speaking. "She's downstairs," he said. "Your wife."

Mohammed made a sharp face and Rosa couldn't tell if it was from anger or surprise. Walking past, he patted her shoulder. "I'll be right back."

Rosa stood. "I must go down also." She followed Mohammed down the shrapnel-littered stairs, the captain going ahead and swinging his lantern. The night was quiet now, no shells going over, just the distant rattle of guns. Like peace, she thought, brushing at the sting in her eyes.

Mohammed seemed to forget her, moving ahead with the captain into the ruins of the ground floor, where a slight woman in a black gown turned her face toward him.

"What makes you take this risk?" Mohammed snapped. "Where are the children?"

She held his hands, brought them to her forehead. "They're with my parents. You are well, my husband?"

"They've backed off, the Christians. We've a brave young woman here, she attacked them alone."

"Kamil came."

Mohammed stepped back, straightened. "And?"

"Your father ..."

"*Speak*, woman!"

"He asks you to come quickly."

"There's no way."

"He wants to see you, before he dies."

Mohammed raised his hand and Rosa thought it was to hit his wife but it was only to run fingers through his hair. "How can I leave here?"

"For a few days, Mohammed." She leaned forward, touching his gown. "When he's gone you'll never have this chance again."

Mohammed spun round, tearing at his hair. "How?"

"You could go up through Aley, the road's open to Sofar. From there cut through the Christians and north along the mountain into Shiite country. You could be there tomorrow night." Again she tried to reach him but he pulled away. "It would be good for you, my husband."

This seemed to anger Mohammed even more. "Go back to your children," he snapped, turning toward the darkness of the stairway where Rosa stood.

18

THE POSTER. Here it was again. The rat-man's skull staring down with hatred on a burning city he had cut in half with his great Crusader's sword. With a shock, Neill realized it could be Beirut.

SPEND A NIGHT IN HELL
FRIDAY 13 MARCH
MOLDOVA 21
COUPLES KR 1,500
BE THERE BY 21:00

Again it was in English. This angered him, as if the poster had been aimed solely at him. Anyway it was too late now, nearly ten.

Down the street a yellow-lit sign, JaegerToefel, swung in the wind. Maybe they spoke German there, German chicks. A tall cool stein of Pilsner.

Inside the JaegerToefel was smoky and hot. Two thin old men were playing checkers at the bar; six or seven more were playing cards at a long table down one side. The barman was skinny and small with a large fluffy black moustache. Faintly the Beatles were singing *"She loves you ya ya ya"* on a radio high up behind the bar.

He ordered the Pilsner and leaned against his stool, against the bar. The beer was a lovely yellow color like early morning sun on fields of wheat. Why would it be in English, he wondered, that poster? It made no sense. If it was Beirut, who was the rat-man?

He emptied his glass and ordered another. Tomás was probably right. He was taking a wicked chance just trying to get into Beirut. Like Michael Szay said, he'd probably end up dead on some pavement, or in a Hezbollah hellhole. Anyway Mohammed would never talk to him.

The waiter set a new Pilsner down on the sticky wet table. Fifteen thousand pounds for one conversation. Maybe he should offer Mohammed five thousand to get him to talk. That way he'd still have Freeman's other ten thousand.

Layla. Did you know, Mohammed, I used to screw your devout Muslim wife?

Did he dare speak to that snake Hamid, the one who made it all go bad, and ask him to contact her, so he could reach Mohammed? Hamid would say no, unless *he* got a little cash, too. Spreading Freeman's shekels around for the betterment of man.

One of the checkers players next to him was telling a funny story and kept backing up, gesturing and bumping him, till Neill stepped on his foot. He halted, hands in mid-air, glanced round at Neill, moved away. Feeling guilty and alone, Neill watched the golden bubbles rise up inside his beer, thinking about Layla, Mohammed, Hamid, Freeman's fifteen thousand, an article about new hopes for peace in Lebanon, Bev and the kids at the dinner table passing round the paper, opened to his article. Even Commors, the deputy news editor, wouldn't dare touch it. Not this time.

After that, why not sign on with Freeman, an analyst or something, keep the paper, or switch back to *The Times* if the paper wouldn't raise him. And Freeman'd use him more, send him back to Ankara maybe, Amman. It was so easy to be a listening post and Freeman was too dumb to know it. He thought it was hard.

The poster wasn't a rat-man, really, but a horrifying man-rodent's skull.

He tried to imagine the fields of barley under the August sun where this beer had come from. On his hands it cast a gentle sunset light. The pores were large and shadowed, the hairs along his wrist a golden gray.

Soon he'd be dead, and this strong, limber wrist would rot and congeal at the bottom of a coffin. These strong legs and gut and eyes and this brain thinking all this and the lungs breathing in, the backbone, neck and skull. All dead. This heart pumping blood, rotting, drying, sinking into the wood.

It was too heartbreaking to lose, this lovely life. This joy, this love, this sun.

One of the men, laughing, slapped checkers on the board. The door squealed and two women entered, muffled in their hoods, talking together, then two men. Out on the street a trolley clanged by; cars were spinning tires in the lightly falling snow; people's boots squeaked on the pavement. Such busy creatures we are, he thought, we humans. So busy in the face of death.

With a strange urge to escape he paid for his Pilsners and ducked out into the fresh snow. A prostitute strolled past and he eyed her without slowing. On the pavement the snow was building into slush that came through the sides of his shoes.

A taxi eased by and he waved it down. "How far to Moldova?" he asked in German. The driver answered in Slovak; Neill tore a piece of paper from his notebook, wrote "Moldova 21" and handed it to him. Get in, the driver beckoned, did a U-turn, and drove through town upriver. Ten-forty, a clock said. Late again, Neill thought.

The tires whammed as the taxi dropped from macadam to cobbles. There were buildings with empty windows now, no pavements, here and there a truck trailer alongside an unlit opened door, men moving without lights, black warehouses three stories high, potholes and ruts laced with ice, once a dead horse at the side of the street, legs frozen in the air.

No cobbles now, just dirt. In and around skeletons of old trucks and piles of scrap timber, wire, and steel, red flash of rat eyes. The taxi stopped. "One thousand korunas," the driver said in German.

"Moldova 21?"

The driver pointed down a wide empty street, toward the river. "One thousand."

"Take me there." Neill pointed at himself, down the street.

The driver moved one hand over the other to signify a car over the street, crashing in potholes, crumpling to a halt. The driver had narrow, sunken cheeks, emaciated skin over bone. He walked two fingers down one of his hands, showed a crossroads. "One." The fingers loped to the next, the next, all the way to five.

Neill could see nothing down the street. *"Das is gefährlich?"* he said – is it dangerous? – made the motion of cutting his own throat.

The driver chuckled. *"Im Bratislava, alle ist gefährlich."*

Neill paid the thousand korunas and got out. The taxi spun round and its taillights vanished the way they'd come. Neill drew his coat close, tripped over a piece of cable, stood rubbing his knee through the torn cloth. No streetlights, barely enough reflection off the smog to show rooftops high on either side, here and there a grim glimmer of window, dark gape of a door. Car lights were coming down the road, stopped a block away, went out.

He stumbled on something hard, moved round it – broken bricks. At the second crossroads several trucks clustered like great dark buffaloes feeding, between them a fire with two men crouched before it.

Ice on the puddles crunched under his feet.

At the fifth crossroads he turned left into the cold sewery

wind off the river. This street was wider, cobbled in places, a skein of transmission cables over tilting dark buildings.

In London you never worry about dark places, he realized, because the crooks are too cowardly to go in them. But here ...

He kept to the middle of the street. The whole thing was crazy but if there was this Moldova 21, he might as well get there instead of trying to go back. They wouldn't have put it on the poster if it didn't exist.

Unless the taxi driver had made a mistake. Or he'd brought him to the wrong place on purpose, radioed some friends and told them where to find him.

The darkness deepened on his left – an alley, at its far end a red glimmer. He hesitated, trying to watch all directions, fearing someone behind. If he went down the alley they'd grab him. But the red light was probably 21 – this must be Moldova. If he went back he'd have to pass the men at the fire, by the trucks. He moved a foot into the alley, hit his knee against hard metal, cold. A car. There seemed to be cars down both sides, a narrow pavement between them.

Silly to be fearful in such a silly situation. Down there, that red light had to be Moldova 21. Or a place with a phone, maybe.

The red glimmer was a light over a red door. Under its aura a Mercedes coupé, an Audi, a Harley with a Portugal license, a Lancia with Stuttgart plates. Reassured, he pushed the lit doorbell.

The red door opened, blocked by a big man in a black jacket, a wild black beard, thick red-rimmed glasses. "You're late," he said in English.

Neill glanced at his watch. "The cab left me. I had to walk."

"Where's the woman?" At the man's back a whitewashed stone stairway dropped toward the sound of heavy metal.

"Woman?"

"You're supposed to bring at least one. This is a couples place."

"It didn't say that."

"You don't read Slovak?"

To Neill his own words seemed ludicrous, a servile postulant's. "I saw it in English."

"Welcome to Hell," the man snorted. "But you pay the couples price."

Another song was playing now, though the first hadn't had time to stop. Neill went down the narrow deep stairs to a wooden door with black metal studs. Now the music seemed overhead. The door wouldn't open.

He went back up but the man with the wild beard and red glasses was gone and the front door was locked. Or was this a different door? Had he come up the wrong stairs? The music was loud, from everywhere at once; it made it hard to think. The man must have locked up – too late, no more people allowed in. Neill shoved the door but it was solid as stone. He went back downstairs, the music fading, but the door was open now on a squat smoky room with couples dancing to Poison between gauze banners hung like cloth walls. This isn't Hell, Neill thought. Not Poison but Scorpions, the couples sliding through smoke and gauze banners. A woman dropped a cigarette, snuffed it with a high-heeled shoe, smiled at Neill and swung back to her partner. At the end of the room was a bar and behind it a movie showing a room of haze and smoke and slowly writhing couples. It wasn't a film but a silk curtain, and beyond it a room of sheepskin, leather, and low couches, men and women making love.

"You didn't come with anybody?" the bar girl said.

"Why does everyone speak English?"

"It's the only other language I know. You take a drink? It's in the price."

He nodded at the two women and the man naked on the floor behind her. "This happen every night?"

She shrugged, unwrapped the cork of a bottle of champagne, pulled the cork, filled his glass and set the bottle beside it.

There were no stools at the bar. He hung his coat over one arm, his back to the bar. The champagne tasted of roses.

Dancers shifted in and out of darkness, the melody changed, occasionally people moved from one side of the silk screen to the other. You think you're wildly passionate lovers, Neill thought, but you're just two flabby people twitching on the floor.

He had such a wearying sense of so many things always going wrong, no let-up. Job and family and fate, remembering when things were different. No wonder. The music ebbed and returned, over the nearer voices, the air thick with cigarette smoke. A woman came naked through the silk screen and took a bottle back into the room. The music broke and couples jostled beside him at the bar, glued to each other or nonchalantly distant, a woman's hot haunch against his thigh as she embraced her lover. Another man raised his partner's dress to her waist while she rubbed up and down against him and they took turns drinking from a champagne bottle. A couple came in the door, leaned to each other briefly, then moved apart. The woman pushed past Neill to the bar, took a long drink from his bottle. She was breathing hard and her black hair stuck to the back of her neck. "Couldn't wait!" she said. "I'll give you some of mine."

"It's all right. I'm not staying."

"Not staying? It's just beginning."

"Why does everybody speak English?"

"I'm from Kosice." She lit a cigarette, waved away smoke. "Lots of textiles. But good schools. So I learned English and Russian, and a little German."

Her lipstick was half gone and her complexion very flushed. She had a round young face with full lips and a rapacious slender body moving with the music.

Neill glanced along the bar. "Where's your guy?"

"Saw someone else he wanted to go in there with."

He looked across the silk screen, couldn't see the man. "You don't care?"

She smiled. "You are too English."

19

HER BODY SLID up and down his as they danced, her thighs clamping his. "Let's go," he said. "The other side."

She glanced through the silk curtain. "Not here." The music died and she went to the bar and plucked up a red and yellow apple, bit into it and washed it down with champagne. Her face was still flushed, her body radiated heat.

Neill nodded at the room beyond the silk screen. "Because of him?"

She put the apple down and held him, moving them back out among the dancers, her body so close there seemed no clothes between them.

Up on her toes she kissed him, soft and deep. "Instead we take a drive."

So many to live with, he thought, so many to love. Her back strong and curvy, a slippery body hot for the rhythms of love. But why, he wondered, does she want me? He could feel her crotch hair against his thigh, through her clothes.

Up the narrow spiral stairs they went into a world of dark red shadows. She had a black lambskin coat and beret, black leather boots, and in the cold air her breath unfurled like a scarf. She got into a Lada, unlocked his door.

Inside it stank of pipe. She started the engine, let it idle while she kissed him, biting his lips, his tongue, teeth against teeth, her fingernails up and down his back. She shoved him away, backed fast down the alley and drove south to an empty wide boulevard curving away from the river. "The road to the Russian base," she said.

She drove with thighs open, rocking her hips to the touch of his hand. "I could go forever," she said, "like this."

"You'll stop before I will."

"I bet you give up first. Twenty-five dollars." She swung off on a side road bordered by barbed wire.

"What's this?"

"The short cut to Vinohrady. At night nobody comes here." She geared down, peering through the windshield, turned left on a gravel track, grass rustling under the car.

At the top of a hill the track widened into a parking lot, rubbish pinned by the wind to the barbed wire round it. She turned off the engine, hands up under his shirt. "I'm going to drive you wild." She broke away, opened the door. "But first I show you Bratislava!"

"I don't care about Brati-bloody-slava."

She got out, the dome light blinding him. He got out and shut the door. "You left on the parking lights."

"Doesn't matter." Her back to him, she stood looking for stars over the city lights. As he moved toward her she turned and extended her clasped hands at him and he saw the gun. "Back up to the car," she said. "Turn around."

He reached up his hands and she fired, the bullet sucking past his ear, the roar crushing his head. "Jesus!" he screamed, holding his head.

"Kneel! There, in front of the light!"

He knelt before one headlight. Against it an insect was splayed, long legs and body. "Please don't –"

"Who are you with?"

"I came alone, I told you!"

"Working with, idiot!"

"I'm a journalist, just going through, not working here."

"Where to?"

"Damascus."

"What for?"

"Cover the Middle East. *Please* don't –"

"Which side are you on?"

"Neither. None of them."

"If I were Hezbollah I'd shoot you for that. Every dead infidel's one more step up the stairway to Heaven. Especially infidels who come pissing on Mohammed's cloak." Her voice backed away. "Or the Czechoslovaks – how do they know you're not a spy? If you were hurting their country, what should I do?"

"Take me to the police. See what they say."

"In Bratislava running to the police is a good way to get killed. You don't have much brains, do you? It wouldn't be a shame to kill you. Get away from the car."

"*Please* don't!"

"Begging for your scrawny little life? Relax, I'm not going to shoot you, much as I should. But it's seventeen kilometers' walk back to the city, and that'll give you time to think about how stupid you were to let yourself be doubled to the most dangerous part of town, where you went on some weird stupid impulse, and where you leave in a car with a woman you've never met."

"I've met you!" He started to rise. "I know your smell."

"Now you do. But you didn't when you should. When I gave you half a hundred clues. You're thick as a door, mate."

The Lada revved and he dashed for it but she spun round, spraying sand in his face, and roared back up the dirt track. He fell on his knees, hands clasped on the oily dirt. He jumped up, listening to the car, but it wasn't coming back. He ran to the edge of the hill but could not see its headlights. Beyond the dark hills Bratislava gleamed, evil and unforgiving.

THE SYRIAN GUNS in the Bekaa were firing at Israeli positions south of Sofar, lighting up the midnight sky. Mohammed led his three men out of the olive grove, seeking a silent path over the crunchy leaves. His heart was pounding – with fear or joy, he couldn't tell. The gun felt heavy and perfect in his hand, the night air clean and cold. God's finger truly points through the gun in your hand, he thought. Cleansing the world.

Beyond the olive grove barbed wire gleamed. He waved the men back, cut an opening in the double fence and squirmed through it. If there was a mine, would he have time to know? Paradise, that gleaming city of green grass and lovely women, was it worth death?"

Before him the land rose into barren plateaus and peaks, umber sharp outcrops and boulders lit by the white incandescence of the rocket launchers.

If God hadn't taught us to kill, what good would we be?

THE GIRL WAS PRETENDING to come, jerking her head back and forth, moaning. "Stop it!" André snarled, shoving harder, bunching her up and driving deeper. Maybe she wasn't faking it, this long coming slowly and her teeth in his shoulder and now this wild angry look through the sweaty hair and on her lips a taste of blood – whose? Not yet he wouldn't come, not yet; the girl stretched out beneath him like a ballerina, now hunching up, a ball of clenching flesh, her legs sliding down his, she writhed out straight again, squeezing herself tight, squeezing it out of him.

He pulled himself away, sat up, trying not to gasp. Sweat and semen glistened in the moonlight on his belly, down into the squat hairs.

She slipped into her clothes. Moonlight was like smoke spilled on the floor. In it he could see dust between cracked tiles. "You want me come back?" she said. "Some time?"

"I'm leaving."

She shut the door softly as she went. Slowly, like a well-trained army, the moonlight moved across the floor, from under the window to the foot of the bed, toward the empty fireplace on the far wall. He went to the window, looking over the tile roofs of many houses and many dreams, to the yellow minaret of Hala Sultan mosque and the silvery sea beyond, and there seemed to descend over it all an almost holy blessing.

He pulled his bag from the cupboard and sat naked on the floor in the moonlight, dismantling and reassembling the Jericho, first eyes open, then closed, till by fingertip he knew instantly the touch of every part, the way each joined the others, until each bullet slipped by itself into the clip and the clip into the gun. Until it came together by itself.

Like this trip, which was disjointed and haphazard at the start and now was beginning to come together by itself. The closer it got, the stranger it was. That he should do this. Or that he should have waited so long. Wrong, what they said. Vengeance should be right away, not cold. Unless you make him live in fear. Unless he knows you're coming but doesn't know how or when.

But this guy doesn't know.

André had waited too long, got too cold, let his anger die. The hatred and pain. No, the pain was still there. But now it was a decision, not a response. A cold decision.

Here, now, was part of the process, talking himself into coming this far. Knowing that once he'd got this far he'd talk himself into going further. Until finally, the whole thing united before him, almost happened by itself.

On his hand were the smells of gun oil and the girl's vagina: out of this we come, he thought, and into it.

He put the gun away and stood at the window watching the moon's phosphorescence on the waves, the mosque with its minaret draped in green lights, the grim black fort, the play of cloud shadows on the gray-green sea, the mast lights of three ships lying at anchor outside the port. Beyond the bay were the refinery lights, then the city trailing into darkness eastward toward Famagusta, the famous Famagusta the Turks had taken in '74 and still held. Cyprus like Beirut was cut in half, east and west, people hungry to kill on both sides of the line.

"Yes," the surf sighed, falling on the sand, "yes," sliding back to rise and fall again. "Yes ..."

The moon slid down the west, yellowed, reddened, and sank among the houses. Slowly, slowly its light faded up the wall, seeming to take him with it when it narrowed to nothing and slipped into the night.

20

HIS FATHER looked so frail and white-bearded on his pallet that Mohammed thought he was already dead. But his father turned his head and smiled. "What a nice surprise!"

"How are you, Papa?"

"I'm glad Kamil found you. That you came."

"I have to start back before dawn, to miss the Christian patrols." He leaned down to embrace his father's chilled thin bundle of bones. The room smelled of an old man's infected sleep, and of smoke from the lemon boughs in the coals. Beyond the wall a lamb was bleating.

"How did you come?"

"We could drive past Aley. Cut through the Christian lines and came up along the mountain."

"I might have seen you. I've been half way to Heaven, tonight. Looked down on the mountain from high in the sky."

Mohammed sat himself closer to the edge of the bed. "How was that?"

"An angel or a *jinni* or something took me right out of this bed, pulled me up in the air so I hung there looking down on myself, as if I was dead, yet I weighed nothing, went up through the roof and could look down on the house and goat pens and the stone wall all round, then the open pasture beyond, the trail to the lake, as if the moonlight was water pouring down the mountains into the lake."

"You thirsty or something, Papa?" Mohammed looked round for the water jug, saw a teapot on the hearth. "You want some tea?"

"I kept getting further away and seeing more and more and finally this whole world was like a big boulder I could see over one edge of. Then it was just a little stone."

Mohammed shivered. "It's cold in here, Papa."

"I saw this war, how it's killing us all."

"No it won't, Papa. It's almost over."

His father's hand rose from the blanket and wavered toward him, settled on his forearm. "Don't *lie*! This is my last time ever. To be with you."

Mohammed felt a tremor of shame down his back. "I'm sorry."

Pulling on Mohammed's arm, the old man raised himself up, caught his breath. "I'm going to die soon. And I understand why this war happened. And how to end it."

"We may not want to end it. You know that. Till we get what we want."

"You're all blind drunks. Can't even see, any of you, that you've already lost everything there is to lose ..." His father's voice, Mohammed noticed, had grown thin and hoarse. "... It's going to kill you all."

"Then we've lost all these men for nothing."

"Anyone who dies dies for nothing. It takes a leader to make peace."

"If it's schism between us then it's schism forever. Until they're *all* dead."

"You know that can never happen. Praise God."

"Because we don't believe in it enough. If we did, Allah would see it done."

His father lay back down, drawing up the blanket. "To learn

the *suras* is to be informed by Allah every moment of your life. Awake and in dreams. Especially in dreams." A lemon branch flared, the bark peeling away, and for a moment the old man listened to it. "But it's no good, unless you listen to what the Prophet is saying."

"You always have."

"Remember the one, *No soul can believe but by the permission of God: and he shall pour out his indignation on those who will not understand.* What do you suppose that means?"

"Many things. None of them merciful."

"But if Allah decides who shall believe, why does he then punish those who don't?"

"*I don't slay the soul which God has forbidden me to slay, unless for just cause.*"

"But think, my son: *Do not revenge thy friend's blood on any other than the person who killed him.* Some man you kill, he may be a shopkeeper, and never have killed a soul."

"*He whom God shall direct, shall have none to mislead him.*"

"When I was seven, as I've told you many times, leading the goats at dawn down to where the river comes out of the mountain, then up the mountain as the sun rose – I could be there now, the juniper needles on the path, strawberries between the sharp stones –"

"The junipers are all gone. Eaten by goats."

"In all my long life, including my love for your mother, that was my favorite time. The river ..."

Mohammed went to the fire and laid some twigs on the coals, poured water into a black kettle and set it on two rocks above them. "Three times now the Christians have hinted peace. If I have to, I'll agree to a truce, until we can destroy them."

"How did they offer this peace?"

"A truce – they lift the siege and we all return to our old sides. Under the UN. But that still leaves Amal, the Druze."

"When I was a boy, we all slept in that other room."

"I remember. You've told me."

"Next door, where the Sillals are now, were the al-Sherifs. Hosseini people. In bed at night I'd hear their voices chattering, laughing and singing, through the mud wall, and I remember thinking that if that wall had been a body's width to the east, I'd be their son and Abdul my brother."

"God did not want that."

"God didn't care, my son."

"How can you say that?"

"There are no just causes. That's what, after half a century of thinking about God, I'm saying."

"You've outgrown the Prophet?"

"If a mud wall separated me from the other side, then Muslim, Christian, Sunni, Shiite – these are not enough to kill for. Not enough to turn Lebanon from Heaven into Hell."

"Hell's what Heaven used to be. We keep looking in the wrong place."

"Remember the imam who was caught in a flood, and he goes up to his minaret to wait for God to save him? The water's rising. A boat comes by, offers to take him. "No!" he calls. "God will save me!" Another boat comes by, he tells them the same thing, "God will save me.""

"You must rest, Papa."

"And then the third boat comes and he tells them the same. The water rises and the imam's drowned. In Heaven he reproaches God: "Why didn't you save me?""

Mohammed, checking the teapot, turned his back. "And what does God say?"

"Fool," God answers, "I sent you three boats."

Mohammed poured a cup, mixed in cool water and a chunk of sugar, held up his father's head so the old man could sip.

"Are you going to cling to *your* minaret?" his father said. "You don't remember that the *Muslim* means *He who submits?*"

21

THE OLD MAN SLEPT. The woman who had been watching over him returned. Mohammed went into the next room, where sixty years ago his father had lain in bed hearing the Hosseini family beyond the wall. He woke his three sleeping mujihadeen and went back to his father. "Papa!" he whispered, but the old man didn't budge. In his blanched face, for an instant, Mohammed saw his own.

"We should stay another night," one of the mujihadeen said, yawning and rubbing his face.

Mohammed swung round, checked his anger. "What about Beirut?"

"Beirut's quiet now. You should take this time."

"We could leave tomorrow at midnight," another said. "It'd be safer."

"You let *me* decide!" He realized his voice was too harsh, tried to soften it. "Hurry!" He went back to his father. The old man's tousled hair stuck up like a white flag of surrender. "Papa!" he said, but again his father did not answer.

"Let him sleep," the woman said. "Wait a few hours."

"Wait?" Why did these peasants never understand? Stuck in their slow peasant ways, the world eating them alive. He nodded sharply to his men and led them out, with one last glance back at the thin white head crowned in white. He turned his face toward the mountain, walked the street of tilting houses toward the lake and along its edge, ducks quacking nervously and swimming their young away from shore.

Here was the place in the swamp at the edge where he'd found the little porcelain vase the French archaeologist had said was Roman, that a woman two thousand years ago had used to store her tears. How, he'd wondered at the time, could anyone weep so much?

They circled the end of the lake and followed the river up the mountain, tree roots like black snakes across the trail. They passed by the shepherd's hut and the trail became steep, the river crashing and booming down its bed. In the moonlight the rocks gleamed with frost. The branches were bare and black, splinters of paler black sky between them.

They stopped for breath where the river came churning out of the mountain into a deep pool then cast itself over the edge. Mohammed walked out on the edge and knelt down to the great white stone that was the section of a Roman temple, one that had been built here to honor the river's coming forth from the mountain, the Frenchman had said, a long piece of carved stone that had been placed above columns.

Mohammed knelt and as he had done so many times traced with his fingers the deep lines someone had carved so long ago in the stone. How, he wondered, had they brought up these huge chunks? For there was no white stone like this on the mountain.

It was hard to imagine those people, so diligent and hard-working, leaving their traces everywhere. And others before them, the Frenchman had said: Greeks, Phoenicians, many others. Where were they now? Against them all, how did you weigh one old man's death? He with his thin white hair like a flag of surrender?

Above the thundering river were the dark mouths of caves where he'd played as a boy, the grass slope his goats had climbed each morning to pastures in the sun. Where was he now, that boy?

The lake below was just like his father had said, a pool of moonlight that had flowed and echoed down the mountains all around.

They reached the first crests before dawn. Early sparrows scattered from goat dung on the path; Mohammed pitied their numb hunger, their scratching at dirt and stone. He tossed the Kalashnikov to the other hand, swinging his legs effortlessly into a sudden climb through basalt slabs with gnawed bitter scrub in their corners. He liked stretching his legs out like this, the feeling he could go on forever, never tire.

Here, where they'd beaten the Christians, a bullet-riddled white statue of their Virgin loomed headless over a vast vertical lunar valley of thorn trees and splintered stones.

Beyond the Christians now. His stomach was empty but that felt good too. You could go on almost nothing, really. Cleared your mind for what you had to do. How to trap them with this peace. Make them beg for their own death.

Death like this crystal morning whose blue air stung his nostrils. *He* must not die before he could trap them. Like the girl said, that girl Rosa, he'd been losing sight of the goal, liberation of the Holy Land. He'd become too caught up in this war of schisms: another Muslim is at least better than an infidel – there his father was wrong.

On the right there were remnants of a stone wall between two boulders. Long-ago separation of the sheep. The liberation of Palestine, the Holy City: first we need Beirut as a base. That's what you must tell Rosa. We cannot move until they're completely encircled. When we have Lebanon, Syria, and Jordan, then Egypt will abrogate Sadat's peace and Israel will be driven under.

Stone walls of a house, the sky its roof, the earth its floor. Beside it a ruined sheepcote, the bouldered, barren earth. He hungered to be back with the first people who had come over these hills of sharp basalt and balsamy scrub and down into the valley below, when it had been grass-thick in the meadows, cedars like soldiers up the ridges, the river like a woman's silver necklace down between them. How many lives in those rock walls, how many young women disrobing for their husbands, how many generations of counting up and never having enough?

He'd be foolish to think the liberation of Palestine would change that. His father taking the goats down to the lake, the Hosseini family beyond the wall, their voices in the night.

He looked back to see his men strung out behind him. To the left, up in the rocks, a quick glimmer of a rifle. He yelled, waved his men down but it was too late; from everywhere rifles fired, shattering the cold clear morning, his men twisting and falling on the path. As he fired at the flash and sound of guns, something punched him hard in the back and knocked him face into the ground.

22

NEILL WANTED TO FIND HELL in daylight but there was no point: the woman was untraceable. And what good would it do to find her?

It was wrong, what they'd done. Scaring him like that. He wasn't *theirs*. He was doing them a favor. If Freeman wasn't such a snide little shit he'd have realized long ago. They didn't care if he lived or died, just wanted him to find Mohammed.

If he did, it wouldn't be how they thought. They'd said they wouldn't follow him, but look what they'd done.

He wasn't doing them any more favors. Like Freeman had said, he'd drop them when he wanted. But not like they thought.

But then, MI6 could have him kicked out of Britain any time they wanted. Freeman had said that too. Just pray, Neill, he had said, that we never turn against you. Maybe that was what he needed: go back to the States, start over.

He was too old to start over. He swung his legs over the side of the bed and hobbled to the bathroom. Anyway, if he tried to find her he'd miss his plane. He sat on the toilet, fell asleep and hit his head on the radiator, stood in the shower, put in the plug and let the tub fill round his ankles. Seven fifteen, and already no hot water.

"I'M SORRY YOUR FRIENDS WERE KILLED. You were very lucky to be just wounded." With his index finger the doctor pushed his bifocals up the bridge of his nose and peered down through them, wrinkled his nose as if his moustache tickled. "And just a little wound at that."

"It's sore," Mohammed said, "to be so little –"

"It missed the lungs – just muscle and soft tissue. A quick in and out beneath your shoulder blade. You have very thick muscles."

"In Ainata I am a mason."

"Soon they'll come to ask you about all that."

"All that?"

"Who you are and where you were going."

"I didn't want to go. But they came to Ainata, the tall one and the one with the scarred cheek. His name's Ahmed. They said we had to send two young men, to fight in Beirut. I have no work now so the village decided to send me."

"Who was the other?"

"He was not really from Ainata but from a farm up on the mountain. Just a kid. He has no family, that's why they sent him."

"It's natural to feel guilty. When they died and you didn't."

"I didn't know the two mujihadeen. I didn't like them. I didn't know the kid either. I'm sorry they're dead but it was just luck."

"Yes, you were very lucky."

"What happens now?"

"Once you're healed you go to a camp. Depends who you are – we might exchange you."

"Hezbollah doesn't even know me. You don't need to tell them. If you trade me then I'll have to fight."

"No trying to escape – it'd kill you."

———

IT WAS THE MALEV Middle East run, Budapest through Sofia, an old TU 44 that flew fast and high and dropped steeply into Istanbul like a pigeon to its roost, took off again across the once-vast forests of an Anatolia now barren and gray, the deserts of the Crusader kings, their castles from the air like pimples on the earth's dark skin.

They'd visited these castles, he and Bev, so long ago. In a past that had shrunk to a tiny memory like the tiny castle so far below. A honeymoon across Byzantium to Ancyra, in a time of their own vague Christianity, south past Caravansary through the gate where Saul quit Tarsus for Damascus, across the plains and hills where later the Crusaders would build their great *kraks* to wall out what they never could defeat.

Castles jutting from the desert like rotten teeth on eroded mountain jaws, walls half fallen and filled with dirt, a village huddled downhill against a bitter April wind, the earth blowing past them in crumbles, small boys running to them with handfuls of coins – gold and silver with faces of long-dead kings, Richard the Lionheart, Philippe Auguste. "Don't buy them," Beverly had said, "it just incites them to dig up more," but once half out of pity he'd given one boy a handful of change for the ancient handful. He'd taken the coins home and they were later stolen by some friend of Edgar's who'd then moved away.

Like the coins, the British mandate too had vanished, nothing but a rainstorm across these peaks and deserts, nothing after a thousand years of Constantinople, eight hundred Ottoman years. From the first tribes out of the African crescent, how many generations of empires won, lost, and forgotten? Like *Judges*, that most honest of the Old Testament books, one long litany of victory, vengeance and defeat.

Across the broad brown desert a single track, and on it a single string of dust blown windward, the wind that had gnawed the dry earth clean of centuries of dead, its walls of empires, their endless battles over what? How many total minutes of human misery and sweat and pain? Animals too – burdened donkeys, hunted gazelles, the last wild horses, wolves dying of poison – all down there, blown away with the sand.

What had he and Bev found and lost there, with their urgent young sex in cold Turkish hotel rooms? Their bitter willingness, at first, to understand each other? What had they paid for, he wondered, that was later stolen and always regretted?

Empires of wind.

MOHAMMED lay on a burlap mattress on a bed of concrete blocks. The blocks were hard and cold through the mattress, and he kept trying to find a better position. When he moved the pain was sharp, cleaving him like a sword. Otherwise it was the dull ache brought on by painkillers, giving him a sort of weary elation.

Overhead a hardened mix of mud and plaster hung down unevenly between the rafters; under the main beam a kerosene lantern fluttered in the wind through the eaves. The wind was sharp and smelled of desert. Why, he wondered, and wondered at himself for wondering, did I stay so long in Beirut, when it's the desert mountains that I love?

What had driven him to quit the barren slopes of Yammouné, its fertile valley, for the festering Shiite slums of Beirut? In Yammouné there had been the beauty of the land but no future. In the Shiite slums there was rancor and misery, but a little work too and, slowly, comprehension.

He took a breath, letting it hurt all the way down into his lungs and across his back. Comprehension, fool that he'd been, of the last thirteen centuries of Shiite bondage and poverty, and how, finally, they might be overcome.

He slowed his breathing; the pain had made him dizzy. Layla would be worried. To be a Warrior of God you should have no wife, no children. The time for changing his people's destiny was now; far more important than a wife, than children. Any man could have those.

But wounded like this he'd never escape. Not all the way back across Mount Lebanon to the Muslim side, down to the Bekaa. He'd have to seem too weak to move for as long as possible, till maybe he could get away.

At his elbow stood an upended wooden case with an extinguished candle and clean bandages. Above his head a crucifix was nailed to the wall; from a nail in a rafter hung a sack of glucose with a drip line to his wrist. Beyond the wooden box were four more beds, in each a wounded Christian. The nearest sat staring at his stump legs, berating them and God. The next kept whimpering, "Halima! Halima!" The third lay motionless with pain and heroin, his face blown hideously away. That one won't live, Mohammed decided. The last seemed dead too, he was so quiet. There had been two others, but a taxi had come up from Qartaba to take them down.

The man in the next bed wept quietly down on his missing legs. *For war shall lay thy legs bare*, Mohammed quoted to him silently from the Koran; this is what happens, Christian, when you will not listen.

The wind sucked under the ceiling as a trap door opened in the corner and white running shoes came down a ladder. It was the doctor, ducking under the beams, his bifocals shining. Nine steps down, Mohammed counted. It's a bunker, he decided. Half underground.

The doctor went first to the one who kept calling "Halima", speaking quietly, holding his hand.

Breathing steadily, softly, so as not to disturb the hole in his body, Mohammed raised his head. The doctor was not carrying a gun. He wore a leather jacket, gray slacks, and the white running shoes. There was blood on one shoe.

The doctor spent a long time with the man whose face had been blown away. Mohammed rested his head. It was too heavy to move. The doctor was speaking now with the legless man. "You can't think like that," he said. "Learn to live for others, now."

"Fool!" the man wailed.

"I wish there were something I could do."

"Find the one who put that mine in the middle of the street."

The doctor checked Mohammed. "It's good you're healing quickly, for soon you must give up your place."

"For where?"

"The camp. New wounded are coming."

Mohammed took a soft breath. "From where?"

"I haven't a clue."

"Yet you heal Muslims too?"

"You wouldn't heal ours?"

"I've never even seen anyone wounded. Before now."

"Welcome to the war."

"If I could pay you back …"

"Do something for someone else, some time. Anyway, you're out of the fighting now. Think about staying out."

"If we all did that you'd win."

"We've all already lost. There'll never again be a Lebanon worth having. A Beirut. We've destroyed them. You and I and our friends. Our separate Gods."

"Beirut will come back. Better than before. Cleaner than before."

"Cleaner is dead. That's what antiseptic means: to clean something you kill everything on it." The doctor replaced Mohammed's transparent glucose bag, flicking the valve with a fingernail to make little bubbles rise inside it.

23

"I WANT to visit the Great Mosque," Neill said. "The Archaeological Museum, maybe go to Amman, up to Palmyra."

"Maybe?"

"Depends how long I stay."

"You've got three weeks. No going north. The road's closed to Aleppo."

"You mean the road through Hama? Where Hama *was*?"

The Syrian Customs man zipped open Neill's bag, spilled it on the counter, a vial of pills clattering. Damn, Neill thought, I forgot about them. No wonder I'm feeling dizzy. "They're for malaria."

"There's no malaria here."

Malaria wouldn't hit so soon, Neill realized, make me this dizzy already. "I may go up the Nile."

The man raised the vial and shook it against the light. "You didn't say Egypt."

"I said maybe."

"The pages in your passport with the Israeli visas – did you take them out?"

"I don't do Israel. Just this side."

"Why don't you tell the truth? How do you expect readers to believe you when you *lie*? If you lie about going up the Nile, who's to believe what you write about Palestine?"

"And you?" Neill said, thinking of Hama.

"Learn to speak the truth." The man shoved Neill's things back into the bag and zipped it shut. "Or don't come here anymore."

Neill's stitches tugged when he swung the bag over his shoulder. "Let me know," he grunted, "when you figure out the truth."

"You speak Arabic – you must know the sacred Koran: *the ungodly shall suffer fearful punishment*. That is the truth."

"You can play anything by the book."

"*The ungodly and unbelievers*," the man stamped his visa, folded his passport and gave it to him, "*God shall render unto Hell*. You know that too."

FEET CLATTERED DOWN the ladder. Three Christians and the doctor. They went to the wounded one who had never made a sound, whose blanket was now up over his face. They pulled back the blanket and one fell down on his knees and began to cry, hands clasped over the body on the bed.

He lurched to his feet, a great bearded bear of a man, his upthrust hands smacking the ceiling, plaster falling down. "Who did this?" he screamed.

"Muslims." The legless man nodded at Mohammed. "Like this one."

"*What!* You have them *here*? In the place where my brother died?"

"He didn't hurt your brother," the doctor said, blocking him. "He's just a poor mason, from some village in the Bekaa."

"I'll *strangle* him!"

Mohammed tried to protect his neck but the man's hands

were too strong, clamping down, crushing. "No!" the doctor shouted, yanking the man's wrists. "He's going to the camps – they're coming to get him!"

The man backed away. Mohammed pulled himself up, trying to breathe but his throat felt crushed.

"When he gets out of the camps he's going home." The doctor was rubbing an injured hand. "Never bother us again."

"And never bear arms against us!" the bearded man screamed into Mohammed's face.

Mohammed massaged his throat. "I never have."

The bearded man stared down at him then twisted away, knelt to lie his head sideways on his dead brother's chest, as if listening for the heart.

"Take the body home," the doctor said. "It must be buried."

"Home?" He raised his face smeared with his brother's blood. "He was the last one." He lifted up the body and carried it up the ladder in his arms.

Mohammed's throat felt burned inside as if a hangman's noose was tight round it. He could hear his heartbeat, irregular as a stone skipping down a mountain.

In a few minutes the doctor came back down. "You shouldn't have said that," he said to the legless man. "He's done you no harm, this Muslim."

"Every Muslim is an offence against God."

"No," the doctor answered. "Every human is an offence against God."

"Or maybe it's God who's an offence against man."

THE HARSH HYPNOTIC smell of roasting coffee filled the narrow Damascus street of tilting stone houses, the stone steps worn down their middle like a stream bed, strange spices wafting out of strange windows, women's eyes behind black slits.

Twice Neill doubled back but no one followed. There'd been no one since the airport. He crossed the Spice Market and ducked under a Roman gate where water ran in an open trench, down more stone-block steps between granite walls, children jostling him and calling like swallows, men shoving up the steps with beef shoulders on their backs, sacks of rice and charcoal, bundled saplings, a beam with a jug of water on each end, two men with a tin full of braziers trailing momentary warmth, a woman's voice loud down a dark passage, another answering.

At a well in the middle of the street a woman had cranked up a bucket and was giving water to a donkey. Neill stopped at a wooden door with black arrowhead studs. He pulled the bell; it rang far back, beyond walls. No one came. He backed up to the well and looked up. The windows were all closed and shuttered.

He went back to the Great Mosque, its immense and supernaturally beautiful dome spiring above the consecrated ground of thousands of years from barbarian campfires to Greek agoras, now a hymn to the glory of Allah: this has always been hallowed ground. He took off his shoes and tucked them in his jacket. There was no light in the entry. When he followed the others streaming into the mosque it was as if the sky had exploded, the domes so far above they seemed to have no limits, really were the darkening sky crossed with bolts of sunset through the great hanging flags and banners inscribed with the *suras* of the Prophet.

Many men were praying and Neill stood out of the way, gazing across the undulating sea of their backs to the far great wall of stone rising up into fading daylight. "Excuse me, brother," he said to a man he bumped standing by a pillar. He felt part of them, he realized, part of this. Coming into the mosque had washed away his Western way of viewing things, he could see, feel, the wondrous aspiration and failure of Islam, that what it tried most to do was what it most failed. But had at least tried.

And he, a journalist who'd done well enough to see the greater lie inherent in truth, the mockery of explanation? Or was that just another reason?

His legs were tired and he knelt, wanting to sit. A flock of pigeons crossed under the dome, wings clattering. If you're exhausted and cynical all the time, doesn't that say something about your life? That something inside you is screaming to get out? If you did what you want, would you be free? Would you still be disillusioned and sour then?

What if your nauseous opinions on the state of the world, like those of most journalists – which you always thought came with the territory, the reason why so many of us drink – what if they're just because you're not doing what you want?

What *do* you want?

What if, like the Prophet says, you *can* change your life?

ANDRÉ went down to the port and paid fifty Cyprus pounds for a single cabin to Jounié. A minibus took him and four Lebanese Christians to the *Larnaca Rose* leaning rustily against its wharf as if trying to summon strength for one more trip. Christians stood in line at the boarding ramp, waiting for the captain to check their papers. The one in front of André was unshaven and swarthy, thick black hair in a squat ponytail at the back of his neck. He carried a black bag and wore a maroon sweatsuit, and kept moving edgily from side to side on his dirty white sneakers, scanning the line.

André's cabin had two comfortable bunks and a desk with a curtained porthole looking across the companionway to the rail and the high cranes of the port. The head stank execrably; a fresh turd floated in the seatless toilet and would not go down when he yanked the chain.

People were smoking and drinking in the small café on the main deck. Down below, three men were playing roulette in the restaurant. "Join us!" one called, smiling, a tall, distinguished, silver-haired man in a gray suit whom André had noticed going on board. André shook his head and went back upstairs.

The boat rumbled and churned away from the dock and through the twin stone groins of the harbor. A gray-white Cyprus Ports Authority patrol boat came alongside and the pilot descended a ladder down the side of the *Larnaca Rose* and jumped onto the patrol boat's deck, his back turned, as if abandoning them to their fate.

They passed three ships at anchor and rumbled out across the black swelling sea, the lights of Larnaca fading to starboard, to port its oil refinery lit up like a great Christmas tree.

The ship churned peaceably through a soft swell, the Big Dipper nearly straight overhead, the North Star to the left. The orange flare of the refinery stack lingered last above the western horizon. The air was damp, the wind cold. A seaman came out and dumped a bucket of trash over the stern rail into the blue-black frothing sea.

A lopsided orange moon rose through the greasy clouds above the eastern horizon. It grew larger and larger, split by the bow mast, casting a whiter and wider swathe across the water, till it seemed they sailed right for it, would sail right off the end of the earth, as if they were already in space.

The Jericho felt tight and hard under his left arm. Richard the Lionheart had once sailed from Cyprus to attack the Holy Land, was captured, finally ransomed, and returned to Les Andelys to build his castle on the hill over the town and the church in the town square. Christians had always used Cyprus to attack the Levant. For arms, a jumping-off place. But this trip seemed not an attack but a voyage to a new life, as if to somewhere he'd never been. Silly, that; how many times already had he been to Lebanon?

After the sea wind his cabin smelled of rust and urine. He lay on the comfortable bunk, thinking how it had been made and bolted into the wall by human hands, in a ship created and run by human hands. People he'd never met carrying him across the sea, while others who had never met killed each other, as he had done also, had been taught to do.

How could it be that in Larnaca humans were friendly and cooperative, while in Beirut they tortured and executed each other? Most people did not seem to hate. It was just the few, by murdering and lies, who split the rest apart. Rooting in the cave of their own hearts.

24

"YOU'D JUST LEAVE HIM?" Rosa said. "Till somebody recognizes him, if they haven't already? You're going to carry that to Allah some day? On your life?"

"They'll take him to the camps." The mujihadeen captain with the sharp beard bent forward to tug at a loose shoelace. "It's easier to rescue him once he's there, or even maybe trade for him."

"Hah!"

"It's not your place, Rosa, to be disgusted."

"Warriors of God!"

The shoelace broke. The captain swore and took off his shoe, fished the broken lace through. "He's in the middle of the Christian sector. We can't just walk in there."

"Without him we have to start all over again! There's no *time!*"

He spliced the lace and put the shoe back on. "You're a foolish woman. Excuse me, that's redundant. It would take two hundred men to get Mohammed out of there."

"I'll show you, then. That one foolish woman is worth two hundred men."

MOHAMMED SLID his body to the side of the pallet and pushed himself up, taking deep breaths to stretch his chest muscles and ease the pain in his back. In the next bed the legless man slept; from a crack in the ceiling daylight blazed down.

The man who had whimpered "Halima!" had been carried feet first up the ladder like the bearded man's brother. On his bed a shell-shocked girl, eleven maybe, crouched face down as if praying, hands clenched to her head, but facing the wrong way, away from Mecca.

He had missed prayers. Three days and nights he'd been here, the doctor had said. But how do you pray in a Christian place? A jet went over, low. Israeli. He waited for the crump of its bombs shaking the earth, but it did not come, the jet's reactor fading through the hills like a stone skipped over water. As each prayer, each life, is skipped across the waters of death, to drown in the great sea of souls. But that was the problem: what is a soul? Even the Prophet admitted to the Jews he had no knowledge of the origin of the soul.

Mohammed thought of skipping stones as a boy on the lake at Yammouné, their ripples merging long after they sank. Like his father before him, and his father's father, stepping from the ember-warmth of the house out into the great star-spangled night, cold earth stinging his soles, his lungs afire with sharp air. Clench-toed, bare-legged, across the stony dung-littered courtyard to lift and slide back the wooden gate that was heavy and cold-slippery, making him fear it would fall on his toes as the goats came butting and shoving out of the pen into the courtyard where for a moment they'd stand wary, ears forward, tails high, defecating and calling to each other. He climbed over the next gate, brushing a hot lump of dung from between his toes, unbolted and swung it aside and the goats scampered out, bawling and mewling, their small hard hoofs thudding the ground, the smell of juniper and sage bushes as the goats snatched at them, the kids dashing nervously in circles on the trail down to the lake, he throwing stones to keep them in line, whistling the strange high birdlike whistle that had come down through the centuries like the land and the house from countless ancestors.

The goats stood drinking ankle-deep along the shore, their ripples merging toward the center of the lake and glinting like knife blades in the starlight. While the goats grazed the bare lakeside, he would skip stones one by one across the water toward the light growing in the east.

His chest was hurting too much so he lay back down. The only excuse for missing prayers was that he'd been unconscious with pain. Did Allah demand prayers then? Was he, Mohammed, taking refuge in pain?

He moved to a less difficult position. Miraculous and life-giving Lord, I am here. I thank You for this life and regret I've not loved You better.

He felt Allah's warm strong hands in his and despite the pain raised them to his forehead. Allah the all-forgiving.

MICK WAITED till the waiter placed the *rakis* and coffees on the table and left. "I recommend you don't."

"It's not that bad. I can't afford for it to be that bad."

Mick brought his chair forward, elbows on the table. Neill raised his cup to keep it from spilling. "I wouldn't chance it," Mick said. "And I'm not carrying your baggage."

"The reason you buggers don't get anything done here is you never take chances. This place is *built* on luck."

Mick pulled a Lucky from the pack in his pocket and lit it with a Zippo, puffing the smoke up. "Luck shifts, mate."

"Anyone who smokes a pack of cigarettes a day knows nothing about luck. You ever see those pictures? Turns your bloody lungs to tar."

"I'm safer smoking two packs a day than you going back to the Root."

"Two weeks. I'm in, I'm out."

Mick blew out a horizontal stream. "She won't speak to you."

Neill shrugged. His stomach was queasy and the malaria symptoms persisted. Nearly every day he'd taken his Paludrine; what the Hell more did they want? "Maybe she will. I've wondered, lately, what it would have been like ..."

"What? Her and you? Total Hell."

"I'm going to see her brother, that ugly beast Hamid. Or maybe I can get in through Amal."

"Amal? If you're talking to Hezbollah, Amal will shoot you. So will the Israelis, the Christians ... He's a popular guy."

"Like I keep saying, he's not that bad."

"Nobody could be. Anyway, he's gone missing."

"Since?"

"Few days. Done it before, apparently. Some new woman, some meeting."

"While I'm there I want you guys to know where I am, and I'm going to tell her you know."

"She couldn't give a shit." Mick slapped the table.

"Shit!" Neill raised his arm, wiped coffee off his sleeve.

"If you'd stuck with her, mate, look where you'd be now. In the thick of it."

"Maybe I still am. Maybe because we couldn't finish it, or live it, whichever, we never got unhooked. In Bratislava I was thinking," Neill brought his chair forward, "that maybe losing her, us both losing each other, broke my heart for good."

"Nah. Hearts are far too resilient."

"I've been seeing this other woman, in Amsterdam. Inneka. She's a little younger than Bev, divorced – we fit really well together."

"What are you going to say to the kids?"

"They don't care, Mick. You don't understand."

"I never lived with my kids. They're just out there, somewhere."

"That's no kind of life."

"I've got a wonderful life. I've got married women and unmarried women and girls and a forty-two-year-old cabinet minister's wife who fucks like a cat. You ever see cats fuck? They leap on each other and yowl and claw for three minutes and it's over. Then she wants to get dressed and go home. Her driver waits outside – poor guy, doesn't even have time for a smoke." Mick flicked ash. "I've got all the illicit substances I want, wine, women, song."

"So?"

Mick looked at Neill, smiled. "Remember Daisy?"

"Daisy ..."

"When you came down to Rome and threw up in the Trevi Fountain."

"Not the Trevi – the one that runs down beside the Spanish Steps. It was my twentieth birthday or something."

"Daisy was the girl we ended up with that night. In some incredibly cold little room up six floors somewhere – Jesus, it was cold!"

"Not my fault I was born in January."

Mick rubbed his crossed arms. "We got in the one bed, with her in the middle, remember? You and I both wanted to fuck her and each kept waiting for the other to go to sleep."

"This I don't remember."

"And finally I heard you snoring so I reached for her. She starts playing with my hand, starts squeezing it, hard, and I'm thinking Jesus, she is *hot*. Her fingers are playing with mine, you know, and I'm thinking this is it, I'm going to fuck this superb blonde – and then I felt up her wrist and there was all this thick hair and I realized, holy Jesus, it was *you*! And all the time we each thought the other was her, she was lying there snoring."

"You're making this up."

"You were drunk."

"When weren't you?"

"Later she told me she'd fallen asleep waiting for us to make a move. She would've screwed us both."

"The tall and slender one? Curly hair and freckles?"

"Daisy. After you went to Beirut she and I got real tight. She was doing research, Roman agricultural systems, some shit like that, pollen and seeds and old plant species. Then I get reassigned, Helsinki of all places. My last day in Rome she and I are sitting in this café with a fountain and music and the sun coming down, and I think, hey, why don't I just stay here with Daisy? Why don't I say no to this job, do something *real* – that's how I thought, then – and I looked at Daisy with the bright sun on her freckled nose and I realized I loved her. But you know what? She was too unusual, I didn't dare marry her, didn't dare ask. See how fucked up we get about women?"

"Trying to get back up where we came from. Doesn't work."

"Man I'm just *driven* by sex. It's not a choice – yes, it is. I could say, OK, no more fucking. But why? It's the best thing there is. But it's a drive, see, has nothing to do with me. Just my genes pushing, these sperm saying, hey, we need to get out, *fertilize* somebody."

"Paradise, that."

"What?"

"Our longing for paradise – I just realized it's nothing more than the cell's memory of the sperm and egg finding each other."

"The one sperm beating out all the others."

"It's a lovely place, between a woman's legs. The source of life. Her magnificent breasts that feed life. Her lovely slender body that carries life into the world ... No wonder we're entranced by it, can't get enough." Neill felt foolish, as if he'd revealed too much. "My grandmother used to toss me on her knee and sing Gaelic lullabies about all the young men the English killed. The very first thing I knew in life was to hate the English. Maybe we hate to make our women love us."

"That's crap."

"I've got over it; if anything, now, I hate the IRA, but I still like to tell that story, and someday I'll tell it to some kid whose mind is looking for something to do with his life and, *bang*, I've helped to start a war." Neill emptied dregs of spilled coffee from the saucer back into his cup.

"Without war we'd be back with the animals. Hand to mouth, jabbering at each other. War's brought us progress, scientific genius, creature comforts." Mick shrugged. "Made us what we are."

"But I'm afraid of this one."

"So don't go." Mick spat a tobacco shred. "What d'you think you've bloody got? Some invisible shield? Like the guy who thinks if he closes his eyes the bullets won't hit him?"

"We all think that." Neill reached across the table, elbow in sticky coffee, hand on Mick's hairy wrist. Absurdly it reminded him of Mick's story how they'd held hands that night, each thinking the other was Daisy. "We're getting old, Mick. Fearing what we never used to fear."

"Then *don't* go!"

"I want to interview Mohammed. Something, a sixth sense – he's got something to say."

"Ask him about those bloody hash shipments out of the Bekaa."

"Everybody's running drugs in this war, not just Hezbollah."

"You've gone soft on the sodding ragheads."

"I'm not soft on anybody, Mick. That's my problem."

"*And I say to you, true believers, take not the Jews or Christians for your friends ...*"

"Doesn't apply to me. Anyway, that *sura* is contested."

Elbows on the table, raised hands clasped in a double fist, Mick leaned toward him. "These ragheads," he glanced round the café at the men in keffiyahs talking at other tables, "it's against their sodding religion *not* to kill you."

"To reach God you've got to step on lots of people."

"You know why? Because God's a killer, that's why. And He loves His own kind."

"He just called Allah a murderer," a voice said behind Neill, in Arabic.

"You've misunderstood," said another. "Listen more carefully."

"He *did!*" The first rapped knuckles on the table. "That's what he said!"

You've done it again, Neill thought. Kneeling before the Lada's moth-spattered headlight, the girl's gun at the back of your skull. Expecting the awful *wham*. "You've bloody well blown your cover!"

"Cover? What the Hell's that? I've been who I am since the day I came. The British sodding Military Attaché and I don't give a sodding damn *what* these ragheads think."

Neill tossed three hundred piastres on the table and stepped into the street. Mick stood on the pavement, craning to look over people's heads. "Down there's Bab el Faraj."

"The Gate of Deliverance."

Mick went down the steps ahead of Neill. "Let's try this little place I know, fabulous food. And down behind the Umayyad Mosque, in al-Qaimarriyeh, a great whorehouse."

Here you are boozing in Damascus, Neill thought. Like the girl from Hell said. Doing every little thing wrong. Imagining English is some kind of shield when it's really a target.

"AND THERE FELL DOWN many slain, because the war was of God. That's how your book says it."

"*True believers fight for the religion of God,*" the doctor answered. "That's how *your* book puts it."

"Do you remember," Mohammed turned on his elbow, head propped on his hand, "your Saint Bernard? The one you've named a dog for, because he gets people drunk in the snow."

"It's not like that. But you can't be expected –"

"*Woe to any man whose sword tastes no blood* – that's what he said. And you made him a saint."

"*I* didn't. And we have to stop using God as a reason."

"You don't *have* a God."

"I don't, no. Not personally."

"So why fight for them?"

"I'm a Christian, it's my heritage. But I've seen how the Maronite bishops thirsted for this war. How they do still, while the hills of bodies rise around them ..." The doctor drew his packing crate closer to Mohammed's bed, sat again. "On your side they're just as bad. These crazy imams and mullahs ranting for blood."

"Plenty to go around."

"That's what I've sometimes thought – war is caused by too many people, we're all crushed together, fighting for space. A detail is soon an obsession, like the disagreement between Mohammed's heirs fourteen hundred years ago that's led, now, to how many million deaths?"

"If one religion is true, then only it can be true."

"If one religion's false, they're all false."

"That doesn't follow."

"We're all the same and all different, we have to follow our own paths. The Koran gives you a reason and a law for everything, so *you* don't matter at all."

"It's not *we* who matter. It's God. Jihad is the sacred war between God and the Devil."

"All wars are holy, because they're damned. All wars are between Heaven and Hell. And Hell always wins."

25

ABOVE THE DISTANT WAVES a darker crest rose for an instant and was gone. Then it was back, taller, across the frothy horizon. Slowly Mount Lebanon rose from the wind-raked waves, its plunging ridges and peaks of snow and ice, then the dark rocky shoulders far below, the steep pine slopes dropping to the first high stony farms, then the white buildings, the first roads, the towns, down to the cities and ragged gray coast.

Jounié Bay was an oily flotsam of green and blue detergent containers and ketchup bottles and beer bottles and chunks of styrofoam, torn nets, vegetable crates, dead sardines and groupers, blue and transparent plastic bags, a woman's black high-heeled shoe in creamy sewage scum.

Behind the port the town rose in a horseshoe of French colonial mansions in affluent gardens and tall nondescript apartment towers jammed among the ancient terraced fields and haphazard palms, linked by inarticulate writhing streets and drooping telephone lines. There was no shell damage. But there wouldn't be here, he realized. Among the wealthy and blessed merchants of the Levant.

The Christian guards in the Customs shed rooted through his rucksack and nodded him through. The rucksack over one shoulder, the Jericho in its holster under the same arm, he trudged uphill past lounging militiamen and whores, and the feel of the crushed rock under his feet was as if part of him had always been here, that he was whole again.

Outside the port's cyclone fence taxis waited in the bright sun. It was ten dollars to the Christian suburbs, fifteen to East Beirut. "No going near the Line," the driver said.

"Anywhere's fine. The Jesuit school ..."

The dirty concrete of bare buildings everywhere. Patches of shore grass between gas stations, garages, junkyards, scraps of orchard. Tanks in a line, guns down, looking sleepy and bored. Graffiti over a tunnel, *Fuck War*, overloaded trucks grinding and belching up the hills, the racket of horns and bad mufflers, sometimes the hiss of the wind, the sea.

There was a burning rubber smell, smoke, a barricade of tanks at Dora, another at the river. The taxi stopped at the first steep streets of East Beirut. "Can't go up there."

André eyed the street of gray tall buildings climbing and curving toward upper Beirut. "Nobody's shelling."

"It's not that. The engine overheats."

There was little damage all the way up Rue Cheikh Ghabi till it turned to Independence, but few cars in the streets and fewer people on the pavements. Many of the shops were shuttered and many windows broken. As he got closer to the Green Line, there were holes in apartment buildings and whole houses rubbled down on their foundations.

A young woman came out of the Emergency entrance of the Hospital Rizk, slender and fast-moving, lovely raven hair, a tan raincoat over a nurse's uniform and white sneakers. God if they're all like you, he thought. She ran to a white Land Rover marked *Croix Rouge du Liban*, yanked keys from her pocket and tried them but none seemed to fit. She took out more keys but they didn't work either. She was lithe and lovely as she bent with each key to the lock. Her black hair was nearly red in the early sun.

"Let me try," he said, slipping the rucksack off his shoulder.

"It's nothing." She backed into the street, glanced up and down, watching him.

"Here." He reached for the keys and after a moment she gave them. She moved to the far side of the Land Rover as he tried the keys. One said Leyland but did not work. He showed it to her. "You've got another like this?"

"It isn't my car. They didn't tell me which key. There's been a car bomb in Ashrafiyeh, I have to get there ..."

He slid his knife up the rubber edge of the passenger window and popped the button, slid into the driver's seat and tried the Leyland key but it still didn't work.

She was in the passenger seat now, her scent of orange blossoms and roses dizzying. "Thank you, please hurry," she blurted. "I've got to get there."

"These aren't the right keys."

"Oh dear."

He wanted to drown in her brown eyes. "Go and get them."

"Somebody's taken them, by mistake." She glanced down the street, biting her lips, fighting back tears. "This war ... Nothing ever works ... Now these people will die ..."

He fished his knife under the steering wheel and cut the wires. "Just separate these two when you want to turn it off," he told her, "touch this third one to them to start it." The motor caught at once, black smoke flaring out of the back. He cut it and started it again to show her. She was ready to slide over, looking up and down the street, up at the hospital. She smiled and he felt his whole face light up, warmed. He hopped out and she reached up and pulled him down by the collar and kissed him, let him drink in her eyes for just a moment before she shoved the Land Rover into gear and drove away.

GOD, YOU ARE *BEAU*, Rosa thought, watching the Frenchman in the mirror as she accelerated toward Independence. She leaned down and pulled the seat one notch forward and unbelted her raincoat as she drove east down Independence past the Lazarist Mission toward the Christian suburbs.

Was she doomed forever to crave this terrified elation of being hunted? This hunger to run?

Through the Land Rover's windows she watched the street jolt past, the shell-caved walls, charred woodwork, shattered shutters listless on bullet-chewed walls, the collapsed balconies making her think of Romeo and Juliet, the faded splintered shop signs like confessions of defeat – *El Ibrahim – Your Best Tailor, Vision Camera, Parfumerie de Paris*. Everywhere graffiti and the xeroxed photographs of missing young men glued to pockmarked walls and twisted lampposts, a pavement sprayed with paint dark as old blood – or is that really blood, she wondered, a tag of music, *"Your love's the hangman of my heart'*, from an open store. What, early in life, had made her so hungry to run?

She'd told Mohammed the truth. Always, when you can, tell the truth. Her father and brothers had been killed. Her mother and sisters too. On that account we're all sisters. But lots of people lost their families and didn't end up like this.

The virtue of war is that there's no time for anyone to have a past. You are for the moment only what you seem. Even brave, if need be.

God he was *beau*, the Frenchman who hot-wired the Land Rover. She realized she was thinking in his language. Some day I'd love to have *him*.

"THERE'S NO BATHROOM," warned the woman at the Hotel des Cèdres. "You have to use the hole in the garden like everybody else. And usually there's no lights or water. But it's a nice room. I keep my rooms clean." She squinted up at him. "You a journalist, somebody like that?" She folded his two fifties into an empty purse and buttoned it in her pocket. "You're too late. Lebanon's gone. Back when you could have said something, you never did."

"I'm no journalist."

"Nobody comes to Beirut now but journalists and gun runners. And since Tripoli refinery isn't working, sometimes traders come, selling gasoline. Have you ever been to Lebanon?"

"Not before now."

"Now? Lebanon's gone, I told you. If you'd ever known Lebanon, how it would make you weep, this!" She glared at him, her mouth pinched, as if he too had had a hand in the death of Lebanon. Which we all have, he thought, taking the key from her outstretched finger and locking the door she slammed behind her.

A pernicious little room stinking of dried sewers and mould. Skinny bed cringing against one wall, crippled table under the window half-shuttered on a sloping rocky garden of three junipers. A curtain in the corner round the toilet that was stuffed with newspapers in a failed attempt to block the sewer smell.

As a base camp it couldn't be better. Situated in the Christian stronghold of steep streets between the Convent of Our Lady of Nazareth and the Franco-Arab High School. And only three blocks from the Green Line. It had taken no shell damage – nobody's target. It might even be safe.

He opened the cracked, taped window, spiders racing for the corners. There were two bullet holes in the aluminum frame. The garden was surrounded by a stone wall; against its far side was a rubbish heap smelling of cinders, wet cardboard, rotten chrysanthemums, and jasmine, over which flies slowly circled.

IT SOUNDED like a Land Rover, crunching and grinding closer uphill, its engine rattle loudening through cracks in the ceiling. Mohammed climbed the ladder but couldn't push the hatch open to see. There was the hard uneven idle of the engine, the crunch of feet on gravel, a woman's trenchant voice, the doctor answering.

There was no way out and nowhere to hide. Breath sharp with pain, he suddenly saw himself clearly, as if from above, the

Warrior of God with his silly half-bald pate, downsloping shoulders and pointed toes, scurrying like a rat in a trap, a fool in a farce. To die is *nothing*; why be afraid?

He sat on the bed. The legless man watched him, chewing his lip. The girl was praying, still facing away from Mecca. Even though she was a Christian and was simply hunched up in agony, Mohammed felt furious with her, her crinkled red-splotched soles and writhing toes.

The trap door squealed open and a woman in a white gown came backwards down the ladder, then the doctor. They went to the girl and the woman tried to speak to her.

The woman's haughty East Beirut accent made him hate her, before she turned to face the legless man and Mohammed saw it was Rosa.

"This is our mujihadeen," the doctor said. "The one they mentioned in Faraiya. Tomorrow he goes down to the camp."

She put a cool hand to his forehead. She wore a Lebanese Red Cross uniform and smelled of soap. She folded down his blanket and checked his bandages. "Can you turn over?" she said, and Mohammed did, her fingertips flitting like spiders over his back. She bent closer, whispered, "Tonight." She turned to the doctor: "It's very good, what you did, bringing him in. I'll note it in my report."

"Please don't. People misunderstand."

"How so?"

He shrugged. "Saving Muslims, all that."

She shook her head. "This war."

"How bad is it hitting you?" he said in French.

"I'm OK, most of the time. You?"

"Going a little crazy. I can see it but can't seem to stop."

"Like the Jews say, if it didn't make us crazy we would be."

"Be what?"

"Crazy."

"Right." He smiled at the wall of dirt, the Christ. "That is a consolation."

26

THE DOG backed away from the garbage pile, licking its chops, half hopeful, half afraid, watching for a gun. A skinny dark male, Belgian shepherd maybe. When it decided André had no gun, it stood waiting for him to pass. He whistled softly, patted his thigh; it wagged its tail low but wouldn't approach. He moved closer and it backed up and knocked over a rubbish bin and ran toward the Green Line.

At the foot of the hill a little restaurant was open, and empty. He asked for wine.

"Ah," the man said. "Before the troubles I had a good cellar, monsieur. Good Bordeaux and a few fine Burgundies – that's not easy, getting a good Burgundy to survive all the way down here. There was Beaujolais, good rosés – do you know the *rosé des sables?*"

"I like it best. That and the *pinot noir.*"

"That's not truly a rosé. Not like the rosés of Provence. The *rosé des sables*, I served it chilled with fresh *crevettes* from the Bay of Saint Georges, in a bed of lettuce from my gardens, new olives ..." The sound of jets was getting louder and he waited for them to pass; the earth shook and the roar of bombs quivered the windows. "Just Israelis," he said, "hitting the port."

André went outside but the Mirages were gone, their thunder streaking southward over the sea. A cloud of dust and smoke was twisting and rolling up from the port.

"You want it bloody, your meat?"

"Bloody." On the wallpaper a shepherdess was leading her flock uphill toward a grove of olive trees. In their shade a man sat playing a flute. All along the wall the same girl kept climbing the same hill toward the same man, frame after frame, the paper darkening with grease as it neared the kitchen. Never did she reach him, never did he stop playing his flute, never did the obedient sheep cease their patient upward plodding.

"Last year's." The man uncorked a bottle of Lebanese Burgundy and poured a glass. His wrist, André noticed, was trembling. But he spilt none on the cloth.

The wine was rough and strong. From the year the yellow Hezbollah truck drove into the French compound and blew it into great pieces that came down on Yves and the others. And yet if he avenged their deaths he'd be an outlaw in their country and in his.

Not a bad wine. It had the taste of the sun-stroked crumbly slopes of Mount Lebanon, a sense of *place*. Like Burgundy – just say the word and you see vineyards and forests and wheat fields and castles and stone walls and slate roofs, the taste rooted in the soil.

Through the open door came early darkness and a guitar's plaint and the tang of lemons and spiced meat – the distant lap of sea on pilings and sand, a woman's voice, a man's answering. The ancient duality, he thought; why revere the inevitable?

He paid the sad quiet man and walked uphill toward the Hotel des Cèdres and there was the dog again, raffling in the rubbish bins. He turned and went back to the restaurant. "You don't have any bones, stuff you're throwing away?"

"Throwing away?"

He reached into his pocket. "I'll pay you."

He went up the hill and put the newspaper of bones and meat scraps and vegetable skins on the pavement. Again the dog backed away, cocked its head. "C'mon, you big-eared thing," he said. It edged nearer, stood by the paper, quivering as it ate. André moved closer and it moved away. He held out a scrap of fat and finally it ate from his hand, then with his hand on its shoulders, then patting the coarse fur down its back. "You're just a pup," he whispered. "What happened to your masters?"

The dog stayed a few feet behind him along the darkened streets lit by candles through curtained windows. At a grocer's he found Israeli powdered milk, a can of ravioli, and some bread. He knelt and let the dog sniff them. "You take care of me, I'll take care of you."

The dog licked his cheek and he wiped it off with the back of his hand. It followed him to the Hotel des Cèdres, hesitated at the door, then came up the stairs to the room. André mixed some milk, ravioli, and chunks of bread and the dog ate it all. He opened the window and the dog stood for a while with paws on the sill watching the garden. Then it turned round and curled up on the carpet under the window and went to sleep.

"I'VE TALKED MY WAY through three roadblocks to here, but there's no chance I'll get you back through them. Instead we have to cross the mountain. *Hurry!*" Rosa jammed the coat over him, glanced at the legless man who watched with a mute, fatalistic inquiry. "*Hurry!*"

"Where's the doctor?"

"Hurry!"

Mohammed shook her. "Where *is* he?"

She pulled a gun from under her Red Cross uniform and gave it to Mohammed. "I have more clips." She swung her pistol on the legless man.

"No!" Mohammed yelled, grabbed her arm and shoved her ahead of him up the ladder into the cold starry night.

"Now they'll have a witness." She bent and locked the hatch. "The girl too."

He realized it wasn't a bunker but a bombed-in cellar. Downhill were the outlines of a few buildings with dim lights, men's voices, a white Land Rover parked at the end of the road. "Where's this?"

"Lasa. We have to climb the Jabal el Mnaitra and go down to the Bekaa."

"What if it snows?"

"It won't. Go!"

Beyond them the dark hills dropped through steep canyons to the black sea. The sea swung round and became the dark hills that came round to the mountain and then the sea again, spinning faster; he stumbled a few feet and threw up. "Hurry!" she hissed.

He felt even dizzier. "What did you do to the doctor?"

"He's fine! *Go!*"

He jabbed the gun against her jaw. "Where?"

She slapped it away. "You can *rot* here!" She turned uphill, walking fast across the open ground past the bombed-in cellar. He stared at the gun in his hand, didn't recognize it, glanced downhill at the quiet dark shapes of houses where people huddled, waiting for bombs and bullets, pain and sorrow. He couldn't see the doctor anywhere. He turned and followed Rosa up the mountain, her shape flitting before him like a faraway white dove.

IN THE HOT SUMMER NIGHTS in the souk Layla would open the damasked curtains to catch the cool breath of the sea, turn toward him unbuttoning her blouse and slipping it backwards off her shoulders, unhook her bra and slide down her long-legged jeans and the white underpants, and loosen her hair, letting it tumble down over her breasts. She'd sit cross-legged before him on the thin mattress on the floor, her body lean and coffee-golden in the candle glow as she crushed hashish into the pipe.

There'd be distant voices from Martyres and the rattle maybe of a Peugeot 403 working its way up Patriarch Way, the chatter of passing sailors and whores, the hushed breath of the sea. There was the smell of orange and lemon trees in the garden, the late wisteria, honeysuckle and oleander, the rosewater on her skin, in her hair, the sweet resiny hash.

How sacred to lie side by side, touching, to love anyone this much. Sacred and unforgettable, her lips tasting like avocado, her tongue sucking him in, sweeter than honey, her breasts soft yet full against his chest, all sacred, the soft hair of her cunt that he licked aside, silky strand at a time, with the tip and side of his tongue for the side was softer, smoother, even more slippery, licking down, licking her wide open, open inside and feeling every shiver inside her, kissing up one side to the smooth inside of a thigh, up to her belly, down the other side, circling closer down into her, her shivers and sweet cries driving him wild.

She came and came again, and again, rocking her cunt against his lips, taking him deeper into her own mouth, her own throat, and each time she came he tasted her anew, fluid and hot against his lips, her lips down over him, softly her teeth, till she could take no more and turned round to slide her body down along him till he was deep inside her, her hair a dark Bedouin tent atop them, her voice rough with hash and love as her pelvis rose and fell, rocking on top of him, and it seemed far too lovely to ever end.

To lie like this for hours, side by side. Again she'd light the hash and they would take turns, hearing and feeling the night and each other and the worn silk bedspread and beyond the mattress the cool pine floor and walls of old stone, her lips down over him like the softest night breeze, like a warm sea, sliding and slipping her tongue round him and biting with her lips down the side, the tip, and above them both the old cracked ceiling was a holy writ in which their fates might be divined, they could see themselves as Heaven saw them, love and bones destined to be dust, drowners drowning in each other's arms, mortal flesh aching for mortal flesh.

"Tomorrow night I can't," she whispered, dressing before dawn, her body dark against first light. "I have to see my brother."

"Come afterwards."

"It's too late. He may make me stay."

"I'll wait anyway. Come if you can."

She squeezed him. "You fool, I love you so."

Come pillow your long soft hair against me, Layla. I've missed you so, all these twenty years. Let me taste the wonder of your lips and the sleekness of your skin. We were both fools, we did what others wanted, not ourselves, too young to know you never get a second chance.

Tomorrow she never came, instead her brother Hamid pounding the door and shaking his fist in Neill's face and putting out his cigarette on the silk bedspread where the night before she'd lain.

"But I intend to marry her. I'll call the British Consul, the Embassy, do everything I can. You can't keep her."

Hamid laughed, a snarling peasant from Saida despite his Mercedes and his trips to Gstaad and a family progressive enough to send his sister to the American University. "You'll never see her again. She's left the university and she's left Beirut. If you ever even try to find her, you fucker," he took a little silver pistol from his pocket, "you're dead meat."

The horror of those nights, Hamid, those days. To live without her was impossible. Going to her parents' farm on the hills south of Saida, the rows of old orange trees going down to the cliffs and sea, and each time at gunpoint to be turned away, feeling her eyes behind the curtained windows. Waiting for days beyond the walls but she never came; weeks waiting in Beirut, but she never came.

Easy to see now what he should have done – quit Beirut as if he were going home, then moved quietly down to Saida, paid informers, learned where she was, freed her. Quickly over the mountains into Syria, buy her a passport in Damascus, two tickets home, and they would have had the rest of their lives together.

But when you're young you're easily fooled; her family's rejection becomes hers, on both sides. They'd been right: twenty years later he was a drunk American journalist from London and she the Mother of the Revolution, wife to the Lion of God.

27

KILLED HIM, didn't you?" Mohammed gasped, trying to keep up.

"For the Lion of God you're pretty weak!"

"I've been shot," he called, realized it was weak to say it, as if needing excuses. How did this woman keep making him appear a fool? "You'd never make a man's wife, the way you act."

She stopped on the trail above him. "I could be yours if I wanted."

He stumbled on a root. "I owe you my life. But not that."

"I said if I *wanted*. And your life hasn't been saved yet."

The path crossed an open starry ridge. There were no trees, no grass, just the wind wailing down the wide bare shoulder of the mountain. He tried to envision his body shut in a box in the earth.

They passed a low stone hut, used in the old days to store snow that turned to ice and could be sold in the valley in summer, bringing it down bundled with straw in the donkey cart, leaving a trickle of darkness behind you on the dusty road, and from the cart's bench seat you see between the donkey's ears bobbing right and left, or down at her back hooves coming back, rising up and going forward, coming back, rising up and going forward, her clickety hooves on the sandy gravel, bits of bitter scrub poking up, the summer air of cicadas, lavender and sage.

The path switched up a steep slippery gully wreathed in mist and he could hear a river's rumble on the far side but they never seemed to cross it. They climbed higher, colder, he took shallow breaths, trying not to stretch his wound, wanting to lean on her, but she was ahead, always moving ahead, accepting no frailty from him, as if he'd fail if he realized how difficult it was.

The river grew louder, crashing down on the rocks above and to the right, wind buffeting them. They crested to a saddle that the wind roared through, and he saw there was no river, had never been, only the wind howling and gnashing at the peaks, roaring through the pass like the million riders whose souls had made the wind, their armor jingling, arrows rattling in their quivers. For an instant he understood war but could not turn it into words, this ancient milling progress toward death and sorrow. We're just not happy if we're happy, he decided. Why?

IN AN HOUR the first muezzin of the day would call and still Neill couldn't sleep. Gone only a week but already home seemed an illusion, as if he drifted aimlessly through sheaves of time.

Yet he missed them. Had to say it. And had to remind himself that life with Beverly would be Hell again three days after he got back. When every word, every kindness, leads to a fight, and each word to make it better only makes it worse.

They had the kids. And some day the tradition of these years together would be something to look back on. To not grow old alone. But would he be like Uncle Vincent, in his eighties, still snarling at his wife?

He'd had no need of sexual binges and thoughtless adulteries to betray Bev, he'd betrayed her enough just in the horrors of daily life. Each little dependency and ignorance and slight, each tiny knife into the pleasures of the other's soul. And there was no point thinking that this time when he came back they could begin again, bridge the last nineteen years. The people they had been were dead, and the new ones didn't love each other. Whom did Beverly love? The occasional lawyer or concert violinist or computer jockey who took the time to spend with her and appear sensitive? The world's most disgusting word: sensitive. Reminds you of a slug or a febrile insect or some little skinny-armed downcast kid, beaten and ashamed.

Why hate him so much, that downcast kid? Because he was you? He's dead, just like the one who married Beverly.

The first bus of the day rumbled and coughed down Bab Sharqi Street toward the gate, its diesel belch rising to his window. If he was going to change his life he would have to sit down with that skinny little kid. Shy little tyke with the endearing smile, the one Beverly had said she'd loved inside him, who had been him, whom he abused.

Feet over the side of the bed, soles on the cold floor, he brushed at something with his toes. Goddamn bugs. Ankles aching, he limped to the bathroom. Forgot your goddamn medication. Some day, the doctors said, a blood vessel's going to blow in your brain and you're dead. Hand grenade inside your head. High blood pressure is *essential*, the doctors said. Meaning they couldn't find a cause. But the cause was obvious: tension, sorrow, frustration, exhaustion, the joys of city life. Not being who you are.

In the bathroom the light flickered, caught, went out, flicked on. In his toilet kit he found his Innovace and popped one, then the two Paludrine, then two more Klaricid for the soreness under his arm that wouldn't go away. Pretty soon you're all drugs, he said into the mirror, there's nothing left of *you*.

No point in starting a new life then dying. No water came out of the shower. Hugging his bare chest he went into the bedroom and dressed. Strange, he'd dreamt all night of Layla and awoken thinking of Beverly.

FIRST LIGHT stenciled the bare trees atop the ridge. Yew trees, Mohammed saw. That once made the strongest bows. Some day this whole earth would no longer be useful. Like the yew trees, intended for a weapon outgrown.

He fell on the trail. No further. She can leave me.

Rosa yanked his ear. *"Up!"*

He took a breath. *"... have you shot ..."*

"That's how you help those who help you?" She was hardly panting, despite the altitude, the climb. "That's Allah's teaching, is it?" She snapped her head back and he thought it was an imperative thrown at him: *Get up.* But it was just her way of swinging back her hair, mocking her own shamelessness, mocking him. Dizzy with height, he felt split between two worlds, a different one in each eye, one that he'd known and accepted and been happy in, another totally wild and different, which invalidated the first, but which he couldn't deny. One was the way he'd learned to see. And the other he saw was true.

"Like you did?" he said. "With the doctor?"

"He didn't *help* me. I had to."

"If you'd told me that, back at the clinic, I'd have shot you."

"We should have been an hour beyond here by sunrise. We're going to get caught in the open by some Israeli jet."

"We hide when we hear them coming."

"Why did I risk my life for you? I had a great dream of you, that's why. But you're not it."

THE SHELLS came pirouetting down in yellow, green and white starbursts with trailing flares blooming over the city, spreading down like boughs of a weeping willow, a jasmine's twisting petals of red, silver, gold, the soft rain of anti-personnel bombs that exploded in random bright daisies in the dawn streets. From the Shouf hills came a drumbeat of artillery and rockets under the bursting shells, and for André it was suddenly just music and brightness, nothing more, just the human accomplishment of making death beautiful, evil beautiful. That's why we love it, he realized, because of its beauty, too evil to be tarnished, its sexual incandescences, its seeds spurting into the raped and battered city.

The Phalange lieutenant shook his arm. "Seen enough?"

"You go back. If you see that dog that was with me, get him to wait."

A 155 came down in the street below, an earthshaking blast then the rumble and crash of buildings. There was silence, then a scream rose up, ancestral, the agony of all the lives lost over many thousand generations, for every burst of pain, animal or man. Over the new falling shells and ragged crump of explosives, over the clatter in the street of the cluster bombs and the rushing hustle of shrapnel overhead, its ping and rattle off the walls, its birdlike cries through the smoky dawn air, the scream grew higher, as though slowly more and more voices had joined in, the voices of all humans of all times, of all the beasts, and he wanted to scream also, add his meager timbre to the wail of time. A rocket came down, spinning and hissing into the building below, its façade surprised and irresolute in sudden phosphorescence. Then it slid like a mask into the street with a great rumble of stone and plaster, baring the soul within, the astonished chairs toppling off the edge, the rooms like a doll's house where you can open the side, burrows. Unreal to think of lives lived there and the great mystery of creation performed in the blue bedroom with the tilting, tumbling bed. Why build them up, he wondered, if you're only going to tear them down?

28

FROM THE SINGLE WINDOW of the goat shed Mohammed watched the road below. Many trucks of men went up and down it but none stopped. A wedge of small spindly cypress climbed halfway up the far slope. The road glistened with rain, the hiss of truck tires and the rumble of their engines echoed up the canyon.

"It's just games between us," the doctor had said. "These wars. If we were all identical we'd find a freckle on someone's neck and that would set him apart. He'd be the *other*. So we'd kill him."

The doctor had saved Mohammed from the angry Christian but Mohammed had not saved the doctor from Rosa.

When ye encounter the unbelievers, strike off their heads.

God commandeth you to fight his battles, that he may prove the one of you by the other.

But what if, as the Hanefi say, this commandment was meant only for the Bedr war, at the beginning of our faith, and not for all time? Now that the doctor's dead, have I like the apostate Walid Ebn al Mogheira hired another to bear my guilt? Who when caught by an arrow refused out of pride to dislodge it from his cloak till it cut the artery of his heel and he died?

"They don't bother you?" he snapped at Rosa, "those Syrian and Christian trucks together down there? Six months ago Hezbollah fighters were dying to protect their Syrian brothers from the Christians, the same Syrians who now unite the Christians and Israelis against us. Six months ago they were all torturing and castrating each other."

"You'd say that Allah does what Allah wills." She pulled her coat tighter about her, shivering. "And what Allah wills is right."

"Why mock me so?" He turned away from the window. "Don't you worry, the way you act, that no man will marry you?"

"You are backward and ignorant, from the Bekaa, where nothing has happened for two thousand years, ten thousand years."

"And you are a wise young woman of the new Palestine, more modern than Beirut and even more corrupt."

"You Persian in Arab clothes, you goat farmer, don't you see?" Her teeth flashed at him out of the gloom. "If we don't change, we turn into Nigerians or something, always going backward!"

He wanted to reach out, strike her. "So you go to bed with Western ways? That's better?"

"Is Islam only the province of fanatics, or can reason enter also? Why let folly divide us? Who is the Prophet's successor? Who *cares*? The Prophet was here and his word is quite explicit."

He felt weak, looked for a place to sit. "I agree."

"Then why don't you live it?"

"If everything is Islam, then Islam is nothing ..." There was just a rock bench, rough, beside the cold fireplace.

"If everything is Islam then Islam's everything." She knelt before him, took his hands. "Bend a little, and you have it all. Don't let Israel divide us, as it always does. Please, Lord?"

His feelings rushed right out of him, wildly, down over her. He touched her shoulder; the act seemed inevitable and wrong, one he'd do no matter what. "What if we made peace?"

She looked up into his eyes. "If we make peace with Druze and Amal and Syria, we can drive the Israelis out of Lebanon."

"I mean peace between *us* ..."

"We're not at war, Lord. But the Israelis."

He pulled back his hand. "You, the Palestinians, *you* brought the Israelis in."

"We were running from them!"

"What if we made peace with them all? Israelis, Christians, all?"

"Not without Palestine!"

"If we got more Palestine with peace?" He felt winded, dizzy; the mountain air was too thin. "As I've said, I'm willing to wait a hundred years, even a thousand."

"I don't have a hundred years to live, Lord."

"But with luck you might have thirty, fifty more. Don't condemn others to die at eighteen, at twenty-one! At three or four."

"We'd rather die than lose Palestine. That's what we've decided. I thought you agreed."

His wound was hurting, wearing him down. "If you could go back to '75, before Bloody Sunday, the first bad times, wouldn't you want to?"

"Not without Palestine!"

"We're all so tired of your goddamned Palestine!" he yelled, hurting his chest. "I don't know a single Lebanese, Shia or Druze, Sunni or Christian who wouldn't prefer things the way they were back then! Before *you* came to Lebanon! No one will win this war now. No one but the Devil."

"We can't stop now."

"You're twenty-two, a Palestinian all your life, and you don't yet see how Israel relishes this strife?"

She stepped round him, glanced out of the window. "In two hours we can go."

"If you didn't hate men so much your life would be easier."

She turned sneering at him and once more he was shocked by her sudden ferocity, terrified for her, what would happen to her.

"Why don't you tell me about your brothers," he said. "While we have time."

Her face was shattered for a second then re-formed with no cracks showing. Once again he expected her fierceness, but her voice was soft, out of focus. "I'm tired, I want to rest."

He felt tenderness again for her, then pain again for the doctor, anger that she'd killed him. Her skin was pale as an ostrich egg – what would she be like to possess? What might it bring him, and what could he lose?

THE RAIN CEASED and low sunlight came under the clouds and fell over the slope as they drove up through gleaming groves of olive and cypress, dates, oranges, and almonds, André in the back beside one bodyguard, another beside the driver in front. The one beside him had a brown suit and a skinny moustache and smelt of nervous garlic and kept glancing back at the cover car. The Mercedes was heavy with armor and wallowed in the curves, its engine gasping to keep up with the lead car on the upgrades.

Rows of grapes loped northward over the coastal hills, the sea beyond them making him think of Phoenicia, of what had been lost, millennia going hungry for a truth, any truth, and never finding one. He imagined Yves driving north here with some Lebanese girl, doing it with her in the bushes, on the beach, in a quick hotel downtown on the Christian side.

The house sat back against the hill, a single-story white villa with a tile roof. They went through the metal detector into the house and General Haroun came out of a side room. His camo shirt was dirty and wrinkled and he was unshaven. He kissed André on both cheeks and led him into a low room of bookcases. "How's your dad?"

"Complaining there's too many Arabs in France."

"I could have told him, ten years ago. Anyway, give him my love."

"He sends his, and Mother too. To Francine also."

"Where you staying?"

"In the city."

"You could be here. What, you're afraid I have too many enemies?"

André laughed. "Fuck your enemies."

"Some of them, probably. You want some coffee, a drink? You staying for dinner?"

"Some of them what?"

"Must be fine young things, worth fucking. Hundreds of them."

"Of course I'm staying for dinner."

Haroun sat back, a cowboy boot propped up on a low table. He had, André realized, a certain heartiness that comes from frequent killing.

An Arab girl came in with two cups of Turkish coffee on a brass tray. "You're wasting your time, *mon cher*," Haroun said when she'd left.

"What's *she* doing here?"

"Nadja? We've known her family for years."

"When you get it, that's how it's going to be – some stupid mistake, like her."

Haroun nodded his chin at André: *be quiet.*

"She's your *enemy!*"

"No one's anybody's enemy. We're all friends who kill each other." Haroun nodded his chin again: *pay attention.* "You're wasting your time with this Mohammed."

"What if he died?"

"You're thinking then we could split the Druze and Amal and Hezbollah and keep the Syrians at bay? But it won't happen. If I've learned anything from this war it's have no expectations. You shouldn't either."

"I'm checking terrain, options. Nothing's decided."

"Nothing's even *possible.*"

"Wait and let's see."

Haroun dipped a sugar cube into his cup, watching the coffee rise up it. "If he could be reached, don't you think we wouldn't have done it by now? You think we're that *maladroit?*"

"Your mistake was thinking Arabs would fight for you."

"That's water under the bridge. We're clean now, tough. With nowhere else to go."

"And fooling yourself if you think you can win. You had all Lebanon and now you've just got half of Beirut and a piece of coast and hills. And they can shove you off that."

"That's just talk."

"France won't come in, Emil. All the bright boys at Matignon are sucking up to Khomeini these days. He's got more natural gas, apparently, than you."

"He's a flaming asshole. I can hardly compete."

"That's how it's going to be decided."

"Then he'll pull his pecker out from under their noses and they're going to be grabbing at nothing."

"History hasn't taught them that yet."

Haroun laughed raspily. "History doesn't teach a goddamn thing."

29

FOR TWO HUNDRED DOLLARS the Syrian would drive
Neill from Damascus at least across the border to Masnaa.
Perhaps even to Sofar, only thirty kilometers from Beirut.
Depending on the Syrians and Israelis, maybe all the way to
Hazmiye – "only an hour's walk from the Green Line".

The road climbed from Damascus through the barren brown
ramparts of the anti-Lebanon past rows of dusty mud and concrete villages with plastic bags stuck everywhere on brush and
fences, dead dogs and rusty cars on both sides of the road. There
were only Syrian soldiers at the border and for fifty dollars they
let him pass.

Down into the Bekaa's broad incandescent green the road
slunk like a tan snake. There were Syrian tanks in the wheat
fields, artillery dug into the orchards, the smell of death, a burnt
armored personnel carrier on its side in a ditch. Up from the
Bekaa into the foothills of Mount Lebanon whole villages lay in
ruins, shell-blasted, uprooted orchards, toppled trees and pylons,
ramshackle shattered houses with gaping roofs and shocked
black-eyed windows.

Like heroin or sex, did violence intensify with social contact?
Is it a disease, he wondered, whose carriers increase faster than

they die till finally, like all plagues it flowers and fades, slowly gathering its forces to rise again?

The road swung round a curve and dipped to the right past a smashed villa in a grove of burnt cypresses by a bullet-stitched wall. Flames soared black and orange from a bus lying on its side, bodies spread like petals round it, a woman running toward him, her head on fire.

The taxi driver braked hard. "Far as I go."

Neill leaped out of the taxi tearing off his jacket and threw it over the woman's head but she fought it, punching him, screaming. He yelled with pain and yanked back his hand where something had melted and burned on it and would not go out when he held it against himself. He fell to the ground trying to smother it and the woman, screaming, fell over him and more of her fire got on him. It's gasoline, he thought, and ran for the taxi. He pulled a blanket off the back seat and threw it over her but she kept burning, smoke and flames shooting up through the blanket.

"No!" the driver screamed. "My blanket!"

The fire on Neill's hand had gone out but the pain was impossible. The woman was trying to crawl, wailing. "They're not all dead," someone yelled, running by.

"Look out, mines!" another called.

"Help!" Neill pleaded. "Help me with this woman!" A great slam of thunder knocked him down. He lay holding his head then slowly stood, before him the skeleton of the bus writhed in red heat. Something else had blown, a bomb maybe, a gas tank. He couldn't find the woman and stumbled from the heat.

Someone was shaking him. "Two hundred dollars!" It was the taxi driver. "Two hundred dollars!"

Neill sat on the ground and tried to find his wallet. It was in the pocket of the jacket he'd put on the woman. He stood but couldn't see her. The driver threw his suitcase at him. "I told you no good!" he screamed in English. "Too far!"

Here was his jacket. Charred down the back and collar. He found the wallet and gave the driver four fifties. More fifties fell out but he stuffed them back. "No extra?" the man shrilled. "For this danger?"

Underbrush was on fire, crackling, thick white smoke contorting in the still air with the black-orange clouds from the bus's burning tires and diesel. People were dragging bodies along the ground and laying them side by side. If that bus hadn't gone through, Neill thought, it would have been us hit that mine. He felt off balance and realized he was carrying the suitcase, put it down, remembered it was his, and picked it up again. "Don't know where ..." he said to a man running by who kept going, didn't even look at him.

A fire truck came screaming and winking its red light. Men ran with a hose but nothing came out. People were gathering round others sitting on the ground. A woman passed Neill, her hands upraised.

"We were just going to Aley, my wife and me," a man was weeping.

Neill walked through the bullet-splintered cypresses and climbed the bullet-spattered wall and over the shoulder of the hill. Beirut spread out below in a jumble of filth and smoke, a vast human excretion aside a crystalline sea. There were brass cartridge casings in the tall grass. You'll step on a mine, he thought, watching the ground.

"I'LL DO IT his way," André said. "I'll blow *him* up."

"You'd die for it?" Haroun popped an olive in his mouth. "Like that kid who blew up your brother?"

"It was Mohammed who blew up my brother."

"Ever wonder what happens to the ones who drive those trucks?" Haroun spat the olive pit into his hand and put it on the table. "Atoms. That's the trouble being Christians: we love life too much to be martyrs." A Phalange lieutenant came in and Haroun left with him for a minute. The Arab girl came and lit candles at two ends of the plank table.

"Too bad there's no electricity," Haroun said, coming back. "I'd play you the new Pavarotti, *Lucia di Lammermoor*. Only heard it twice since Francine got it for me." He spat another pit, drained his Suze and set his black holster belt into his hips. "Anyway, you jokers hear that kind of shit all the time, up in Paris."

"I never go to the opera."

"Story of a girl in love with this guy, but her parents make her marry another one, some lord. So on their wedding night she kills him, goes mad."

"That's why I never go to the opera."

"Speaking of opera, Paris is pissed."

"What did they say?"

"They want you out. Head or feet first. Just thought I'd tell you."

"Did you tell them I was here?"

"You crazy? But somebody will."

André got up. Out of the corner of his eye he caught the girl moving in the kitchen, flash of chestnut hair, the aura of lamb and spices. "I never should have told them I was coming. See what I get for being straight?"

"You should get out of it, *mon brave*. Like Paris wants."

"That's what they told me. Can't you see? They're just establishing distance?"

"Ex-commando runs amok – is that the message?"

"I have a line to these scramblers Mohammed could use."

"He's got no money. Anyway, he's lying low for some reason. Hasn't been seen for a week."

"I'll find a way to reach him. But then I'll need *matériel*. I can't just walk in on him with a little Jericho from Larnaca."

"Nice gun, that. But you won't need *matériel*. Because you're never going to reach him."

"I'm losing faith, Emil, in your desire to kill Mohammed."

Haroun glanced up at him and André had a sense of being caught in mirrors, through a swing door. "I'm beginning to think you need Mohammed alive," André added. "As if he's the only guy dirty enough to make you look good."

"We're the *brains* of this country. All that keeps it from being just another filthy overpopulated dysfunctional Muslim nation."

"All that hash you're selling in France – are you getting it through him? Out of the Bekaa?"

"How would *you* have us pay for weapons?" One foot over a knee, Haroun ran a fingertip down a stitch in his boot. "Of course Mohammed's good to have. But he draws too many people. When we don't squeeze him it makes us look weak and ineffective."

"You've been trying to look like that ever since Sabra and Shatila. That's where you lost this war."

"We did that as a favor."

'Kill two thousand old people, women and children? It lost you the war."

"It'll never end, this war. No one ever wins or loses, everybody's getting too much out of it."

"Except the ones who die."

"So far, they haven't counted." Haroun tucked his stomach tighter into his Wyoming belt. "We Christians," he leaned forward, "we have two, maybe three kids, care for them. Send them to the best schools, all that. Muslims, they have ten, twenty kids, throw them out on the streets to sell Chiclets, then say it's not fair, you Christians have all the advantages."

The girl passed in the background, from the kitchen down a hall, tall and willowy, and André wondered if Haroun was screwing her, his big hairy pungent chest in her face. Would he be sweet, affectionate? Not like when he killed the four teenagers caught with Uzis, shooting three in the face, stopping to ask the last, "Why aren't you afraid?"

"Because I have no need of substance," the boy had said.

But the boy's corpse had been hard to kill, kept jerking up its knees. And André had gone with Haroun and the Phalange back into the fight for the Shouf hills, crossing the Nahr Barouk in darkness, its chill rattling over the stones and sparkling with stars, the smell of high explosives and burnt earth, and André had knelt to drink from the river, wondering what the boy had meant, to have no need to *be*.

"You'll never get Mohammed," André said, "unless you let me do it."

Haroun swung down his foot, leaned forward, a man getting down to business. "*Let* you?"

"The only way is a vehicle. To take out his building. At least a thousand pounds."

"We don't have a Tehran connection."

"You can find *plastique* anywhere. I could buy C-4 in Paris but I couldn't get it down here."

Haroun spat another pit. "*He's* the one with all the high explosives. Buy it from him."

30

MOHAMMED stood in the door, blocking the night. "Snow's coming."

"It's better," she said. "They can't see us."

"We can walk right into them. Or they can follow our tracks."

"The snow will hide our tracks."

"Until it stops. Then we've got an arrow pointing at us."

"Next thing you're going to tell me," she snapped, "is *Mektoub*: it is written!"

"I didn't say that."

"But you *think* it! You say I have no faith but see how you waste yours. The Koran was never so precise. Those are *your* fears, *your* strictures."

Outside there were no stars, just the cold blanket of clouds hugging the earth. She closed the door behind them: *I'll be who I will.*

Another truck came grinding up the road, gearing down nastily, spitting noise and fire. How easy, Mohammed thought, to throw a grenade down on those forms huddled in the back. War's not hard at all; killing's easy, it's getting along that's hard. Rosa brushed past him down the hill and he sensed her litheness beneath the coat and nurse's uniform, her smooth, scented body. We're out here in the dark, he thought, with no path.

Each time he slipped and fell going down the gravelly damp slope it drove wild pain through his chest. She floated below, never slipping, never looking back. His hands were gloved in rime. Up the canyon the wind came full of ice.

The road was slick with freezing mist. If trucks came up now, he thought, it would be so easy to hit them. She went down the far side of the road into a ditch of broken rock and then up through the sparse cypress and already he was panting and his chest felt as if someone was twisting an arrow in it. The land was so steep he had to grab roots and outcrops to pull himself up. How she hates me, he thought, hating her.

The snow came down in soft fat flakes that made her scarf glisten, got in his mouth and eyes, slicked the lichened rocks. He followed her up out of the cypress, where the slope eased to a flat high ridge and the snow thickened. His arms and head were light and his legs felt disconnected.

The slope flattened to the broad belly of a ridge of chipped stone and boulders that vanished and reappeared in the driving snow. Her shape flitted before him like an angel's – the Arabs had thought angels were daughters of God, till the Prophet called them *infidel*.

Face down, he bumped into her. "From here on," she said, "stay in my path. My line of travel exactly."

The stones were like broken walls of a bombed-out city; once a night bird flew squawking away, rocks and pebbles clattered in the wind that ate through his gown and bandages and into the hole the bullet had made in his side, deep into him, cold against his heart.

She turned back, facing him, gun at her waist as if she would shoot him, and he had an instant of fear, only half seeing her through the blowing snow. I don't know you, he thought. But you saved me. Why is that?

"Wrong way," she said. "I'm getting lost in this snow."

He was shivering, terribly cold. "Got to go down."

"It's all mined. Both sides. Damn this snow. I never thought ..."

He felt fury, wanted to shoot her. "What did you think coming up here would bring you?"

"I do what I do for Palestine. Not for you!" She shook snow from her shoulders. "Wait." She slipped into the snowstorm, and he called but she didn't answer. Snow scurried round his ankles, wind carved his shins.

She came out of the blizzard. "Follow ten steps after me." She moved to one side among the rocks, holding her hand above her as a signal, but he couldn't see it, got lost, and she came back for him. "Can't you do better?"

"Shut up and leave me."

"These rocks are full of caves."

He followed her tracks; crumbling and snatched by the wind, the fleeting white filled and erased them. "Where are you!" he yelled, glancing round, wind and snow in his face, at his back, knocking him down, coating his face, like death, he thought, like death.

"Found one!" She grabbed his arm.

It was body length deep, the front open to the wind, snow building against one side. "Go in first!" she yelled.

He squirmed in till his feet bumped the end. The ground seemed like ice but was only frozen earth. She squeezed in beside him. "We must wrap up together in both coats."

The wind rose, grinding rock on rock, sucking the snow from the earth, fleeting veils across the night, raging white banners with cold razor edges. The whole world will be like this someday, he thought. He imagined his dust blown by the blizzard across the naked, frozen earth.

The snow built up against the far side of their hole, blocking the wind. The cold earth warmed to their bodies; inside the coat his hands were warm, touched hers. "Tomorrow, in the snow," she said, "it'll be hard to know the way. To not step on mines."

Something sharp bit into his back – a rock. Her breath was warm against his neck. He thought of the Christian doctor, his tired gentle hands, his kind and hopeless eyes. She moved her feet and he felt how cold they were, held them between his ankles. What if everything I've believed is false? he wondered. And only this is true?

THE ARMORED MERCEDES took André back down the mountain, now only one guard car ahead and none behind. A squall had come off the sea, wetting the windows, the headlights sparkling on the white-painted stones alongside the road. Rain here meant snow up in the mountains – good skiing, in the old days.

He wondered if the dog would be waiting when he got back. It hung around all the time now, tail between its legs at every sound of guns but getting fatter, some good food easing its worried mind. Leaping on the bed in the mornings to lick him awake – got him mad at first but then he realized it was good to be getting up so early.

The Arab girl kept flitting before his eyes. She moved on bare feet as if out of the past somehow, something he remembered. And Haroun screwing her only made it worse – like one small part of her was saved for Haroun and the rest was bared and hungry.

No, she'd have a guy somewhere, some skinny Arab with wild eyes, in a keffiyeh, all muscle and hate, a worn-out Kalashnikov and a dirty little knife. Fun to fuck her though. No one since Larnaca, the night he'd found the Jericho. A bad idea having the Jericho up front with the guard, but that was the drill. They'd give it back when they dropped him off. Naked without it. If Haroun wanted to deliver him to the French now would be the time. Then he'd never get to screw that girl. Not that he would anyway, she was Haroun's. What a name, Nadja. Makes you want to screw her just thinking of it. Just saying it.

I'm fearing the French, he realized, my own country. As if they're enemies when they're *la France*, for whom you've sworn to fight and die. But *la France* is all of us, Yves and all those other guys in the Beirut barracks who gave their lives for perfectly nothing. Every man who has died for France would agree: pay Mohammed back.

France is what *we* do. *We* are *la France*.

The rain had stiffened, pummeling the road and bouncing up wildly in the headlights. Going to be a nasty storm in the hills. He remembered Haroun and the others in the fight for Jabal Sannine, the great flank of Mount Lebanon in swirling drifts, fear and bullets, bright blood on the new snow.

31

FIRES GLOWERED in Shatila where Christian and Israeli shells were landing. Bright low comets of jet afterburners crossed from south to north, their thunder racing behind them.

"They're not shelling Ras Beirut," Saddam said. "We can go all the way."

Neill leaned out of the VW's window. "Where are they hitting?"

"Can't see over the hill. Down by Martyres maybe. Along the Line."

The back seat full of oranges rumbled and rattled as Saddam swung right into El Rachidine toward Rue de Rome. "Which side of the gardens are you on?"

"Drop me anywhere. I'll walk it."

"I'll take you. Which side?"

"Arts et Metiers."

A building had fallen, blocking the street, the red lights of fire trucks sliding through the rain and the steam and smoke and skidding off the buildings on both sides, people gathering and *fedayeen* holding them back, a bulldozer and more *fedayeen* burrowing at the ruins. "They don't care who they hit," Saddam said, backing up. He braked, oranges rumbling backward. "Hey!" he called to a boy on the pavement. "Whose was it?"

The boy shrugged, looked up. "It just came down."

"Where are you going?"

"Saroulla."

'Get in. I'll drop you at Hamra."

Neill put his suitcase up on his knees and squeezed against Saddam as the boy wedged in beside him, twisting sideways to shut the door. Neill had to bend his leg aside so Saddam could shift into second. "Let me out in a couple of blocks," he said.

"You're brave enough to come here, try to tell the world what's happening, to help us, speak our language like you do – I take you anywhere you wanna go."

"It won't help," the boy said. "You just make it worse."

"Probably I do," Neill said.

"No!" Saddam shook his fists. "What we need is people knowing about this. What if the whole world," he threw up his hands, making Neill want to grab the wheel, "worked together? And any time war started we stamp it out, like fire in the forest?"

"In my country," the boy said, "for a century we had no forest fires because we put them out, but then when a big one came it was so hot it even burned away the soil."

"See?" Neill said. "Now you'll have no more fires."

Saddam stopped in the middle of Arts et Metiers, the garden on the right. The boy got out and then Neill; the boy got back in. Neill took four fifties from his wallet. "No, no!" Saddam waved them away.

A rocket sizzled over and Neill dropped to the street. It hit with an awful clatter to the east, by the Museum. Neill stood and handed the four fifties into the car, hunching his shoulders as the next rocket started in.

"No, I really don't want to," Saddam insisted, shoving into first gear.

"You deserve it. Anyway, I get it back." Neill dropped the

notes on the dashboard and dived to the ground as the rocket seared over but hit further down. The VW's one tail light blinked and wobbled down Arts et Metiers and turned left into Emile Eddé, the brake light glinting as Saddam halted at the barricade.

Neill settled his suitcase on the pavement and put away his wallet, thinking that he shouldn't have forced the money on Saddam. He'd refused the gift of love and given the poison of money. Reimbursed money. In his own little way he'd contributed to war.

There were nicks in the wrought-iron fencing of the Jardin Public and pieces torn out of the palm trees by bullets. The façades along Arts et Metiers looked beaten up, black eyes and scarred stucco, shutters hanging disconsolately, the smoky night bright through splintered eaves.

But the Harad house was still standing; through the leaded diagonal holes of the living room windows there was candlelight down the edges of the curtains. The black wrought-iron gate was gone but the fence stood, bent in places by machine-gun bullets. Bullet scars marred the front; one corner of the second floor was gone and the lovely French colonial balcony over the front door had collapsed into the patio. The front door was gone and boards were nailed across the hole. "Nicolas!" Neill called. "Samantha!"

The candle went out. "Nicolas!" he called. "It's Neill. Neill Dickson."

There was no answer and he felt frightened and backed across the pavement. There were no lights on the street. How could you run, he wondered, with all these burnt cars to bump into that you can't even see? It's like Hell, he thought, just like Hell.

"Neill!" Nicolas called. His voice came from the side of the building, the garden. "Quick! Over here!"

Neill went through the empty front gate and cut across the

garden, the soft soil making him nervous for mines. "What the Hell are you doing here?" Nicolas whispered, reaching out.

Neill broke away. "Christ, I've missed you. How's everybody?"

"OK. Just fine." Nicolas squeezed his arm. "Sammy will be ecstatic."

"How's her folks?"

"They're fine too. Went to Kuwait. Hurry, let's get inside. The front door's nailed up – we go round here."

Neill followed him into the greater darkness between the buildings. "Can I stay with you tonight, till I sort things out?"

"Tonight? You can just *stay*. Nothing would make us happier." Nicolas guided him down the back stairs. "You have to excuse us, no water or gas or electricity and most of the time we stay in the basement."

"Nice guy," Neill laughed. "Telling me to come back down and then I do and you shut off the fucking lights and water. Nice guy."

They went into a black passage that Neill remembered had once been the back stairway up to the maids' rooms. There was a door into the kitchen and then another corridor smelling of wax leading into the wide dining room with the long table and a candle and two plates at one end. Sammy stood with one hand on her chair, as if not sure whether to run or hide, till she saw it was Neill. She put the revolver on the table and ran forward to hug him. "How are you, dear?" he laughed, swinging her around.

"Oh Neill, Neill, how lovely to see you!" She leaned back to see him clearer. "What? Why?"

"Doing a piece on the war. I'll explain later. Thank God you're fine."

"Blessed be Allah we are fine. Blessed be Allah you are here. For us, but not for you."

———

"GOD TELLS SOME PEOPLE to do wrong, then sends them to Hell?"

Mohammed folded back their coats and crawled forward to check the snow falling faster and faster beyond the cave. "You know the answer to that."

"To punish them for doing what He says? Like me. You think I'm going to Hell for the way I act, don't you?"

"I'm not always right."

She rolled to her knees. "When are you wrong, then?"

"God's the one who does no wrong."

"How comforting to those in Israeli jails. And everywhere else."

"Most of them understand."

She crawled forward, beside him. "What if they *don't*? What if they're tired of *understanding*? What if they're tired of God and just want Palestine?"

"That's why they don't have it. God's the one who's tired of human lies. That's who God is." Mohammed squirmed backwards into the cave, shivering. "I've never known it so cold."

"Get used to it. You're going to be dead an awfully long time."

"You don't believe that."

"Do you actually believe in some kind of paradise?"

He watched the snow coming down, each flake alighting like a bird. "Always. In every way." He felt a pain in his guts, shifted his hips.

"That's a shame. You need to see through men's illusions to lead them."

"I never asked for war!"

"You just wanted it more than other things, that's all."

He shivered. Easy to die out here tonight. Why let her get under his skin? Why let her turn things upside down with her questions? Didn't she know that questions are just for those who have no answers?

If the snow stopped now they couldn't move for fear of

tracks. He'd be stuck with her. He was a fool to be so open, suggestible. She just took advantage, lost respect. He stared again out of the cave, hands trembling. How could she make him so angry?

The snow had risen halfway up the cave mouth. Soon their breath would make a hole – a hole someone could see. He checked his watch, 11:12, promised himself he wouldn't look at it again for half an hour, at least till after 11:30.

After 6:30 there'd be light to see, they could travel in the snowstorm, and maybe nobody would see them. If it didn't wane.

She'd got him this far when nobody else would. Of course they would. It was easier for her, as a woman, that was all. "That doctor you killed –"

"It was him or you. Take your choice."

"I take him. That I should die."

"No wonder Palestine's enslaved, with people like you to defend it."

"That doctor, knowing I was Shiite, saved me from another Christian who was choking me."

"Why?"

"Because we'd shot his brother."

"War's like syphilis. It just goes round and round."

"You're truly shameful."

She eased up next to him, shoulder to shoulder. "The question is, what made the doctor save you?"

"That's what I'm trying to understand."

"See?" She nudged him. "You're softer than me."

He was lost in her change of mood. "How did they die, your brothers?"

"That's another story." Out of the darkness she took his hand. "For another night."

32

NEILL KEPT HIS HAND in a pan of water but the pain didn't
ease. Samantha coated it with fat and wrapped it in an undershirt but that only made it worse. The pain was alive, throbbing
and burning and stinging and shooting up his arm like electricity
with every pulse. "Can you imagine," he kept saying, "what *she*
felt?"

The shelling stopped and by flashlight Nicolas led him
through dark streets and up stairs, knocking at each door till
someone opened and sent them to the third floor right.

The doctor was a small woman with gold-framed glasses and
silver hair, in a pink puffy bathrobe. "Come into the light," she
said.

There was a lantern on a mantel and a fire of rubbish and
brush in the fireplace. "Yes," she said, holding his hand to the
lantern, "you've really burned it."

"What could have been on her face, the poor woman, to have
burned like that?"

"Skin. It was her face melting, and it fell on you."

As they went home shells started drifting down from the
Shouf, cracking randomly in the streets. They ran, Nicolas
leading and shining the light behind. Once inside, Neill had to

hold the wall, dizzy and afraid. The malaria, that was it. He *had* to take his goddamn Paludrine.

A shell came in short and hammered the next street. "Mother*fuckers!*" Nicolas screamed. Neill ran after him into the cellar, skidding feet first down the steep stone stairs, wrenching his ankle. He hobbled toward a twitching candle where Samantha sat knitting and a man and woman crouched on the floor over a little boy, more people behind them.

"They're from next door," Samantha told Neill. "This cellar's deeper." Another shell was coming in louder and louder and louder, right down on top of their heads. This is *it*, Neill thought, diving. How crazy to come all this way just for this.

There was perfect silence.

WHAM.

Roar and crash, thundering walls, clattering stones, wailing glass inside his brain and blowing out to the end of the universe. I've been killed, he thought, astonished. The heat shook and slammed him down, a wall of shelves toppling on him, cans of food. The dirt floor stopped shaking. With a wrenching groan of iron beams bending, holding, then easing, the concrete floors of a building in the next block cascaded one by one into the street.

Then another *crunch*, not so near, new dust tumbling before the candle, the little boy's eyes upraised in frozen terror to the ceiling.

"Who *is* this?" Neill yelled. "Why the Hell are they shelling *us?*"

"Anybody." It was a man with a Turkish moustache, a fat wife and two children behind, then an old lady in a black shawl, her arm round a boy in a baseball cap. "It could be anybody. Who'd stop them?"

ANDRÉ WOKE from a dream that had made him warm and happy. The dog was growling softly in its throat, its nose at the window. What had he been dreaming? Why the dog growling? He slid the Jericho from its holster, ducked to the window, reached up one-handed and popped it open. The dog leaned out, paws on the sill, the fur on its neck raised, teeth bared, a snarl in its throat.

He crouched far back into the dark room and stood carefully, looked down in the street and saw dogs trotting away, their pelts glistening in the rain.

He sat back down, cradling the Jericho in his lap. Get an idea stuck in your mind and straightaway it poisons you. The idea *la France* is hunting you. Because Haroun said. Haroun with his little Arab pussy, warning you.

If they're after you it's just to show some distance. Or do they really *want* you? For planning to kill Mohammed? For breaking the ultimate rule: always do what *they* say.

He sat cross-legged, hearing the pulse in his temples, the steady shelling, now in West Beirut. What if the purpose of life is for God to test your virtues: how good are you?

How *badly* could they want you?

THE SNOW STOPPED before dawn. Under the last stars Mohammed could see a bleak snow-clad hill and the rough flank of a higher ridge to the right, straight ahead a sharp sky and the far pale crests of Mount Lebanon. "We'll never get back," he said.

"Not if we leave now," she said. "We must wait till tonight. Unless it snows again."

"I have to go outside."

"We can't. Any low-flying plane will see the tracks."

"Just round the corner of this –"

"No. Do it at the back of the cave. We have to. Cover it and wait till tonight. I'll go first if you're shy. Face out the front and cover your ears."

He did as she said, uncovering his ears to hear her urinate at the back of the cave. She came back, laid down beside him. "That's better."

It had always horrified him, the idea of women excreting. Why did God put it *there*, her paradise place, between two places for excreting? It was truly unholy to touch a woman. Yet the Prophet said respect women, who have borne you, for Allah watches over you. It made no sense.

You're not supposed to question, he reminded himself. Was he some infidel, running always to questions like a kid to its mother's teats? Man had pre-eminence because of the advantages God gave him over women. Man the seed of life, woman the dirt it is planted in. She is unclean but must be taken as such.

With a handful of snow he performed his ablutions, knelt toward the rising sun. Muslim means *he who submits*, he repeated to himself. Muslim is *he who submits*.

NEILL SAT ON THE BED in his room, banging his ears to clear them, could barely hear.

"I'm sorry," Samantha said, sweeping the floor. "To get shelled your first night. It's not like this every night."

"I'd like to kill them," he said, cocking his head against the roar in his ears, his words seeming to rise from the bottom of the sea.

"They did us no harm, thank the Lord. Just this glass."

In the cracked mirror he saw he had a sharp cut across one cheek, like an African initiation scar, from a piece of flying window. He'd got it in the street, coming back with Nicolas, hadn't even known it. More than twenty years a journalist and never been hurt. Now twice in one day. Here in Beirut when everybody said stay out. Except Freeman with his little transmitter under your arm.

Where were they now, these invisible beings who watched over his transmitter? A chip in a satellite, two ragged Arabs on some hill with a little radio, who? Now, in all this danger, why? What use to them? When London didn't give a damn what happened to him.

"Nobody's shelling now." Samantha swept the shattered glass into a dustpan and tossed it out the gaping window. "Nicolas has gone to the office. There's talk of a new ceasefire and if they get together he'll try to film them for the news. Let's go out and try to find some food. Maybe there'll be carrots – or some salve for your hand."

In the next street a building had fallen, crushing three cars. A fat man was digging in the ruins, glancing up at the loose concrete. A child's broken plastic gun lay in a smashed doorway. At the corner they went into a shop where the man with the Turkish moustache stood behind the counter, stacking packets of Marlboros.

"That's all anybody does here," Neill said. "Smoke."

"It calms the nerves," the man said, a pen clenched in his teeth. He took the pen out and put it behind an ear, glanced at Samantha. "How's your place?"

"New broken windows. How's yours?"

"The windows were already gone." He came round the counter and set a table and three chairs out on the pavement and brought out pitchers of thick strong coffee and hot condensed milk. "Just like the Sixteenth," he smiled. "A café on the Bois."

"The Bois are full of junkie hookers now."

The man shrugged. "See, I was right to come back. If we make it, we can look back, say we were here."

"If it ever ends," Samantha said.

"Look at it this way: we're investing in peace. If we can fight long enough, kill off everybody who wants to fight, maybe we can have peace for a while, build back up."

"To tear it down again."

"Every fifty years a war. For five thousand years. Ten thousand, maybe. Since there was man. What are you going to change? You just get in the rhythm. Ten years of war, fifty of peace."

————

IT WAS A BLUE 1957 FORD with high tail fins, a fat American car. The paint faded but clean, a few nicks, one long dent down the right side. The trunk was big, with more space if he needed it under the back seat and in the doors. The oil in the crankcase wasn't too dirty and the engine didn't run too rough and there was hardly any smoke out the exhaust. The tires were bare but not too uneven. A sun-faded green cardboard cedar of Lebanon hung from the mirror.

"It's a nice car," André said. "Why you selling it?"

"Why do you think?"

"Where you going?"

"Perhaps France. Or London. I'm a jeweler. If I can get a job –"

"Just you?"

"My wife and four kids and then my mother-in-law and father-in-law and maybe others."

"You'll have to sell a lot of cars."

"Everyone says the best way is Larnaca to Athens which will let us in on a tourist visa, then from Yugoslavia to Trieste. Do you think so? Those hills between Yugoslavia and Italy, do you know them?"

"Mountains. In the north, near Austria."

"Excuse me for asking, but do you know anyone who'd write us a letter?"

"Letter?"

"Explaining we have nowhere and are good workers and will pay as much as we can, if we can stay."

"No one would read it. It'd make no difference."

"I'll give you a hundred dollars off the car if you can write such a letter."

"I don't write letters."

The man shrugged. "You're crazy coming here."

"I'm betting the war's nearly over. Now might be the time to come in, get ready to invest."

"Invest? This war's just beginning. They're going to tear down every brick. The only ones who come out ahead are the ones like you, selling arms."

"I'm not selling arms."

"You can do what you want. I wouldn't tell."

"You don't need to give me a hundred. I'll write your letter. For someone in France. If you get there."

He parked the Ford in front of the Hotel des Cèdres. The car had 391-67 on its plates; both sets of digits added up to thirteen. His lucky number. He'd have bought the car for that alone.

33

SUN WARMED THE SNOW and water dripped off the rocks; they had to dig a trench in the mud to keep it out of the cave. Then the wind turned cold, the snow crust froze and the water hardened into icicles. Snow began to fall.

The ground was frigid through their doubled coats. Her hands would not warm even when he held them. "Shivering's good," she said. "It warms the body."

With a crunch of steps a man moved past, his head visible through a notch between two rocks, then his legs through another, his rifle over his far shoulder, his boots wrapped in rags, snow like a cloak down his back. Then came another, bent over under his weapons, the wind snatching chunks of broken snow crust from his shoes and scattering it through alleys of stone. Christians, nine in all, filing past like ghosts.

"They've saved us," Rosa said, "we can go back in their tracks."

"Tonight. If we don't freeze first."

She fought her shivering. "How you talk like a Muslim!"

"How's that?"

"A mother's boy, needing reassurance!"

He opened his shirt and cupped her hands against his chest, her fingers like frozen sticks. "Don't be so harsh. *I* didn't kill them."

She bit her lip to stop shivering. "Who?"

"Your brothers. They were killed by someone, so you hate everyone."

"If there's any God other than a completely impotent one, then it's God who killed them."

"Trying to make you understand just makes you wilder."

"The only one who can understand for me is me." She huddled closer, shivering, her breasts and thighs cold against him. He tried to hold her up on him off the frozen ground but the bullet hole began tearing and he rolled back on his side.

"We could truly freeze up here," he said.

"Like sleep."

To get close is to stay warm, stay alive, and if God didn't want us to, He wouldn't make us want it so much. Or is it just to torture us, test us? Her body so little, after all, so slim, such young breasts and such a shame to die.

"When I was a kid I had a puppy," she whispered. "He used to climb into bed with me. All night so warm beside me."

It shocked him to think of her as a girl, long innocent black hair down her slender back. "How old were you?"

"I must have been nine. We'd just moved to Mount Hermon. My father got him to help me forget my friends in Nazareth."

"You had no new friends on the Mountain?"

She shook her head as if brushing aside a hair or his query or the thought of having friends. "In the village there were only boys. Like I told you, they threw stones and called me names."

He tried to see her hiding in her house, fearing the stones. "What did you do?"

"Helped my mother. Did what girls do."

He had no idea, he realized, what girls do. "What's that?"

'Keep the race going. While you men tear it apart."

"But you're here too. At war."

She burrowed tighter. "I'm cold."

He was sliding into a delicious peace, couldn't stop. He slipped his hands down her hips and up inside her gown, thinking this is just, this is fair. The backs of her thighs so chilled and thin in his hands, slipping down her brief clothes while she, silent, raised up a knee so he could pull them free.

Even her core was cold, her smell. "What are you thinking?" he said. "You're so silent."

"This isn't how I wanted it."

"What did you want?"

"I was going to be distant, showing by my silence that I didn't approve of you."

"You still don't approve?"

She waited for a moment. "Scarcely."

He swallowed the slight. "You've made me less approve of me."

She drew to him like a puppy. "I can like you although I don't approve of what you do."

"Whatever happened to your little dog?"

"The boys who threw stones killed him. They put his head on a stick."

Tears stung his eyes. I haven't cried for years, he thought. I haven't *ever* cried. "Christians?"

"Druze and Christian and Shiite. It was a mixed village – this was Lebanon, remember. The place where we all lived together."

"You hate them still."

"Why should I? They've killed each other off."

"So what's this mourning for Palestine?"

"Palestine is where the Israelis chased us out and we had to go to the Mountain. Where everything would have been different."

The sting behind his eyes was gone. She was as close as his

clothes, touching his skin, her skin warming from him, and this is how we keep alive, he thought, this sinister touch, this skin.

But no matter how deep you are inside a woman, what do you touch? What is sin?

Sin is what it means to be free.

A CAR CAME SPLASHING the gutter and they ducked into a stairwell. "And tell her for me," Neill said, "that my talking with her husband is one way to show he still matters."

Hamid shrugged rain off his coat. "I don't do this sort of thing."

"You need the money. I need the story. We're the ultimate couple."

"You're so coarse." Hamid's bushy eyebrows made him seem to be looking from under two dark storm clouds. "I've always hated that about you."

"People hate everything about me. "Specially those who know me well. That doesn't change a thing."

"You think you're tough, saying that?"

"I'm as scared and dumb as everybody."

"Mohammed's not scared. And he's not dumb."

"All the more reason for me to meet him."

"Wait till you have hot metal going through you, see how you boast."

"You had your chance years ago to be a human being and you blew it. Now you've got another chance."

"She didn't belong with you. That's what caused this war, *all* the wars – Christians like you."

"I'm scarcely a Christian."

"The Crusade's not over, is it? You people are still coming over here to win back your fucking Holy Land. It's *our* Holy Land, you fucker, not yours. We *live* here. Not you."

"You can have your goddamn Holy Land. Just get me to her."

"He'd be crazy to talk with someone like you. I'll tell her that."

"I can do him more good than you ever could. Tell her that, too."

With a snort Hamid turned away. Neill watched him diminish down the pavement into the rain. Painted on the wall was an American flag with Jewish stars and a huge fist through the middle, with the golden city of Mecca atop the fist. I'm becoming, Neill realized, a person I don't like.

34

WITH ROSA'S NAKED belly and thighs against him how warm she was! Warm and soft and holding tight as a magnet, her sex hair sticky with sweat and sperm, her skin slippery like olive oil and sweeter than honey. Old men are right, he realized, to love young women, they are the gift of God. Her body so lean and long and never-ending because his hands could not leave it, where there was only one place and that was inside her, only one feeling and that was she. Long after he could come no more he was still locked hard inside her, trying to slide deeper, her teeth in his shoulder, her claws up his back.

It's not this that's evil, he realized, but its absence. If you submit, it must be also to what you feel, that too is God's will.

When he woke the new snowfall had broken the cold and she slept warmly against him. Nearly five. In an hour he'd have to wake her. The Makarov she'd given him on one side, she on the other, he lay with neither cold nor pain, watching the snow drift down among the darkening rocks.

Crazy, what she and he had done. Forgetting the danger, everything. Wild as two newlyweds. Wilder.

Never had he been to this place of total forgetfulness before. This place of total concentration. Not even in prayer. He took a deep breath, realized he was still winded. Exhausted yet strangely rested. Could watch all night if need be, over her. This strange hateful child for whom so suddenly he was responsible. For whom he wanted no more pain.

Telling himself not to fall asleep lest he endanger her, he lay watching from the cave while the solitary snow sifted steadily down into the ghostly dusk. Although no men passed he kept seeing them, an endless line, snow caping their heads and shoulders, their backs bent under guns and swords, cloth-wrapped feet trudging the cold slippery snow. *In'salah*, the will of God. Back to the start of time. *In'salah*.

A shadow came up behind but vanished as he turned. Each way he looked, it hid behind him. Its blade drove into his spine and he shook himself awake.

Near night's faint glow on the snow. She moved, still naked against him, and he wanted her, in terror. The snow was still sifting down. What was that? A footstep? Just wind scurrying among the rocks. The line of her hair black as a veil above the pale brow. Oh God, he thought, how beautiful.

The shadow rose up behind him. *"Nothing,"* it spat, "is deadlier than love."

IMAGINE finding Black Label here in Lebanon. But that's the thing about war, Neill decided. Either there's everything, supermarkets as full as Saigon's in '65. Or there's nothing at all, Hanoi in '69.

He'd been going to stay off liquor but that was the kind of intellectual decision he was always making to screw himself up. Nearly everybody drank, he just had to watch it. He'd have no trouble watching it here, at fifty bucks a bottle.

It poured cool and golden into the cracked white cup, swirling fine shadow, smelling like oak root, turf, musk, all together. His sinuses cracked as they opened, sucking it in. Nothing this good could be bad for you. Warms your tongue, slides cool fire down your throat, you can taste a thousand places ...

The first Katyusha came over whistling like a dove. He snatched the Black Label but the rocket kept going, far away now, a monotonous thud, the air and scraps of window shaking. Out there maybe someone dying, their spirits floating up into the air.

How strange to sit at this desk in Nicolas and Samantha's guestroom with its empty windows, in the candle's wavering light, like a supplicant, a mendicant, a hermit, this cup of transitory gold in his hands, while out there others died. And when he died they'd be going about their business, unable to help him any more than he could them.

What if when he died there'd be time to look back? If he saw that he hadn't lived his life well? Hadn't done what he could? Instead of being a nobody reporter at the seamy ends of the earth, what if he'd *done* something?

In the mosque in Damascus he'd promised to change his life, improve his character in some way every day; had that too been illusion, both the reason and result?

This was the way to lose it. Sanity's just a convention: once you start asking questions like this there's no end to where you can fall. And what does it bring you, getting to the bottom of things?

He'd stop at three glasses. God, it tasted good. All those shutdown lines in your brain coming back to life. The signals going through again. What if he could make enough on this trip to take time off? Working for Freeman could net him twenty thousand a year, maybe thirty. Say thirty. Could live on that, up in the Lake District, a slate-roofed little place with an uneven rock-and-briar wall, looking out over sheepcotes and green valleys.

His underarm stung as he reached forward for the cup. Leave me alone. Shut down the thinking machine. Just for a while.

His watch said 4:56. In four minutes he'd promised himself

he'd leave. Hamid wouldn't stick around. He wouldn't himself, Neill realized, if he were that scared. He needed an extra little hit, really, to face Hamid. Hamid a true turd on the face of God. Neill tossed back the fifth whisky and gave it a chaser, slammed the cup down cleanly on the table. Hamid source of all my sorrows. Nearly all anyway. He put the bottle under the pillow and went downstairs but Nicolas and Samantha weren't there. They were somewhere going through the foolishness of filming another peace talk for the television station that could not show it because the electricity was dead. He went outside into darkness. Another rocket came over softly hissing, drawing near but kept going, went over the hill.

Hamid opened his door before Neill knocked, led him into a low red room with beams. "She's a fool. She'll see you."

"When?"

"After this, never come near me!"

"*When*, man?"

'Go back to your place and wait."

"Today? Tomorrow?"

Hamid moved behind him, opened the door. "Do me a favor?"

"I owe you one?"

"Lay off the bottle. If you stink of liquor she won't even look at you."

"HEY YOU! It'll soon be dark. Time to go."

Rosa stretched, still asleep, looked up and saw him, drew closer. "I'm so tired ..."

Mohammed had again a crushing sense of strength and helplessness. "Just a few more miles. Soon downhill."

"The minefield."

"You know the way across it. We have their tracks."

"I've been worried those soldiers we saw were laying mines."

He hesitated. "I hadn't thought of that."

"Two of them had shovels."

"I didn't see them."

"Your mind was elsewhere."

"It still is. You have completely befuddled me."

"I thought I'd hate you. But you're still a boy."

"Every conversation I start with you goes somewhere else." The small of her back was so thin he could hold half in one hand, her fingers up his spine electric, her arm so soft and strong under his, round him. His penis tingled with delight. This had to be right, to be so good.

35

THE CAFÉ DE PARIS was open but there was no coffee. Neill sat on the terrace with a Pernod. Few people came by and there were no girls and no one he knew. A cold wind licked his ankles. He had been thinking about a line so difficult to translate in the ancient Arab poem of Qays, a young man who loves the beautiful Layla. She is stolen away by her parents and ceases to love Qays, and he becomes Majnun the Mad, wandering the desert, spurning God and man in his thirst for his beloved:

> *I dream a lovely maiden of pure light*
> *Tall and slender, her limbs of fiery passion –*

No, that wasn't it. The poet *meant* "fiery passion" but he didn't say it. Damn Arabic so complicated, more full of meanings than English. How do you say *she plants love in my heart, waters it with the desire pooled in her great eyes*? Any way you try it in English sounds silly.

Crazy to be thinking of poetry while Beirut tore itself apart. Hadn't he like Qays been wandering a desert of his own, rejecting life because love had rejected him? Becoming Majnun the Mad, forgetting that love once it's lost is nothing but a poetic device?

A waste to think such things. A waste of time. He saw Freeman's prim displeased mouth. Freeman wanted *results*. The stuffy self-worth of a man who has never bet all he had and lost. *But have you?* Neill asked himself.

He tucked two dollars under his glass and crossed Rue Hamra, thinking of the traffic in Bratislava that had nearly killed him on Staromestska Street. Here there was no traffic, only danger, yet despite the war little damage but for broken windows, the refuse piled on the pavements spilling into the streets, the smell of charred rubber. He took Rue de Caire, each step deeper into danger but kept going, alongside the silent American Hospital and up Clemenceau past the closed-up Orly Theatre to the University gate. Over its wide golden stone arch the words carved in Arabic and English:

THAT THEY MAY HAVE LIFE
AND HAVE IT MORE ABUNDANTLY

Barbed wire and machine guns blocked the gate. Beyond them the yellow stone edifice of College Hall, where in a seminar on classical poets he had met Layla, was no longer there at all – just a black hole as if it had never been, nor they.

He went down the boulevard with the trim yellow stone church behind the wall and took Rue John Kennedy toward the beach, down the stairs thick with rubbish and broken boughs where once in the overarching shade of tall trees she had kissed him for the first time, and the taste of her mouth had been the opening of a whole new world, one from which even at the time he'd sensed he could never return. There was a body in the grass, swollen and stinking; around it clouds of flies buzzing angrily at his approach. Some day, he thought, you won't wait till we die before you eat us.

There was an exploded car in Van Dyck and a bludgeoned

building before it, then on the seashore boulevard the two-winged American Embassy with its middle crushed in, the concrete floors hanging down like veils, children kicking a soccer ball across the rubble where people still lay buried – typists with three children at home, an old lady with mops and brooms reflectively chewing her gums, young foreign affairs majors on the way up. The cooking fires of Shiite squatters twinkled on the shattered balconies where bright clothes and bed sheets hung.

The sun was sinking like a flame into the sea. Once they'd stood hand in hand before it, stunned at the magnificence of life. Where are you, Layla? Without you I can't sleep, can't ever rest. He followed the smashed empty seaside boulevard where they'd walked so many times, felt her hand in his and remembered the strolling Sunday families, their children holding ice creams, the minty breeze off the sea and the smoke of broiling meat, old men playing backgammon on the concrete wall along the rocks, boys slapping cards down on upended boxes, the fruit and balloon sellers, girls lying bare-breasted on the golden rocks, the fishing boats rocking on the crest, the red, green, and white sailboats beyond. What is it about Paradise that condemns us to destroy it?

He was letting this obsess him. Layla. Keeping him up nights. Had to stop.

Behind one of the concrete pillars in the ruined hollows of the Artisanat, several *fedayeen* were taking turns with a woman. There was the stink of urine drying on the pillars, of piles of feces on the concrete floor, a burnt and bullet-riddled Volkswagen van. He kicked a cartridge case and it pinged across the floor, making him fear the *fedayeen* but they didn't notice.

A Palestinian in a red keffiyeh was driving a red BMW madly up and down the boulevard, spinning in circles, the tires shredding, smoking. The last red speck of the sun sank in the horizon and a wind came up quickly, cold on his neck. You shouldn't be here, he thought.

Ahead, the blunt ruins of the Hotel Saint George on its rocky point were like the stocky remnant of an old chateau, the bare burnt walls where once had been verandas and jalousies and red awnings tasseled in gold, the hideously scarred rooms where lust had been a constant visitor and every illusion about love must have come to dust. Where twenty years ago they'd sit out on the terrace under the stars, after he'd finished waiting tables at 2.15 a.m., hearing the lap of the sea and the soft solace of buoys, talking about the future and how good it was going to be.

Where were they, the other students who'd also worked the short hot summer nights, eight hours straight, four tables each? Sleeping from dawn to noon, then afternoons on the hot beaches, the hash and sun and the hot sweat of making love in the sand, long sultry days and wild nights, never sleeping, never wanting to, never getting enough of girls' hot sweaty slippery bodies, the taste of them, their cunts, their hungry cries.

It was getting dark and he was crazy to be here. Turning up his collar he hurried past the shell of the Holiday Inn with a rocket hole under "Holiday", the Christian cemetery where the near buildings had been bulldozed, the cypresses and grave-stones buried under rubble where children played at war, making him think of the archaeologists some day who'd find this perfect example of a late twentieth-century Christian cemetery crushed under whole flattened buildings, and think how primi-tive and vicious they were, back then.

The *souk* was gone.

Acres and acres of crushed buildings and vanished streets that once had been an ancient bazaar of shops, tenements, whore-houses, jewelry stores, *ateliers*, bars, hashish and opium dens, French bakeries, locksmiths and lawyers' offices, goldsmiths and smugglers, with its Phoenician walls and Roman streets and Crusader alleys sticky underfoot with centuries of blood.

There was no street where he once had lived on the top floor over La Croissant de Paris, in the little room with the worn silk bedspread over the mattress on the pine floor, with the French window letting in the night, Layla young and tanned in his arms.

But where did they go? If even where they'd been was gone, where were they?

He felt nauseous and wanted to sit down and throw up or weep, it was the same thing. Three men were coming downhill through the rubble; instead of turning aside he walked straight past them and they did not stop him.

There was a firefight somewhere, to the south, the salvos tailing off and erupting again. Rockets began to swish over, coming from the dark tall hulk of the Holiday Inn – Hezbollah, maybe, firing at Phalange. Pieces of sharp thin metal were falling, and a soft rain.

THOUGH LAYLA matters most, Mohammed thought, Rosa's the one who saved me. He picked up his gun. "Wait till I come back."

"Giving orders already? Now you've had me?"

"Go first, then, if you like."

"We'll both go." She tightened the coat over the nurse's uniform, scrunched out of the cave mouth and turned right along a string of rocks overseeing the trail. He waited a minute, then went left, also working toward the trail.

No one was visible across the whole broad ridge of snowy dark boulders. The other men's tracks had been softened by wind and half-filled with new snow. Mohammed followed them and met Rosa in the middle. Girl-like, she cocked up her head. "Let me go a hundred yards ahead?"

"Who's giving orders now?"

"We spread the ambush distance, and you're clear of mine shrapnel, if I hit one."

"I'd be the world's worst coward!"

"You're the one I came here to protect, not me."

He moved past. "Just stay in my steps, a good way behind."

There's no point in worrying about the mines, he'd wanted to say, because if it's fated for me to step on one then, *in'salah*,

I will. It won't do any good to worry. And if I do step on one, I'll be either dead or maimed, and if I'm maimed you'll have to shoot me.

Chances were there would be no mines in this path, only elsewhere. Chances were those men had mined below, then come up this path. She'd said they were carrying shovels but he hadn't seen them. No experience – she'd take anything for a shovel.

NICOLAS' and Samantha's house was dark. Neill let himself in the back door and climbed the stairs to his room. Loudspeakers echoed in the street. He lit a candle and sat on the bed, poured a glass of Black Label, put out the candle. If Layla was going to send for him, it wouldn't be tonight. It was damn cold, the wind sucking through the empty windows, constant rumblings of war. Your heart gets numb, all these dying people weighing it down. He saw the woman's burning face, felt it melting on his hand, saw his building in the souk explode, him and Layla inside it. He went to the window. Only two flights if he fell but the concrete down there could crush your skull. No point in worrying about jumping because he wasn't going to jump. The dark hole leered up at him. *You will if I want you to*, it seemed to say.

And if he'd been with Layla, all these years? He saw her walking up the path toward College Hall past Marquand House, so slender and unconsciously lithe in her slim skirt and blouse and long dark hair, with a new black bag over one shoulder, smiling toward him, into the sun. He saw her in the crowded souk, holding up a dented brass coffee-maker with a carved bone handle. "It's real Bedouin!" she whispers in English, so the grizzled Druze shopkeeper won't understand.

Downstairs the back door squealed, Nicolas and Samantha's footsteps in the corridor. He put the Black Label under the pillow, lit the candle, and went down.

Nicolas and Samantha were holding each other, broke apart

as he came into the room. "What's new?" he said, slowing, trying to sound jovial.

"It fell through."

Neill snickered, wanting to inoculate them against defeat. "It would've been what – the seventeenth failed ceasefire?"

"It's not that. Every day without fighting's a success."

Neill started to speak, held it. A fist hammered on the plank front door. Nicolas waved them down on the floor, went into the hall. "Who is it?"

"Hamid! For Dickson. Get him out here!"

Nicolas looked at him helplessly. "Maybe you shouldn't go."

"It's to see *her*," Neill answered. "Any message?"

"No," Nicolas smiled. "Not after all these years."

"Be careful," Samantha said.

Neill went down the back stairs and round through the dark garden. When he got to the pavement it wasn't Hamid but two mujihadeen. "Let's go," one said in English, jerking his gun.

"Where's Hamid?"

"You're coming with us."

"Hamid sent you?" he said in Arabic.

"Don't be such a pussy," the first answered. "Who else would want you?"

"Wait!" Neill gestured at the house. "Let me tell them –"

"Nothing doing."

They fitted a black hood over Neill's head and walked him into the street. "Beat it!" one called, and someone's steps scrambled away, high heels.

"Don't!" a woman screamed.

"He's just going for a visit," the mujihadeen said. "He'll be right back."

They trotted him down the street, tripping over cracks in the concrete. One gripped his burned hand and when he tried to pull away held tighter. They stopped, a car door snapped open and they shoved him in between them, a wide plastic seat smelling of fish oil, rust and dust. The car lurched forward pinning him to the back of the seat. A Mercedes diesel's rough roar, the shocks gone, wheels banging in holes, jolting him left, then right, up the hill and over the top, down and up other streets, no end, once an ambulance screaming by, the smell of hot honey and spices – a shop somewhere. He tried to remember the turns but lost track, the car bottomed through ruts then jerked to a stop, a hurried conversation with someone through the driver's window. It lurched forward, uphill, always uphill now, stink of open-air sewers, burned rubbish, dead animals – he was back in Shatila.

Up an alley, round something in the middle of the street, the driver cursing, the car tipped, sliding Neill against one of the mujihadeen, the driver revved and pulled through, tires screeching, the car braked hard, dumping them forward then back then forward again as it drove over a mound and stopped. They walked him up seven steps and across a concrete porch into an empty-sounding room with a low, echoing ceiling. A door clicked shut.

"Take it off," a woman said.

Fingers yanked the cord at the back of his neck, pulled off the hood. He held his hands over his eyes to shield the light. "You have five minutes," she said.

He faced her, blinking. "You could have just given me the damn address. Why this hush-hush? This silly blindfolding? I'm not your enemy."

She was two dark eyes out of a dark slit. "You've used fifteen seconds."

36

"HOW ARE YOU, LAYLA?"

"We're here to discuss my husband." Her voice, which he remembered so sweet and light, came deeply out of the black gown.

"Every day, Layla, for more than twenty years –"

She shook her head. "We'll only speak Arabic, so Feisal and Rastaf understand."

He glanced at the two mujihadeen who'd brought him. "Then I'll speak English. Just to say your name, Layla –"

"You now have four minutes."

"Do you re*member*, Layla?"

"If you're this crazy I'll tell my husband not to see you."

Every time she said "my husband" his heart clenched. "You're the love of my life, the brightest happiness. The greatest pain."

"Has so little happened in your life," she snapped in English, "that you're willing to live in such a tiny part of your past?"

"It's where *you* lived!"

She stood. "That's insane!"

He caught at her arm, her cowl slid back and underneath it her hair was lustrous chestnut black; she swerved aside holding her veil, and it seemed crazy to him that this woman whose body he had known so well would now hide her face from him. One of the mujihadeen shoved him back. "You're going to get hurt," he said.

"Send this jerk out!" Neill said in English.

"You're lucky he doesn't understand. He'd shoot you."

"Why don't you stop this? I know you better than your own husband!"

"You're crazy!"

"And you're the Mother of the Revolution. Did you spawn this war?"

She hesitated. "It spawned itself. To stop it we'd have to give up completely. We, Lebanese people, thrown out of Lebanon. Syria wouldn't take us. Jordan wouldn't take us. Only Iran would take us. Can you imagine anyone wanting to live in Iran?"

"If Mohammed – or you for that matter – could explain your side in the foreign press –"

"We don't *care* about your foreign press. It's as crazy as your gambling and immorality and usury and heroin and crime and all the other silly things you do."

"Do you remember what you and I did, Layla? Have you been to the British Museum where half the history of your land was preserved before it could be destroyed by camel thieves, nabobs, and assassins? Do you realize what's happened to your fine Muslim culture? Why are you stuck in the Dark Ages while the rest of us go to the moon?"

"I trust you enjoy it – living on the moon?" She nodded at the mujihadeen. "If and when we decide, Mohammed and I, that he should speak to you, we'll let you know. In the meantime stay where you are."

"I saw Tomás in Bratislava. He sends his best. And Nicolas and Sammy send their love."

"When we want, we'll come for you."

"And all our other old friends would send their love too, if your husband hadn't killed them."

"Poor Neill." There was no wrath in her voice, just an exhaustion that made his heart break. "You don't understand a single thing."

THE TRACKS IN THE SNOW dropped down the ridge to the right, deeper into Christian territory, far down the mountain's west flank to where the snow thinned, became dark ground. The wind and stars were sharp, snow crystals tinkling across the crust.

Mohammed waved and Rosa came up, stepping in his steps, holding her coat off the snow. She stood before him, couldn't stop shivering. We've got to get off this mountain, he thought. He pointed at the tracks. "They came up from Lasa."

She looked past him down the ridge. "Damn them."

He raised a cold hand to her brow, for an instant was willing to die to protect her from the minefield, saw his legs in bloody pieces on the ground, his cock that had been just inside her torn to shreds. "Trial and error, this is called."

"We'd better follow them down."

"Back into their territory? So in the morning they're all around us?" He slid the Makarov into a pocket and held her cold cheeks in his chilled hands. "When we get off here we'll celebrate, just you and me." He couldn't stop shivering. "A little memory of what we've done."

She bit her lip, shivering. "I already remember."

He turned from her up the ridge, bending his knees into the deepening snow of the great ice fields, climbing east toward the crest of Mount Lebanon, away from the Christians below, away from the soldiers' tracks and into the minefield. "Same distance," he called, "as before."

ANDRÉ TURNED THE KEY, opened his door and it leaped for his throat – the dog, furry and warm, licking his face, chewing his arm when he tried to force it down. "Stop!" he laughed, and the dog sat quivering with joy, tail slapping back and forth. He shut the door, knelt down and hugged the dog. "You're all I have to come home to." The dog reached out a front paw and put it in André's hand.

He went to the window – nothing in the yard, felt the bed – it was warm where the dog had been sleeping, so there'd been no danger. He drew down the shade and lit the candle.

The dog came and put its chin on Andre's knee. André patted its head – such smooth short fur over the hard muscular skull. "Yeah, big fellow, we'll go out." He caressed the dog's soft mane, behind the ears. "How about a little scouting mission, on your old turf?"

It was seven fifteen, already dark. Six fifteen in Paris. *Métros* full, people and lights and motion and laughter, women with slim thighs going home to lovers and friends. Monique coming home to Hermann after an afternoon in bed with whom? *Magret de canard* and string beans flown in from Kenya, lettuce from Spain, avocados from Mexico, Swiss silver and English bone china – what do you talk about when that's all there is between you?

I'm thinking I can't do what I came down here for. That's what I'm thinking. A draught quivered the flame and he moved the candle to the bedside table. On his pillow was the bone the dog carried everywhere, its favorite possession.

He checked the set of the Jericho under his arm, slipped on his leather jacket, put a spare clip of shotshell cartridges into a pocket, called the dog, snuffed the candle and went out into the Beirut night.

AS MOHAMMED shoved his soaked and frozen feet one by one through the crusted snow he was very careful to increase his weight carefully, slowly, hoping to feel the metal of a mine before he touched the detonator, wherever mines might be in this eternity of snow and wind, the little sphere or disc of explosive chemical in a compressing coat of sharp hard steel meant for him.

He'd studied all the photos, the arcs of kill, the arcs of maim, how many bodies you could get for how many dollars in Larnaca or Cairo or Rome or New York. That made it worse, somehow, as if the Prophet was going to show him how he'd gone astray, give him a bit of his own medicine. If we get out, I make a promise, he decided, to find some way to peace.

Because he'd been so careful he was shocked when it clicked under the snow, loud as a child's tin snapper. It was impossible that a sound so innocent could be so deadly; he wanted to step off nonchalantly, saying don't worry, I won't take it to heart.

Twisting round without moving his foot, he waved Rosa back. "Mine! *Mine!*" He realized he was losing control and quieted himself, forced down the need to jump, to finish it rather than have this horror, shivering so hard his foot would surely slither off the little metal box. Face what will be, he told himself; you're going to die.

37

HE COULDN'T STOP his ankle from quivering or steady his toe and heel against the soil, couldn't keep his foot from shaking the mine. If it had a fuse or timer it'd blow any second. "Go back!" he yelled at Rosa, waving his arm, voice snatched by the wind.

Could he dive aside? Lose his legs only? If it were timed, wouldn't it have blown by now? Under his instep the crumbly soil was sifting, the mine sinking. He kept pushing down harder on it, but that could make it blow too, trying not to lose his balance in the wind and to keep his foot steady under the snow on the mine. He waved her away but she came right up as if it was nothing and he wondered, how can she be like this? She just doesn't care about her life, that's all. Why would anyone do this, bury this hard piece of agony and death for people they've never met?

She knelt. "Keep your foot still!"

"Get back! I *order* you!"

"Hold *still!*" She dug snow and dirt from round his foot, then deeper. "The little metal ridge, on the side – it's American."

"The one that jumps up?"

"It has a ten-minute back-up fuse."

"How long has it been?"

"Five minutes, maybe. Seven." She leaped up and ran, and he lurched to call her, didn't want to die, *wanted* her, wishing she'd said goodbye, waiting each thousandth of a second for the mine to blow, his whole body shriveling away from it, seeing his whole life not in little pieces but as God would, all at once. So this is how they judge you, he thought.

It was easy, viewing it all at once, to see where he'd gone wrong: the pride, the stupidity so viciously defended, most ruthlessly against those he loved; how he'd failed them absolutely except in the most superficial ways. If there's no holiness with your family, none of that deep happy love, then you have none at all. He thought of his father dying alone.

Rosa came dashing back with an armload of rocks and built them up round his foot and ankle. "Go!" he screamed. She ran away, coat sailing in the wind. The wind was trying to push him off the mine. If he could soar now, like a bird. Now it explodes. Now. Ten minutes now. He tried to remember back to when he had stepped on the mine but it was very long ago. So much and nothing. Now it explodes. Chunks of his body and blood spraying through a hail of white metal. Who would make a thing like this, to do *this*?

She ran back, built the wall of rocks further up his shin, shoving away snow, three rocks deep. Maybe I could live, he began to hope. Just lose a leg? He'd take that deal now, any deal with God, promise to change the life he could see in this vast diorama, the little it added up to. He saw the faces of the men he'd sent to death and how ill it suited them, had hurt them, how many he'd pained, and for so little. It came in a flash so strong he could not argue it down. I *will* make peace. Spare me, God, and I'll find a way to make peace. A good peace. Do *You* want peace, God?

"Just leap straight back." Rosa placed the last rock on top of the others. The wall was two feet high, six to ten rocks deep. "Now!"

"Get away!" When she'd run back about thirty feet, he dove sideways over the wall, hit the ground and rolled up and ran through the snow, Rosa safe ahead, no blast.

He caught her and they stood gasping, half crying, knee-deep in snow under the implacable stars. "Dud!" she kept saying. "Dud!"

Her body was life, *his* life. "Reborn ..." He couldn't speak.

Welded to him, she looked up into his eyes. "For what?"

THE DOG trotted, sometimes ahead sometimes behind, stopping to piss on corners and lampposts, down Nabaat, the cemetery gloomy on both sides. West Beirut was beginning to get hit, rockets dropping from the hills, Syrian, Christian, or Israeli. They made André want to turn back but now's the time to find a way in there, he rebuked himself, when nobody's watching. You can always get out when it turns hot.

The dog bounded ahead, nose to the ground. The street dipped and narrowed toward the stadium; two men came out from doorways on each side, Phalange, and warned him to go round by the Lycée, there were snipers in the stadium.

"Palestinians?"

"Geagea's men. Crazy Christians."

There was no point getting caught in some battle between Christian militias over a drug shipment. He went back uphill and swung round by the Lycée, down the hill by the Hotel Dieu. "You're crazy to cross over," said the Phalange captain at the Museum barricade.

"My wife's parents live by the Conservatoire."

The captain handed back his passport. "Everybody coming through here says they're going to see family. With all these blood ties you wonder why we're fighting."

"Lots of stuff coming over tonight?"

"From us?" The captain shrugged. "Don't stay out late."

André stepped into the wide empty half-lit bowl of the Museum intersection feeling the rifles trained on his chest, the dog romping unawares beside him making him fear it would step on a mine. Or did it know where not to step? The Amal barricade loomed closer and he felt they were waiting till they could have his body before they cut him down. This is foolish, he told himself, people cross here every day.

The Amal fighters on the other side were like skinny kids compared to the Christians. They didn't speak, glanced at his passport and laughed, waved him through.

He took Rue Basta uphill toward the Conservatoire. More shells were coming over, heading downtown, and there was the rumble of Israeli offshore fire, hitting near the port. A 155 hissed down and smacked into the next street. He started running, the dog loping beside him; things were falling, metal and glass, in a choking cordite stink. Up a side street something was burning – two cars, a truck, people yelling. A man waved at him – help. You shouldn't do this, he thought, running toward him.

There was a distended flaming Mercedes with its doors and trunk gone, its roof peeled up, a red truck squeezed flat, a collapsed building. The man was yelling in Arabic but when André spoke French he just yelled more, pointing to a hole where two other men had jammed a steel bar under a fallen slab; they waved, flames flickering on their faces. André followed the man down into the hole – a cellar stairs. There were children crying beyond the slab. Together, the four of them pushed the slab aside enough for people to squirm and drag themselves out and scramble up the stairs.

The people from the cellar stood in the middle of the street in the light of the burning Mercedes, counting each other and crying and staring up at the remains of their building. Another 155 was coming in and they ran against the wall. It hit somewhere near in a scream of steel. Yet another was coming and there was nowhere to run, all these people crushing against the next building. Luckily it hit a roof with a *whip snap crack* and a great white silence trying to suck them up, and another was coming.

He ran after them toward the stairway of the next building, not liking it because it was old and made of sandstone. He tried to call them back, the rocket's scream louder and louder down over his head. I'm fucked anyway, he thought, diving down the stairs, and the son of a bitch hit somewhere else with an awful thud, shaking loose bricks and floorboards, the stairs shuddering, and another one was coming down, you could hear it over this one's roar, a sharp dying scream – it knows it's dying, wants to kill us too, why are they doing this? Jesus, where the Hell's the dog? And it crashed like a jet plane, the earth lurching, new bricks and boards tumbling down. This, he thought, is where you buy it.

"THEY'RE HITTING over by the Conservatoire." Nicolas closed the window, pulled the curtain.

Samantha relit the candle. "And the Israelis are shelling the port."

"Amal's got some Hezbollah cornered there," Neill said. "Wants IDF to finish them off. That's the easiest way."

"It's always bothered me to sit drinking wine while a few blocks away people are being hunted to death with high explosives."

"Does no good to cry." Nicolas shrugged. "Besides, it's lousy wine." He drained his glass and poured another. "In a crossfire today between pro- and anti-Arafat Palestinians, this eleven-year-old kid gets hit and is lying wounded in the middle of the street. His parents keep getting shot at when they try to get him till finally the father dashes out waving a white shirt and they wait till he picks up the kid then they blow him away with a fifty caliber. Right in front of my secretary's eyes – she was pinned down too. So anyway, the militias pull back and the wife gets her husband and son, and others drag away the dead before they start to stink. And my secretary apologizes because she's twenty minutes late."

"Sooner or later," Samantha said, "we'll bring people together. But first we have to stop fighting."

"It'll only stop when it's imposed from above," Neill said. "That's what I learned talking to Layla. *They'll* never stop."

"They've got the least to lose."

"They've always had that – the least."

"I agree, that's part of the problem." Nicolas was rubbing his eyes, flexed his arms behind his head. "So what else did she have to say?"

"You'll never win them over to a negotiated settlement. Not till they lose a lot more people. Or if they lose Mohammed."

"You suggesting this?"

"He may represent valid and serious concern for people who've never had a voice. It's easier to integrate him than hunt him down. If you do, you're going to get burned."

Nicolas raised his hand, listening to planes coming in from the southeast, louder, closer. Neill wanted to get down on the floor but Nicolas and Samantha sat there as calmly as if it were a noise on the radio, of what it sounds like to get strafed. The jets swerved to the south then north. Mirages. You could hear them deepen and settle into their runs like a snake striking and there was a sharp snap and the sky lit up like lightning in a total white silence and awful *bang*.

"Allah!" Nicolas said. "How they are getting it!"

"Who?" Neill wanted to yell *Aren't you afraid?*

"The Palestinians down by the Conservatoire. Getting their poor ignorant brains blown out. That was a vacuum bomb."

38

THEY CAME DOWN from the mountains to a narrow saddle between two peaks. Lower down the snow thinned then was gone, the soil damp and rocky, here and there bits of goat-gnawed grass. To the right a trail dropped down Jabal Nakiba toward the Christian side; to the left another path descended Dahr el Kadib toward the Muslim side. Distantly to the east Mohammed recognized the shapes of the mountains on the far side of Yammouné valley. "I was here," he turned to her, "right here at this crossroads – less than a week ago."

She tugged his sleeve. "Let's go."

The path dropped steeply eastwards into Yammouné valley. They were in Hezbollah territory now and there were no more mines and no patrols. They came down past where the river comes pouring from a hole in the side of the mountain and down over the pieces of Roman temple, where he had knelt just a few days ago, before he'd *known*. They followed the goat trail down into sleeping Yammouné at midnight, the town silent but for a single lamb calling for its ewe and the soft cool chuckle of the stream and the smell of banked fires, oak charcoal, and fresh dung, of dry earth and straw.

His father's house was locked and dark. He knocked softly

on the neighbors' door. "Yeah!" one whispered, down from the eaves.

"It's me." Mohammed stepped back into the street, for them to see.

"You're too late. He's dead and buried, bless his soul."

He didn't expect how badly it would hurt, nor the guilty sense of freedom. "When?"

"It's been two nights."

"Where's the key?"

"Mother Zazid's."

"Where's that?" Mohammed felt guilty not knowing where she lived, the woman who'd cared for his own dying father.

"Across the lake."

Hens began to cluck. "Do you have food? For two days we haven't eaten."

A woman answered. "We'll bring you something."

Mohammed tried to climb to his father's sloping roof but his bullet wound was too sore so Rosa did it, tiptoed along the ridgepole and down through the hayloft. He heard her bare feet cross the tile floor; the lock squeaked open. "Welcome home."

"Don't joke." He stepped past her into the darkness smelling of cold ashes, dried tea leaves and old bread.

A teenage boy he barely recognized came in sleepily without knocking, with a candle, a basket of cucumbers, cheese, and bread, and a bucket of cold tea. "It's what we have."

"May Allah bless you, bless his name," Rosa said.

"You don't believe that!" Mohammed said when the boy left.

"Neither do you. Let's eat."

It was gone too soon, leaving them hungrier. Beyond the wall the lamb had found its ewe, the hens stopped clucking. They undressed and crawled under blankets on the straw mattress where his father had died.

"To sleep in a bed," she sighed. "Such luxury!" She slid her hand up his ribs. "I'm sorry about your father."

"At least I had a chance to see him, one last time."

"What did he want to tell you?"

"He wanted to make peace. The doctor wanted me to make peace. *God* wants me to make peace."

"No one knows what God wants."

"If I'd never come to see my father I'd never have been wounded and you would never have found me. I'd never have known ..."

She tickled his ribs. "Known what?"

"How much I owe you."

She snuggled closer. "Nonsense."

He kissed her temple, the skin so soft, the hair so soft, the hair so fine. This is the flesh, he thought, that saved me. By which I am reborn.

THEY HAD BEEN SHELLING so long André could not remember, could not think. There was no air in this sweaty fearful *cave* where somebody had vomited and the sewer main was broken in the wall, and there comes a point, he realized, when you just no longer care, when the next shell comes down straight for you. It was coming now, loud and angry, won't miss this time, you already know how it'll feel, how it will blow you apart or knock the building in on you, squashing you an inch flat between concrete floors. Is that what happened to *you*, Yves? Is that why they'd never tell us?

In between the falling shells and the searing jet runs with their awful crunch of buildings and crackle of anti-personnel bombs you could hear the screams of people trapped in a building somewhere, more and more frantic, till either they got out, André decided, or the fire overcame them. Shells were coming down in tandem now, several batteries, shells hitting two and three a second, their constant, uneven *wham-wham wham* making the ground shake crazily. Things kept falling but still the building hadn't been hit. Maybe it's good luck, he thought, to hide under a place that's sure to come down.

"It's *them* again," wailed an old woman in the dark in front of him.

"*Quiet!*" someone hissed in French. "Grandma hears something."

But everyone could hear it now, the double-thrusting jets, the fiery air screaming over diamond wings, another Mirage on the same run, low over Christian East Beirut and up the hill into the West. "It's the big one!" someone yelled, and for two or three seconds there was just the jet's departing roar then everything crashed in, crushed in his head, sucked out his mind, into the white.

AFTER MIDNIGHT the shelling died off and Neill stood at his paneless window watching the last of the bright Israeli afterburners streak up into the southwest sky. Behind their roar was the constant crunching of flames; the Israeli Army had shut off the water into Beirut and now the city was burning, so hot the stones themselves were catching fire.

"Where are you, Layla?" he said to the night, remembering *layl* means *night*, that she was out there, somewhere, nearer than she'd been in years, almost within reach. Any night now she could be among the new ones entombed under some building, shot down in some street. When he was so close. What if, he thought, I could take her from Mohammed?

The sky was full of smoke, pink on its undersides from the fires up by the Conservatoire. Up there people are trapped and burning alive, Neill thought, and here I stand helpless by my window. That's what I've been all my life – outside the pale. Depersonalized, not able to give, not able to take. He thought of Nicolas and Sammy sleeping in the basement, wondered, does it screw up your sex life, all this bombing?

Come close to me, oh beloved of my soul; the fire is cooling and fleeing under the ashes.

Where are you, Layla?

39

THE AIR WAS AFIRE, impossible to breathe. Huge heavy concrete was crushing André's chest into the floor. Chunks of concrete jabbed up into his back. When he realized where he was, the terror made him thrash and beat at the concrete but he could not move it. You're down here forever, he realized. Entombed.

"Don't fight," a woman whispered. "Uses air."

"*What?*" He could barely speak, he was shaking so crazily with fear of this concrete slab on his chest.

"Calm down," she said. "They'll find us."

He took deep breaths, trying to calm. "Where are you?"

"Over here in the corner. The floor – or something. It's bent down on us. Where are you?"

"On the floor. There's a floor on my chest. Who's with you?"

"Two kids."

"The others?"

"The building fell in. I think they're all dead."

"How are the kids?"

"They're fine. I've told them exactly what's happened and that we must be quiet and save energy for when the rescuers come."

THE LAND FAR BELOW was tanned and crinkled under the blue light, speckled with the shadows of small white clouds, the air sharp, cold and very thin. Mohammed could see the wide curving earth and every path and house upon it. He dived and rose on canyons and peaks of wind and cloud, perfectly alive.

The cry came again and he realized it was a lamb in the stables. He wasn't free, couldn't fly. The lamb was calling its mother and should be suckling – what did it fear? He took the Makarov, slipped from bed, opened the door and went naked down the corridor and stood in the darkness watching out through the window to the garden.

The small moon hung in the mulberry branches like a hapless skull. The garden of bare peach and pear trunks and freshly turned strawberry beds gave nowhere to hide. Moonlight glittered on the broken glass set like fossil teeth in the top of the wall. He went to the door, opened it and peered round it. The narrow street lay in moon shadow, smelling of flowers and manure. Again the lamb bleated.

He shut the door and relocked it, the dark house quiet and warm, a lingering odor of his father, of thyme and drying cheese, the cool dampness of the well in the garden. His feet rustled over the stone floor. Be silent, he thought, don't wake her, wishing she were awake, wanting to talk to her. Soundless, he entered the corridor.

He sensed the gun, ducked and dove forward to snatch it before it fired, twisting it, twisting her wrist, hand clenching her throat.

"Let me go!" she hissed, yanking at one wrist.

He dropped his hands.

"Where *were* you? I damn near shot you!"

"I damn near shot *you!*"

She sat naked, trembling on the floor in his arms. He made her get up and they went back into the room. He lit the candle. Her face was white. "I almost shot you," she said again.

"What were you doing?" He picked up her gun; she had mounted a black silencer on it. "Where'd you get *this?*"

She got under the blankets. "I keep it in my bag, like that. I woke up and heard a noise in the hall. You were gone – I was afraid they had you."

"*They?* Who?"

"I don't know! Get into bed. Sometimes I worry about everyone."

He lay beside her, the bed still warm. I could have been dead, he thought, and my bed still warm.

Before dawn he rose and washed, said his prayers, his back stretching and limbering as he knelt forward, face to the ground. It bothered him that she could see him, she who would not pray. "Why am I with her, God?" he asked, smelling her musk on his hands. "What do You want?"

He finished the prayer. She sat naked, cross-legged, brushing her hair. It made a ripping sound, like a fire spreading. She's a *jinni*, he thought, she can help or kill you. The backward people of Yammouné still believe that if a *jinni* wants a young man she'll condemn his beloved to death. But Rosa doesn't want *me*.

"In half a day," she said, "we'll be back in Beirut. To who we were."

"I was wondering, could we stay up here?" He shrugged. "I suppose now it's my house."

"If you've come back from the dead," her eyes warmed him, for an instant, "then it's to drive *them* out. Palestinians and Shiites together – we can do it."

His arms felt weak. It's still the wound, he thought. "If we go back –"

"*If?*"

"We'll get a lift with somebody, go by Baalbek and Zahlé. After that I don't know what I'll do with you."

She stood in one motion, elastic. "Nothing! I'm on my own."

"But I don't want that!"

She smiled, watching him. "Jealous?"

"You've slept with other men." He trembled, not wanting to hear.

"So did Mary, the Prophet's servant girl, before she gave him a son."

His insides congealed. "We didn't –"

"Don't worry!" she laughed. "Anyway, the Prophet never married her."

"Of course not."

"But when his wife complained, he threw her out and banished all his other wives, and only lived with Mary. Then people criticized him, so he had a new revelation that it's fine for prophets to do this but nobody else."

"I'm no prophet."

She cocked her head, biting her lip. "Why?"

"I can't find my own way out of the desert, let alone anybody else's."

"Neither could the Prophet. He just did what he wanted. As with Mary. And told everybody to do what he said, not what he did."

His head spun. Once again she was contorting things. He wanted to sit down but that would seem weakness. To whom? To her? He sat on the floor.

"Hey!" She rushed to him.

The room was going round. If she saw it as weakness that meant she didn't care for him and then he couldn't chance being himself. But what if he *could* be himself, all the way? Nauseous dizziness washed over him. When it lessened he pushed her away and stood. "When we get to Beirut I start anew. The path of peace –"

"Lie down, you fool," she clicked her tongue, "pushing yourself!"

The ceiling stopped spinning. He smiled up at her, heart full of joy. "You're the one who's been pushing – *"Oh, don't stop!"* he moaned. *"No, don't, not now …"*

She slapped him. "Pig! I should leave you to them!"

"Who?" he laughed.

"Everybody who wants you!" She tried to stalk away but the room was too small so she bent and snatched her underpants and stepped into them, yanked them up. With sorrow he watched them cover her luscious black crotch, the bra hooked over her lovely tight-nippled breasts, the robe like a curtain coming down. I'm a fool, he thought, not knowing why.

NEILL WOKE to the recorded plaint of a muezzin out of a loudspeaker across the Jardin Public. He thought of Layla waking now, warm and drowsy, Mohammed snoring beside her. She probably has to take a piss, he reminded himself. Just like me. He had to piss too much to go back to sleep now that he was awake, thanks to the muezzin. His burnt hand still hurt against the rough bandage. *Our God*, the Bible says, *is a consuming fire*.

Once he got up and wandered down the stairs to the outhouse in the back yard, he might as well stay up. Another tired meaningless day. Another day closer to death. Waiting for Mohammed. For Layla, really. Like he'd been doing all these years.

Another day of helping Nicolas and Samantha look for food – we're right back in the hunter-gatherer mode, he thought, maybe we never left it – and trying to make contact with other people who might know Mohammed. People he hadn't seen in years, hadn't wanted to. Why had he become a journalist when he *hated* people? Actually, he realized, it made perfect sense.

If he didn't speak to Mohammed, Freeman was going to want his money back. Freeman didn't give a shit about Layla. Neill hugged his arm against his ribs.

He sat on the edge of the bed, bent over rubbing his neck. Another day. He really *did* have to piss. He stood, found his trousers and pulled them on, trying not to jiggle his bladder.

He went down the echoing dusty stairs, trying not to wake Nicolas and Samantha, and out the back corridor. New blue daylight glistened over the trees. Already dawn, he realized, and no shells, no rockets, no sound of guns, no wail of ambulances or bray of fire trucks.

War's like the Devil, he thought as he hopped barefoot across the cold crinkly dew-wet grass. Sometimes it just gets tired of tormenting you. Those are the times called peace.

40

MOHAMMED STEPPED FROM his father's house into the sun-bright street. The air was cool, down from the ice sheets of the mountain and perfumed with the spring herbs of the valley, the warm smell of charcoal in the village hearths, the fur and dung of animals, the onions hung on stone walls to dry in the sun. "Cover yourself," he said, turning to check that Rosa had hidden her hair completely under her scarf, that the veil covered all but her eyes and that the gown fell to her feet.

A boy and two little girls passed, holding hands; he did not recognize them, nor the crippled old man driving goats down the street, waving a bent stick. He went into the shop's cool spicy shadows but did not know the woman behind the counter. "Good morning, young man," she said; he realized she was the sister of a boy he'd gone to school with, up the hill.

"You're the shopkeeper now?" he said.

"Yacoub's dead – you don't remember?"

"Of course ..."

"And you're still fighting."

"Perhaps soon we can stop."

She was cutting the stems of garlic bulbs and tossing them into a basket. "Don't believe it."

"I need a ride to Baalbek and Beirut."

She looked up from the garlic, the curved knife in her hand. "You're not of here any more, are you? You belong to Beirut, the war."

"Nothing owns me but God."

"That's what you all say but look what you've done to us!"

"God owns us all."

"No God would do *this* to those He loves!" She let the knife clatter to the counter. "The farm by the lake, they're sending a truck to Beirut with vegetables. You and the Mother of the Revolution, there, can ride with them."

"She's not –"

"It doesn't matter. They'll be happy to send you both back to the war."

THE MADNESS RETURNED and André couldn't stop his hands from smashing at the concrete, his spine from trying to arch, pry it up. Finally beaten and exhausted, he lay gasping, head twisted to one side.

She was hitting a rock steadily against the wall behind her. *Tunk*, it went, *tunk tunk*. "I had friends in Rue de Mexique," she said. "Their building fell in on them and they were caught in a basement like this, curled up in a shower stall, the caved-in floor on their shoulders. It took three days to find them. All the time they kept signaling, like this."

He licked sweat off his lips, couldn't bring his arms up his sides.

"If you fight it," she said, "you won't last."

He listened to the steady cadence of her knocking, like an arrhythmic heart. "How are the kids?"

She said something in Arabic, one answered. "Fine," she said.

"I don't know how they stand it."

"They already have ten years of war behind them."

"What do you tell them?"

"Pray to Allah."

"You're Muslim?"

"They are."

"You're not their mother?"

"Their teacher. The shelling started while I was running them home. We ducked in here. You live here?"

"I live in Paris. Down on a visit."

"Must be nice, Paris. Peaceful."

"We had a bombing last month – Muslims."

"One bombing a mouth – that's Paradise." She cleared her throat. "We shouldn't talk so much."

"You thirsty?"

"A little."

"You have to drink each other's urine. You can last a day longer –"

"That's silly."

"It's true. They told us that, the Army. They wouldn't lie."

She kept up the steady knocking. "When we get out of here, I'll buy you champagne."

"If we get out of this …" He did not finish, not knowing what to say. What had happened to the dog?

"How old are you?" she said.

"Twenty-seven."

"Married?"

"No. You?"

"Twenty-two. I was married but my husband died."

"Wait! *Stop*! That sound!"

She stopped. There was nothing but the dullness of the great weight leaning down on top of them. Then in the distance *tick tick* like the sound of someone's watch in another room. "It's *them!*" she said. "I told you!"

MOHAMMED got down with Rosa from the vegetable truck and watched it rattle away, holding his breath against its last burst of sooty exhaust. In front of them, Beirut seemed the same under the dark clouds of war, making him hunger for the dry cool air of Yammouné.

Rosa had taken off her veil and gown; seeing her breasts outlined beneath her dress made him excited and ashamed. "I'm going home," he said.

She smiled, like the sun. "Run to her, after I've saved you."

"They're my family, they'll be worried."

"Not enough to come after you like I did."

"I still don't know why you did."

"Nor do I." She shrugged. "A mistake."

He took her hands, the gesture seemed to shock her. "Anyway," he said, "I thank you for this new life. This chance for peace."

She glanced up at the contrails of fighters far above. "If I'd known that's what you wanted I would have left you."

Feeling strangely alone he climbed the crest of Beirut toward the apartment on the Rue Maalouf that he had commandeered from a Greek Orthodox family to lodge his own. Seeing the church of Saints Peter and Paul on the corner made him wonder at his aloneness, at why humans bothered to fight. We don't love life at all, he thought, we just love to destroy it.

THE TINY *TICKING* noise had vanished but the teacher kept beating her rock against the concrete wall till the rock broke into pieces and then each of the pieces crumbled. "I can't see my watch," André said. "Do you know what time it is?"

"Mine's broken."

"Must be day outside."

"They'll be coming. They always do."

André tried to envision this mysterious *they* who would at great danger to themselves dig down in shattered buildings to retrieve survivors pinned under sliding tons of concrete and stone. "Unless there's new shelling. Anyway, they'll have lots of people to dig out, after last night. It'll be a long while till they get to us."

"Do you remember what street this is? Were there any buildings knocked down, blocking it?"

"It's off Basta. They hit every building on this street. Never have I seen such bombing."

"It was much worse in eighty-two. Every time they got some Palestinians cornered, they'd drop a vacuum bomb."

"Last night, some of that was Syrian."

"And Christian. We Christians are the worst. We started this by not sharing Parliament although the Muslims were the majority."

"You could say *we* started it, the French. There's always a million guilty for everything that's wrong."

"It's people," she said. "That's what's wrong."

"I FEARED TERRIBLY for you, my husband." Layla squeezed his hands, raised them to her brow.

Mohammed snatched them away, wondered will she want to make love? The idea disgusted him. Was it because she'd talked to that Englishman? The one there'd been a rumor about, years ago. "You really love me that much, Layla? After all these years? Or do you just love who I *am*?"

"They're the same."

Irritated he turned away. Why was returning such a defeat? When all along he'd looked forward to it? "To others I'm the Lion of God and all that foolishness, and people do what I say not because of who I am but of who they think I am."

"I don't care what people think."

"You don't seem to understand, Layla." He liked having his back to her like this, his words booming back from the walls at her. "This girl who saved me, I'm keeping her with me."

"As you wish."

"You don't care?"

"Does it matter? Should I?"

"That's what has always irked me most about you, Layla. Sarcasm. The way you never say what you feel."

"You've told me many times you don't care what I feel, that it's my problem. I agree."

"Layla, please understand. I've been hurt and I'm wondering if we can end this war."

"If you try you'll be killed. Like everyone else who's tried."

"I'm being told by *God*, Layla."

"Then you can't help yourself." For a moment she said nothing; he picked up his rifle and slid it over his shoulder. "So talk to this English journalist," she added. "Maybe you can use him."

41

THE *TINK TINK* sound of steel on concrete had returned but seemed farther away. "They're back digging!" she cried.

He tried not to talk too much, too thirsty. "When we get out – we'll go up to the Casino. Have dinner. Looking out over the bay –"

"Stop! Don't do this."

"What would you eat, right now?"

"I would've said lobster, but have you ever seen them, the poor things, thrashing in the pot?"

"If you worry about that, Anne-Marie, you'll starve."

"People are digging!" She hammered louder, in rhythm, waited; the other skipped a beat, followed the rhythm. "See?" she kept saying. "See?"

André told her the Morse code letters for SOS and she hammered them out and the others repeated them note for note.

"They don't know what it means," he said.

"They're just repeating," she stopped knocking, "everything I do."

"Buried," André said. "Just like us."

———

THE SHELLING HAD DESTROYED all the buildings around the Conservatoire. Neill stood watching the rescue crews and bulldozers digging out the corpses, once a whole family still alive, all crying and holding each other. Over one rubble-filled basement a single column of concrete stairs spiraled up several flights and ended in a half-step over the void. *Stairway to Heaven*, the words came to him bizarrely.

If they could only see this, all the people letting this happen. If you could only write it well enough, they'd see. What the Hell did they think the world was coming to as they went about their profitable mortal businesses, propagating money, children, carbon dioxide, effluents and hazardous waste?

They? Him too, everyone. The next century was going to be a horror like none in history: warring billions of swarming hordes tearing everything down in their hunger, the technical horrors, the diseases, the weapons of Armageddon. While a few unraveled the riddle of aging, the toxins of death, traveled to new planets, learned to speak with machines, the barbarians were going to be tearing it all down faster than it could be built.

The shelling started again in midafternoon and Neill ran home. He took the Black Label down to the basement and sat at Samantha's typewriter but could think of nothing to say.

He finished the whisky. Finish *this article*, he promised himself, and you can buy more.

The hardest was the beginning: *"I wish you could all be here ..."*

When the article was done, it was five hundred words that went from a statement of theme to detailed description and out the other side to clear conclusions and a final demand to the reader: *make us stop.*

Like Icarus falling from the sky while the farmer ploughs his field and we all go about our business, the Lebanese are dying in their cellars barely a quarter mile from me. There is nothing I can do to help them but to write this. If we are the cells of a greater body then each cell must feel, share in, and try to prevent the loss of any other. As Beirut dies, so does our world.

Feeling free of everything but sorrow he went to the window and listened to the shelling. When it seemed to slow he went up Emile Eddé to the Commodore and called the story in. "Wait a min'it!" the girl on the other end in London said, chewing her gum. "Yer talkin' too fast."

He tried to speak slowly and clearly but the line was very bad and he kept asking her to repeat it and that made her angry but finally she seemed to get it all down. "Can you switch me up to Editorial?" he said.

"Editorial?" She snapped her gum. "This is the typing pool, honey. Those blokes've all gone home."

"DO YOU THINK there's something after this?"

He was thinner, André realized, could slide a little toward her under the slab. "I'm a Catholic but I don't think there's anything more."

"I keep wondering, will I see him? My husband. Will I ever see him again?"

"You'll see him, Anne-Marie. If we die, you'll see him soon, but I don't think we're going to die because the shelling's stopped again and soon they'll dig us out."

I'm starting to believe in *them*, he thought. On the boat coming from Larnaca it seemed strange that people would build a boat for others to travel on, perfect strangers. And now I'm dreaming that others will dig down into this mountain and find us.

The *tick tick* was back and he wanted to slap out at it, silence it. What right did they have, wanting to be saved?

Anne-Marie was talking to the two girls in a low throaty Arabic that made it seem impossible this same voice could speak French.

"What did you tell them?" he said.

"One's getting very feverish and we've nowhere to go, we're in our own wet ..."

"That's fine. That's who we are. Now we know what it's like to be human."

"It's not so bad, being human. I want to live, want these girls to live!"

"What was he like, your husband?"

"He was afraid all the time –" She stopped, spoke to the girls. One was arguing back, plaintive. "He was a photographer and had to go out every time there was a street fight, a bombing. He tried not to show it, but at night he'd tremble. All night beside me in bed, trembling."

"It's all right, Anne-Marie. It's all right."

"The bombings broke his heart and the fights scared him to death."

"Why didn't he quit?"

"He felt if people saw his pictures of how awful the war is maybe they'd want to stop it."

You don't learn about war in the newspapers, he started to say, but there was no point. The newspapers only printed the nice shots. The bodies under blankets, trailing a little blood. Not the heads on bayonets, the women slit from jaw to crotch, the disjointed limbs of children. "I wish I'd known him."

"You don't need to say that."

"I don't have any friends like that. I wish I'd known him. I wish you had him still."

"If he was here, he'd dig right down, get us out."

"What happened to him?"

"A car crash. In the rain. Hit by a truck. Going up to Dora for some meeting."

One of the girls was weeping almost silently; the other joined in. "Don't let them," he said.

"Why not? Why can't they feel what they feel? It's such an awful death." She too started to cry. "It's such an awful death ..."

"After we go to the Casino we'll drive up the coast –"

She halted through her tears. "It's bad luck, saying that."

"It's *good* luck. Showing God we want to live."

"Have you ever been to Byblos?"

"When I was a boy. I remember ruins and cliffs going down to the sea."

"With the golden Phoenician city and the Crusader castle and wild poppies and the water so warm and sweet in the bay ... André, it's the loveliest place on earth. If we ever get out, I swear it, we'll go there."

"And we'll make love in the tall grass going down to the sea, Anne-Marie. I swear that too."

"You shouldn't say that." For a moment she was silent. "Yes, maybe you should."

"I promise you, Anne-Marie. I promise God. If we get out, we'll do that."

"What are you like?" she said. "Are you tall?"

"Two meters. Almost."

"I'm one eighty. I was two centimeters taller than my husband, even in flat shoes."

42

THEY CAME QUICKLY when they came – bulldozers shaking the earth, the concrete slab creaking over him. She kept hammering the wall and stopping and hammering and stopping, and someone hammered back.

A shovel or pick, clanking the earth. Every time they stopped, she hammered. Every time they started again they were closer.

"Tell them," André called, "not to shake this slab."

There was the *rat-tat-tat* of a jackhammer and the nearer *clank* of shovels, then something crashed down on the slab making him yell out and the air was full of dust and he realized he could see. Gray grainy light making him blink.

"André?"

"Can you see?"

She was calling out in Arabic, the same word, over and over. The noise stopped. A voice, a man's voice, coming down a tunnel from far above.

"Please!" André couldn't help himself. "*Please* get us out."

"They're coming!" she called. "I've told them not to shake the slab. They're going to dig in from next door."

MOHAMMED'S MUJIHADEEN came to Nicolas and Samantha's back door and took Neill, sleepy and cold with a black hood over his head, to another car, not a Mercedes but a smaller, jolting sedan with an importunate whining engine. They drove across early morning Beirut, the streets already loud with trucks, car horns, boys hawking papers – "Jumblatt declares truce!" Strange how it goes on, he thought, in the middle of the war. Like new cells growing while you die of cancer. The farmer plowing his field. A jet went over, low, he couldn't tell which kind. Never, he realized, have I felt so bad. It's going to kill me, Beirut. Breaking my heart.

They walked him up fifty-nine stairs and down a long corridor that turned twice. They stopped and knocked. "Who's that?" a man beyond the door said.

"Your grandmother, dinkhead!"

The door opened and they shoved him into a room with a carpet and the smell of coffee. There was a short-wave radio receiving in the background but he couldn't understand it. Someone snatched off the hood. The lights were bright. He rubbed his eyes. There were a lot of mujihadeen with Uzis. They led him down a corridor to another room where a lean, balding man with a full beard, dressed in a white robe, sat on cushions in the corner. The two mujihadeen who were with him got up and left. "Sorry to wake you so early," he said. "Can we get you coffee or tea? Some bread?"

"Coffee and bread. Might as well be sleepy with a full stomach."

"Sir down. We have half an hour."

"You're?"

"The one you've come all this way to see."

"You don't look like your picture."

"They're all mistaken, the intelligence agencies. Even yours."

"I don't deal with MI6, the CIA –"

"I hear from Michael Szay in Bratislava that perhaps you do. He warned me to avoid you."

"I asked him to find you because I hope to tell your side to the West. Michael doesn't want that."

"Why not?"

"He likes selling you guns. He likes the war the way it's going."

"Everybody uses Lebanon to get something for himself. Britain, France, you ..." Mohammed tried to settle himself on the sofa. "So tell me. Where do *you* think this war's going?"

THE RESCUERS BROKE through the next basement and jacked up one side of the concrete slab an inch so André could slide out. He tried to stand and fell down. "Get her."

"We're fine," she called. "Don't worry."

They tried to jack the floor up higher but it was pinned by debris above. Someone wrapped him in a blanket and gave him hot sugared tea and bread. They dug a trench out of the floor with the jackhammer but could go no further because the hose wasn't long enough. André crawled back under the slab, past the place he had been pinned, but could not reach her. The concrete was rough like sandpaper and cold as the bottom of the sea. He was sure it was going to fall on him.

"Anne-Marie!" he called. She did not answer. Someone came in with another length of hose and a short skinny crippled man dragged the jackhammer further under the slab.

"He's going to shake it down on us," André said. The others were shoving pieces of plank on top of each other to hold up the slab.

The jackhammer chattered, the hoses hissing, the generator in the street outside revving and dying down. The jackhammer noise stopped, the slab shivered, slid lower. Voices echoed under the slab, hers, the jackhammer man's. They grew louder, Anne-Marie's voice coming toward him, and he took her hands as she crawled out from under the slab, a tall, pretty, short-haired woman squinting in the generator lights, two little girls behind her.

A camera flashed. "That's forty-two today!" someone said in French, slapped André's shoulder. The jackhammer man came sliding out, dragging his tool and hose.

"Thank you," André said to him. "Thank you, God!" He knelt and Anne-Marie with him. Hugging each other and the two little girls, they wept and prayed in French and Arabic to God and Allah for their salvation.

"YOU DENY bombing the American Marines?" Neill said.

Mohammed's eyes turned on him. Exactly like a hawk's, Neill decided. A blue-eyed Shiite hawk. Something else for Freeman to chew on.

"A month before the American and French barracks were bombed," Mohammed said, "do you remember what happened?"

"Let's see, that was October eighty-three. In September?"

"In September, as you would count it. When Ronald Reagan ordered the USS *New Jersey*, the *John Rogers*, and the *Virginia* to shell the Muslim and Druze villages in the Shouf. Have you seen what they did?"

"I'm American. I don't dare go to the Shouf."

"They killed five thousand people, nearly all women and children. They killed my brother and his wife and their seven children and her parents, and half the people in their village. My brother and his wife were cooking dinner for their family when the shell from the *New Jersey* hit their house. And while my cousins were digging through the ruins, trying to find *their* children, French planes killed them with phosphorous bombs." Mohammed looked away, and Neill had a moment of pity for him, realized he was trying not to weep. "You Westerners think because we are Arab we do not feel?" Mohammed said. "You think that the death of an American child is more important than that of my four-year-old nephew?"

"I left America after Vietnam," Neill said. "It hasn't changed. I'll never move back."

"Have you ever seen what a phosphorous bomb does to someone? Or a high-explosive shell the size of a car? If you had, you would understand why Hussein Musawi said that if America kills our people then we must kill Americans."

Neill reached out, his hand on Mohammed's wrist. "I'm not your enemy."

"You're a journalist. What I don't understand is why your newspapers won't tell the truth."

"American newspapers will never print the truth about what caused this war."

"But you are here representing a British paper."

"In Britain most of the newspapers are owned by very rich conservatives and staffed by people with little experience and lots of opinions."

"But yours is supposed to be the best, liberal –"

"Liberal in England means seeing things through a cloud of preconceptions. Having a lot of ideas you've never tested because you went from university to a nice desk somewhere and you've never seen much of the real world."

"So you see why we've taken prisoners – hostages you would call them. We have no faith in your ability to police yourselves, to say the truth and act upon it. Knowing you are very sentimental and will raise a fuss about one person in a Hezbollah prison while you help to kill thousands of innocents in Lebanon, even let thousands of your own innocents die on your roadways, we've decided to act on your sentimentality by taking an occasional prisoner."

"So who bombed the Marines, the French paratroopers, the US Embassy?"

"If you knew, would you print it?"

"I'd try. But before I left London my editor told me he couldn't be even sure he'd print this interview."

"What would make him decide?"

"If he felt the story had a UK draw. Said he's tired of hearing about Beirut."

"You mean he's tired of hearing about Arabs."

"My editor, like much of Anglo-Saxon England, scorns Arabs."

"And you?"

"I scorn the human race."

"Seven years I've fought the Christians. I've fought the Syrians and the Druzes and the Israelis and Amal. I've killed people from across the sea and people from my own village. I've killed people whose faces I've never seen, and I've killed the friend who shared his goat cheese and bread with me at school every noon. I shot him in the face ..."

"I'm learning war and religion are the same thing. It's best to be what we want, not what we're told."

"If you asked the Druze what are their terms for peace, what would they say?"

"As we've said – their hegemony and punishment of Christian war crimes."

"No, I mean with us."

"They'd want you back where you were. Out of their hills."

"They would compromise a bit?"

"Surely."

"What if you got a good compromise and came to us and we said yes?"

"What have I got to do with this?"

"You're one of the few journalists here right now who has any credibility with us."

"I don't have a whole lot, right now, with the other side."

"Why? You're certainly not pro-Arab."

"Westerners have a complete inability to understand this place. Anyway, nobody wants to hear the truth if it's inconvenient."

"Once somebody has said something to the papers it's harder to back out."

Neill shook his head. "You don't know the human race."

Mohammed smiled. "Talk to the Druze – Walid Jumblatt. He says he wants peace."

43

THEY WERE CHUBBY, DUSTY LITTLE GIRLS with wan faces and long chestnut braids. "We're all soaked and filthy," Anne-Marie said. "Didn't want you to see me like this."

"We're human, Anne-Marie. We're alive."

"Everyone else in the building is dead."

"The ones who were knocking, they're still down there –"

"I told the rescue team. They're looking."

Behind them the street swarmed with diggers in the maw of each gutted building, one building completely gone, only the stairway sticking up into bright morning. "Let's get the girls home," she said. "Their parents will think they're dead. My building has a generator. If there's water we can heat some."

A Mercedes had stopped out on Basta. Palestinians, one a young woman with a camouflage T-shirt and tanned muscular arms, a black scarf over raven hair, silver earrings, a silver bracelet, a Kalashnikov. Two other cars were with them and they all got out and came down the street toward the flattened buildings. The Palestinian girl with the AK47 was familiar, he couldn't stop looking.

You. No, that had been Christian East Beirut and this was Muslim West, and that girl had been Christian – the Lebanese Red Cross. He'd hot-wired her Land Rover ...

She walked past, glanced at him quickly, glanced away.

"What's the matter?" Anne-Marie said.

"Seeing spirits." He looked into her eyes and there was no hiding there, just hers looking strongly into his. I could live with someone twenty years, he realized, and never know her as well as I know you.

"CAN YOU REACH WALID, see if he'll meet me? Tell him I want his thoughts on peace. What he'd give for it."

"You're wasting our time, Neill. There's been a hundred peace attempts. A thousand."

"I don't give a shit about peace, Khalil. I'm doing my job."

"You've got this agenda always, ever since I know you." Khalil Hussein's thick glasses twinkled, making him seem merry. He patted Neill's hand. "The betterment of man."

"Just like you, Khalil. That's why I came to you."

Khalil Hussein shrugged. "I can't help you. Nobody can. This is Beirut."

Almaza Pilsner, the bottle on the café table said. *Produced in Lebanon with the assistance of Amstel breweries in Holland.* Just a few days ago, Neill realized, I was drinking Amstel by the Amstel. Why did I come here?

"I'll talk to anybody high up in PSP. Doesn't need to be Jumblatt," Neill said.

"What does Walid get out of talking to you?"

"I've seen Mohammed twice now. He says if we can pull in the Druze and Amal we might make peace. Do what you can."

Neill stood and dropped ten dollars on the café table. His head spun fiercely and he wondered whether it was malaria or blood pressure. "I don't sell guns and I don't sell people. But I'll tell his story, if he wants."

He crossed the patio of café tables and turned left on Rue de Californie, so dizzy he feared falling down. He walked to the corner and straight across Rue Bliss. Has nobody ever done this before? he wondered. Tried to talk peace with them all?

ANDRÉ CARRIED THE PAIL of water into the kitchen and put it on the stove. She turned on the gas and it lit, a low fitful blue. The water sparkled beautifully in the galvanized bucket. She was shivering and he took her in his arms, realized he was shivering too. There was nothing to say and no need to say it, just holding her thin and shivering in his shivering arms. We two bits of flesh, he thought, bits of feeling, thinking flesh, back from death.

"It'll never boil," she said, hugging her arms together. She glanced up at the barren shelves. "You want a cookie? I have cookies."

He smiled at what she'd said, then smiled again thinking that whatever she said in her rough-throated accent would make him smile. He dipped a finger in the water: cool. She shrugged, looked into his eyes, bit her lip.

"It's warming," she said.

He kissed her, behind the ear as she turned into his shoulder. "Such an optimist!"

She was crying, her shoulders shaking. Women are the stronger, he realized, because they cry. "We'll go away from this," he said, thinking of the people knocking, down in the *cave*. "I swear it."

"This is my home. I have children to teach. I missed three days of classes. I don't *want* to go away."

"Then you're crazy." The water got warmer before the gas ran out and he sat in the living room while she washed in the kitchen. *This* is crazy he thought, and went into the kitchen.

"You scared me!" she said, bent naked over one leg raised on a chair, rubbing it with a piece of wet towel. Her spine was impossibly long and went down into narrow full buttocks and long, long legs, a tuft of dark hair between them.

He took the piece of towel. "Let me wash you." You're mine, he wanted to say, and I am yours, but there was nothing he dared say, not wanting to harm it. "In Paris," he said, "we could just stand in the shower."

"Imagine, all that *hot* water beating into your shoulders!" she sighed. "Ooooh ..."

The people in the cellar, André decided, they'd surely be rescued by now. When they both had finished washing he tossed the towel over the chair and kissed her, her body all damp up his, skin to skin, feeling the fur in her crotch and the hard nipples against his chest and the lovely skin down her long back and the strong spine and buttocks and everything was holy, everything was good, her short hair and little ears, her lovely wide lips and big teeth and strong hips and such lovely long legs, their coolness up against his.

"My God," she whispered, "how beautiful you are. What a lucky woman to have a man like you."

"It doesn't matter, that –"

"I already know what *you're* like. That's what matters." She drew her hand up the side of his ribs, feeling each one, up around his shoulders. "But to get this too ..."

The air was cool, a mix of night and sea. This is a moment that changes your life, he realized, her eyes closing, her mouth eager, her fingertips sharp in his shoulders and her lips full against his, her teeth seeking his lips, his tongue, biting it but letting it through, to hers, and it's over now, he thought, suffused in her smell, I have her, have her forever, want her for ever, all I ever wanted, all these crazy thoughts cascading through his brain, thoughts he'd never admitted and now he saw that each was true, she was lovely, knew more than he, understood more than he ever would, she the crucible of life that he must honor and protect and love fully in rage and pain and despair and joy, and can *you* really do that, he thought, are you up to this? Because if you are, why are you here?

You're here because you came *for* her.

So now you've got her, why don't you go?

44

ALTHOUGH HEZBOLLAH IS *clearly in a continually stronger position,* Neill wrote, *Mohammed has stressed his distaste for the war and its impact on Lebanon. Although he has defeated the combined attacks of Syrian, Israeli, Christian, Amal, and often Palestinian forces, he has committed himself to what may be the most important peace overture of this war.*

By offering to keep his perimeter if other forces maintain theirs, by promising to relinquish arms if others do, Mohammed has broken through the long impasse on force and territorial negotiations. He has promised to work toward open elections and to live by the result. He has offered to send his Hezbollah fighters to help rehabilitate Christian areas, and asks that the Christians, Israelis, Americans, and Syrians help rebuild Muslim areas they have destroyed. Initial Syrian response has been positive ...

It was a lovely sunny day with no trace of war, pigeons cooing on the pavements, white clouds dashing across the sky. Last night he'd blocked his window with the table for fear of jumping out in his sleep – it's just the depression of all this horror that's made me like that, he told himself. It won't last.

A car went by dragging its tailpipe. The newspaper seller on Emile Eddé had opened his kiosk and Neill bought last week's

Figaro, the Pope on the front page, holding up his hands. Come help *us*, he thought, you're the one who caused this. You and your kind.

It took half an hour to get through on the radio phone from the Commodore to London. "Glad you called," said Commors, the deputy news editor.

"What do you mean?"

"That piece you sent, Neill. I can't accept it."

"It's the way things are!"

"We want impartial reporting. Not the Hezbollah line. If I wanted that, I'd send for their press release."

"Damn it, they're the focus of all this. The reason every peace attempt has failed is because Hezbollah's top dog and no one'll talk to them."

"I've talked with the FO, Neill, and Hezbollah's definitely *not* top dog as far as they're concerned –"

"What does the FO know about Beirut? They got out the moment it got hot."

"I've always feared you have too much ego to be a good reporter. Now you're saying you know more than the British Foreign Office?"

This is where you blow it, Neill told himself. Where you lose this job. "Tell me what you want. I'll write it."

"Fall out of love with Hezbollah."

"I don't even *like* them! I hate them all!"

"That's a problem, then. You *have* to empathize. Anyway, we're a little full this week, the miners, a backbench row, the PM's going to Belgium ..."

"Jesus, may she stay there –"

"We're thinking of pulling you back, Neill."

"*Back?* Why?"

"Beirut's just not fulfilling our needs right now. There's good stories closer to home. You're costing money."

Neill looked down at the torn dirty carpet, not seeing it, scuffed it with his toe. "Don't know if I'd *come* back."

Across two thousand miles of cable he felt Commors shrug. "Your decision," Commors said. "Call us after tomorrow. By then we'll know."

"In the meantime, you want me to send this last story, about the peace offer?"

"Sure," Commors said. "Go ahead and send it. But I can't promise we'll use it."

"LAYLA IS *MY* WIFE!" Mohammed whispered. "While you are not."

"*I* wouldn't be!" Rosa snapped.

He drew back, his hands retreating into his robe. Now I've hurt him, she worried, so finicky under his roughness, I must remember ... His disapproving way of tucking his chin back against his neck, his beard flat against his chest, made her hate him even more. Remember who he is, she told herself; the hard part's already over. "You'd rather be with me than her. Why don't you say it?"

Under his robe he folded his hands like a good imam and she hated him again. Remember what he's like, she repeated. She shook a cuff free and poured his coffee, slipped in the sugar. *I could kill you*, she told him with her eyes; he wasn't looking.

"I know it's hard for you," he said.

She gave him the coffee. "Nothing's hard for me."

He looked up, amused. "I can't imagine what you mean."

"I thought you were a defender of Palestine, a Warrior of God."

He sipped the coffee. "And you don't think so any more."

"I still need you," she said. "I want to change you, make you see."

It was as if she'd struck him – the thing he'd least expected. He couldn't help himself. "And I need you."

"Then why run to her?" She tucked her gown and stood.

"I don't!" He slapped the floor. "Sit!"

She glared at him: *this is where I have you.* She sat. "Every obedience is a favor. Remember that."

"I don't want to give you up."

"You make it sound like alcohol, some filthy habit –"

He reached out, scaring her, clasped her ankles. "Don't waste this time." He twisted his arm to check his watch. "Already I'm late."

She stood fiercely and swirled away. "Don't come back." She spun round. "I wish I hadn't bothered to rescue you!" She watched his face, her eyes watered. "No, I don't wish that!" Wiping savagely at her eyes she stalked out.

He wondered if he should call her back and decided no. Learn to manage your life without love. Everyone else does.

He was late again anyway. Layla would be furious in her own insidious way. His lung pained, the wound a hole razored out of him anew. Does it ever end, this being bent down by things? Bent down by what's on our backs and what's inside us. Our own great weight. And blindness. Bitterly trying to see the ground. The pain of knowing we will die.

That's what breaks our hearts, he realized – the moment as children we understand we're going to die, that there *is* death and it will have us. That moment breaks our hearts for life. To know this mysterious ecstasy must pass. At any moment.

He took out the Makarov and checked it. Eight bullets glistened in the magazine. Eight deaths. Who had made them? Who would make death for eight perfect strangers?

He stood, old pains shooting up his legs. From how many troughs of concrete going up how many buildings on his back? On the backs of others, good young men with strong hearts, from poor families, climbing that mountain to early death.

He'd been thinking too much. It brought sorrow, challenged things. So many voices to hear – which one is right? He nestled the Makarov under the gown against his heart. Always imagined it might some day block a bullet, save his life. But when the bullets came there'd be many and one little gun over the heart wouldn't block them all.

Time to go. A married man. *Mektoub*: it is written. He swallowed, his throat sore. He shouldered his few clothes, his Kalashnikov. These are what bear us down, he thought. Thinking of the Christian doctor, he went down the stairway to the main tunnel, its sallow walls creeping with slime evilly candle-lit, the air choked with resinous fumes. There was thunder overhead as a truck passed. They could blow you apart, he realized, even down here. Implode you. He ran up the steps to a brighter room where two mujihadeen saluted. "God be with you," he said absently.

"The car's ready," one answered. He had broad moustaches and bright black eyes, was swinging his prayer beads.

"So am I." Bright sun outside. Bright trees, flashing light off passing cars. The mujihadeen moved past him to open the car door but a smack like a cannonball smashed him back into Mohammed, knocked them down, Mohammed's ribs breaking on a low steel fence, the man's shuddering body on him. The air was loud with smashing bullets and people screaming and now a Kalashnikov firing and Mohammed realized it was his own men firing back, machine-gun bullets hitting the car, sheets of glass and chunks of metal flying. Another salvo hit the building behind him, tiles and bricks crashing. A bullet hit the man on top of Mohammed, skittering him sideways. Mohammed dashed for the building but bullets raked it and he dived into a concrete drainage trough, bullets spraying dirt. They've got me, he realized. Betrayed.

"TONIGHT WE'RE GOING TO THE CASINO. And drink champagne."

"I have to be up early –"

"I don't want you walking there every morning, Anne-Marie. It's too dangerous."

"How else am I going to teach? It's my job. I'll starve."

"I'll send you to France. Right now."

"Right now? *Heil, mein Kommandant!*"

He felt guilty, a fool, a man who steps too blindly. "It's safer."

"This is my world, remember?" She took his hand. "There's talk of a ceasefire that might last. They can't go on this way."

He looked out of her kitchen window at the rough-roofed assemblage of buildings, alleys, and light wells overlooking the Beaux Arts. Have they got our neighbors out of the basement yet, he wondered, remembering the faint *tick tick* of steel on concrete. "Half of Beirut's still standing. Why stop now?"

She reached out her arms to him, and it's so automatic, he thought, taking her in his arms, as if we've always done this. "Let me finish the school year," she said, her fingertips gentle up his back, softening bruised muscles. "Then we'll see?"

For an instant he saw how her lovely kindness would always be tempered by awareness of what was best, not for her but for those she loved. That the value of actions, the depth of love, is shown over time. It was impossible anything could be so warm, so electric as her body all the way up against him. "I just want what's best for you."

"You fill up my heart," she said. "That's what's best for me."

His heart felt it would stop. "Me too."

She kissed along the edge of his jaw, down along his throat. "You wait, I'm a bitch and sharp-tongued and ... You just wait and see what I'm really like ..."

QUICKLY AS THEY'D COME they'd gone. Just two, one with a machine gun and one an AK, waiting for Mohammed, knowing he'd come here, to catch him in a crossfire. And what had saved him was the dead mujihadeen with the thick moustache and bright eyes. "I don't even know you," Mohammed said, kneeling over his body.

"*Hurry!*" Amali grabbed his shoulder. "We want you out of here."

"How did they find me? There hasn't been a change in our personnel, a contact, for a week –"

"The one who came twice to see you, damn him. And first to your wife. He could have sent a signal –"

"*Who?*"

"The English journalist. With his silly questions, stinking of drink and ignorance."

45

WHEN ANDRÉ REACHED THE CORNER of Rue Basta he wanted to go no further. The street where he and she had been buried was empty, its ruins bright in the sun. There was a car-wide path through hills of rubble, a bidet perched atop one pile, pieces of wall on either side sticking up like stumps after a forest fire, chunks of concrete suspended on reinforcing steel like hanged men. He thought of the Palestinian girl, her slender tanned muscular arms, the Kalashnikov, wondered where she was.

A motion in one building made him reach for the Jericho but it was just an old woman sitting in a stairwell, rocking and weeping. "Let it be," he said to her in French but she did not look at him or answer.

He found the cellar stairs he'd run down when the bombing had begun; they were still blocked so he went down the stairs next door and through the wall the jackhammer had cut.

Light came faintly through the hole in the wall, dusty. Something was dripping, a broken pipe maybe, splashing slowly into a puddle. The slab was before him, half visible, enormous, waiting as if it had called him back, would get him this time.

He sat on the edge of the slab and listened. *Plunk-plunk*, went the leak, *plunk-plunk plunk*. He dug a brick from the broken wall, knelt down and thumped the floor, waited, thumped again, the beat Anne-Marie had used. Even the sound brought fear.

Tick tick, came the faint response of steel against concrete.

IF THE NEWSPAPER wanted Neill to return to London he'd take a leave of absence. He was going to see this through. See Layla again. They couldn't just send him way down here then yank him.

This damn place. That once was Paradise. Everyone so afraid. Natural to drink, keep the spirit alive. A pun, that. If he couldn't live without booze, it wasn't going to kill him. If he hadn't been drinking, would he have had the courage to stick it out here?

Freeman would have to pay the second installment, for Neill had met Mohammed. Not once but twice. Met him wired. "The way to peace is understanding," Mohammed had said. "Each of us learning to understand the other, and the part of ourselves that doesn't want to understand."

Neill felt affection for him, briefly, as toward any other shred of feeling, thinking matter. He felt an expanding warmth that covered all creation, even the evil. The sore under his arm stung every time his clothes grated against it. It's because you're coming down sick, he realized. Malaria. Fever worsens the pain.

Once you catch malaria it stays with you till you die, the *Plasmodium falciparum* parasite waiting in your liver for the next time you weaken, the next time reinforcements arrive from new mosquito bites. Like the virus of war inside the soul, waiting out the dull years of peace.

Like this damn transmitter under his arm. Freeman had said two stitches and that had been a lie. Had said he wouldn't feel it and that was a lie. What else did Freeman lie about?

In Neill's pain and nausea everything seemed a failure, a mistake. Was Freeman even MI6 at all? He could be CIA, Mossad, Iranian, Russian ... Once he'd mentioned Sandhurst – was that too a lie? Like the transmitter that wouldn't hurt, the virus lying in wait, a malarial parasite counting the days.

As soon as he got home he'd have it out, the transmitter under his arm. And deal with the paper. If they were going to be like this he'd take another job, go back to teaching. The thought of tiers of expectant faces in the lecture hall depressed him. Coming in with so much hope. It's because they're so young and horny, he realized, still believing in the future.

He capped the whisky and slipped the bottle back under the pillow. Nicolas and Samantha were strict enough Muslims not to like heavy drinking. A little wine was fine; maybe they were right?

It wasn't really Scotch, but some Egyptian concoction, in a bottle labeled "Highland Grouse, Ten Years Old Fine Whiskie" and sold at the price of the real stuff. But it had the active ingredient. He went out and closed his door, couldn't find his wallet in his pocket, went back inside and saw it on the desk. "Active ingredient, Hell!" he said, went downstairs and out the back into bright day.

He bumped into a man with a sack of potatoes or something, begged his pardon, and turned toward Rue Hamra. Spot of coffee, couple of rolls, just the thing. No shelling. Lovely clear day and no killing. What's wrong with these people?

He chuckled at the thought, aloud. A woman passing turned to look at him, a bundle of clothes and pots and pans on her head. "No shelling," he explained, pointing at the sky. She went on, flat feet slapping the pavement, a small mangy black dog trotting after her.

The Café de Paris was closed so he went to Movenpick. Two men sat at different tables. One had a *New York Times*. "That a new one?" Neill said in English.

The man glanced up. "Two weeks ago," he said in a heavy accent.

"I'll buy it from you, when you're done."

"Missing home?" The man had a wary, beaten air. "Here, take it."

A white Mercedes stopped outside and a man got out and entered the café, nodded at Neill, came over. "He wants to see you."

"Who?"

"Same as before – you don't recognize me?" He was winded, sweaty, one of Mohammed's men.

"Let me eat."

"We have to go. You'll eat there."

"I've got nothing to write with."

The man felt him for weapons. "We've everything you need."

As Neill stepped into the rear of the white Mercedes another mujihadeen came up from behind and got in the other side, forcing him to the middle. One pulled out a black hood. "Same as before."

The car moved away from Rue Hamra, over the crest of Ras Beirut and downhill. There was sun on his right knee, so they were heading south, toward the airport. The car was bouncing, moving fast, the two men beside him sweating. He made a joke in Arabic but no one spoke.

They stopped. The front passenger got out. Flies were bumbling and buzzing against the rear window. The engine idled, unevenly. Inside the black hood the air was thick with his hot breath, the whisky.

A shell screamed over and crashed into distant buildings with a great *crack*, making the Mercedes quiver. First of the day, Neill thought.

The front passenger returned. The car lurched forward, ducked round something, and purred in low gear down a hillside of narrow streets, the muffler echoing off near walls of houses.

"Why are we in Shatila?" Neill said. No one answered.

The car braked, turned, accelerated, stopped. One man pulled him out and another grabbed his other arm and they walked fast across a resounding low space like a parking garage, down forty-one steps past a room where a radio was playing *"Yours was the hand I sought"*, and into an echoing room with a bare concrete floor. Neill yanked off the mask. "Next time *he* can come to *me!*"

"There won't be a next time." Mohammed came into the room in a white robe. One side of his face was dark, as if bruised; he walked bent over. He sat, motioned for Neill to do the same. "You thought we wouldn't make the connection when you planned this?"

"Planned what?"

"Whom did you tell where to find me?"

Neill stood. "Absolutely nobody. I *told* you –"

"Don't yell."

"I bloody will goddamn yell if you say crazy things!"

Mohammed turned to one mujihadeen. "What did you find?"

"No guns, transmitters, anything. Just clothes and a few books and writing materials, some notes of Damascus and here, something about a woman with her face on fire." The mujihadeen turned to Neill. "A bottle of whisky under the pillow."

"And there's nothing on him?" Mohammed said.

"We checked him good. But he keeps throwing out an echo."

"Echo?"

"On the receiver."

With a grimace, Mohammed stood. "Go through his clothes, whatever. Find it." He turned to Neill. "You fingered me. That's all right. Part of the game."

"That's nuts!"

"We're going to have a serious talk with you. You might think about explaining now, save us all the pain."

46

"THERE'S NO WAY," the fireman said.

New shells were coming in and André waited for them to hit. With each one the earth shuddered. "But I can hear them knocking."

"People are buried in basements all over Beirut. They're knocking but we can't find them."

A Mirage, nearing. The fireman snatched André arm and yanked him down behind a truck. The Mirage went over, the building shaking. "Fuckers!" the fireman said.

"Give me a shovel then."

The radio was squawking. More Mirages were coming in, in sequence; the earth began to tremble. André imagined the pilots in their warm shielding cockpits in the crystalline sun, toy streets of the smoldering city below.

"We're out of shovels – we can't buy them, can't find them. We're digging with our hands."

THEY CUT THE TRANSMITTER out of him with a razor. There was so much blood he thought they'd cut an artery, but it subsided, drooling down his ribs. His hands and shoulders were numb, his bare skin freezing. "They said it was for my own good, to save me if something happened."

"Who's they?"

"I never knew. Thought it was MI6."

"You've been working all these years for them and you never *knew*? You consider yourself a journalist? A man?"

"This is nuts. I want my consul."

The man laughed, took up a canvas chair and sat on it in front of Neill, settled his maroon sports coat comfortably round his shoulders, put one white Adidas up on a frilly cast-iron table where a cassette recorder turned steadily. "Let's go through it all again. From the start. Every single act and word. Between you and them."

"If they're MI6, you expect I'll tell *you*?"

"You don't care, you're American. Anyway, they lied to you, then kissed you off for a chance to hit Mohammed. God arranged that another man should die. Salim Drahad – you must remember his name. You're his executioner."

He was *so* thirsty. Couldn't breathe. "Three times we've gone through this." His voice sounded as if it belonged to someone else, an old man's.

The interrogator's black chest hairs stuck out of his blue shirt under the maroon coat. He had a worried lawyer look. His lean high-cheeked face had perhaps two days' beard; his gold wire-frame glasses seemed to pinch his nose. The ceiling bulb gleamed on his bald head with the few strings of dark-gray hair patched across it. With a thumb and forefinger he pinched his lips; his mouth was incredibly small.

"Freeman's always been the one," Neill said.

"*Free*man."

"And this Dr. Kane who did it. At Gatwick."

"What else have you done for them? Who else have you betrayed?"

"I just made reports. I keep telling you but you won't listen!"

The cassette recorder clicked as the tape ended. The man

held up one finger. A mujihadeen put in a new tape. Neill couldn't remember if it was the fourth tape or the fifth.

"Tell us again. About the reports. This time leave nothing out."

"It was every trip to eastern Europe. They wanted to know who the good dissidents were, the ones we could trust –"

"*We?*"

"I assumed the country – Great Britain –"

"*Great* Britain? That started World War One so it could sack the Ottoman kingdom and take over Arab oil?"

"See it how you want."

"Who else did you do 'reports' on?"

"I didn't do reports on people. They were on places, the mood of a place. Prague in eighty-two – that kind of thing."

"And here?"

"I've interviewed lots of people."

"Tell us about them. We know most of them, but you don't know which ones. You leave one of them out, and we'll shoot you." He leaped out of his chair and screamed, spit spraying, into Neill's face, "Right away! We'll *shoot* you!"

"I can't remember everyone I've spoken to in fifteen years."

"In Palestine."

"Just finding the ones who want peace."

"How many do you suppose you've reported on? Those who want peace?"

"Just a few."

"Six? Ten? Fifty?"

Neill shook his head. When he turned to the right he could see a valley with distant rounded elms and split rail fences and a broad shallow stream down the middle with brindled cows on the near side.

"Do you know where they are now?" the man said. "These Palestinian lovers of peace?"

"The Middle East's a dangerous place."

"Keman Fahul blew up two days after you interviewed him."

"That was the Druze! You know that!"

"Hamrani died in an ambush, Kaffez was gunned down in a parking lot. Besmíl – you know what happened to him. His family's still grieving. As are we all. Al Fahz and Sallem – blown up in Tunis. You talked to them all."

"You blame *me*? You want a revolution, then you're going to get killed!"

"Not by *your* friends. Not anymore." The man held up the little silver transmitter. "They think you're right here, your friends. But they don't know we've found you." He waved the transmitter. "Now it's going to go somewhere and wait. When your friends come they'll be sorry."

THE KNOCKING WAS FAINTER but hadn't died out. André tried to climb down into the other basements but they were blocked. He ran outside and saw a man coming down the pavement with a tablecloth full of things. André asked him to come down but the man didn't speak French. Some Palestinians were patrolling the street and André waved them over but they didn't speak French either. One of them handed his rifle to another and followed André down the stairs and through the hole in the cellar wall. André knocked on the floor. He waited, trying to quiet his breath. The Palestinian said something. "Sshhh!" André said, and there it was, *tick tick*, steel on concrete.

The Palestinian lay with his ear on the floor. He took a knife from a sheath on his arm and tapped the shaft on the floor, the same rhythm as the distant knock. "They don't know SOS," André said, forgetting the Palestinian didn't speak French. The Palestinian yelled up out of the basement and the others came down and listened. They argued, pointing different ways. One left and came back with a stethoscope.

They knocked again but there was no answer. For half an hour they knocked, but there was never any answer.

———

THEY SHOVED NEILL into a little dark room with a draught under the door. His underarm stung and the smell of blood was nauseating. He'd let Freeman convince him, *when he hadn't wanted to.* Why do you do what you don't want, he silently screamed at himself. Why don't you *listen?*

He couldn't find the answer, could see every moment of the last taxi ride with Freeman: a girl riding a bicycle, her long black scarf up round her chin, a paper cup wind-bounced along the curb, the taxi's worn leather, frayed stitching, the driver saluting another on Albert Bridge. Freeman's fleeting hand on his knee, a benediction: "Go easy, Neill. That's what you must not forget: go easy."

Into this good night. The dark, in pain, waiting for what might be the end.

They wouldn't do that. They won't shoot you.

Freeman was just what Neill did to pay for Amsterdam. Money. When he could have been at home with the only family he'd ever have. In the mosque in Damascus he'd promised to get better every day and look what he'd done.

They wouldn't shoot him. The paper would help, the government, the same government he was always cursing. Will you really stoop to *that?* he wondered. He had to stop this worrying, just wait. They were going to beat him again but maybe not as badly.

The ceiling was so low he couldn't stand, walls at his elbows and back. No handle on the inside of the door, just a metal plate. He felt along the walls, the low ceiling. The floor was straw sticky with used diesel oil, concrete underneath. A little air came through a square duct high in one corner. Faint light came through the crack under the door. Squeezed down on his knees with his face hard against the oily straw, all he could see through the crack was a span of dusty brown and white tiles like farm fields seen from a plane, the horizon a white, scuffed baseboard. His underarm hurt; he sat on the upended bucket. A sick shiver ran up him, greasy. Malaria.

He'd been this stupid all his life. Always would be. Had to learn to live with that. If he was going to improve his life, what better time than this? If you're not happy, what good is it to be free?

"You'll never be happy," Beverly had said, "till you find the boy inside you. The one you hate."

He saw Freeman's strained face and small eyes, the cultured smirk. "What I meant," Freeman had said, "is I don't know how far we can leverage for you."

"First time you want," Neill had answered, "you'll drop me dead."

47

ANDRÉ WATCHED Anne-Marie cut the baguette, the lovely way her wrist turned. "I don't like you crossing the Line," she said. "Why not stay here?"

"I have to check my place, see some people. Find my dog."

"I'm sure he's gone, poor pup." She put the slices of baguette in the straw basket and brought it to the table.

He reached out and tickled her navel through a gap in her blouse. She slapped his hand and went back to the sink, brought over the steaks. He thought of her navel, bumpy and hard, how once she'd been connected to her own mother there.

"I keep hearing them," he said, "signaling us in the *cave*." He could feel the air going in and out of his lungs, the fresh air. "Do you?"

"All the time." She knelt on the dirty kitchen floor, her head on his knees.

"We're eating steak and drinking wine. And they're down there trapped and dying." He looked down at the steak in its pool of seared blood. "I just don't get it."

They stood and clung to each other, two halves of a whole, each trying to shield the other's pain. "All the years we might live," she said, "we'll never live through it."

She was long and close in his arms, and he thought this is how it would be if you have her all your life, always this reservoir of good faith, this sharp kindness, the rough throaty accent that made him love to hear her speak. "Come with me to France."

She leaned back, smiled. "And turn into a prostitute? That's what happens to Lebanese girls who go to Europe." She tickled his waist. "Already you are eating too much. Feel this?"

"That's muscle."

"That's *fat!* You think just because I'm some stupid Arab girl I wouldn't know? Why would I go back to France with someone like you?"

"Because I love you."

"You'll always be jealous, thinking I loved my husband more."

"Do you?"

"Now still, but maybe not always. Why are you smiling?"

"I love the sound of your voice."

"If I make you a tape, will you leave me alone?"

"I'm never going to leave you alone."

No one else, he realized, matters. Not the people like Christian St. Honoré who like you as long as they need you, the people who like you till it's time to kill you. People like Monique who only like you if they can screw you, people like *her* husband who like you only if *they* can find a way to screw you.

Her body part of his, as his of hers. It's better you're a widow, he thought. For in some strange way I've been a widower too, and never knew.

"IF YOU WANT TO UNIFY THE ARABS, attack Israel," Rosa said.

"They'd crush us," Mohammed said. "It's not the time."

"For you it'll never be the time."

"In 1982 they came to southern Lebanon, and we had no hatred for them. And they blew up our villages and killed our children, although we were at peace. Don't say, Rosa, that I don't care about Israel." He let his hand sink into her shoulder, feeling the lithe muscle under the taut skin. "You saved my life, gave me the chance to learn from death. You don't know how much I've learned."

"They've just tried to kill you and you want to talk peace! Without your help, we can't win!"

He sat back, hand on his knee, looked out of the window at the gathering night, tucked his djellabah tighter. "It's all tied up in death. My father's death, which took me to Yammouné, the doctor's death after he'd saved me from the Christian whose brother died, the deaths of my three men on the trail up out of Yammouné, the deaths of all our people in these last weeks of attacks. The mujihadeen who died yesterday because he caught the bullet meant for me. My standing on that land mine, and you came and built the wall of stones –"

"I didn't do it for you, Lord, I told you that, I did it for Palestine!"

"It was certain death. Standing there, I made a promise to God ..."

"You care more about God than man."

"Of course."

"That's still caring for yourself. Your private reverie of God."

"I need you to help make peace. I've sent people to others in Hezbollah, to the Palestinians, the different Christians, the Syrians. Will you go and see Karam Al-Nazir, set up a meeting?"

"If I won't?"

"Peace is just another way, remember, to win a battle."

"Not when it makes you lose."

"IT'S A PROMISE we made, my brother Yves and I. If ever one of us got killed the other would avenge him. Just a kid thing. When I was eleven and he was eight."

Anne-Marie tugged back her hair; the gesture made her seem infinitely lovely, infinitely removed. "And you're going to stick to this, something you said when you were a kid?"

"You'd break *your* word?"

"From back then? If I had to, yes!"

His body ached not to leave her. Without you, Anne-Marie, I can't even breathe. "You've got this commitment to teach these kids – that you won't walk out on."

"But mine is for life. Yours causes death. And each new death causes more death."

"Don't lecture me!"

She looked into his eyes and he realized hers were filled with tears, and felt agonized shame. "Every war," she said, "is rooted in past wars. Every murder comes from past pain."

"Suppose this person who killed my brother kills many others unless he's stopped?"

"There's no just war."

Why are we arguing? he wondered. Why, when in minutes I'll be gone? He tried to hold her but she moved away. "We're paying," she whispered. "Beirut, you and me. No crime goes unpunished. Especially the crime of justice."

He stopped at the door, took her hands. "I'm going to miss you terribly. Think of you all the time."

She smiled. "Silly."

"You be careful, tonight, tomorrow."

She looked up into his eyes, sad and angry. "I just go to school and back. Look for food. Nothing else."

"I'll be back in two days. Sooner if I can."

Her anger melted; she threw her arms round him. "Don't go! Please *don't go!*"

He saw Christian St. Honoré's silly little school smock sailing in the wind. Christian'd lost something that André found – what was it? Was he, André, just going through with this now because he'd told *them*, Christian and the bright boys at Matignon, that he would? Not for Yves?

He waited till she closed the door and slid home both bolts, then went down the three dark flights out into Rue de France, turned and looked up at the gray silent building, her shuttered curtained windows. Already it felt too long without her; he imagined a 240 hitting her building, boring down through three floors before it exploded on hers, the building coming down on what was left. Get her out, he told himself, thinking of all the people in Beirut who wanted to get out and couldn't.

The sun was setting through oily smoke of fires in the port, the distant crackle of Kalashnikovs like a carnival somewhere, over the next hill. Three F-15s pulled out of a dive, wings flashing sunlight over sprays of flame and plumes of white smoke. Somebody down there, he thought, burning alive.

He stopped at the street off Basta. Shadows were falling over the ruins, cold and windy, rats scurrying down the dark basement stairs ahead of him. He thought of himself dead under the slab, rats gnawing his leg. He crawled under the slab and knocked, listened, knocked again, but nothing came back.

He crossed the spine of Beirut down to the Museum. There were no Palestinians on the Muslim side, only Amal, who yelled at him in Arabic then let him through. The same captain was on the Christian side. "How's your family?"

"We got stuck in a basement together."

"Sorry about that."

"Not your fault. You told me watch out."

He climbed the Rue Hotel Dieu and round the Franco-Arab High School and down to his street. A few cars were circulating like fish with glowing eyes in submarine canyons. Shells were firing from the Mountain into the Shouf. Everybody, he thought, hates everybody.

His hotel still stood uneasily beside the cavity of its neighbor, splinters of floors like black spider webs against the gray walls. A dark low shape streaked downhill toward him, hit before he could pull the gun – the dog, the crazy dog, licking him and whimpering, trying to crawl up into his arms.

He knelt, hugging it, rubbing its neck, feeling the spine and ribs through the thin coat. "I'm going to have to fatten you up again, aren't I? Where have you been?"

It bothered him that the dog could never tell him where it had been. He stood, spine feeling exposed, and glanced behind him, seeing nothing.

48

"GUY LIKE YOU PISSES HIS PANTS at the first taste of pain."

Neill watched the toggle switch under the man's left hand. Up meant more and down meant less. No matter how hard he tried, he couldn't make the man keep it down. "How does a moral criminal, an infidel like you," the man edged the power up, "dare carry the Koran?"

"Because it teaches –"

The man spat into Neill's face; it got into his mouth and eyes, ran down his chin. "We wouldn't take you!"

"The Prophet says –"

"You killed a Warrior of God!" the man screamed. "You tried to kill Mohammed!" He was red-faced, the veins at his temples rigid. For a moment it seemed an act, as if he'd smile, then he smashed Neill hard in the mouth, a thick fist with a heavy ring. Pain roared into Neill's eyes and he saw the red darkness up inside his skull, pain shooting down his neck, his arms. "Stop!" he screamed, spitting blood. "I didn't hurt him!"

The man stood there shaking his hand, glanced at the Rolex on his left wrist. "It's nearly four a.m. How long do you want this to go on?"

"Please, I've *told* you! I'm on *your* side!"

The muscular hand with the hard ring came up and smashed into his mouth again. "Only God is on our side."

THE DOG GROWLED low and steady, paws up on the windowsill, banging its muzzle against the glass. André rolled out of bed and snatched the Jericho, tripping over a shoe as he snaked across the room to the darkness beside the window and the glass smashed into his face and he thought he'd broken it till he heard the gun's *crack!* as the bullet whistled past his ears, whacked into the ceiling, and he thought, shit, it'll kill somebody, diving flat, the desk tumbling. He scrambled for the door knocking down the dog and yanked it open, jumping back but no one fired. He went fast and silently down to the first floor and ran to the back, trying to keep from panting. He could hear nothing. Upstairs the dog was whimpering. That's good, he thought, they'll think they got me.

Silently he edged round the lounge which stank of old stained couches and tobacco, dirty tiles underfoot. With horror he saw the front door was wide open.

He dashed out through the door and spun round to fire but no one was there. He sprinted down the alley expecting the great thud of a slug in his back but none came. He ducked round the alley, waited. Far away a truck was starting, gravelly-voiced; a shell passed overhead weeping like an angel. Sweat fell off his brow to the ground. He shivered.

Daylight was creeping wet and misty into the alley, hushing footsteps in the next street, the tinsel of voices through a half-opened window. Cold stung his bare legs, his feet against the chilled ground. He thought of Anne-Marie asleep in her warm bed, his absence beside her. If they killed him he'd lose her. Forever.

With the pistol against one thigh, he edged back up the alley, using rubbish bins, a burnt Fiat, a pile of sand for cover. From across the street he could see the front door was still open, dark inside. The sidewalks were empty, open, another street rising to the left past the garden behind his building, from where the gun had fired.

If it was just one gunman, who fired once and ran?

Why?

Again he thought of Anne-Marie, how he'd let everything drop because of her. You almost died, he thought. And every second could be your last. If you get out of this you're going to do what you came for.

A dark shape sliding out of the door made him raise the gun but it was the dog running toward him, crouched low, tail down. He felt one-handed, patted its nose; it licked his hand and he pulled the hand away. Still no motion out on the street, just a distant hum of traffic.

Again he wanted to go forward but the thought of Anne-Marie held him back, almost tugging his shirt. A screech of metal made him swing to shoot but it was only a shutter rising on a window across the alley. An old Peugeot barked its way down the street, kicking up dust and smoke, a skinny bearded man at the wheel. Out of the unshuttered window a boy stuck his head and whistled. Another shutter rolled up, someone whistled back. The boy saw André standing there in his underwear, saw the gun, ducked from the window.

The hotel woman came down the steps, plastic bag over her arm. He wanted to call, ask her to check his room, but why would she interfere, catch the bullet meant for him? Get out, that's what she'd say. Don't ever come back.

Another face at the window, vanished – a woman's. Trucks up the alley, mufflers rattling like coal down a chute. Soon someone would pick him off, just for having a gun.

He walked straight across the street and up the hotel stairs with the whole world aiming at his back in his flimsy undershirt, his legs and feet bare, the tiles filthy and cold. What a silly way to die. The dog darted ahead up the stairs and stood grinning at the top, wagging his tail, happy to be home.

No one on the stairway and no one in the corridor except a little girl he almost shot as she came up behind him with a bag of bread. No one in his room.

He called the dog and locked the door. There was no hole in the window. It was not possible – he'd *seen* the shattered glass!

Could she have fixed it already, the landlady? Was it a dream? Stunned, he reached for it, lunged backward but no bullet came. He stood with his back to the wall. The dog leaped on the bed, turned in a circle, and lay down. André reached out: the glass was gone.

Already the landlady had broken the pieces out of the window frame and swept up the floor. But the bullet's angry dark mark was still in the ceiling. He backed from the window, snatched a blanket from the bed and sat in the corner, Jericho across his knees. It's going to get sold, he thought, looking at the lovely gun. It's going to get sold just like it was sold to me, to some new guy who'll wonder how the last one died.

49

ROSA had a way of sideways chewing her thumbnail, her eyes lost beyond the wall, making Mohammed wonder where she went, her face so passionless. A reserve of darkness within her that he rarely sensed, a cold hole that froze him. Then, warmed by her body, he forgot the dark behind her eyes, this watching eternally from a grave.

He'd taken this path unbehest. God couldn't be blamed. So much of him had failed – his fear of women, his passion for them. Was God tempting him, or merely bored?

"He had the transmitter," she said. "Who cares why? Kill him."

"Such a silly man. Believing in fairness."

She shrugged. "He couldn't be that dumb, thinking it was just to protect him." She peered at her thumbnail, chewed carefully on the other edge. "So kill him."

"I pity the new Lebanon if it has no mercy."

Again the dark look in her eyes made him shiver. "Not the new Lebanon," she said. "The new Palestine."

"The one you said I don't truly believe in."

"Only women love the earth they come from. Not construction workers."

"I was a goatherd in the hills. Don't talk to me of place."

She watched him, head cocked, fingers playing with a thread of coverlet. "You know how I know your heart isn't tied to your land? Because if I could be in Palestine I would be. You could be in the heart of your land and you're not."

She watched him try to slip his hand into his robe, forgetting he was naked. The hand like a furless puppy sneaked under the sheet. Somewhere inside him, she thought, lurks a coward. She stared into his eyes, saw him shiver.

He ducked down into the covers, reached out and touched her elbow. "I've never known anyone who tears me down like you do. Turns me into a child. Yet sometimes I feel more a man with you than any other place."

She slid the covers from her waist, bent forward stretching her back, feeling the muscles tug, let go, her breasts pillowed on the sheets. "The one you have to feel a man with, poor Mohammed, is you."

"SORRY, no coffee."

"What is there, then?"

"Sorry, there's nothing."

The man's craven sorrow made André want to hit him. He realized how cruel this was. "And you've got nothing to eat either?"

"Try down by the Abattoirs, monsieur. The Quarantaine." The man's hair was dusty, his face lined with old fear, a mix of pain and desperation, his shirt smudged and burnt. "Why do you stay, monsieur? Why don't you just go home?"

"I'm here for someone who can't leave." It seemed a good excuse till he realized the next question was why couldn't she leave – what was she doing and for whom, and how could this information be used or sold? And if someone had shot at him, why would that be? "But now she can," he added, "in a few days."

"May the Lord protect you till then."

André looked both ways out of the door: no one unusual in the sparse flow of passersby. It's not the unusual, he reminded himself, that kills. Checking back and circling, he went down to the port through the slippery, littered streets, found a café with no coffee but some fried fish and beans. Not a bad breakfast, he reflected, after somebody's tried to shoot you. With his bicep he clenched the Jericho, to feel it against his ribs, but it brought no peace. Like half the people here, he thought, you've got a price on your head.

This brought no consolation, that anyone can step out of the mist and kill you. He ordered more beans and put the plate down for the dog. Slowly, like lines being drawn by blind men, the shattered docks and jetties took form out of the fog, seagulls crying and wheeling over rubbish dumped by a truck into the bay.

He had a crushing sense of helplessness so overwhelming he barely knew what he felt, just empty dread. Someone had shot at him and now he had to change his base camp. He had to watch out they didn't trace him to Anne-Marie. And any time they wanted they could just slap a stick of *plastique* under the Ford and wait for him to turn the key.

He thought of Christian St. Honoré as a little kid at the Institut Suffren, the shy kid with skinny knees in need of a friend on the Champs de Mars. "We're going to do what it takes to stop you," St. Honoré had said in his office full of antiques on the Rue de Varenne.

He thought of Yves but Yves seemed weary and annoyed with being dredged up for all solemn occasions like some *jinni* out of a lamp. "We're always just what you want us to be," Yves said, "now that we're dead. Personally I don't give a shit about vengeance. You want to avenge me? Then kill the whole goddamn human race."

"You know what day it is?" André asked the café owner.

"Wednesday."

"Of the month."

The man went into a back room and returned. "The twenty-first," he said. "Twenty-first of April."

She wouldn't leave till the end of June. And only if he promised they'd return in September. But if he did what he came for they could never return.

He paid and walked along the shore toward the ruined yacht harbor. Gulls were fighting over something swimming through the waves – a rat that had been dumped with the rubbish. It was hurt, swimming in circles. Each time it raised its head above water to catch a breath or find the shore, the gulls dived on it, pecking its eyes. The surf tossed it ashore in a cloud of flapping wings, and it crawled, dragging its back legs, up the sand. The next wave beat it down and the gulls crowded round it, screaming and tearing.

He threw a rock at them and they pulled up, circling, shrilling. But why take the rat's side? he wondered. Didn't it kill to eat too? Don't we all?

War the nature of life. Love just a trick to keep things going. Like gulls killing a rat. Cockroaches mate too, consider it significant and beautiful. When it's only two bags of cells shuffling genes.

Do what you came for, he decided. But don't expect to know why.

A GUARD WAS PACING the corridor; his footsteps slid to a stop outside Neill's door. Neill waited but nothing happened; he bent down and looked under the door, saw part of a gray tennis shoe, then a dark black block set down on the floor beside the shoe: a rifle butt.

"I'm thirsty!" he called in Arabic, his ear against the door so when the rifle butt hit it the *wham* went straight into his brain. He sat on the floor holding his ear. The door screeched open and three men pulled him out into the bright corridor, pinned his arms behind him, gagged him and lashed his wrists. They yanked the hood over his eyes and hustled him along the corridor and back up the forty-one stairs, letting him trip and fall to his face then yanking him up, laughing and kicking him. "You're going to die now, spy!"

His knees smashed into something hard and someone spun him round and shoved him and he fell back, hitting his neck on a ledge – no, a car's trunk lid. They shoved him inside. "Make any noise and we'll take you out and drag you behind the car. Till there's nothing left."

The car drove for what seemed a long time, bumping and banging over potholes; his head lay on a sharp metal bar – a jack maybe. It kept jabbing him, the spare tire's steel rim banging his face.

He tried to hear the distant talk of the men in the car but the muffler was too loud and the wall of the trunk too thick. One wheel, the right rear, had a constant squeal, as if a rabbit or some other little animal had been caught up in it and was slowly grinding to death.

The car slowed, swung left, climbed a little hill, sliding Neill and the spare tire and jack first to the right then backwards. The grinding loudened; the car stopped, eased forward, swung left again, down a steep slope and halted. The motor died. The doors opened, shut.

He waited. After a while when nothing happened he began to count his heartbeats to tell the time. After several thousand heartbeats he gave up. What if the car had a bomb and they were going to blow him up? Frantic, he shoved up on his knees, back bending the trunk lid. It creaked but wouldn't give. He caught a foot on a tail light wire, hearing it ping, feared what they'd do. They'd done this before, put people in cars, left them in a building to blow up, and they get torn to pieces and then the building falls in on them and no one ever bothers to look.

The saint buried alive – who was he? Never canonized because when they opened his coffin they found him doubled up inside it, horribly contorted, the coffin lid slashed by fingernails. He'd been buried alive, they'd decided, and his anguished position showed he hadn't accepted God's will, had fought it. And therefore was no saint.

Neill imagined the saint wakened by the clods of earth thunking down on his coffin, the hard airless box with no room to move, screaming and yelling as the dirt rained down and nobody heard. With the gag on, Neill couldn't even scream; if he was doomed he was doomed, nothing to do about it.

They wouldn't just leave him like this. He was too valuable to them to die. He tried to slow his breathing, conserve some air, but there wasn't enough. He saw the kid with the ugly freckled face and the wall-eyed squint, his spindly frame hunched against the January wind. Where's your father, kid? I hate you, kid. See what you've grown up to be?

50

HAROUN'S ARAB GIRL went to get André a coffee but didn't come back. There was the sound of doors closing and a jeep snarled away in the night; Haroun came in, tugged up the black holster on his Wyoming belt, sat and poured a calvados. "Know what they did, those fuckers?" He downed the *calva*, poured another and one for André, swung his cowboy boots up on a hassock, dropped them back down. "A friend of mine, a doctor –"

"I still think," André said, "that girl is dangerous."

"They killed him for no reason. He saved their man's life, and when they came to get their man they cut the throat of the doctor who saved him! How are you ever going to make peace with animals like that?"

André rubbed the soft fur behind the dog's ears. "Animals aren't like that."

"First we thought, like they said, he was just some shepherd from the Bekaa. But then we wondered why would Hezbollah send this chick all dressed up like Lebanese Red Cross for *him*? Then we learn." Haroun leaned forward, poked André's knee. "It was your goddamn Mohammed."

"He's not mine." André shrugged. "It's *your* war."

Shrugging, Haroun mocked him. "It was *yours* too."

"That was France. Not me."

Haroun shook his cigarette impatiently; the ash fell to the floor. The world's nothing but a cigarette ash on its way to the floor, one of André's superiors had once said, a man broken-hearted by the memory of Algeria: what France in ignorance and temerity had abandoned.

"So now you've got some hot new pussy," Haroun said, "you forget all about Yves. Why is it that soon as a guy's prick gets hard his will goes soft?"

"Maybe it was being in the *cave*. Seeing what it's like. Maybe I'm just pissed at being shot at. On your turf."

"Everybody gets bombed, shot at. Don't take it personal."

"Maybe when I have someone I see life differently. I care. Worry about her."

"She's a widow, right? Best thing *for* her's a good fuck." Haroun put a record on the turntable. "Goddamn Callas. I hear this goddamn Carmen ten thousand times and she still brings tears to my eyes."

"Only thing'd bring tears to your eyes is a kick in the balls."

"You're like my own kid, you know? And your dad, dear to me as my own brother."

"I remember when you and the Syrians were brothers –"

"They knifed us in the back." Haroun spat into the garden, tugging up his holster and scanning the Shouf hills, whence cometh, André thought, our salvation. In the form of Druze 130s.

"I've been thinking, Emil. About vengeance."

"The Syrians have killed every Lebanese nationalist they could. They don't *want* us independent –"

"Today's friends are tomorrow's enemies. Is that worth dying for?"

"I'll find you *matériel*. You just get Mohammed."

"You've got a thousand guys with a better chance."

"My guys aren't French. You've got *entrée* – those scramblers would give them a real advantage against the Israelis."

"I don't really have the scramblers. And maybe I'd just make things worse."

"Killing Muslims never makes things worse."

"First day here I saw a Red Cross girl. Lovely, makes your prick sting just to see her. Helped her start her Land Rover –"

Haroun rubbed his craggy big-nosed, thick-browed blunt face. "Where was this?"

"Then the day we got out of the *cave* I thought I saw her again ..."

BOOTS THUDDED toward the car; the trunk lid sprang open, hands yanked Neill out and propelled him across the floor and down what seemed a corridor. A door screamed open.

"Do it!" someone hissed.

A hand snatched off his hood. A knife came at his throat, cut through the gag and it fell to the floor. His mouth felt unhinged, wouldn't close; the light blinded him. They cut the ropes round his wrists and fire spread down his hands into his fingers.

It was a little room with a sink on one blue-painted wall and an empty flue hole high up another wall with a spear of light down it.

"Be sure to let us know," one mujihadeen said in English, "anything you need –"

"I need to piss," Neill said in Arabic.

The man's knee crunched into his groin and he fell doubled over on the floor, gasping, trying not to scream. "That'll make it better," the mujihadeen said.

HEARING THE CALLAS Haroun had never played, André let the Ford float slowly down the foggy hills, moths battering the lights. A bottle glinted on the shoulder; he stopped and stood it on top of a white concrete post in the car's lights, backed twenty steps and fired, the Jericho punching his palm, the bullet sailing off a rock into the valley beyond, the acrid taste of flash-suppressed powder and primer floating in the mist.

He brought the Jericho down carefully on his left palm, tried to imagine the concrete post was the Palestinian girl. He squeezed again, the post convulsed and the bottle sailed into the bush.

His footsteps sounded loud as he crossed the road to the post. The bullet had taken a six-inch chunk out of the middle. He knelt beside it; the world grew so silent he could hear the dew coming down like smoky rain against the ground, the far tolling of a ewe's bell.

NOTHING BETTER than the absence of pain. He could stand, hunched over, his jaw half numb unless he moved it, tried to open his mouth. Teeth broken but he couldn't tell which. Just breathe, he told himself. Slowly. In and out.

Maybe now they'd leave him. He could be happy here, just in the absence of pain. The sink to piss in, urine laced with blood staining the flat porcelain. The tap dry, but a water jug on the shelf, water with flecks of rust and dirt and tasting of stagnant warmth. The room's wall of scaling blue paint and the flue hole filled with the songs of sparrows, larks, and doves, the crushing perfumes of lavender and pine. A cock crowing amid a distant crying of children, hush of wind in pine needles.

Out here in the middle of nowhere: had to be the Bekaa. Twenty miles, maybe, from the border. Maybe they'd send him back to Syria, let him go free. People like him, you didn't just drop them off the end of the earth.

This peaceful bed, if the pain would go, these boards on a steel frame, a Palestinian shawl for a pillow, a worn rug for a blanket, too short so his ankles stuck out at one end or his neck and shoulders at the other. He wanted to hunch up but couldn't for the agony in his crotch. It'll go away, he promised himself. Everything goes away.

Free. For an instant he didn't understand then realized: alone, at peace, nowhere he could go and nothing he could do, no money to earn, no roles to play, nothing expected, nothing possible. For the first time in his life. If he could get over this pain, if no more came, he could be free.

In a way he'd stopped caring about his body; it wasn't *his* anymore, wasn't anybody's. He was free of it too, not any *body*; it didn't matter what happened to it, he was going to leave it soon. He saw his body after death, the rot starting in his eyes, the rubbery skin, bile from the mouth, how the swelling body grunts and farts as the gut digests itself and the juices of death spread their sweet perfume. This body I've tended with so much care and abuse, as if life were just practice for what comes after. Instead of an end in itself.

51

HAROUN TOOK ANDRÉ to a street near the port smelling of sea wind and burnt buildings. There was a string of small shops and industrial warehouses on the landward side; in front of one several Phalange were loitering. They stood at slow attention when Haroun's armored car arrived; he got out and strode ahead of André into a half-ruined building that had once been a shop of some kind, car parts maybe.

There was a counter along one side and across the back and a trapdoor to a stairway behind it. One Phalange pulled up the trapdoor and led them down the slippery stone stairs to a low room smelling of cordite and oil. There were boxes of machine-gun belts along one side and rifles stacked on shelves along the back. The Phalange went to a pair of suitcases on the opposite shelf and opened one.

It's like money, André thought, or heroin – the brick-sized bundles wrapped in white plastic, and like money or heroin it can do such harm. He wondered what Anne-Marie would think, of how he and she had lain for three days under thousands of tons of concrete, and now with these little white packages someone else was destined, perhaps, to be caught under a collapsed building.

Haroun picked his nose and wiped it on the shelf. "I hate this shit. Scared stiff of it."

"It's our stock in trade, Emil."

"Lies there and then one day it blows. And you're gone."

"Where'd you get it?"

"Four Hezbollah brought it into Jounié in a flower van. They hit three places before we got them. This is what was left."

"They were trying to say it with flowers."

Haroun carefully shut the suitcase, pushed André ahead of him up the stairs. "It's yours now. To do what you came for."

They went out of the ruined shop into the light. Far up a pair of Kfirs were pirouetting in bright morning sun, playful and innocent, the sound of their reactors distant as rain over the sea. André thought of Anne-Marie in her half-empty classroom, the shattered windows and strips of ceiling hanging down, the blackboard on which with a piece of ceiling plaster she declined "to have" and "to be", the two interchangeable verbs of Christian thought, for a frightened assemblage of little Muslim children who might never grow up. This weekend we'll drive up the coast, he thought, where those planes don't go – if I can get across the Green Line. And if she and I can then get back through it together. It'll give me a chance to think about the *plastique*. About what I'm going to do.

"Goddamn Israelis," Haroun said, nodding up at the Kfirs. "Stay way up there and let us do the nasty shit, the house-to-house."

"They came in low enough when they dropped that building on my head."

Haroun opened the door of the armored car, tipped the seat forward for André and the dog to climb into the back. "Yeah, but if they hadn't you'd have never met this babe you're so hot about."

I never thought of that, André realized. Are we always so dumb about our fates? "You're pissing me off, talking like that."

"I'm trying to. Get you back on target."

"This deal isn't easy."

"You're so lucky, with those scramblers you're going to try to sell him."

"Give me some time to think."

"Think fast."

"I've got to change my base, everything, because of that guy who shot at me. Is there somebody around your place who turned Hezbollah on to me?"

The armored car lurched into gear, snapping André's head back. "That," Haroun said, "is one fucking stupid question."

A FINE LITTLE ROOM, really, with the sounds and smells of spring down the flue hole, its blue walls and sink, the mice that came out at night to rattle and squeak, mating and fighting and raising their young to mate and fight and raise *their* young. To the mice, he thought, their own battles and loves are all that count, not the blinding thundering wars we wage around them.

Best were the sparrows chittering and screeing in the eaves, building their springtime nests, fighting over love; sometimes one would land on the edge of his flue hole, fluffing its feathers and cocking its head to peer down curiously, a stalk of grass in its beak.

When there was food he'd step on the foot of the bed and stretch up to spread a few lentils or flakes of bread at the top of the flue hole. Sometimes the sparrows ate them, almost out of kindness, he thought.

At least the sparrows lived off the world, not each other. None was trying to suck the maximum out of his fellows, none was selling useless things at prices heightened by advertising, creating false hungers, so that those who bought them had to work harder and were even more driven and unfree in the hideous circle of debt and work. None was destroying resources to drive prices higher, none murdered his fellows or hunted for the pleasure of killing ...

It's *we*, he thought ruefully, sitting on his cot, wrapped in his rug, who work too hard, constantly defeated, worn to death trying to make ends meet. For eleven years he and Bev had been paying their mortgage, their "pledge of death" on that three-bedroom stone and brick pile with the bare yard that the dog dug up and used as a toilet and the gray skies glooming over, the litter and dog turds on the pavement and the stinking dirty hedge bitten by winter winds.

And because of that fine invention of Anglo-Saxon usurers known as compound interest they still owed the same amount as when they'd bought it. While the bank made a nice profit for the directors with Daimlers and top shareholders with weekend places in Kent and summer estates in Scotland, ready to lend it out anew to other young couples aching for "their" first house, begging to jump on the same treadmill. While life leaked out between their fingers like the warmth sneaking out between their walls and windows, and the only time you get caught up enough to enjoy it is when it's time to die.

Even worse, after how many more years – seventeen? – the house would revert to some "aristocrat" because two centuries ago a farmer's eleven-year-old daughter was sold to his illiterate ancestor with five hundred acres of strawberry fields. So that the "Duke' and others like him, who had never known a moment of honest work or worry could sneer down their slender noses at *us*, we who sweat and fear and worry and try to make ends meet, and die in the wars they wage for profit. Even the Muslims, crazed as they were by silly God-rapture and their terror of women, at least they'd outlawed usury: *they who live by usury shall not arise from the dead.*

And here he was in a Muslim prison. Why? Because he too had loved money enough to do what he had known was wrong.

Missing Layla. After all these years. Condemned like poor Qays to wander the desert.

And poor Layla. Everything that had gone wrong in Islam could be discerned in her sad fate. We humans stupid enough to take anything for happiness. Like me, elated when there's a scrap of goat sinew in my lentils and old bread. Willing to call so little life. Willing to forget what life can be. And when you're in chains you think all that matters is to be free.

Had it been real or was he imagining it? Had he for years fantasized a glory that hadn't been there? Layla's eyes, the turn of her head toward him, of her soul toward his, as if it would go on eternally, her smooth firm hand in his, her smooth young body under his?

Hot Beirut afternoons in his little room at the top of four flights over La Croissant de Paris, the afternoon sun's lemony brightness and the chatter of shopkeepers in the narrow cobbled street below coming through the wide damasked window, the far hush of the sea and the scents of the hills, all destroyed by madmen and buried in rubble, and now only he and she remembered them, he with sorrow, she in hatred and shame.

Strange that imprisoned in this little room with the blue wall and sink and mice and songs of sparrows down the flue hole, he could see the world so clearly, what had gone right and what wrong, what doomed you and what didn't, how easy it was to grow old without ever understanding, and die blind. Funny, he thought, here I am in prison learning how to be free.

52

RIDING IN A LAND ROVER into the Shouf hills reminded Rosa of another trip just weeks ago in the white Land Rover of the Lebanese Red Cross to bring Mohammed over the mountain to freedom, making her feel disgust, and then irritation for feeling it. The driver had wide moustaches sticking out from the sides of his face and this irritated her too, that he could be so caught up in his own image with a war going on. The Land Rover was old and rattled too much, the canvas rear seat had broken and she had to keep shifting her weight on the curves to keep from tipping, making her feel nervous and out of place.

They passed through one demolished village after another, the militiaman in the front passenger seat reproachfully announcing who had destroyed each one, as if somehow, indirectly, she were responsible. "This was Israeli planes," he said, as they crossed a battered hamlet where one huge tree trunk stood branchless and charred at a crossroads of broken, upjutting walls. "This one the Americans got," he said two miles further, where the Land Rover circled the jumbled ruins of perhaps fifty homes and farms. "It got so hot the road caught fire."

"We've all had losses," Rosa said.

"Losses?" the militiaman snapped back. "This was not losses but annihilation."

"*You're* still here –"

The militiaman shook his head, said nothing. The road snaked higher, steeper, through groves of eucalyptus and pine, occasional white farmhouses pinioned to the crests, here and there patches of white sheep among the broom and heather. It seemed to her strange that in the midst of war there should be such disconnected places of peace.

The soil turned to chipped white stones and awkward white boulders like the countless bones of dinosaurs. Sixty million years they lived, she thought; that's almost forever. We'll be lucky to survive another hundred.

There was a barricade ahead and she had to get out and be checked again for weapons, another strange man's hands on her body. "If I wanted to kill Al-Nazir," she said, "I wouldn't come in here like this."

"How *would* you do it, sister?" the militiaman said.

"Why should I tell you? Someday I might need to do it."

'Karam Al-Nazir isn't going to be killed by some Palestinian woman."

"Don't tempt me."

"I thought you were here on a Hezbollah mission," he smiled, "of peace?"

"Wasn't it Karam Al-Nazir," she smiled sweetly, "who said that only killing brings peace?"

The Land Rover lunged up the last few hundred yards to Al-Nazir's HQ like a chamois scaling cliffs, halting to wheeze and steam at the top. The HQ lay in a circle of stone walls and machine-gun nests, the black barrels of 155s and 57mm ack-ack guns jutting out of camouflage netting in sandbagged positions, tanks crouching on their treads like fat, bored toads.

Two more guards checked her at the door and one led her down a long hall of polished tiles and into a room with a painting of sunflowers on one white-painted wall. There was a leather couch and coffee table and large bright cushions against the wall facing a window whose glass had been patched with Scotch tape. An older fattish woman came in and took Rosa's hand. "How are you, dear?"

Rosa couldn't help smiling, seeing the woman's kindly round face and feeling her warm hands.

"They're awful," the woman said, "these guards, feeling you up. But we have to, four times just this month someone's tried to kill Karam. Once the Christians sent a young woman just like you – she had a poisoned knife and tried to jab him."

"What did she say she was coming for?"

"Said she was a journalist, some Italian paper. Of course it wasn't true. Here, come sit down." She tugged Rosa's sleeve. "I'm Madame Al-Nazir. My husband will be right in." She sat plumply on a cushion. "So tell me, what's a Palestinian girl doing with Hezbollah?"

"We have nothing against Hezbollah."

"Surely you do. They've chased you out of West Beirut –"

"The Israelis chased us out of West Beirut."

"Yes, but think about Tripoli, how Hezbollah fought you there, how they joined with the Syrians against you in the south ..."

"War is war. Mohammed has asked me to speak to you of peace."

Madame Al-Nazir smiled. "I'm too old to believe in peace."

"I'm still young."

"The young grow old."

"Not in war."

A boy with a thin moustache brought in tea. Madame Al-Nazir poured two cups and handed one to Rosa, who waited till the older woman had sipped hers before she touched her own. Madame Al-Nazir smiled. "Don't worry, dear, we won't poison you. We want peace as much as you. I thank you for coming."

"It's Mohammed who asked me to come. He believes if we

can unite, we can keep the Christians and Israelis at bay and force the Syrians out."

"We had no battle with Hezbollah. It was the Israelis who destroyed our land."

"Because they wanted you to drive us out."

"When they'd already driven you out of Palestine –"

Steps sounded in the corridor, old and hard. Rosa felt fear cold and sharp in her spine, wondered why. "Well, dear," Madame Al-Nazir stood. "Here he comes."

A FIREFIGHT had broken out between two groups of Christians near the Jewish cemetery, salvos screaming among the tombstones, grenades cracking with white-red flashes, a truck with a red cross lying on its side aflame, bodies burning in the middle of the street. André stood at the far corner hoping it would end so he could cross, but more and more men were coming on each side, a cluster of Geagea's men setting up a machine gun to sweep the inside of the walls. With a grimace of annoyance André whistled to the dog and climbed up through the dirty bombarded street to the car, in the hope of finding another way round.

NEILL WAS NAKED in a snowstorm and crawled downhill through deep drifts to the frozen edge of the sea and barefoot out across the cracking ice till he fell into the frigid water and dragged himself out on an ice floe and lay shivering in the wind, but there was only the one blanket and no way he could huddle on the simple board bed that would give him any warmth.

Someone was coming, he could hear the rattle of the engine then realized it was just his teeth chattering. He realized he was waking and tried to stop, unable to move he was shivering so hard, staring up at the blaze of freezing sunlight the flue hole cast down the wall.

"WHAT KIND OF A MAN is this Mohammed," Al-Nazir said, "sending a woman to do his work?"

"He's sent people to see the Palestinians, the Druze, the Syrians, even the Christians."

"The Christians? He has no shame, your Mohammed."

She smiled. "No peacemaker has any shame."

"And you believe it can end?"

Rosa glanced at the painting of sunflowers, the ack-ack guns in their camouflaged nest beyond the window. "You've lost three sons and two daughters. I shouldn't have to convince *you* of the need for peace."

For a long time Al-Nazir seemed to be inspecting the spotted wrinkled backs of his hands. "May their memories be blessed," he said. He sipped his tea, watched her in silence.

"I meant no harm. I too have had losses. My father, mother. My three brothers."

"God grant peace on their souls."

"Hah!" Rosa scoffed.

"If you don't believe in peace, what *do* you want?"

"For us all to unite. Against the Israelis."

Al-Nazir's mouth curved down in distaste, revealing black teeth. "Even the Christians?"

Boots echoed in the corridor and Rosa felt again a strange fear, as if she were a prisoner and her executioner neared. A tall dark-faced man came in and scowled at her. He was dressed in dark olive-striped camouflage and wore a knife strapped to one boot. He was slender and tall and his arms under the rolled-up sleeves were very muscled. "This is my son, Suley," Al-Nazir said.

53

"**LET'S GET AWAY** from this war," Anne-Marie said, "go up the coast to Byblos. It's so lovely, the spring flowers."

Something was wrong with the idea of him and her driving up the coast, the Ford's bad shocks making the rear wild on the curves, the slick brakes making it hard to stop, somebody coming up behind them with a bullet for him, an extra for her. "We'd have trouble getting back across the Green Line."

"The Museum checkpoint's open, one of the other teachers said. She went through this morning."

"I had enough trouble coming the other way."

"So I'm just your woman for here? Not to go anywhere with? You can sleep with me but you can't be seen with me? Is that it?"

He felt like a heel found out. "You're all I think about."

She caressed round his ear, little finger in and out of the hole. "So take me *some*where –"

To be alive, awash in her hair, her warm length pillowed on top of him, welding skin to skin, heat to heat, juice to juice. *God anoints thee with the juices of love*, didn't the Psalm say; it's what we're living for – how did I forget? "You already take *me* somewhere –"

She nibbled his lips, his chin. "You're hard as stone – a huge stone warm from the sun."

"Sleep on me all the rest of your life –"

She pulled up, looking down on him, breasts light on his chest. "Do you suppose we'll really ever get married, have kids, all that? And you'll come home with bread under your arm, and on weekends we'll go to the country?"

With a curl of her hair he caressed her cheek. "No reason why not."

"I can't imagine it."

He curled the lock of hair around her ear. She wrinkled her nose. "Three hours," he said. "By plane."

"Another world."

"We're going to be married in Normandy, in a church built by Richard the Lionheart –"

"He slaughtered eight thousand Muslim prisoners, Saladin's men, not far from here, in one afternoon. I'm not sure I'd want to be married in *his* church."

He imagined Yves' quick scorn to hear he was getting married – "some camel-keeper's orphan, some broad he shacked up with in Beirut –" No, Yves, he decided, you're dead.

She was so long atop him, slender and strong. Two bodies one skin. Flesh of my flesh. He raised her up with both hands, their bodies barely touching. "Oh," she said, "you make me *so* excited –"

"I HEAR SHE'S CRAZY about killing Christians, this Rosa."

"She came through their lines and got me, when nobody else would."

"No one knew where you were –"

"*She* dared to go looking, that's all."

"And now she's set up this meeting with Al-Nazir –" Sheikh Khamal plucked an olive from the bowl, chewed it ruminating, spat the pit into his hands and dropped it on the floor beside him. His old blind wrinkled face turned up as if seeking something on the ceiling whose rushes and beams reflected off his black glasses. "We're surrounded by infidels. They support us till they no longer need us, our faith, our brave young men. Then they kill our brave young men, trample our faith, and go back to running the world as they always have."

Mohammed shook his head. *"They who buy this life at the price of the one to come, woe unto them."*

"They've been running the world for oh so long."

"It's different now." Mohammed leaned forward. *"We're* running things. In Beirut –"

"Half of Beirut. Temporarily. A part of Lebanon."

"We have Iran!" Mohammed realized this was not what he'd meant, that he no longer *cared* to have Iran.

"How many times have we carved out a little piece before the infidels cut us down? What happens when Iran runs out of oil and we can't buy any more weapons?"

Mohammed cupped his hands and blew into them, the fingers so cold. Is it warm in Heaven? he wondered. Do our old wounds hurt still, after we die?

"You're tense, Mohammed."

"I was wondering, are we warm in Heaven."

"Heaven's never a sure thing."

"Surely you –"

Sheikh Khamal cocked his head, a wide smile on his thick dark lips. How white his beard's grown, Mohammed thought. You, too, so soon gone. "I don't give a fig about Heaven," the Sheikh said.

"In a sense it's all I ever think about."

"That way you'll never get there. God wants us to live *this* life, to do good now, not plan on the next."

"The question that has come to worry me since I met that doctor, the Christian –"

"I remember what you told me about him. He was a good man."

"To kill – is that doing good in this life?"

"To God even an infidel's life can be precious. You know well the ancient dispute: *be they Jews, Christians, or Sabians, those who believe in God, and the last day, and do right, they shall have their reward with the Lord.*"

"But *they who follow any religion but mine shall perish, on the last day.*"

"We *all* say that, all religions." The Sheikh chuckled, felt for the bowl, took another olive. "How little we need to appease our hunger: a few olives, a piece of bread, a little water, figs from the tree of Heaven. Our souls, too, so easily sated ... a few lies –"

"I'm trying so hard to understand."

"This girl, Rosa, obsesses your soul? You who were happy with your lawful wife?"

"Now that I've known Rosa I see I was never happy with Layla. But I try to make Rosa go. My heart aches so."

"I too, dear boy, have tasted the sweet flesh of young women. In this life there's nothing finer." He was silent a moment. "Nothing finer," he repeated. "Don't worry so about temptation. Your heart's good, be loving."

"And holy war?"

"War's not bad, though many call it so. There's far too many of us on this little earth. Like rats in a box we breed and go mad, kill each other. Men lust after men, women after women. I don't understand why God lets us overfill the earth. Even I, blind because my father married his cousin – like so many in the Bekaa, blind this way." He seemed to be having another conversation, with his long-dead father, when he'd been a boy eighty years ago in Chmistar, a pauper's blind child stoned and spat on. Is it from that, Mohammed wondered, that he learned grace?

"Is it only by pain," Mohammed said, "that God teaches?"

Again the Sheikh smiled and Mohammed sensed it was not for his question but for the old man's memories. "He touches us most through love, through joy. Like this young woman whom you can't tear yourself from. God teaches us best by the joys of the flesh. Isn't the most sacred thing we do simply to carry on the seed, generation after generation? The word of life? If we didn't lust so much, we simply wouldn't *be*."

"Yet you say war's good –"

"I say I understand it. Now that I near the door from this world to whatever comes next I think about the ancient days, the old prophets, when this was truly the land of milk and honey. The time of tall grass and wild animals everywhere to eat and streams of cold clear water, when you could walk for days and never see another soul under the bright blue sky."

"You can see it, that blue sky?"

"Very well. Sometimes, too, I can see the ancient times perfectly, which is better than seeing the present. And so seeing, I see we were better off then, that this's the reason for war. We're driven naturally to fight when there isn't enough. The strongest and most evil win."

Mohammed felt cold again. "I'll meet Al-Nazir."

"It could bring peace. The peace your Christian doctor spoke of. Just think of all the time you'd have to enjoy this young Rosa then. You might even marry her."

"I've forgotten what peace is like."

"War is simply turning the soil, my son. Peace is each new harvest."

54

AS ANNE-MARIE HAD SAID, there was no trouble getting through the Green Line at the Museum. They circled northern Beirut and Dora, little traffic on the road to Jounié, past the port where it seemed to André years ago that he had stepped off the *Larnaca Rose* onto the asphalt of the Holy Land. They drove past the casino and north along the coastal hills, the Ford laboring on the upgrades, yellow daisies and red opium poppies bright along the roadsides, the dog sticking his head out the rear window, ears flapping in the wind.

"When I was a girl we'd drive up here for weekends, all pile in the Renault and Father would throw the tent in the trunk and we'd camp on the beach. Back then the road was smaller and there were hardly any houses going down to the sea."

"How did they die, your parents?"

"Like everyone, a bomb."

"When?"

"Two years ago." She reached along the back of the Ford's seat, fingers in his hair.

"If you think about it long enough you wear it down. Like my brother. So you don't really give a damn."

"I won't do that. By numbing ourselves to death we numb ourselves to life. Denigrating death by denigrating life."

Going north in Christian territory there was no sign of war but for the troop transports grinding south with hopeful young faces clustered along the sides, the checkpoints every two miles, a certain sense of sorrowed emptiness and shame.

Beyond Byblos the road turned in from the coast through magnificent green valleys past a Crusader castle half dismantled, its great stone blocks being crushed to make concrete. They were deep in Christian territory now, with fewer checkpoints. "Where are we going?" André said, but she shrugged and smiled and for an instant he wondered is this it, would she set me up?

He kept looking in the mirror but there was never another car behind. Beyond the bay of Chezka she told him to take the road up into the mountains toward Amioun. "Where to?" he repeated.

The road climbed steeply, the sea soon spread out like a brilliant blue painting far below, the hills unfurling roughly, red-soiled, down to iridescent coastal valleys where greenhouses glinted like diamonds. A burro stood saddled in the shade of a new slab floor in an unfinished house, there were stone houses with red shutters and roadside shrines of the Virgin and water sparkling everywhere, in ditches, sliding across the road, in deep canyons with straight cliff sides a thousand feet deep. There were pines and sage on the hills now, out of the rocky maroon earth, and beyond and above the hills Mount Lebanon's white walls of ice and snow blocked half the sky.

In the towns the stone houses were overgrown with fuchsia, oleander and wisteria, set in orchards of almond, lemon, lime, apple, pear, and peach trees all in blossom, with porches of grape arbors cantilevered over carved wooden beams. Everywhere water glistened, gleamed, and sparkled through flashing meadows, great waterfalls hung from the crests of the hills that looked down on the emerald sea. In one garden a man in a conical straw hat was planting seeds while long-haired white goats munched reflectively in the pasture below. There were red poppies among white- and purple-blossomed trees, a white cat sleeping in a rusty wheelbarrow in the sun, a great white church dominating a green valley, golden light pouring through the pines. "We could live here," André said, "and never come down."

"There's no war here. Unless you have a husband or a son."

"I have neither. Neither do you."

Her hand lay on the inside of his thigh. "But I want to. I want to have you."

In Hasaoun, a lovely stone-paved village of twisting alleys and rock-walled orchards that reminded him of Briançon, perched on the edge of the grand canyon of the Abu Ali River, a man was selling vegetables from a loudspeaker van. Rubbish and wrecked cars clogged the flashing streams, a bullet-perforated VW bus lay at the side of the road. "We're closer to Hezbollah country now," she said.

Still the road twisted and climbed, the icy crests of the mountain never nearer. The trees thinned, vanished. Higher and higher the road twisted past villages of flat stone houses with old people at their windows, farmers tilling terraced fields behind mules, the sea spread out below the hills like a dream, something remembered but never true, and he wondered, were we ever down there, were we ever in Beirut, in a hole under tons of concrete? If you could heal that, he thought, this would be the way.

Tall trees clustered in a crotch in the hills, the mountain wall far above. "The cedars," she said. "These are nearly all that's left." He parked the Ford by the side of the road and she led him over hardened waist-deep snow to a stone church set in the shadow of the cedars. Dry goat dung lay scattered over the stone floor; on the wall a plaque announced the visit of General Weygand, "Haut Commissaire de la République Française en Syrie et au Grand Liban", on 26 September 1923. On a table gnawed by goats a book lay open, and someone had written "Little Jesus pray for us."

Sun slanted through the mosaic of the cedar branches in the song of the wind; new grass surged up through patches of sun-warmed earth; needles, boughs, and cones littered the snow. The air was cold and thin. The dog scampered and rolled in the snow, barking with delight.

A wide-trunked cedar towered over a snowy ravine. "See!" She pointed to a rusty sign that said Lamartine and his daughter Julia had cut their names in the cedar's bark when they had come here in 1832. "They call them the cedars of God," she added, breathless from the height, her cheeks flushed with cold. "Lamartine said the cedars of Lebanon know the history of the earth more than history itself ... Imagine what it was like, up these miles and miles of mountain on horseback."

He thought of the big old tree, in its thousands of years, humans living and dying round it like mosquitoes. A part of it had fallen, its reddish-chestnut bark the color of her hair, its sweet eternal odor of incense and myrrh on the sharp wind. Not knowing why, he took a piece of its broken wood and put it in his pocket. As if for luck.

The Ford coasted easily down the hills it had agonized up. "The Bible," she said, "tells how the Pharaohs of Egypt sent to Lebanon for the cedar to build their ships and pyramids. For five thousand years we've supplied all the Middle East, North Africa, and part of Europe with wood. And now there's just these few, along the crest – little ones. Just think how big they once must have been!"

The cold had revived something in her he hadn't seen before, a girlish spontaneity, making him wonder what she'd have been like without so much grieving, for parents and a husband dead. "I love you so," he said. "I'd give you up if that would bring your husband back. If that was what you wanted."

She didn't answer, her hand on his leg as they drove down out of the cold to the pines and reddish umber soil of the lower hills. I wish I'd learn to shut up, he thought, the caves in the cliffs across the Abu Ali River reminding him that man has never been safe from man. Through radio static an old song was playing – *Oh baby, baby, it's a wild world*. He saw his brother Yves before he'd left for Beirut for the last time, pulling his big black Honda up on the sidewalk of Boulevard Montparnasse. Yves shut off the bike and stood stretching, unbuckled and pulled off his helmet. He came into La Rotonde and put the scraped black helmet on an empty chair. "We've waited half an hour!" Sylvie seethed.

Yves leaned over the table and kissed her, hugged André and sat, took a drag of her cigarette. "They're going to completely screw us, these *emmerdeurs*."

"You're talking about our country's finest minds," André said.

Yves drained Sylvie's *demi* and waved at the waiter. He looked hard at André from under his thick golden brows. "They're going to send us in there to hold hands with people who want to kill us. When *we* can't shoot back." Yves waved again at the waiter. "What kind of world is this, when you can't shoot back?"

55

BACK IN BLYBLOS they took the street from the highway down past houses, shops, gas stations, and warehouses, on one side a line of huge sun-whitened Roman columns towering over the entrance to a garage, the hood of a truck leaning against one column while a man hammered it straight. There was a wall of great stone blocks half-covered with a torn poster of a woman taking down her stockings, wind-torn orange groves with apartment buildings half-finished and deserted rising among them.

"Turn here," Anne-Marie said. It was an alley lined with yellow walls, the blocky heights of a Crusader castle visible beyond the rooftops. A cobblestone path led up wide eroded stone steps into the castle's grave calm, amid the distant hiss of the sea, the scent of oranges, sea grass, lavender, and moldering stone, with broken walls and stairways emptying on sky.

From a battlement westward spread the turquoise sea, rumpled with foam; before it lay walls of carious stone and toppled columns, purple geraniums, daisies, yellow buttercups, and blood poppies pulsing with warm sea wind. Between the walls paths wandered, the soil littered with chunks of terra cotta. He picked one up; it was shaped like an arrowhead, a heart. "They used them as fill between the stone walls," she said. "It's a piece of roof tile, that." She turned it over in his hand. "See those lines – for drainage."

Warmed by the sun, it lay red and compact in his hand, still sharp along the edges. "How old is it?"

She glanced at the zigzag wall from which it had come. "This is the early Phoenician part. About five thousand years."

Stunned he stared at the little chunk of earth that human hands had mixed with water and baked. His arm stung suddenly and he looked down, saw a mosquito and smacked it, leaving a bloody spot. Time seemed disjointed; he imagined himself the last man, in a capsule in outer space, doomed to live alone forever, alone but for a single mosquito in the capsule and if he killed it he would be always alone, so instead he feeds it with his blood and it makes more mosquitoes and he feeds some of them also and so, from generation to generation, is never alone. Is that love? he wondered. Does it feed on you?

"Imagine," she said, "Beirut is only an hour away."

He felt it stab him, thinking of the short sword, the *gladius*, of Roman soldiers. For close work. Why am I here? For you, Anne-Marie. For you.

Thinking of the Romans who had lived here two thousand years ago, in a city then three thousand years older, he imagined a centurion walking these walls, trying to understand the past, like himself a warrior in battles not his own, fighting to aggrandize the possessions of others at the risk of his life, the loss of all that love had made worthwhile. He imagined the centurion in love, thinking *I was nothing before*.

Hand in her hand, he bent to pick up an old coin in the dirt but it was the back of a machine-gun cartridge. They followed a path down to the bluffs overlooking the sea rippling over mossy seaweeded rocks and strings of kelp rising from the depths. The bluffs were eroding into the sea, baring Phoenician walls, and in them chunks of pottery and tile used as filler; he picked up the neck and handle of an amphora that lay on the sand, trying to imagine the person whose hands had formed it. Could they, he wondered, ever have envisioned this? He felt suddenly helpless before the mystery of time, thought what Anne-Marie had said: by dismissing what we don't understand or fear don't we numb ourselves to life?

There was no one on the beach, no one to see except a few fishermen in their little blue and red boats far out on the swell; he and she took off their clothes and and swam through the translucent water that clung salty to their skin, seeing chips of tile and pottery caught in tendrils of swaying seaweed deep below. They made love on the warm sand, and afterwards as they dressed he noticed a shepherd boy playing a flute on the bluff. Nothing else was visible from the beach except the wind-rippled grass and ancient battlements, the fierce blue sky and the sea turning molten as the sun fell down upon it. We've gone back, he thought, thousands of years.

The hotel was nearly empty, the restaurant quietly echoing footsteps and the lap of the waves. How strange to sit at a table and eat fresh lamb and string beans, the way most people live, with so little fear. Through the restaurant windows they could see the fishing boats at anchor in the cove and the southward curve of the coast beyond, a distant smudge that might have been Beirut. He thought of Haroun's two suitcases of trimethylene trinitramine in the basement of the auto parts shop; it was like an unpaid debt.

Barracks, maneuvers. Drinking, laughing, fighting with the best soldiers in the world – he and Yves had done it because there'd been nothing in their lives.

The sun went down in splendor across the sea, and he thought of the moon rising before the bow of the *Larnaca Rose* as it brought him to Beirut, how little he'd known then, how much he'd learned. It's the only teacher, love, he thought, taking her hand. How sad she'd been, he could see it now, in her eyes, her face, like the remnant of an old tan, the darkness under the eyes, the stiff skin. Her worn hands. It'll all come back, darling, he promised. The happiness.

The wine sat untouched in her glass, like blood.

"HE'LL SPEAK TO YOU," Rosa said. *"I'm* just a woman."

There was a crackle of small-arms fire in the next street; Mohammed brushed at it as if at a fly. "How does he look?"

"Older than I thought. Lame. His teeth don't fit. He hates you."

Mohammed nodded sagely, hands inside his cloak. Wrath rose inside her.

"That's to be expected," he said.

"You think you can just *infect* everyone with this dream of peace?" She could not keep it down, the anger. "Al-Nazir, the Druze, Amal – they'll destroy you!"

"Have you really understood this war, Rosa? How it destroys us all?" He caressed the lapel of her gown between his thumb and fingers – like a child, she thought, sucking its thumb. "I think of you," he said. "All the time."

"You shouldn't!"

Even in pain his glance was mild, without fire. "Because you don't feel the same?"

"I don't feel. I've told you that."

"Palestine has to be more than an idea, Rosa. Live it with your body, with your heart."

"My heart's in Palestine. Not here with you."

"Your heart's in the ground. Already dead."

"Think what you will. You have me, what more do you want?"

"For you to *want* me."

"Why should I want anyone?" She thought of Suley Al-Nazir.

His hand scurried from his cloak, caught hers. "Dear Rosa."

Her teeth ached to tear his face, her nails to rip his eyes.

"Dear Rosa," he repeated, "we've so little time."

The firing died down; there was a distant thump of shells. "But when you die, dear Mohammed, don't you get automatic entry into Paradise? When I die, can't you drag me along with you? Just like Mary, the Prophet's servant girl?" She let her eyes sink into his; his were shallow, tremulous, furtive. "Or have you been fighting, dear Mohammed, under false pretenses? Not believing in Paradise?" She smiled, watching him shiver. "Have you been tricking God?"

His hand burrowed into her clothes, seeking her breast. She let it wander, annoyed to feel the nipple harden. Mohammed stretched along her, a cold hand timidly up the inside of her thigh, and she drifted back to Suley the son of Karam Al-Nazir, his hard muscular body, imagining his upraised angry prick.

ANDRÉ LAY WITH HIS LEFT ARM under her head, the sheet and blanket rising and falling with their breathing, the dog snoring at the foot of the bed. He could hear the whisper of the waves from the breakwater and a hiss now and then of lonely tires in a distant street, once the cry of a gull, startled, out of the night. Far away a radio sang, a cheap Arab dance swallowed and spat out by the wind.

The candle glistened in the windowpane but he couldn't see out, just the darkness beyond the glass, though it seemed he could look straight into Heaven, to the bottom of space, the utter blackness. He was startled again to realize how meaningless humans were there, the cold grave of love. It doesn't matter, he thought. Doesn't even matter that it doesn't matter.

Tomorrow after he dropped Anne-Marie off in West Beirut maybe he'd cross back over the Green Line and see Haroun, tell him it was no go, he could keep his *plastique*. Yves was dead; André couldn't bring him back. If anyone had killed Yves it was *la France*.

La France, that never turns against its own. *Never* deserts its own.

56

THEY HAD NO TROUBLE crossing back through the Green Line. André left Anne-Marie at her place and drove back along Rue Basta till he came to the street where they had been buried in the *cave*. He left the Ford on Basta and walked to it, but when he got to the building it had been bulldozed in and the one beside it also, there was no going back. He stood for a long time looking down, wondering who was still buried there, remembering what it had been like under the slab.

A dying sun crimsoned the ruined city. He thought of all the high explosives it had taken to destroy Beirut, of the people buried in so many cellars. When Anne-Marie's father was a boy, she'd said, there had been a field of cows behind his convent school above Emile Eddé, and when the nun opened the windows the smell of cow dung came into the classroom. Now for miles beyond Emile Eddé were buildings and streets, some ruined, some waiting to be ruined. The field of cows would never come again.

He walked back up the street; a woman was coming down, carrying a rifle. He thought about ducking into a building but there were no buildings left. He stopped in the middle of the street. *"You!"*

She smiled; it warmed his face like sun. "My little Frenchman! What are you doing here?"

He glanced at her Kalashnikov, the silver bracelet on her right wrist, her breasts beneath the camo shirt, the lithe compactness of her. The dog backed away growling, the fur on his back raised. Will she kill me? he wondered. Does she know? "I could ask you the same."

Again she smiled. "War makes strange bedfellows."

It was there already, the invitation. She could kill me, he thought. He wondered without reason was she the one who shot at me? Why would she? "How's your Land Rover?"

"I never found the keys."

I should tell Haroun, he thought: this is the one who killed the doctor. But it didn't matter, somehow; she was no less right than Haroun, the others. Why take sides against her? Even if I do kill Mohammed, that's personal; after that I'm getting out of this, it isn't my fight. "I got buried here." He pointed behind him. "We'd just been rescued when I saw you, the second time."

"And now you're back for more?"

He was silent, not wanting to tell her of Anne-Marie.

"You can get shot," she said, "just being here. What brought you to Beirut?"

What side, he wondered, is she on? "I was looking for Hezbollah."

"That especially can get you shot."

"Do you know where the command post is?"

"Why?"

"I might have business with Mohammed."

"He doesn't speak French."

"Are you with them?"

"Nobody's with anybody in this war, as you've seen. Are you a spy?"

"I thought I might have something he could need."

Two Mirages went over, the noise making him flinch. She smiled good-naturedly, adjusting the rifle on her shoulder.

"You're a virgin – couldn't you tell they were headed elsewhere?"

"Anybody can kill anybody here – there's never any reason."

"So you're a weapons dealer, wandering from one side to the other?"

"No. Can you help me find Mohammed?"

"Not unless you tell me why."

More planes were coming over, the ground shaking with their roar. "They're hitting the port again," he said. He looked at the Kalashnikov. "Why don't you empty it at them?"

"Maybe I'm here just like you – on a pretext." She shrugged; her every move was sexual. Why, he wondered, fresh from making love with Anne-Marie, does she excite me so?

"There were East Germans training mujihadeen in this street." She looked up at the battered buildings, the sky through their gaping rooftops. "Are you part of them?"

"I'm not part of anything." Shells were coming down in the port, Israeli, maybe – no, he decided, for some were falling short. "We should get out of this before one hits us."

Once more she smiled, and now he saw something behind it, like the skull under the skin. "My place," she said, "or yours?"

"My place is way across the Line."

A shell landed, closer, the ground shaking, roof tiles clattering into the street. "Come!" she yelled, running for a doorway. Another shell came screaming down. He expected her to go down to the cellar but she ran up the stairs; all the apartments were empty, smashed, till she found a closed door on the third floor and kicked it in. It was a bright little apartment with a kitchen, then a hallway, living room, and bedroom. The dog crouched in the kitchen, quivering. She dismounted the clip of the Kalashnikov and slid it into her pocket.

"Why up here?" he asked, breathless.

"Better blown to bits than crushed – no?"

"That day I saw you, I'd been two days pinned in that basement."

She turned and came into his arms and she was like a sister, a second flesh, no way he could prevent her. His body felt on fire. "I've got someone," he stammered, feeling foolish.

"Don't we all?" She reached up on tiptoe to kiss him, breasts hard against his chest, her mound shoved against his prick. She kissed him, beneath the softness of her lips the hardness of her gums and teeth, her mouth sucking him in, tasting like rose water, what her other mouth might taste like, her raw desire like high voltage searing into him, welding them, their bodies rigid together, hot together. *I've got to stop*, he thought helplessly as she tore apart his shirt, buttons pinging across the floor, another shell dropping in the street. Under her camo shirt and jeans no bra, no underpants, just her beautiful brushy cunt and lithe strong breasts with dark round nipples reminding him of bullet holes in the window frame of Anne-Marie's apartment. She backed up, naked, pulled him down on the bed. The building shuddered as another shell hit the street; she yanked down his trousers and took his prick into her mouth, licked it with the side of her tongue, and pulled him down on top of her. "Hurry!" she cried. "Goddamn it, hurry! Before we die!"

THERE WERE MORE AND more sparrows. Even in this dark tomb of a room you knew it was spring. Even the mice knew, mating and battling frenziedly in the walls. If the mice had dug through the walls, Neill wondered, why couldn't he? If the swallows could come and go, chattering and disputing over food and nests, the little voices of their young peeping out, couldn't he? If spring was coming?

As soon as he stopped shivering he'd crawl to the foot of the bed and stand holding the wall and try to smell the warm scent of spring through the flue hole. That'd be better. To know it was there. If he could climb out into that sun, lie on the sun-hot earth in the sun's bright heat, wrapped in many blankets – if there were only blankets – then he wouldn't be so *cold*. But no, you couldn't kill this malarial cold, it started in the bones and worked its way out; his soul was absolute zero and everything it touched turned to ice.

He was going to die here. No blankets but this one thin rug. A bed of ice with a blanket of ice in a freezer where the breath froze in his lungs, and exhausted as he was he couldn't stop shivering and it made him even colder.

Nice sun. Get out in the nice sun. Lie in the warm sun. Rise from this frame of wood and ice and slip down the long funnel toward the white-orange heat that was so bright and did not burn. Huxley's last words dying, "God is the sun", and didn't Bev say that woman in the car wreck had gone out of her body and could look down and see herself but didn't want to die, and turned back from the light?

He tried to imagine himself from above, an old sweating white-skinned man with his beard growing out gray, gray to the roots of his hair, his skin like pale cheese, cold and pallid. The old man sighed and his ribs puffed out and he took a shallow breath and sighed again. Neill noticed he wasn't shivering, but that was natural – the last phase before death.

The last phase before death, when the body has given up fighting; the body knows what's best, the body *wants* to go up to the sun.

Lying on his side the old man drew his arms up against his chest, hands folded under his chin. Then he was bones in a half-open grave, radius and ulna against the ribs, splintery little finger bones up under the jawbone that hangs open, teeth missing, in that last shocked grin of death. Then he was just dust windblown across the Lebanon hills that were not Lebanon any more, or anywhere, for those who named them named no more.

And the earth drifted through glacial dust storms toward the reddened sun, fell into it like a windblown flake of sand into the sea. The great cold universe hunched its shoulders and lurched on, stars and constellations were born and died, swept away, till that which could come forth came forth no more.

Yet he did not feel alone. This is what it is, he realized, to die. He *had* died, the earth, the sun. The universe had darkened into other forms and times, yet he did not feel alone. Did not feel *without*. Maybe nothing ends, he thought.

How silly then to kill ourselves. Like a drowning man whose life passes before him he saw why he had come to Beirut – it had been the pain, the every day knowing Beirut was happening and doing nothing to stop it. Knowing Layla was here, the agony of being without her when she was in danger. Thinking somehow he might help, when they were all fine people and it was so sad they should kill each other. When pain for one hurt just as badly as pain for another. With every hand you raise against your brother you wound yourself. And because he had not been doing anything to help, he had been raising his hand too against his brother. To not help is to hurt.

He'd come to Beirut telling himself it was to find out who had bombed the Marines, when all along he'd known. We all did. And saying it was to get away from Bev, to see Inneka on the way, and make more money from Freeman to support two wives, two lives and all the booze he consumed per week, per year, when that too was only to stop the pain. The pain of Layla, of seeing the photos of so many bodies on so many streets of the only town that had ever been his home.

Layla who had stayed inside him since the last night in the little room up over La Croissant de Paris, with the souk smells and sounds and sun and moonlight through the damasked window, the little room that was gone forever now. Layla whose absence poisoned all else: *Desire assassinates me*, said her broken-hearted lover, Qays. *What good does my heart do to love, not being loved?* But was not Layla also his love for life, and her absence its death? But if we lived forever, dear Qays, we'd never love at all.

The Layla who had moaned naked beneath him, thrusting her body up to his each time she came – she'd died long before the room in which they'd made this love had crashed in fire and dust. But she'd stayed like a diamond in the core of his heart, slicing it with every beat.

Now in this little cold room with the blue wall and the stain of sun down the flue hole, both she and the boy he had been had died for good, like the room in the top floor of the souk, vanished under bombs and time, just another story.

If the diamond was gone, if the past had died, could *he* now live? He woke and realized he was no longer shivering. He lay in warm light, unthinking, then realized there was no light, but he was warm, that the fever had passed.

57

"THE ISRAELIS ARE CREAMING YOU with these French laser-guided bombs ..." André waited for Rosa to translate.

"How would you know?" Mohammed's answer came back.

"I've been creamed too." André glanced at Rosa. "She can tell you – I spent three days buried in a cellar."

"I told him," Rosa said. "Otherwise he wouldn't see you."

Mohammed spoke angrily. "He asks," she said, "why are you here, when you all think we blew up your barracks."

"They weren't *mine*," André answered. "France is always willing to put her soldiers' lives on the line. For nearly nothing."

Mohammed seemed all sharp angles and pain. André wondered what had made him so. Is that what war is – exorcising old pain? Thus making new? "I can deliver the scramblers in two weeks." He sat back, watching Rosa from the corner of his eye. "Maybe sooner –"

Again Mohammed spoke. "He still doesn't understand why," she said.

"I told him, I've got a score to settle on another side. You give me a hundred kilos of *plastique*, you get the scramblers." He stood; settled his leather jacket on his shoulders. "I'll come back tomorrow; just send word down to the Museum to let me through."

Mohammed cocked his head strangely, pursed his thin lips into a narrow smile. Has he seen through me? André wondered. "He wants to know," Rosa said scornfully, "what you think of the chances of peace."

"Peace?" André smiled back, following her lead. "Peace sucks."

BEFORE, THERE WAS NEVER enough time; he'd always hated to see it pass. Now, finally, there was time enough.

Time to do his sit-ups and push-ups and one-arm push-ups and knee bends and running in place and isometrics against the blue wall. Ahmed, the boy who brought his single meal each day, with his cheery smile on his long dark-haired sunny face, would ask him "how's it going?" in his ruddy Bekaa accent, glancing back at the guard with the Uzi, and Neill knew Ahmed wanted to stay longer but didn't dare, feared the Uzi.

There was time to think about the little boy inside him, the one his father had beaten when he was drunk and ignored when he was sober. It was so easy, Neill saw, to turn out like your own father; true, he'd hardly ever hit Edgar and never Katerina, but when had he done much more than ignore them? Caught up in his own dear dramas, as Beverly had said, of love and death.

When the little boy inside you grows up alone, he realized, there's no way you ever excise the pain, you just learn to recognize it, try to keep it under control. Like a man with only one leg, you accept what's missing and try to live without.

There was time to think about Bev and what had gone wrong, kept going wrong, time to realize that with Inneka the only thing that kept them together was being apart, time to realize that with Layla he had been trying to ease the little boy's pain. But that you can never get deep enough inside another to fill the hole inside yourself.

When – or if, he reminded himself – he ever got out of here, what next? Could he go back to the newspaper, seeing it now for what it was: like all news media an amalgam of useless pre-occupations cleverly yet ignorantly proposed, a comic sheet for intellectual cripples who hunger to follow some simple story from day to day – which PM was screwing whom in one sense or another, the folly of importance, the illusions of politics and fame. When a society is well ordered it is only because each person down deep inside faces the sad child awaiting death, the mystery, the truth.

Now, for the first time, without booze, without sex, he had accepted, he thought, who he might be. It was only justice that he was in prison: he'd been a fool, had taken Freeman's word against his own intuition, had craved more than he had.

There was almost all the time in the world to think what might come next. But it was better just to live, in the song of the sparrows, the scents of spring down the flue, with the footsteps of his guard like the memory of death beyond the door.

"MY FATHER AND I talked it over with the others," Suley Al-Nazir said. "We agree only to a meeting, us and Mohammed."

"That's all he wants," Rosa answered.

"A neutral place."

"The problem is safety for both sides."

"He comes with ten people, so do we. No weapons."

With fascination she watched the corded muscles of his arms, the abrupt hard way he checked his watch, moved to stand. He was truly frightening, this one, no ass-kisser of peace like Mohammed. "What do you think about Palestine?" she said, her voice quavery, annoying her.

He swung on her, as if somehow she'd insulted him. "You should know better –"

"Obviously I don't."

"There'll be no peace till Palestine's reborn." He yanked a

cigarette from his pocket, lit it. "Any fool knows that – even the Israelis."

"And them?"

He seemed more and more irritated by her questions. "There'll be no Palestine till Israel's gone." His men kept coming in and going; she'd have no time with him, a pity. "Can you do anything beside ask questions?"

"I can fight, when I get half a chance."

"Hah!"

"You heard about the Life Building, behind the Byblos Cinema? Forty-two Christians ..."

He watched her, saying nothing, spitting smoke.

"I was the one," she said. "Alone."

His eyebrows raised. "*You?*"

"Ask Mohammed."

"Allah!" He smiled. "With a few more like you we might win."

"We *can!*"

"So why come round peddling peace?"

"That's Mohammed. *I* have no need of peace."

"Is this some silly trap?"

"No." She stood, making ready to leave. "But it could be. If there were someone so hungry for peace it got in his way, he couldn't see clearly. It might be time to pass him by, move on to others with less divided minds."

"People who care more about Palestine than peace?"

"People not afraid to win."

He snuffed his cigarette on the side of his boot heel, sat back down. A messenger came in and he glanced at the note quickly, waved the man away. "Or it might be time to entice me with such words into a trap of your own."

She imagined his thick lips rasping over her breasts, down into her belly. His jaw was like a blade, the muscles of his neck standing out like ropes. Is there any part of him, she wondered, that isn't hard? "Whatever I do," she said, "I do for Palestine. Take that how you will."

58

"**THE MINUTE** Mohammed's dead, I want Anne-Marie out of here."

Haroun turned angrily, bent over a map. "Just because she's a fucking Christian."

"Find a way. You want Mohammed gone, *you* make sure she leaves."

Haroun returned to the map, his back to André. "This isn't some military régime. You know the drill. She's not even on the Christian side of Beirut."

"I told you where she lives. Send some people, tell her you need her in Paris. Tell her it's for peace. A peace offensive."

Haroun was sketching in where he wanted the shells to hit, deep beyond the souk, near the Phoenicia. "You can reach that?" he asked the artilleryman.

'Goddamn right," the artilleryman said.

"You send him up to Heaven," Haroun told André, "and I'll see she goes to France."

"Let me do it," the artilleryman said.

"You've been trying for weeks!" Haroun snapped. "The Israelis, or the Americans – somebody – actually caught the fucker in an ambush two weeks ago and –" Haroun waited for the sound of departing shells to diminish – "even they didn't get him."

"I'm going," André said.

"Romeo!" Haroun called. Another artilleryman with a scarf round his head came in from the next room. He unwrapped one side of the scarf and André saw it held rubber buffers over his ears. "André's ready," Haroun said. "Tamp that stuff in well, where nobody can see it."

Romeo switched the toothpick in his mouth from one side to the other. He had on a dirty T-shirt and jeans with torn knees. He looked like the kind of kid, André decided, who plays a guitar for coins on the *métro*. "This is serious," André said.

"So's Romeo," Haroun answered.

They went outside; the roar of artillery was too loud to speak, to think, to breathe; André ran for the Ford with Romeo behind him. They got in and André rolled up the windows. "I hate fucking explosives," André yelled over the roar of more departing shells.

"So do I!" Romeo answered.

The dog was quivering on the floor and trying to cover its long pointed ears with its paws. "Don't worry, *mon cher!*" André yelled. "It'll soon be over."

"No, it won't," Romeo answered. "Anyway, I'm not worried."

"I was talking to the dog." André drove down out of the Christian hills into East Beirut, feeling uprooted and alone, vaguely aware of something out of place. He turned along the waterfront and stopped at the wrecked auto parts shop.

"Give me an hour," Romeo said.

"My ears. They're all screwed up."

"You should wear plugs. Like me."

The dog ranging ahead, André climbed the hill to Ashrafiyeh and his hotel. He watched it for a few minutes but there was no one unusual around, and no way they would have waited this long for him to return. With the Jericho ready, and letting the dog go before him, he silently climbed the stairs, packed his few belongings into his rucksack, locked the door and walked back down to the waterfront.

"I'll go with you as far as the Museum," Romeo said.

"No need."

"I'm headed that way. And just to show you there's no worry."

"Where is the shit?"

"In the door panels and under the back seat." He handed André the keys. "You drive."

"Damn shame." André ran his hand over the Ford's chrome strip above the door, along the faded blue roof in which the dawn sky was palely reflected. Suddenly this car seemed more important, tangible, than man. He got in and cautiously turned the key, expecting it to blow. As if unwilling to participate, the car wouldn't start.

"Hey!" Romeo called to two Phalange guarding the front of the auto parts shop. "Give us a shove."

Hesitantly they pushed the Ford and the engine caught at once. Stomach full of butterflies, André turned the Ford around and headed uphill. "I don't like driving it. Like this."

"Don't hit the brakes hard. Keep a steady slow speed. Watch for holes in the road. Don't pull up on the curb."

"Jesus! Is there anything I fucking *can* do?" Nervousness was making him swear, André realized.

"Just blow the son of a bitch to Hell."

"Damn shame," André repeated.

"Don't let anybody ride in the back."

"I goddamn well don't even want to ride in the front!" André realized he was starting to sound cowardly and resolved to shut up.

"Just you, *mon cher*," Romeo said. "No one else to do it."

"If I blow myself to kingdom come, my ghost is going to make life very hard for you."

Romeo shifted his toothpick. "Plenty of ghosts after me already. One more won't hurt."

"You truly know this stuff? It's wired right?"

"I've spread Muslims all over Beirut. They call me the Candy Man – divide 'em up into little pieces, just like candy, for the birds to eat." Romeo took the toothpick out, poked it into André's chest. "You park this mother in front of his HQ, get yourself some distance, a good viewpoint, pull up the antenna on your transmitter, wait for that fucker to come downstairs, and press this pretty little orange button. The transmitter will send a signal to the receiver wired to the blasting cap embedded in the RDX – you know all that."

"I know all that."

"If you get in trouble, set your transmitter, like I showed you, to automatic. Then even if you're not there, anybody touches the car, it blows."

"Damn shame," André repeated, not knowing exactly what he meant. He saw the Boulevard St. Germain in Paris, imagined walking down it hand in hand with Anne-Marie. Soon this would be over. For her too.

Both sides knew him at the Museum now; he had no trouble crossing. "You gotta be a gun runner," an Amal kid said, in crippled French.

"I work on one side," André said, "and I'm in love on the other. What would you do?"

"I don't believe in love," the boy answered.

André followed Basta toward Mohammed's HQ, driving slowly, watching in the mirror for cars behind. The Ford swayed a bit, down on its springs. He felt bad about the car, as if this were a betrayal, somehow, of the car, of the man who had sold it to him. The Ford was old and out of shape but had never failed him and now he was going to blow it to shreds to kill another human because that human had killed another human, and so on.

He eased to a stop where a mujihadeen was directing traffic. A big Mercedes truck thundered to a halt inches behind his bumper. Its engine was out of tune, its massive grille vibrating – could the noise alone set off the *plastique?*

The mujihadeen waved him on. André slowly pulled away, the truck rattling impatiently behind him; he shifted into second, the truck pulled out and rumbled past, its passenger scowling down at him. Maybe they're carrying explosives too, he thought, everyone here seems ready to blow everyone else away. You could say it's Muslims against Christians, Druze at Israeli throats and vice versa, but if anybody wins, in weeks they'll be tearing at each others' throats. Down to the last two men, and when it's all over one of them will stand bloody over his brother's body. And say *I* won.

He imagined Mohammed eating, taking a shit, smiling, not knowing death was hours away. He drove down Capucines and parked three blocks from Anne-Marie's apartment.

She came to the door with wet hair in a towel. "There's water!" she said. "I've washed my hair!"

He ran his fingers under the towel through her lovely hair. So strange, he reflected, to be excited because water runs out of the tap, but he'd become a little that way too, delighted with a few leaves of lettuce or a piece of beef. He kissed her; she pulled back. "There's coffee, too," she added.

He kissed her again.

"No," she said, "there isn't time ..."

He felt a surge of anger toward this school that kept her from him, kept her in Beirut, these little Muslim children. "Just a quick one."

"No!" She ducked under his hand and turned back into the kitchen. She's seen through me, he thought, feeling the horror of guilt again. He saw Rosa naked pulling him down on the bed, felt anguish and desire. I've lost you, he said to Anne-Marie, almost aloud.

"I'll be home at five." She was briskly rubbing her hair. "I'll feed you something good." She came forward, kissed him, her lips wet with spatters from her hair. "Then we can make love all night."

"I've seen Haroun." Just the name made her recoil but he pushed on. "He's sending a new delegation of Beirut citizens to Paris, to ask for help." He was saying anything that came into his head now. "Help for peace. He asked me if you'd go."

Her face sharpened. "You *know* I can't!"

"I said I'd try to convince you."

"Haroun – what's he know about peace? He's a murderer! He was one of those behind the Shatila killings, he murdered little children, old women – two thousand of them!"

"You're misjudging him, he wants peace."

"Only if he's losing, and he's not lost hard enough. Not yet. *Never* would I go on any mission of his! Who am I anyway? A no-body! What good can I do?"

"You're misjudging you too. You're a perfect example of why we need peace – lost your husband, parents, friends ..."

"So have we all!"

"And it isn't just Haroun," André improvised, "there's bishops, government people."

"*Bishops!*" She spat out the word. "I may be a Catholic but they're the ones who started this, those horrible priests in their monasteries. It's because of them I've given up the Church!"

He sat on a kitchen chair. "Anne-Marie, please. Please go."

She knelt before him, hands on his. "Dear darling what's the matter?"

This was the moment he could tell her, about Rosa, the explosives sitting in the Ford, waiting for Mohammed. He got up, brushed past her, looked out of the window. Sun was pouring into the street; it frightened him. "Nothing!"

Again she took his hands. "Whatever it is, please darling tell me. It doesn't matter – if you'll say."

He saw Rosa's mouth round his cock, her compact lithe writhing body beneath him. The bite she'd made on his shoulder was like a tattoo. How could he make love now with Anne-Marie? "Nothing," he repeated. "Don't be silly."

A truck rattled down the street. If he was going to have Mohammed it would have to be soon. At the door he took her in his arms; even this seemed false. "I'll be back when I can."

"I know you will darling. Don't worry, I'll be here."

The stairwell echoed with his footsteps. The hangman's tattoo, he thought, not knowing what it meant. He went out into the dawn-bright street that smelled of rubbish, sewage, explosives, death. Yes, he remembered, it's the death drumbeat of a hanged man's feet. I've seen it. He went up the hill in the warm sun, got into the Ford and drove it to Mohammed's street and parked it in the shade, up the hill from the HQ. There was no way anyone could come up from the HQ without passing it.

He called the dog out; strangely, it lingered, did not want to come. "Come!" he insisted, slapping his thigh. With the transmitter in his pocket he climbed the rest of the block to the crest of the hill and found a vantage point in a gaping rocket-shelled kitchen. The wallpaper, he noticed, was the same as Anne-Marie's.

Warm sun poured down the eastern hills; it was going to be a lovely day. The dog restless at his side, he sat back in the shadows, watching the Ford.

59

ROSA WENT DOWN the bright morning street, Kalashnikov slung loose over one shoulder, toward Mohammed's HQ. She'd seen Suley again but he wouldn't warm to her, stayed cold and rigid, fixing her with his close-knit black eyes, the tendons standing out like steel cables beneath the skin of his arms, the huge Magnum on his hip like she imagined *he* would be. Don't you have pity for anyone? she'd asked, thinking of herself, and he'd said no more than a viper under my boot. Why, do you? Truly if we're to win, she'd thought, he's what we need. But winning wasn't *it*, somehow, it wasn't what she wanted, not with him. I'm getting soft for him, she realized, just like Mohammed is for me.

From his rocket-blasted kitchen window André watched her go down the street. The Ford gleamed its valiant faded blue; he imagined it sucking in and blasting out in incandescent heat and orange flame, doors and roof flying; she was ten yards from it, eight, five, one –

Your sperm is still alive inside her, he told himself, don't be crazy, wanting to kill her … He put aside the transmitter, hungry to push the orange button, wondering why. It's Beirut, he decided. Just drives us mad.

Rosa continued down the street, watching pigeons pirouetting in the blue sky, thinking of Suley Al-Nazir and what he would do if he had a piece of Beirut and the southern suburbs, like Mohammed. He wouldn't let the Israelis sit there, that was sure. Wouldn't let them run their Centurions in and out, playing traffic cop and big boy on the block, blowing up every little thing that displeased them.

Mohammed was sleeping when she reached the seventh floor of his command post. She pushed her way through the acolytes and radio men and a clump of filthy mujihadeen being debriefed after last night's shelling down by the Phoenicia, smudged with blast debris and spattered with the blood of their comrades.

"I've been up all night," Mohammed rasped, rubbing his eyes. "But it's nice to see you. Been up two nights straight, come to think of it."

"The Al-Nazirs want to meet on middle ground, west of Baabda. They said they'll call and give us an area and then we pick the site. That way nobody can ambush the other."

He rubbed his face, his beard; this irritated her intensely. "They won't betray us?"

She let her nails sink into her palms, shoved her Kalashnikov further aside. "No chance."

He rubbed his hands together. She slid slightly back, out of reach. His odor was foul in the dirty, closed-in, sandbagged room. "You still don't like it, do you?" he said.

"I think we get more with terror than kindness."

"We've had ten years of terror. What has it brought us?"

She forced herself forward, knelt before him. "Please, Lord, give up this foolishness of peace."

He shook his head, looked into her eyes. She wanted them to burn him but he didn't flinch. "You killed the doctor," he said, "when you didn't need to."

"They would have recognized you! You'd have been executed, or spent the rest of your life in some Christian hellhole. I rescued you."

"Allah would have preferred to give me up, rather than him. That I know."

"How soft you get! Dreaming of peace and Allah's love for infidels!" She stood. "You've been eaten from the inside out, Mohammed. All that's left is shell!"

With long fingers he was combing out his beard. She snatched up her gun, started for the door. "If I have, Rosa, it was you."

"Hah! Just like you, blaming a woman for what you're not."

HOW STRANGE, Neill thought, at a time like this how every moment becomes precious. Nothing's alien, not the ants with their constant trail across one edge of the floor, touching feelers as they pass, not the sparrows or the flakes of peeling blue paint down the wall, or the flat metallic taste of the water that first had given him diarrhea but now seemed familiar, impossible to imagine otherwise. We need so little to live; we spend so much effort trying to be happy when it's actually so easy.

Remember, he told himself, that what seems simple now will once again be impossibly complex back in the real world. How, if I get back, can I keep *this* with me?

He remembered the little boy so clearly now, the one hidden inside him all these years. The bruised little boy had learned to lie for safety, never to be himself since to be himself would bring down rage, had learned never to trust women because his mother had never protected him, to hate men because his father had hated him, had used booze to lie to himself about his pain. And because he lied to others he lied to himself and therefore did not understand the world or himself because he saw neither clearly, neither correctly.

He'd not been the kind of person who brings joy to others' lives – too preoccupied with grave questions of death and purpose, forgetting that everyone has the same questions, the same fears, hears the same executioner's boots coming down the same corridor. All we have, he realized, is love, sex and laughter in the face of death.

Chittering and chattering, the sparrows took off and landed in the eaves above the flue hole. He had managed to widen the hole, left his little tribute of rice and lentils every day, which they would now take from his hand. Still he had the feeling they did it out of kindness, as if conscious of his fate.

All along, Neill saw, he had been trying to live his life to the full, to reach some imaginary point of completeness. He had not realized, all these years, that he'd already reached it: to live your life completely is simply to have and love a family, to pass on, in joy and understanding, the magic gift of life.

BY MIDAFTERNOON the sun had swung round to pour into André's blasted kitchen, and he sat sweating with heat. Truly spring was here. A bullet twanged over the housetops, then a rattling salvo, and it seemed so strange to want to kill when everything was coming to life. He thought of all the bodies rotting in their graves, people who had laughed and sung and worried about money and made love and had all the time in the world. For what had they died? When they could have been alive in this warm Beirut afternoon with the smell of honeysuckle and lavender and the sun sinking into old stone.

When he and Anne-Marie got back to France he wouldn't have to think of this, nor would she. Beirut would be behind them.

The sun grew motionless in the blue clear sky. As he waited, the buildings, the hills with their lacerated streets, tilting power poles, chunks of cars and stone and crippled trees, the redolent shifting sea with its crests of aquamarine and white – all seemed to be waiting too, as if the moment were eternal, and nothing would ever happen, ever change.

Like a cockroach picking its way daintily through trash, a yellow Fiat ascended the street, nosing this way and that among haphazard piles of concrete and stone, fallen trees and lampposts, an exploded rusted truck. There were four men in it but he could not make out their faces. Ten yards before the Ford, the Fiat stopped.

The Ford sat silent and blue in the sun-bright street. The Fiat's driver got out and moved a piece of metal from the road. He was wearing sunglasses and a cowboy hat. He got back in his car and shut the door; a moment later the door's sharp thud reached André. The Fiat continued up the hill and stopped under André's window.

Trying to see yet not be seen, he leaned out then ducked back. The driver and three other mujihadeen got out of the Fiat. They all had rifles and one had a radio. A rocket went over, whistling, missed the port and blew a funnel of water upward in the bay.

Someone was coming up the street – a portly man with his veiled wife and a little boy behind. Not now, André prayed to Mohammed, don't come now. Sounds echoed from below as the four mujihadeen started up the stairs. André drew the Jericho and backed against the kitchen wall.

The portly man and his wife and son passed the Ford and continued up the hill. The four mujihadeen were on the floor below, still climbing. The dog began to growl. André glanced at the transmitter; if they got him, next thing they'd do was check the Ford. Maybe Mohammed would be with them. He switched the little orange button to automatic.

The mujihadeen went past Andre's apartment and climbed to the next floor; he could hear their footsteps overhead. They wanted, he realized, a guard post overlooking Mohammed's HQ. He could hear them talking and laughing, one sang a bit of song, over and over, till another yelled at him.

He had a sudden feeling of total aloneness, as if these four men who shared this gutted half-burned building with him were not members of the same species as he, not even of the same universe and being.

A woman and two children were ascending the street. The two children, girls, kept skipping ahead, toward the Ford, and the woman beckoned them back. They ran back to her and she took each girl's hand firmly in her own. They won't touch the Ford, he told himself, tried to move the orange button back from automatic, then remembered Romeo had said once on automatic you can't go back.

The woman neared the Ford. She was tall and walked quickly; something familiar about her, the girls too. Anne-Marie.

60

ANNE-MARIE AND THE GIRLS were ten feet from the Ford. "No!" he screamed, but over the thud of artillery there was no way she'd hear. She saw the Ford, pointed to it, moved toward it. She went round the driver's side, pointing again, waving the girls closer. "*No!*" he raged, half falling out of the rocket hole. There was no time to run downstairs; he fired the Jericho again and again, hoping to hit the street, drive her to safety but it was too far. Her hand touched the door handle and the car seemed to crouch, recede to nothing, became a white-red flash, pieces flying everywhere, bouncing off the buildings, far up into the sky, its roar thundering up the hill, the stairs shaking as he ran down them screaming, yelling, crying, falling and running on, the mujihadeen clattering down behind him, yelling at him. Someone was firing at him as he ran down the middle of the street but he did not care, thinking kill me, please kill me. The Ford was a crushed remnant of incandescent metal in the middle of the street. He fell to his knees, arms raised, choking and screaming, fell over a chunk of corpse he thought was her but it was too small, was one of the girls.

There were pieces of her everywhere, on a splintered tree,

sprayed across the pavement. In the gutter blood ran like a spring. He tore at his throat, his face, searched frantically for her pieces, a finger wedged with splintered glass, a shred of bloody hair against the pockmarked street.

He found the Jericho and pointed it at his head and fired but it was on safety; he pushed the safety off and the bloody gun slipped from his hand. Blind with tears, he could not find it. "Anne-Marie, Anne-Marie," he wailed, found the gun but someone kicked it from his hand. "Kill me!" André screamed. "I did it!" But the mujihadeen simply stepped back and nodded for him to stand; other Hezbollah were running up. He lay over the pieces of Anne-Marie's body trying to staunch the blood.

Someone kicked him in the ribs. People were yelling, hands grabbed him, dragged him along the street clasping her torso. A rifle butt smacked his head, another. There was a marble lying in the gutter; he scrambled for it, could not reach it. It was her eye, staring up at the sun.

SULEY TOUCHED ROSA'S CHEEK. His rough hard hand sent shivers down her spine; a warm flush radiated from her belly. She blushed, backed away. "I'm going to give you a radio frequency," he said. "When Mohammed chooses his site, I want you to call us at once. There will always be someone there to take your message."

"You expect me to betray people just like that?"

He smiled; again she felt the tremor down her spine. "You know it's not a question of betrayal. I'm asking you because I trust you, and not Mohammed. I want to make sure he doesn't surround us, betray us –"

"I may not know. I may not be with them then. I'm not Hezbollah."

"I know that. Nor am I – we have something in common."

"And your father?"

"He may not come either. He's getting old; it's between me and Mohammed."

"What is?"

"Who holds West Beirut. Who is willing to deal with the Christians in order to gather our forces for the Israelis."

"And you will do that?"

Again he reached out, roughed her cheek. She felt a little girl, protected and enticed. "My father would do that," she said.

"Where is he now?"

"Killed by the Israelis."

"Perhaps we can average him for you."

"He and all my brothers."

"Yes," Suley said. "And all mine too."

TWENTY-ONE DAYS Neill had marked on the blue wall, under the sink where no one would see it, each day scratching one new line with the handle of his spoon as soon as he'd finished his meal. That way there was no chance he would become confused and make two marks in the same day, as he may have done the first few days.

Like a monk he had divided his day into distinct parts. Awakened by the sparrows' calls as first light began to sink down the flue, he would sit cross-legged on his bed and try to recall his dreams. As he recalled each new dream it led him to recall the others, hoping this way not to lose them, although he nearly always did, or they became indistinct and ran together, or only the most striking remained. For a while then he would bow his head and give thanks for life, not sarcastically nor with remorse, but simple thanks for another night passed, another day begun. He would fold his blanket and begin his stretches, first the legs, then the back, then the arms and shoulders, the neck which was always stiff.

When his stretches were done, he would take deep breaths, trying not to think, though the thoughts always came sliding in, or overwhelmed him like a waterfall. Then he would stand, stretch once more, and begin his walk.

To vary his walk he would switch from clockwise to counter-clockwise, sometimes changing direction each hundred circuits, often walking randomly, a few times one way then some the other. Each morning he would try to do five miles. It was seven steps round his tiny room if he did not take big steps; each circuit of seven steps made about three yards, each hundred and fifty circuits a quarter of a mile. There were six hundred circuits to a mile, three thousand circuits to five miles, but he could only do a hundred or so at a time; they made him dizzy, no matter how often he changed direction. In two hours, though, he reckoned he could walk five miles.

Exhausted, disoriented, and sweaty, he would sit on the bed and rest. He refused to lie down at this point because if he did he would fall back asleep and wake depressed. Depression was a constant and resilient enemy; each tactic that he used against it turned back on him; like a guerrilla army, he told himself, and he battled it with a combination of constantly changing tactics and total resolution.

After he had rested from his walk, he would do his poetry lesson. This was simply attempting to remember all the poetry he could, first in English then in Arabic and German, scraps of French and Spanish. At first there was little he recalled, not even a full Shakespeare sonnet but only pieces:

Shall I compare thee to a summer's day?

... rough winds shall shake the darling buds of May ...

But soon they were coming back in bigger and bigger pieces; like the dreams, the more he remembered the more he could re-member. Not only Shakespeare but Donne, Herbert, Housman, Gray, Shelley, Wordsworth, Eliot; and not only the English but Ben al Yayyab, Ziryab, the great poets of the Moorish enlight-enment, and Goethe, Schiller, Heine, Baudelaire, Verlaine. By midmorning he'd finished his poetry lesson and locked both new and old away in his mind, and began his swim, which involved lying across the end of his bed and doing the breast stroke with his arms and a kick with his feet. This was very exhausting; after a short while he would be forced to lie on the floor and rest.

After the noon muezzin's call, he began his religious instruction, first remembering as many *suras* of the Koran as he could and trying to see the meaning of each, its connection with the rest. This was difficult as he remembered so few; even Ahmed, when he asked him, would not enlighten him, glancing nervously toward the door where a guard waited stolidly with an Uzi.

After the Koran he tried to remember the books of the Bible and anything he could of each; the Old Testament was much like the Koran, he found, and the New more confusing because the tale was told from so many sides.

Religious instruction ended with a period of what, refusing to call prayer, he termed simple meditation: going beyond what he had remembered of the Koran and the Bible, he sat still and tried to fall back inside himself down the long corridor of time to a wider sense of life, the world, trying to see things in the whole, as a god might. As in his early morning meditation, he tried not to think, go beyond the flesh, the self, and as in the morning, he kept cycling right back to himself, an ant across his knee, a fly around his head, a clatter of sparrows above the flue.

At the muezzin's fourth call he would go, as he termed it, out for a run, which involved a simple jog in place, at first a thousand steps, then two thousand, till by now he had reached ten thousand steps.

Then came the time he loved best. Sitting on the edge of his bed, though never lying down, he would continue the recall of his life. First he had tried to remember every birthday, for they were the easiest, then other important days, his marriage, the birth of his children, changes of jobs, meeting every woman he'd loved, every friend. He tried to remember his happiest days and saddest, and what had made each so, every great meal, every marvelous night in bed with a new woman, the most beautiful landscapes, the loveliest songs.

Punctually after the muezzin's last call Ahmed would bring him dinner. This he lingered over long as he could, sometimes tasting each grain of rice separately, each flake of bread. No matter how scant the meal he always set a bit aside to put up inside the flue early the next morning; no matter how hungry he was, and there was never enough, he kept this link with others, with the sparrows, his key to life.

After dinner was free time; he lay on his cot and thought about his past, what had gone wrong and why, what if he lived he might improve. You can't amend old wrongs, he realized, the ones you've already done. But you can watch out for new ones.

He thought constantly of Bev and the children, knew he was missing them horribly but refused to give in to it. He had accomplished, he now understood, the most important thing in life, creating a family, but he had failed utterly because he had not given them a stable loving life. What if, he often wondered, he and Bev like the poor Lebanese had all these years just been fighting their own unnecessary holy war?

Despite the rhythm and determination, there were days when nothing worked; despair crushed him, he lay on his cot and tried not to think, not to live, barely caring to rise when he had to urinate in the sink or defecate in the bucket Ahmed emptied so faithfully each evening.

Today he'd been thinking of the night club, Hell, in Bratislava. He'd gone there because the poster of the rat-man skull cleaving the flaming city in half had reminded him of Beirut. He had gone to Hell for the same reason he had come to Beirut, to try to heal his own divided past, much as he had hoped that by talking to Mohammed he could aid the Lebanese reconciliation. But his own divided commitments, not only to the paper but also, secretly, to Freeman, had condemned this act before it had been undertaken. If we are going to tread a mean, he realized, we must do it openly, have nothing hidden.

He had worked secretly for Freeman because he thought he needed money but the money had been only to maintain his own divided life. He was married and had children with Beverly; what right or purpose had he in creating a life with Inneka as well? She like everyone wanted a deep love in her life, and her relationship with him ruined this possibility.

Like Beirut, his own life had been cleaved apart; by ending up in what someone had called a Hezbollah hellhole he had despite himself been unified.

Maybe Beirut and Lebanon might also someday be reunited. Or was the need to war genetic? The self-reinforcing heredity of the killer as survivor?

He had finished his long-distance run; it was hotter than usual and he had only done six thousand four hundred and eighty-seven steps when there was a rumble of a car and the rattle of gravel; doors slammed, there was silence then the sound of a heavy sack being dragged down the corridor.

Ahmed opened the door. Two mujihadeen dragged the sack into the room, forcing Neill back on his bed. It was not a sack but a sandy-haired man covered in half-dried blood. One of the mujihadeen pointed his AK47 at Neill and pulled the trigger; it made a loud click as the hammer came down on an empty chamber. "Soon," he said, "you'll know what a real bullet feels like."

61

AFTER THE MUJIHADEEN had gone Neill pulled the sandy-haired man up on the bed, unwrapped the barbed wire tying his wrists, washed the blood from his face and hair, took off his shirt and washed the blood from his chest and back. He had been punched and kicked many times; his front teeth were snapped off, bloody stumps, his ribs broken, one of them poking through the skin. He was French but spoke good English, better than Neill's French; when Neill asked him what had happened he just turned away, wrapped his head in his battered arms and stared at the wall.

Ahmed brought supper early but the Frenchman did not eat. Neill made him drink water, tried to clean the infection round the rib hole in his chest and the bruises on his face and body. The pain of his broken teeth must have been enormous but the Frenchman did not say. To Neill's questions he would only answer that he had murdered someone and deserved to die.

That night Neill spent on the floor, beetles and mice scuttling over him. The Frenchman did not seem to be sleeping but made no sound except an occasional sigh. At one point he seemed to be weeping but when Neill went to him he was silent, did not answer.

In the morning, surprisingly, Ahmed brought a cup of coffee and several chunks of bread. Neill soaked the bread in the coffee and fed it to the Frenchman one piece at a time, while the Frenchman in a flat listless voice began to tell his story. The air was already thick; it was going to be a hot day. With two of them in the tiny room there was barely air to breathe.

By the third day the Frenchman began to sit up, tried to move around in the tiny room. He was too big and too hurt; there was no way Neill could stay out of his way. "I thought I could have vengeance," the Frenchman whispered, "and love too. But the more love I had, the less I cared for vengeance. I did it because that's what I came for, I thought. But really all along I came because I had no love. When you have no love you'll do anything. Nothing matters."

"You were just caught up in what you felt you had to do." Now that he, Neill, had found a core in his own life, it seemed impossible that he could not help another poor soul seeking his.

"*She* got punished because *I* wouldn't learn." Tears were running down the Frenchman's face, around the scabs and bruises. "She must have gone back to her apartment for lunch, hoping I'd be there," he said after a while. "She must have picked up the two girls on her way back to school, from their parents. On top of killing Anne-Marie, I killed the two little girls who lived through that hell with us, in the cellar." His hands reached out in supplication. "Why? Why kill them now, after they've been through so much, after they *survived*?"

"*If God should punish men for their iniquity He would not leave on earth a single living thing.*"

"What's that?"

"The Koran. That's the local view. Life is full of horror." Neill sensed he was sounding sanctimonious. "We have to live with whatever we get."

André stared at him. "What if you lost the one you loved? What if you killed her?"

"In a sense I did, once. In a sense, several times."

"In a sense!" André mocked.

Neill nodded. "You're right. I'm a fool. The trouble with pain is that nothing alleviates it. Except time."

André swung his feet over the side of the bed, grimaced and stood. "And death."

THE PHONES WERE DOWN in West Beirut and Rosa finally ran all the way down Hamra and up to the Commodore and used the radio. As Suley had promised, someone was waiting, and answered on the first ring. "It's to be on the first floor of the offices across from the old British base east of the US Marine post at Lima," she said. "That's where Mohammed wants to have it. His CP is going to radio Suley when we get there. There'll be ten of us, as agreed, in two cars."

"When?"

"In three hours."

"Is he bringing weapons?"

"Just in the cars. Not inside the building."

"We'll be waiting for his call."

The line went dead. I too, she felt suddenly, I too will end like that, the sudden numb buzz. Long before Palestine is won. She remembered a diary she'd written as a girl; after the Israeli attack on Mount Hermon she had buried it in an empty shell casing in the field where she had buried her parents. "I'm going to die soon," she had written in an angry schoolgirl scrawl. "You who find this diary remember me, and that I died for Palestine."

They left West Beirut in two Mercedes, Rosa and Mohammed in the second. Something was going to happen, she could sense it. Each time a new phase had begun in her life she'd had the same feeling. I'm through with you, she said silently to

Mohammed, who rode peacefully, not intervening in the others' conversations, his hands tucked inside his gown. Suley won't kill him, she thought, he has too much spiritual following. The Al-Nazirs, who are more committed than he, will just use him to their ends. And I will help them. He may be married to the Mother of the Revolution but she does nothing for Palestine; her revolution is based on the development of the individual, she says, but she's too dumb to realize an individual can't develop with a boot heel on his throat.

62

THEY DROVE SOUTH PAST THE RUINS of Shatila where the Christians had slaughtered the Palestinian women and children after the men had agreed to leave and the Americans had promised they would protect their families. When other Palestinians had joined those who remained, their Muslim brothers the Shia Amal had attacked the camps, bombing and shelling till the starving survivors begged their holy men for the right to eat their dead.

Why, Rosa wondered, should *we* be the dispossessed and outcast of the earth? When we were, as this craven Mohammed once said, little more than thieves and camel stealers, one tribe among hundreds sharing the same roots? Where, how far back, were we divided, and why? Or are all humans divided, and tribes only an excuse for killing, as the Catholics brought their holy war, *For the Cross – "Croisade"*, to the Holy Land, teaching us the meaning of jihad?

There was no purpose in such questions; unlike vengeance they led nowhere except to further questions. If I don't die, she thought, will I someday have a husband and children? It is incomprehensible; I do not even like the idea, there's something sad in it, defeated.

The road leveled among a line of blasted façades; the driver slowed where the British Army base had been and parked before a small two-story building. The men in the first Mercedes went into the building and came out moments later. "It's clean," one said.

Mohammed got out and strode up the steps. "Call them," he said to the driver of the first car. "And tell them where we are."

He led them into the echoing empty room. He could not calm his rippling stomach, forced a heartiness to his voice, a calmness to his manner. It's nothing, he reminded himself, but a simple confidence trick. No matter how careful you are, there's always a way to trick you; if the Al-Nazirs did not want to talk peace, they would try to murder him here. If you want peace, he had told himself again and again, you have to risk death.

It had been his father's dying wish to speak to him of peace that had brought him back to Yammouné, that had then led him up the mountain into the Christian ambush, that had caused the deaths of his three men and brought him to the Christian doctor who had first saved his life from the wound then saved it again by protecting him from the man whose brother had been killed. And in return for saving his life, Mohammed through the hand of Rosa had brought down death upon the doctor. He glanced back at Rosa, hard and beautiful as ever, and recently more so, more willing to cut him down, hating his dream of peace. Again he thought of the doctor, as if he could speak directly to him across the wall of death: you saved my life; now help me spread the vision you taught me.

There was a long narrow table in the center of the room; one end of it was charred, although the rest of the room was untouched. This is a good place for peace, he reassured himself, trying to keep his fingers from clutching each other in the shelter of his gown. He saw his father as he had seen him the last time in Yammouné: his tousled white hair like an upraised flag of surrender.

In fifteen minutes Suley Al-Nazir and nine of his men came,

Suley striding in first as if he had no worries in the world, scorned all fear. He's like me, Mohammed thought, the way I used to be. Suley wore Israeli combat boots and camo, the ever-present knife on his calf, irritating Mohammed, for this too was a weapon, but then again, it was the kind of thing he would have done, five years ago, at Suley's age. He took Suley's hands in his and kissed him on both cheeks, feeling Rosa's eyes like knives between his shoulder blades. "Here we are, my brother." He looked into Suley's hard black eyes. "It is time to talk of peace."

"We have suffered too much," Suley said.

"I am sorry for your suffering. We are one kin who have been torn apart, turned against each other."

"By whom?"

"You know the answer to that. We've been their victim as much as you."

"*You*'d give up, then?"

"Together we can gain more ground. Haven't we been divided by our enemies so they can more easily defeat us?"

"No." Suley reached down and in a single motion pulled the knife from his boot. "You joined our enemies against us."

Despite himself Mohammed glanced at the knife. He was a foot from it; Suley could kill him before he could jump back. "You know that's not true!"

Suley's arm shot out; the pain ripped apart Mohammed's gut and he grabbed Suley's wrist; something smashed him back and he heard the crash of guns and as he fell he saw Druze militiamen shoving into the room, their guns blazing.

The roar of guns grew very far away and it was cold, colder than the ice river that flows out of the mountain at Yammouné over the lintel of the Roman temple, colder than Mount Lebanon's winter snows, and he felt he was flying, could rise above the cold and snow and heartache up into the bright blue dome of Heaven.

Suley's men lined up Mohammed's mujihadeen and shot

each one. Two of them still groveled, gasping with agony, on the wooden floor. Suley stepped across the other bodies and shot each in the head.

"You disgust me!" Rosa yelled. "Mohammed wasn't their fault. They were all brave, even this fool!" She nodded at Mohammed's dead captain, he with the sharp beard and narrow lips who had mocked her when she had first come to see Mohammed, who had not wanted her to go after the sniper in the Life Building. "You betrayed me!" she screamed, reaching for a militiaman's gun.

The man backed away. Suley bent to wipe his knife on Mohammed's robe. "No one could betray you."

"These men did you no harm."

"They were scum, Christian lovers. They had no place in the new Lebanon."

"I pity, then, the new Lebanon." Who had said that to her once?

"*You'll* never see it!" Suley yanked her long hair, her silver barrette flying; her fist smashed into his crotch as he pinned back her head and jammed the knife into her throat. She fell choking, writhing, across Mohammed. Grasping her throat in both hands she stumbled to her feet, raised her two bloody hands as if crucified and ran at Suley. He kicked her in the face and she toppled back, tripped over Mohammed, rolled to her knees, tried to stand, fell forward and lay still.

"Shit, boss," one militiaman said, "she was a nice piece. We could have had her first."

"She was a desert viper," Suley wiped his knife again on Mohammed's gown, "that should be killed the instant it's seen."

63

"DYING'S EASY," Neill said. "But it's poor expiation. Instead of wanting to die, why not try to bring more peace into the world? Like many who have suffered deeply, bring more happiness to others."

"That's rot."

Yes, Neill realized, almost everything I say is rot. "If you hadn't been down in that cellar with her, maybe they never would have found her."

André turned on him. "Why don't you just shove it?"

There were many things he could say, Neill thought, none of them worth a damn. André's arrival had completely changed his own preoccupations, but he was just as likely not to live this out. He had his own fate to consider. He felt a flash of anger at André for coming in, breaking up his routine. It's that kind of selfishness, he told himself, that made you what you were. What good is understanding if you can only maintain it alone?

The muezzin's last call came and went but no dinner appeared. Neill felt displaced, hungry, angry. André felt too sorry for himself, he decided; we've all had sorrow. Look at me – I've overcome it.

At last the food was coming; the thump of boots in the corridor. The door flew open. It was a mujihadeen he'd never seen, three more behind him. His boot came up and smacked Neill against the wall. *"Wait!"* Neill yelled in Arabic, clasping his ribs. The others pushed into the room, kicking and hammering with rifle butts; there was not enough space and they moved back outside.

The first man remained. "Each of you tried to kill Mohammed. Now he's dead. In retribution, one of you will be hung at dawn. Slowly." He gave Neill a last savage kick. "We leave it up to you to decide who."

The door shut, the bar fell back across it; the boots clumped away. I'm still hungry, Neill thought. How can they mean, hang us? We're foreigners. Europeans. They can't just kill us.

"Cocksuckers," André said. "I wish I had killed him."

"They can't mean it."

"Of course they do. They killed my brother and fifty other guys, more than three hundred fifty Americans –"

"But that was retribution for shelling all those villages!"

"So this is in retribution for killing that jerk. Somebody finally got him."

"He wasn't a jerk. He wanted peace."

"That's what I said: he was a jerk."

Lost in memories of Mohammed, Neill barely heard. How had he died? Had it been Freeman again? Freeman who had put the transmitter in Neill's arm not to keep him safe but to track down Mohammed, to kill Mohammed? Who was Freeman? All along Freeman had implied he was MI6. By working for him, how many times had he said Neill was doing his adopted country a favor? But Neill had never verified it – how could he? Was Freeman truly MI6? Or Mossad, a drug dealer, the CIA, KGB? When did you ever know? Weren't they all the same?

"Don't worry," André said. "I'll be the one."

Still caught up in Mohammed and Freeman, Neill didn't understand.

"Serendipity," André said. "These fuckers want to shoot somebody, they can have me."

Neill crawled to his feet. The sound frightened the sparrows, their wing beats clattering away. "If they're really going to do it –"

"You think this is some kind of game?"

Neill could feel his fine resolutions slipping away, the wisdom he'd gained in his weeks alone. "We'll draw for it."

André snickered. How can you hate somebody so fast, Neill wondered. "*Draw* for it?" André mocked. "What is it you do in your country, play bingo? Shall we play bingo?"

Suddenly Neill stopped hating, felt only pain for André. "We each tried to kill him."

"You didn't know. I *wanted* to."

"Do you still?"

André said nothing. One by one the sparrows began to land outside the flue. "No," André said. "I never want to kill anyone again. Except me." He sat up, and Neill saw his face was freshly bloody from where the mujihadeen had just punched him. The blood running down both sides of his mouth made him look like a Japanese actor in a morality play. "I'm a soldier," André said, "it's my fucking job to die."

Neill felt washed by an incredible wave of tenderness. "I'm a journalist. If anybody goes, it should be me first."

André flashed a smile garish with blood. "You can tell all about it. You can write a book."

With his fingernails Neill pried loose a little flat rectangle of tin stapled to the side of the bed. He laid it on the floor and scraped one side of it with a sharp pebble. "This side is heads, the scraped side is tails."

"Don't be silly."

Neill stood over him. After his weeks of exercises and walking and running he felt strong, capable. "We're going to have an even chance."

André snorted.

"We *are*," Neill persisted.

The light, he realized, was dying. He tossed the piece of tin and caught it coming down. "Heads or tails?"

"I'm the one. You're wasting your time."

"I pick tails." Neill opened his hand. "Tails it is." I'm going to die, he thought with a shock. It did not seem strange, only frightening.

André sat up. "You cheated. You saw it."

"I did not. You had your chance to call."

"You're serious, aren't you? A serious fool." André took the piece of tin. "Best of three. Call it!"

The piece of tin flashed up into the flue's light, pinged down. "Heads," Neill said.

"Heads it is."

"That's one out of three." Neill tossed it. "Call it!"

"Tails."

It came down, bounced across the floor. "Heads it is." Neill said. He covered it with his hand. "Guess it's me." There was a hollowness in his shoulders, his voice too light. He felt incredibly alone.

"Sorry," André said, "it doesn't count."

"Sure it does."

"I didn't see it before you grabbed it. I won't take that."

Neill wanted to hit him. "Listen, you're off the hook. Go back to sleep!"

André got up; there wasn't enough room, standing, for them both. He shoved Neill backwards, surprisingly strong. "If you play with me, you play fair." He snatched the piece of tin; it bent, cut Neill's hand. André straightened it on the floor, under his shoe. "I'm going to throw it thirteen times. Pick one side, now."

"I already won."

"Pick one side!"

Neill sucked at his bloody palm. "Tails." He shook his hand. "But we still take turns, tossing it."

"We let it land on the floor. No touching."

Neill glanced up at the flue. "I can barely see."

"Then give up now."

"Toss it!"

It came down heads. "See?" André rasped "*See?*"

André tossed it. "Heads again! Give up now?"

Three more times it came up heads. "That's five to nothing," André said. "Five out of thirteen."

Neill realized he was beginning to hope. If it truly came out against André then he, Neill, would live, fairly. They'd each have had an even chance.

André took it from his hand and threw it so high it clinked off the ceiling. "Tails," Neill whispered. "Five to one."

"All I need," André said, "is just two more –"

Neill tossed it and it bounced down heads. "Six to one," André said, voice hollow. He laid it on his thumb and spun it upwards; it came down and bounced under the bed. "Heads," he called, reaching under.

"Let me see!"

André slid back out and Neill crawled under. At first he could not see the piece of tin, then could not tell which side lay up. He pulled it out. "Liar!"

"You turned it over!"

"Six to two."

"I won't take that, you turned it over."

"I wouldn't cheat."

"Sure you would. What guilt are *you* trying to get rid of?"

"We don't count it then. If it goes under the bed we don't count it."

"All right. Six to one and I throw again." André spun it upwards again and it came down and bounced across the floor and off the wall. "You won that one," he said. "Six to two."

Offhandedly Neill tossed it. This would be the end. "Six to three," André said.

There was no way it would come up tails three more times,

Neill reassured himself. He was still going to get off, it was going to be André who died.

Up it went, out of André's hand, down. Tails again. "Six to four," Neill said. He did not trust his voice, had to whisper. He took the piece of tin. This was going to do it. He spun it extra hard; again it bounced off the ceiling, came down hitting his knee and rolled into the corner. "Six to bloody five."

"You're screwing with it," André said. "It's mine, I won already."

"You bastard! You did not." OK, Neill told himself. It's going to come up tails two more times and *I'm* going to be the one who gets hanged.

André flipped the piece of tin between his fingers, like an amateur gambler with a coin, showing off. "This is my seventh." He tossed it high.

Neill leaned down to see the piece of tin in the faint light. No doubt about it. Tails.

"Six to goddamn six," André said "You're screwing with it."

"It's going to be mine," Neill said, hoping it would not: the bastard wants to die, so let him. He took up the piece of tin. "My throw."

"No putting it under the bed."

"Screw you." Neill tossed it nonchalantly, a low one. It plunked down fast, leaped up and turned over.

"You cocksucker," André whispered. "You cheater."

"I won fairly." Neill felt like he was flying, out of touch with everything. "Three times I've won. All along, it's been my turn to die."

64

NEILL sat with his back against the blue wall. Beside his head the tap dripped steadily into the sink, like a heartbeat; the mice rattled in the walls; the people and animals of the village settled into sleep. Once a plane went over, very high, its sound trailing north-ward, away from Lebanon, and he felt his heart go with it, came back a moment later to this tiny room with the crude Frenchman on his bed and the boot heels of the guards beyond the door.

He couldn't have let himself get talked into this when the Frenchman didn't want to live and he didn't want to die. Maybe it wasn't real, he kept telling himself, just a ghastly joke – let you fear all night then not kill you.

He was an internationally respected journalist for a famous British paper – they wouldn't kill somebody like that. He looked up to see if the Frenchman was sleeping – no, he never slept, just lay there looking at the ceiling. Thinking of this girl he'd blown up because he was trying to avenge his brother. Just the way the Lebanese War had started, back in 1975, Bloody Sunday, an eye for an eye. A virus that just needs to infect one or two people and see how fast it spreads. *For the violence of Lebanon*, the Bible says, *shall cover thee.*

He'd promised himself in the Damascus mosque he was

going to change his life. Yet he'd gone out drinking with Mick the same evening, gone to the whorehouse down by the Gate of Deliverance, he and Mick smoking hash with four girls, two for each.

Even before that, in Bratislava, when he'd gone out with the girl from Hell and she turned out to be Freeman's agent, holding her gun to his head as he knelt before the headlights of her Lada on the hill above Bratislava, warning him that this was not the way to live, that if they had to, *they'd* kill him.

Now he was going to his death not even knowing who Freeman was, the man who had condemned him. No, he thought, I condemned myself. Freeman's just part of the faceless evil that surrounds us – call it MI6, the CIA or KGB. On every level I was warned.

Wasn't that what his failed marriage with Beverly had been also – a warning? That he was not living his life right?

How would they do it? he wondered. Stand him on a chair with the rope round his neck, hands tied behind his back, then kick the chair out from under him? That way he'd never fall enough to break his neck, just hang there choking.

Bev and the kids wouldn't really care he was dead. As she'd said, they'd prefer that he go rather than stay, how could he blame them?

"You awake?" he said.

André rolled over, looked at him. "Of course."

"Do you know how they do it? Do they push you off a chair? Do you choke, or does your neck get broken?"

"They'll push you off a chair. Or they garrote you."

"What's that?"

"Wrap a wire around your neck and twist."

"Oh God ..."

"Only takes a couple of minutes."

Neill stood and unzipped his fly to piss into the sink but nothing would come out. He kept having this terrible need to piss but each time there was nothing, or just a few drops.

"You should let me be the one," André said.

Neill shivered. He wanted so badly to say yes, go ahead, you be the one to die. But tossing the piece of tin had been fair; three separate times he'd lost. If he were truly going to change his life, as he had begun when he'd been here alone, then he had to stick with what he'd said. Tossing the piece of tin had been fair; he could not go back on that, not without living the rest of his life in shame.

It's better to live in shame, he reminded himself, than not to live at all.

ABOVE THE GREEN LINE the flares and rockets made it light as day, even brighter, a titanium incandescence. The dog glanced once more behind it and dashed across the Line's smashed streets and buried buildings, the smell of death and cordite everywhere. It ran up the hill into East Beirut and through the streets loud with falling metal and singing bullets to André's hotel. The front door was closed; it settled down in the alley to wait. When someone came out of the door the dog raced into the lobby and up to André's door. There was a different smell there now, no sense of André. Confused and indecisive, the dog circled the corridor and ran back down the stairs. It looked around outside but could not find the Ford. Tail hanging, head low, it trotted back down to the Green Line and crossed again, panting with thirst, dizzy with hunger, and along Rue Basta and up Capucines to Anne-Marie's apartment, climbed to her floor and sat down to wait outside her door.

ANDRÉ WAS WORRYING about the dog. He' taken on responsibility of the dog and but hadn't fulfilled it because he'd been divided by too many other wants. Just as he'd taken on the responsibility of Anne-Marie and had destroyed her because he had not been centered on her, even though she was all he cared about. The thought of her made his body cringe, his heart congeal; he could not breathe, the pain choked him so badly.

Death would be like morphine, better than sleep; only it could stop the pain.

He forced himself to imagine what she had felt like, that last mini-second. Had she felt at all? He made himself believe she had. How could you not feel, to be blown apart?

There was nothing after death and no way he would ever see her, be near her, feel her near him, hear her voice with its rough lovely tones. What, he kept worrying, had happened to her body? It drove him crazy to think of it lying in pieces in the street, the rats eating it.

She and he would never have children and never grow old together; he did not mind for himself, he could stand anything. What he could not stand was that she had lost the gift of life; he had snatched it from her, murdered her.

It was getting late. The Englishman sat immobile in his corner by the sink, waiting to die. Putting a good face on it though. Not a bad man, just silly, out of touch with himself, the world. And what about *you*? André said to himself. How much more out of touch can anybody be than you?

Soon they'd come and take the Englishman away. Hang him by the neck till dead. Because someone had convinced him to carry a silly transmitter under his arm, and then they, or someone else, had tried to kill Mohammed. Everybody had wanted to kill Mohammed. He too. But what if Mohammed hadn't been the one who bombed Yves' barracks?

Life is completely random; the only punishment for our crimes happens in our hearts. Just as I by losing Anne-Marie am punished for the crime of interfering, of vengeance, ignorance. Or maybe we just get punished accidentally, the way some people die in earthquakes or plane crashes.

It did no good to think. That was simply trying to avoid pain. And pain is our only teacher, so thinking is a way of never learning.

He did not care whether he ever learned or not. There was no reason to ever take a breath – just the body doing it, automatically. Anne-Marie, he begged, seeing her lovely face with its firm kind mouth and deep dark eyes, feeling her lips against his, her breasts, the long soft coolness of her skin, please help me dear Anne-Marie.

65

THEY CAME BEFORE FIRST LIGHT, an ugly hare-lipped long-bearded Hezbollah with the others who had beat him and André. "You've chosen?" asked the ugly one.

"Goodbye," Neill said to André, who stood uncomfortably. "Good luck." Neill walked out of the door, light-headed.

"This way," one of the Hezbollah said, almost solicitously. As Neill turned, something smashed down on his shoulders and he fell, thinking as he dropped into unconsciousness, they've shot me, they've killed me here and now. It took forever, falling; there's nothing to it, he realized, being dead.

André stood over Neill rubbing the sides of his hands where he had hammered them down on Neill's shoulders. "Just knocked him out," he said in English, but the mujihadeen only stared, astonished, covering him with their guns. André pointed to himself. "I'm the one."

They did not seem to understand; he pointed at Neill, that they should drag him back into the room. Neill was beginning to move. André turned quickly down the corridor, the mujihadeen behind him.

One of the mujihadeen pulled Neill into the room, ran out and shut the door. Neill heard the bolt drop and tried to stand;

whatever had happened to his shoulders had numbed his whole body; his muscles were slack, would not work.

As soon as he could he dragged himself to the door and pounded on it. His fist was heavy as a chunk of lead. No one came; there was no noise but the sparrows in the eaves. Slowly daylight began to sink into the room.

He felt betrayed, cheated, elated, terrified it might be a mistake, that they would soon come for him, guilty that André had gone in his place. Once again he hadn't been a man.

The numbness went away. He paced the tiny room, banged on the door. There was no air; he wanted to sing, laugh, weep. Dear André come back, he kept saying, knew he did not mean it. If you don't mean it, he told himself, shut up.

The room grew brighter. He imagined André with the rope round his neck, being pushed off the chair, hanging in midair as the rope got tighter, tighter, arms lashed behind him, chest heaving, body screaming for air.

Still no one came. He drank from the tap, threw up bile. He sat on the bed and tried to pray for André, give thanks. Dear Lord, I'm sorry, he said. That I didn't understand him. Didn't even like him. When he was better than I am.

No, he wasn't. Neill paced again. If he was going to renew his life, he must stop tearing himself down. He'd kept the bargain. Gone out into that corridor ready to die.

He fell asleep and woke wondering where he was, crushed with shame when he remembered what had happened. No, he reminded himself, you can't do that. I'm sorry, he told André. I'm so sorry.

The last muezzin's call came and went. The door creaked open. Ahmed slunk in and put a plate of food on the bed.

"What happened to him?" Neill whispered.

"Gone."

"Gone?"

"Gone." Ahmed swerved his head to see if the guards were watching. Their voices were further down the hall.

"They killed him?"

Ahmed shook his head: be quiet. "Some very top Hezbollah came and took him in a car."

"To shoot him?" Neill's stomach turned queasy at the thought.

Ahmed shook his head, glanced at the door. The voices were coming. "They gave him back to France. Some big people there wanted him back."

Neill stood stunned, mouth open, unable to speak. "What," he said finally, "about me?"

"It was the will of God. *In'salah.*"

The voices neared. Ahmed put his finger to his lips, stepped out. The door shut, casting the room in darkness.

Neill ate the food mechanically. The darkness deepened. He paced, lay down, sat, went to bang on the door and halted mid-step. Would they kill him? After they'd let André go? It didn't seem possible.

Should have remembered, the French never abandon their agents. Not like the CIA or MI6. That they'll abandon national policy to get back one man. Even if like André he wasn't an agent.

I was the one, he told himself. Three times I lost the toss. Then I let him go to die. No I didn't. He surprised me. Maybe that's why they let him go. For his courage.

If the French saved André won't someone save me?

The night took forever, would never pass. I've always been here, he thought. In this room, the night. He looked out on life and it seemed he understood every little thing, why people war and do not love, why the world breaks down.

Dear Lebanon, dear foolish humans – don't even realize that the love of war comes from the war of love.

He felt like a god, a speck on the wall in a little blue room in the Bekaa, under the burning sun, the cold night. Time did not matter.

Something fell from the ceiling, a piece of plaster maybe. It disturbed the sparrows; they cried and worried for a while, grew silent.

He could say that if he got out of this he would be a different person, but it did not matter if he ever got out. Nothing mattered.

Slowly light drained into the room, the blue wall and sink took shape, the low hunched door. It was like the gate of death, that door, the gate between our mother's thighs through which we fall into the world. Screaming, blind, terrified, not understanding. When do we ever change?

Something had fallen in the corner, down from the ceiling, a little piece of pink-gray plaster. He bent down to pick it up; it was a baby bird, unfledged. He thought it was dead but in the warmth of his hand it began to move, turning its sightless eyes, its open beak, up to him, uttering tiny cries. He cupped it in his hands, warmed it with his breath, smiling to think how God had breathed life into the world. When it had revived he climbed up on the bed and raised it through the flue hole. The sparrows outside began to sing excitedly; he carefully laid it beside the top of the hole, his fingers feeling the warmth of the sun. When he removed his hand a sparrow was peering down the hole with little bright eyes.

He would have to pick up where he'd left off. That was our only power in this life: determination. He would begin this day as any other, in meditation, the stretching, his long walk, the reflections on the Bible and the Koran, running in place, the poetry.

The day passed as any other. After the muezzin's last call, Ahmed came with a plate of beans. He seemed sad and would not speak; Neill pressed him. "I fear for you," Ahmed said.

"They're going to kill me?"

Ahmed said nothing, head averted.

"When?" Neill said.

"In the morning." Ahmed glanced at the guard behind him, went out and closed the door.

So that's it, Neill told himself. He wished he had asked Ahmed how they would do it. But he already knew.

It was almost worse than death, this endless waiting. But isn't waiting for death what we do all our lives?

Late at night he must have dozed, he dreamt he was walking along a beach when a flock of sparrows burst forth above him and some circled into a crown over his head and landed on it. He walked along the beach with Beverly and Edgar and Katerina, with the crown of sparrows over him, and one stayed on his head; he even lifted a small grass seed for the sparrow to eat. This is the one I saved, he thought.

They crossed the end of the beach and went up into the trees. There was a house and a path of white stones between a spit of rock and ocean on one side and the beach on the other, and he thought how easy and perfect it would be to travel up this path of white stones in the sun.

THE END

MIKE BOND BOOKS

GOODBYE PARIS

Special Forces veteran Pono Hawkins races from Tahiti to France when a terrorist he'd thought was dead has a nuclear weapon to destroy Paris. Joining allies from US and French intelligence, Pono faces impossible odds to save the most beautiful city on earth. Alive with covert action and insider details from the war against terrorism, *Goodbye Paris* is a hallmark Mike Bond thriller: tense, exciting, and full of real places, and that will keep you up all night. "A rip-roaring page-turner." —*Culture Buzz*

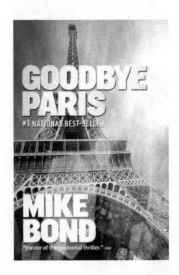

SNOW

Three hunters find a crashed plane of cocaine in the Montana wilderness. Two steal the cocaine and are soon hunted by the Mexican cartel, the DEA, Las Vegas killers, and the police of several states. From the frozen peaks of Montana to the heights of Wall Street, the Denver slums and million-dollar Vegas tables, *Snow* is an electric portrait of today's America, the invisible line between good and evil, and what people will do in their frantic search for love and freedom. "Action-packed adventure." —*Denver Post*

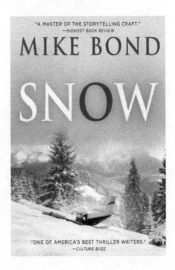

ASSASSINS

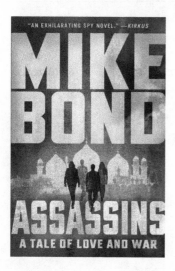

From its terrifying start in the night skies over Afghanistan to its stunning end in the Paris terrorist attacks, *Assassins* is an insider's thriller of the last 30 years of war between Islam and the West. A US commando, an Afghani warlord, a French woman doctor, a Russian major, a top CIA operator, and a British woman journalist fight for their lives and loves in the deadly streets and lethal deserts of the Middle East. "An epic spy story." —*Honolulu Star-Advertiser*

KILLING MAINE

Surfer and Special Forces veteran Pono Hawkins quits sunny Hawaii for Maine's brutal winter to help a former SF buddy beat a murder rap and fight the state's rampant political corruption. "A gripping tale of murders, manhunts and other crimes set amidst today's dirty politics and corporate graft, an unforgettable hero facing enormous dangers as he tries to save a friend, protect the women he loves, and defend a beautiful, endangered place." —*First Prize for Fiction, New England Book Festival*

SAVING PARADISE

When Special Forces veteran Pono Hawkins finds a beautiful journalist drowned off Waikiki he is caught in a web of murder and political corruption. Hunting her killers, he soon finds them hunting him, and blamed for her death. A relentless thriller of politics, sex, and murder, "an action-packed, must read novel ... taking readers behind the alluring façade of Hawaii's pristine beaches and tourist traps into a festering underworld of murder, intrigue and corruption." —*Washington Times*

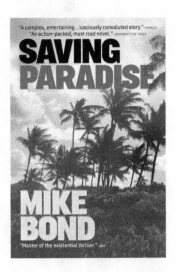

THE LAST SAVANNA

An intense memoir of humanity's ancient heartland, its people, wildlife, deserts and jungles, and the deep, abiding power of love. "One of the best books yet on Africa, a stunning tale of love and loss amid a magnificent wilderness and its myriad animals, and a deadly manhunt through savage jungles, steep mountains and fierce deserts as an SAS commando tries to save the elephants, the woman he loves and the soul of Africa itself." —*First Prize for Fiction, Los Angeles Book Festival*

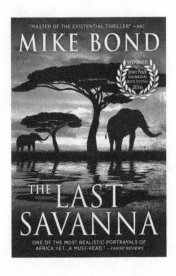

HOLY WAR

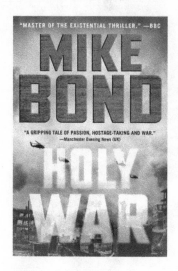

Based on the author's experiences in Middle East conflicts, *Holy War* is the story of the battle of Beirut, of implacable hatreds and frantic love affairs, of explosions, betrayals, assassinations, snipers and ambushes. An American spy, a French commando, a Hezbollah terrorist and a Palestinian woman guerrilla all cross paths on the deadly streets and fierce deserts of the Middle East. "A profound tale of war ... Impossible to stop reading." —*British Armed Forces Broadcasting*

HOUSE OF JAGUAR

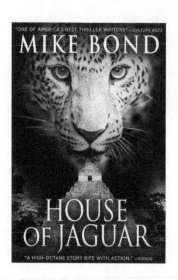

A stunning thriller of CIA operations in Latin America, guerrilla wars, drug flights, military dictatorships, and genocides, based on the author's experiences as as one of the last foreign journalists left alive in Guatemala after over 150 journalists had been killed by Army death squads. "An extraordinary story that speaks from and to the heart. And a terrifying description of one man's battle against the CIA and Latin American death squads." —*BBC*

TIBETAN CROSS

An exciting international manhunt and stunning love story. An American climber in the Himalayas stumbles on a shipment of nuclear weapons headed into Tibet for use against China. Pursued by spy agencies and other killers across Asia, Africa, Europe and the US, he is captured then rescued by a beautiful woman with whom he forms a deadly liaison. They escape, are captured and escape again, death always at their heels. "Grips the reader from the opening chapter and never lets go." —*Miami Herald*

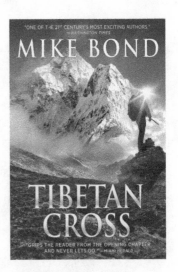

THE DRUM THAT BEATS WITHIN US

The tradition of the poet warrior endures throughout human history, from our Stone Age ancestors to the Bible's King David, the Vikings of Iceland, Japan's Samurai, the Shambhala teachings of Tibet, the ancient Greeks and medieval knights. Initially published by Lawrence Ferlinghetti in City Lights Books, Mike Bond has won multiple prizes for his poetry and prose. "Passionately felt emotional connections, particularly to Western landscapes and Native American culture." —*Kirkus*

MIKE BOND is the author of nearly a dozen best-selling novels, a war and human rights journalist, ecologist, international energy expert and award-winning poet. He has been called "the master of the existential thriller" *(BBC)*, "one of America's best thriller writers" *(Culture Buzz)*, "a nature writer of the caliber of Matthiessen" *(WordDreams)*, and "one of the 21st century's most exciting authors" *(Washington Times)*.

He has covered wars, revolutions, terrorism, military dictatorships and death squads in the Middle East, Latin America, Asia and Africa, and environmental issues including elephant poaching, habitat loss, wilderness survival, whales, wolves and many other endangered species.

His novels place the reader in intense experiences in the world's most perilous places, in dangerous liaisons, political and corporate conspiracies, wars and revolutions, making "readers sweat with [their] relentless pace" *(Kirkus)* "in that fatalistic margin where life and death are one and the existential reality leaves one caring only to survive." *(Sunday Oregonian)*.

He has climbed mountains on every continent and trekked more than 50,000 miles in the Himalayas, Mongolia, Russia, Europe, New Zealand, North and South America, and Africa.

For film, translation or publication rights, or for interviews contact:
Meryl Moss Media
meryl@merylmossmedia.com or 203-226-0199

CPSIA information can be obtained
at www.ICGtesting.com
Printed in the USA
BVHW071108010421
603929BV00001B/41

9 781949 751161